LOST

Books by E. G. Lewis

The Seeds of Christianity™ Series

ROAD TO BETHLEHEM — *A Prelude*
WITNESS — Book One
DISCIPLE — Book Two
APOSTLE — Book Three
MARTYR — Book Four

The Mountain Memories Series

PROMISES — Book One
LOST — Book Two

Christian Non-Fiction

At Table with the Lord - Foods of the First Century

All Things Christmas - The History & Traditions of Advent and Christmas

In Three Days - The History & Traditions of Lent and Easter

LOST

A Novel

By

E G Lewis

Cape Arago Press
P.O. Box 771
North Bend, OR 97459
www.capearagopress.com

ISBN 13: 978-0-9825949-4-0
ISBN: 0-9825949-4-1

1. Fiction: General   2.Fiction: Mystery

LOST is set in sight-saving Georgia 11 point type for reading ease.

LOST is dedicated to the memory of
Steven D. Bergthold
February 28, 1946 — December 16, 2006

Steve was a first reader of an early, and admittedly flawed, version of this book. His enthusiastic support for my tale featuring "two Vietnam vets and a kick-ass Indian scientist," as he termed it, became the impetus that drove me to revisit and revise, edit and polish the manuscript through its multiple iterations. By bringing this novel to publication I feel I have validated his faith both in the appeal of the underlying story and my ability to tell it.

Grant him eternal rest, O Lord;
And let light perpetual shine upon him.

Amen.

The author wishes to thank the staff of U.S. Coast Guard Air Station North Bend, Lloyd's of London, and Cruise West, Inc. for providing details that ensured the accuracy of the narrative.

"It is not the critic who counts, nor the man who points how the strong man stumbled, or where the doer of deeds could have done them better. The credit belongs to the man who is actually in the arena; whose face is marred by dust and sweat and blood; who strives valiantly...who knows the great enthusiasms, the great devotions, and spends himself in a worthy cause; who, at best, knows the triumph of high achievement; and who, at the worst, if he fails, at least fails while daring greatly, so that his place shall never be with those cold and timid souls who know neither victory nor defeat."

—Theodore Roosevelt

ONE

It's high time someone set the record straight.

And since Tom's still recuperatin', Derek's left the country, 'n' Claudia's busy in New York, I suppose the task falls to yours truly.

There were a bunch of differing opinions flyin' round town that fall. But then, that's only natural. Pine Crest is a small town and folks in small towns do talk. Let's not beat around the bush... they like t' gossip.

Now for some people it was plain 'n' simple; they thought Tom had lost his mind. Others attributed it to the grief. Lord knows there was than enough t' go around. A lot of folks in Pine Crest got a heapin' helping, but none more than him. Still, everyone agreed he'd eventually get over it, pick up the pieces, and go on with his life. At least in the beginning that's what they thought. As time went on and he persisted, well, those theories sorta went out the window.

Unlike most folks, his actions didn't worry me a bit. Ya don't really know what a person's made of 'til you've seen 'em under pressure. And believe you me, I've seen Tom under pressure. See, me 'n' *Sarge* — Sarge is what I've always called him— go way back. We were in 'Nam together.

Not that he was in my unit or anything. He led a small recon squad and spent his time trackin' lost patrols or findin' downed aircraft. Lucky for me he was nearby the day a land mine gnawed away a big hunk of my leg. Have ya ever seen how much blood a body pumps out when ya sever a major artery? It's a frightful sight, let me tell ya...especially when it's *your* blood.

Before I knew it, he was there beside me whippin' off his belt 'n' makin' it into a tourniquet. Far as I could tell, he didn't worry much 'bout steppin' on a mine himself, unlike some others who dithered whilst I bled t' death.

Folks here in Pine Crest, only know what's on the outside. They see Tom Jenkins the newspaper editor. Not that they don't respect him for what he's accomplished. Over the years, they've watched him build that little paper of his into a respectable publication. They've also seen his syndicated columns popping up in lots of big city newspapers.

But that's the superficial stuff. Me, I know him better. After all, he's the one who saved my life. Might say I owed him a debt I could never repay. I wouldn't blame ya a bit if ya did; I felt the same way until not too long ago.

Strange ain't it, how fate can turn on the convergence of unplanned, co-incidental, seemingly insignificant or unrelated circumstances? Rain on the eve of an important battle, studyin' the wrong chapter for a history test; or simply bein' in the right place at the wrong time.

It reminds me of makin' rope when I was a Boy Scout. We started with three pieces of twine that we stretched and twisted together with a clockwise motion. Once they formed a strand, we divided it in thirds and twisted those strands together goin' counter-clockwise.

Right about now you're wonderin' why I'm tellin' ya how t' make rope when the local hardware has as much of it as you'll ever need. My point is, most catastrophes begin with good intentions. Yet once those unrelated events get twisted around each other, just like the rope, it takes a bunch of unravelin' to separate 'em again.

But I'm getting' ahead of myself. We need t' crank the ol' clock back a ways 'n' begin at the beginning. Not here in Pine Crest, Oregon or New York or Annapolis or even London, but in Delhi, India.

TWO

Delhi, India—*August, 1995*

The Indian scientist led his two visitors on a circuitous path through a labyrinth of hallways in one of the university's buildings. The trappings of academia gradually fell away and their surroundings grew shabbier the farther they walked. Their trek ended at the last door in a dim corridor.

Brandon Steele studied the rusting metal door and the slim, dark-skinned man who'd led them to it. He frowned and shot his boss a questioning sidelong glance. Winston Ridgely gave a nearly imperceptible nod, but remained unperturbed.

Dwarakananth Maheshwari's hand disappeared into the pocket of his white lab coat. Removing a fountain pen and several sheets of folded paper, he gave his well-dressed visitors an apologetic smile.

"Before I allow you in, gentlemen, I have something for you to sign. You must agree to neither disclose the existence of this technology to any government, corporation, or individual, nor will you discuss it with any other person."

He uncapped the pen and extended it to Ridgely.

Ridgely frowned at the paper. He twisted the pen in his fingers, bristling. "Is this really necessary, Dr. Maheshwari?"

"Yes, Mr. Ridgely, I am afraid it is. Were it not, I would not ask it of you."

As Chairman and CEO of the multi-billion dollar defense contractor, RCI Corp., Ridgely was accustomed to making the rules rather than abiding by them. "You've worked with RCI as a consultant in the past. We never required *a priori* nondisclosure agreements. Our relationship has always been one of mutual trust."

"My dear Mr. Ridgely, we are splitting hairs here. If I did not trust you, I would not have invited you to come to India. And you, in turn, trusted me enough to make the trip. This process is still in its developmental stages and not yet patented. Would you have me leave my intellectual property unprotected?"

The idea had taken shape several years earlier while he waited to takeoff on a flight to Europe. It was early, but already intensely hot when he boarded. As he waited, Maheshwari, the head of the University's Physics Department, idly watched waves of heat shimmer above the tarmac. In the distance, he noticed the disembodied tail of a British Airways jet floating above the dry grass as it taxied on the runway. It was an *Ah-Ha* moment.

Ridgely bit his lip for a moment then sighed. After what seemed like an interminable wait, he pressed the form against the door and scrawled his signature on the designated line. Ridgely passed the pen to Steele, RCI's Executive Vice-President, and he did the same.

Maheshwari eased the papers back into his pocket with a smile and unlocked the door. Its dry hinges screeched in protest as he folded it back against the wall. A mild, but persistent animal smell mingled with the not unpleasant odor of fresh hay wafted up the stairwell and settled around them.

"My laboratory is in the basement," he said softly. "Tread with care, these steps can be most treacherous. Should you slip, it could result in serious personal injury. More importantly, it would negate all of our efforts to maintain secrecy."

Seeing an opportunity where no one else did, Maheshwari's idea, this dream of his, caught his imagination and held it. He knew he must prove it out and put it to practical use. And to do so he had to cross the line between theoretical and applied physics.

When he sought research funding, he was dismayed to find that even a sterling reputation and high position weren't sufficient to secure a grant for such a fanciful notion. Frustrated, he did what any driven man would do, he funded the research himself.

Winston Ridgely peered over Maheshwari's shoulder at the concrete steps disappearing into black oblivion. "It looks more like a dungeon than a laboratory. We could have provided you with better lab space than this."

Maheshwari shrugged. "I required a private place. My associates and I adapted this abandoned storeroom to our purposes. We have taken every precaution to insure no one knows of our work." His dark eyes nervously darted around the narrow hall behind them as he returned the keys to his pocket. "Discovery remains an ever present possibility."

He was still speaking when two men in their late twenties and an equally young woman rounded the corner at the far end of the corridor. Ridgely noticed them first and touched Steele's arm. The two men eyed the approaching trio suspiciously.

"Those are my assistants, Abhijay Patel, Raheel Singh and Sivanee Kaur," Maheshwari said with a smile. He flipped a light switch and a string of naked bulbs under battered metal shades sprang to life. He grasped the pitted metal handrail and cautiously stepped down. "Come. Let us see if we can make your long flight worthwhile."

His little team sprang into action as soon as they reached the bottom of the stairs. On his way to the security pad Patel flipped a few switches flooding the large, windowless room with bright light. After disarming the security system, he went to a nearby computer and inserted a command erasing the log entry. University records indicated no one had been in the area for over a year.

Meanwhile, Singh circled the room removing the large blue sheets draped over their electronic equipment. After careful folding, he stacked them beside a row of dusty document storage boxes lining the shelves of one wall.

Steele, unprepared for the wretchedness of their surroundings, crossed his arms and mumbled something to Ridgely.

Maheshwari's head jerked up. "I should warn you, Mr. Steele, I have extremely acute hearing. You find our accommodations less than impressive?"

Steele's cheeks colored, but he said nothing.

"Since the university would not fund my research, we have been forced to operate on an extremely limited budget." Maheshwari patted his back pocket. "I believe this is what is known as pulling oneself up by the bootstraps. As I explained to Mr. Ridgely on the telephone, what we have here is merely a small prototype. Proof of the concept's validity, if you will. Concentrate on the results not the surroundings."

"He meant no disrespect," Ridgely said.

"And none taken. Many great things have sprung from humble beginnings. The famous Mr. Edison lacked the expansive laboratories and office buildings of glass and steel you deem so necessary to conducting valid scientific research. Your esteemed Silicon Valley was birthed in a wood-framed garage used by Misters Hewlett and Packard. Charles Kettering did his pioneering work in his garage as well. Rest assured; we will undoubtedly find a multitude of things on which to waste your money if our work moves to RCI's facilities."

Ignoring the men, Kaur moved along a row of cages, inspecting her charges. She opened a door, removed one of the animals and pressed a stethoscope to its chest.

Maheshwari walked to where she stood with Ridgely and Steele trailing behind. "Kaur here is our animal person. She is an Associate Professor of Veterinary Medicine at the university and visits each day to check on her charges."

When the time came to test their prototype on living subjects, Maheshwari's tiny group realized none of them possessed the required skills. They needed an animal person and Kaur was added to the team.

He turned his attention to the animal nestled in her arms. "And how are our junior partners today?"

She removed her stethoscope from the White New Zealand rabbit's chest and stroked his dense fur. "Gautama could not be better." She sat the plump rabbit on a scale. Waited for the dial to settle, and recorded the weight...4.264 kilos.

Her black medical bag waited on the metal table beside

them. She'd already spread a fresh surgical drape over the tabletop and arranged her instruments. Small-needled hypodermics waited alongside bottles of sedatives.

Turning to face the visitors, she motioned toward the row of cages. "All of these animals are SPF, Specific Pathogen Free, and bred for laboratory work. We acquired them individually from separate breeders. None of them share any parentage. I checked each of them for health problems, genetic defects or other anomalies when we began. I have carefully monitored and recorded each animal's vital signs. These records will enable us to determine if the experiments Dr. Maheshwari is conducting trigger any physiologic changes."

Maheshwari silently scanned the bank of cages.

"They are all ready, Professor," she said, anticipating his unspoken question.

"Shall we use this one?"

"We can. It makes no difference. As I said, any of them will do."

Maheshwari directed the men toward the center of the room.

The rabbit's pink eyes followed them warily.

Meanwhile, Kaur plunged an injection needle through a bottle's rubber seal and withdrew a small amount of sedative.

Singh sat with his back to the men, concentrating on the semi-circle of computer screens in front of him. A tangle of wires linked the computers and a thick, black cable snaked over to a small metal device about five feet away.

Maheshwari patted the gray box with pride. "This, gentlemen, is our prototype."

"What does it do?"

"My dear Mr. Ridgely, you would not believe me if I told you." Maheshwari smiled at Ridgely's indignant expression, and wondered what Ridgely would do when Singh flipped the switch causing the box along with its rabbit to vanish from sight.

THREE

Annapolis, Maryland—*October, 1996*

Dr. Jeremy Tilden eased the door back and tiptoed into the dimly lit room. His wife, Mary Jane, known to the world as supermodel Claudia Monet, sat at her desk in an oasis of light. He noticed she hadn't bothered to draw the curtains on the bank of windows overlooking the now dark Chesapeake Bay. A pile of ash covered coals emitted a faint red glow in the stone fireplace, a reminder of an earlier fire.

The intermittent tap of a computer keyboard broke the hushed silence as Jeremy noiselessly crossed the plush carpet. Brow furrowed, she frowned at her computer screen. Stacks of collated printouts and presentation folders lined a nearby coffee table.

Stepping behind her, he drew a wisp of blond hair aside and nuzzled her neck. "Good evening, Mrs. Tilden. It's way past your bedtime."

She leaned back and swiveled her head to kiss his cheek. "Maybe so, but *Claudia Monet* has a deadline looming. I'm almost there, honest."

The office was part of a three-room post and beam addition they'd tacked onto the back of the colonial farmhouse purchased the previous year. Living in Annapolis put them equidistant from Jeremy's work at The Johns Hopkins University School of Medicine in nearby Baltimore and her brother's law office in Washington, DC. Three commercial airports, Reagan National, Dulles International and Baltimore/Washington International, lay within a fifty-mile radius. Their proximity and her private jet made her frequent trips to New York an easy commute and provided a quick start for longer flights to London or Paris.

Jeremy pointed to the lower right corner of the screen. "In case you haven't noticed, there's a little window down there that tells you the time."

She feigned surprise. "Well, whaddaya know? How could I have missed it all these years?"

"Where's Trevor?"

She covered her mouth, stifling a yawn, and motioned toward a leather couch by the fireplace. A small boy lay curled up against a pillow with his arm around a Teddy Bear. Mousse, Claudia's Chocolate Persian cat, slept beside the boy on the quilted throw she'd put over him.

"He conked out hours ago. I intended to take him upstairs, but never quite got around to it."

"Still working on the proposal?"

"I've been re-running the numbers on my financial model to check the alternate financial outcomes I factored into the program."

Jeremy took a seat beside her. "Are you considering utilizing bigger ships?"

Her lips tightened and her nose crinkled when she shook her head. "No, the last thing the world needs is another floating hotel. I like the idea of smaller. It's definitely the way to go. For one thing, the capital requirements are much less. Everyone I've spoken with agrees the intimate atmosphere of a smaller cruise ship would be a big selling point." Her eyes returned to the screen. "I'm searching for the optimal balance between investment, risk and return."

Jeremy scratched his head and chuckled. "The idea of an optimal balance reminds me of the magazine article they did on you last year. Remember them overlaying your picture with those blue lines? They concluded people consider you beautiful because your face conforms to the golden ratio of...um, what were those numbers called again?"

"Fibonacci numbers." Her eyes remained on the screen. "DaVinci did something similar. You've seen the naked guy in a circle with his arms and legs splayed out. Those ratios explain why most models are tall, we meet the ideal."

"So the brain comes as optional equipment."

She gave him a playful poke. "Watch it fella, you're heading onto thin ice."

Jeremy rubbed her shoulder. "You worry too much. You've got the Board in the palm of your hand. Give them one of your winning smiles and they'll approve anything you want."

Straightening in her chair, she turned and rested an elbow on the desk. "I want my ideas to prevail on their own merit. And for your information, I wear a business suit to board meetings... with slacks, you male chauvinist pig."

"Deny it all you want, but you know you can twist just about anyone around your little finger."

"Why does everyone assume all I can do is look good in front of a camera? Perceptions like that are the reason I work so hard. Is it wrong to want people to respect me for my accomplishments? My looks are an accident of nature; I can't take credit for them. Would you want someone to think you were a great medical researcher because you're handsome?" She waved her hand and chuckled. "Not that you are, or anything. That was just a theoretical question, so don't go getting the big head over it."

Knowing he'd hit a sore spot, Jeremy dropped the subject.

She rolled her shoulders and rubbed her tired eyes. "What kind of a nut schedules *two* Board meetings in the same week?"

"When it's over, you'll be glad you did. It'll save you a second trip to Europe. C'mon, let's turn in."

Jeremy scooped Trevor into his arms while she powered down the computer.

"How was your evening?" she asked as they climbed the stairs.

"Lonely."

FOUR

Offices of Paradise Getaways, London, *October 1998*

Rudy gave Claudia a hug before he started applying her makeup. "You need to relax, Honey. It's only a Board meeting. They may not buy your plan, but they won't send you to the guillotine."

He and Claudia had completed a photo shoot in New York the previous week. When she returned to Annapolis, Rudy, who'd done her make-up and hair for years, accompanied her. Representing a cosmetics company made her a walking billboard for Souvanée cosmetics. She wouldn't attend their Board meeting without looking her best.

The following morning Claudia kissed Trevor and Jeremy good-bye and she and Rudy headed for Baltimore-Washington International. Greg Harris, her pilot of six years, was there to meet them. He introduced her to Christopher Allen, their co-pilot for the flight.

Claudia traveled in a custom Cessna Citation X. The sleek craft, desert sand with chocolate accent stripes, was a top-of-the-line business jet. Capable of near Mach speeds, it cruised at 50,000 feet and could do New York to Paris in a little over six hours. She'd earned her pilot's license five years earlier. Instrument-certified, she was fully qualified to handle the twin-engine jet and frequently did. However, on trans-Atlantic flights she preferred having a second pilot aboard for safety's sake. And, since this was a working trip for her, she'd only take the controls in an emergency.

"We'll be taking runway 33R as usual," Harris said when she boarded the plane.

"Any weather?" Claudia asked.

Allen shook his head. "Clear as a bell."

Following a smooth liftoff, Harris maintained his departure heading for a mile to comply with noise abatement regulations then executed a gentle banking turn. A few minutes later they passed over the Delaware coastline and headed across the Atlantic bound for France.

Following her two-day meeting in Paris, Claudia flew to London and checked into a hotel. She'd once owned a condominium in the city, but shortly after she took control of Paradise Getaways, Ltd., she'd sold the penthouse at Putney Wharf for £4.25 million and transferred the funds into company accounts to provide additional working capital.

She and Rudy ordered room service and ate a quiet supper in her suite. Afterwards, he checked his watch. "The East Coast is five hours behind us. If you want company, I can stay."

"Don't stay on my account. I'm too wired to be good company. I'll see you first thing tomorrow morning when you come to do my makeup."

At 10:30 London time she called home and spoke to Trevor and Jeremy. It was late when she hung up, but sleep eluded her. Never one to rely on pills, she passed the time staring out at the London skyline as she rethought her presentation and tried to guess what the following day would offer.

She'd held the title of Board Chairman since taking the company away from her ex-husband, Michael Cole, but her role had been essentially one of a caretaker. No other approach made sense. Under Cole the company had violated every precept of prudent management. They'd made under-the-table payoffs to booking agents, bribed and blackmailed government officials, and falsified the company's books.

During the transition period only the strength of her reputation and that of her Chief Operating Officer, Admiral Reginald Schoonover, kept the liquidators at bay. Against all odds the troubled company managed to hang on. They were forced to restate their earnings reports and stockholders threatened to sue. There'd been regulatory issues to deal with, fines and levies to pay, and restrictions placed upon their ability to raise capital. With the Admiral handling day-to-day operations and her brother, Brian, providing legal advice, the company made a hard-won recovery.

Eventually British authorities agreed to let her take the company private. While it removed the threat of additional stockholder suits, it left them deeply in debt with no access to the capital markets. Twice she'd mortgaged personal assets so Paradise Getaways could meet its payroll. To everyone's great relief, the government lifted their regulatory restrictions ahead of schedule. Now the company could finally begin to consider new initiatives, stretch its wings and fly.

Yet she still worried. Being a caretaker was one thing. It was quite another to exercise real leadership. Her proposal represented a bold departure. Would a group of men who'd weathered such a storm have the courage to raise the sails and tack into the wind? Or had their narrow escape left them gun shy and afraid of risk? She'd know in the morning.

Claudia entered the Boardroom wearing a blue pinstriped suit. She had a long-sleeved white blouse with ruffled cuffs under her single-breasted jacket and a cornflower blue scarf folded loosely around her neck. The outfit contrasted nicely with her sapphire and diamond earrings. Her hair and makeup were flawless, her tailored suit and silk blouse tastefully stylish.

"Good Morning, gentlemen," she said, crossing the room. She took her place at the head of the table and called the meeting to order.

They spent the morning on routine matters. Following a catered lunch, she took the podium. "Your meeting packet contained preliminary figures on my proposal. I'd like to spend some time fleshing those numbers out. I also have additional information for you to consider before we vote."

She began by recapping the struggles of the past several

years. Ignoring the negatives, Claudia instead focused on the company's achievements. Then she discussed the need to strike out beyond the confines of the tried and true and take reasonable risks to grow the company.

As she circled the room extolling the benefits of her plan, she distributed financial estimates and projected slides illustrating the type of ships she proposed to add to the company's fleet. When it came time for a vote, she won their unanimous support.

"Bravo!" Admiral Schoonover rose and shook her hand. "Your plan is insightful and well-thought out. I'll organize an implementation team immediately."

The full Board rose and applauded her efforts.

Claudia swallowed the lump in her throat and beamed with satisfaction.

Eighteen months later, Claudia and the Board gathered in San Francisco to launch the new ships. Christened the *Paradise Explorer* and the *Paradise Voyager*, plans called for the *Explorer* to sail south with a stopover in San Diego before heading for destinations in Mexico. Her sister ship, the *Voyager,* would sail north, stopping at Vancouver, BC on its way to Alaska. Over the winter months when inclement weather made the northern cruises impractical, the *Voyager* would join the *Explorer* on the southern routes.

FIVE

Pine Crest, Oregon—*May, 1997*

Content to find a quiet corner where he could sip his coffee and read, Tom paid little attention to the comings and goings in the Sugar Shack until a shadow loomed over his table. He gave a start then smiled. "Oh, it's you, Eddie."

"Mornin', Sarge." Rain had turned Eddie Beltzer's tan Carhartt jacket dark across the shoulders and the bill of his John Deere cap spattered beads of moisture on the tabletop when he sat down.

He was the only person in Pine Crest, in the world, who still called Tom *Sarge*. It was an acknowledgement of mutual time spent in Vietnam. Eddie had noticed Tom's car in the parking lot and decided to stop at the Sugar Shack to share coffee.

"I didn't hear you coming."

"'Course ya didn't; I wasn't draggin' my boot like I usually do. Got me a brand new leg." Eddie grew up in Idabel, a small town in southeastern Oklahoma, and still retained his soft, Texarkana drawl. Tom accepted this without judgment. Less charitable individuals in town labeled Eddie an ignorant hick. Nothing could be further from the truth. Though he kept a low profile, Eddie was nobody's fool.

He lifted his pant leg revealing a shiny silver rod. "It's top of the line, titanium shaft and stainless steel joint with space-age bushings."

"How do you like it"?

"So far, so good." He gave him a wary grin. "I've only had it a few days. It's like learnin' t' walk all over again."

"How much did that bad boy set you back?"

"Let me put it this way, the folks who make these things are mighty proud of 'em." Eddie tilted Tom's cup. "Looks like ya need a warm-up."

He rose and walked over to the coffee station.

Tom watched and noted his greatly improved gait. The old leg had been heavier, forcing Eddie to lift and swing his foot with each step he took. This little kick step gave him an uneven, boot-scuffing gait. He still needed to flex his new knee, of course, but it operated so smoothly that the action was hardly noticeable.

Eddie lifted the pot off the warmer and grabbed an empty cup from the honeycombed dishwasher rack beside it. He refilled Tom's cup first, leaving a dark trail of coffee on the table when he transferred the spout to his.

"Not to worry, I'll get that right up." He wiped the drip with a flannel shirtsleeve before filling his cup, and handed off the pot to a passing waitress.

Eddie slid a small, metal cream pitcher in Tom's direction. "I know ya insist on the real stuff."

Tom nodded his thanks.

Opening his bakery sack, Eddie inventoried its contents and removed one bleeding raspberry filling. "Looks like we got us a leaker here." He caught the bright red glob with his tongue and sucked it into his mouth. "Mmm, I do like jelly donuts."

He slid the sack across the table. "No need t' be shy. There's a bear claw in there with your name written all over it." Eddie flipped the folded newspaper over as Tom reached into the sack. "Son of a gun, The Wall Street Journal. Ya still writin' for them?"

"Now and then, if and when they ask." He alternated bites of the bear claw with sips of coffee, savoring the contrast between the sweetness of one and the bitterness of the other.

Both men knew he was being politely modest. Tom had become a national spokesman on issues affecting the Pacific Northwest. Big city papers frequently asked him to provide commentary for their Op Ed pages and his syndicated columns appeared regularly from Seattle to San Diego.

"You know The Wall Street Journal brought me to Oregon, don't ya?"

Tom smiled and shook his head. "You're entitled to believe

whatever you want. Personally, I think it was just a co-incidence."

"How many times do I have to tell ya, there ain't no such thing."

"So it was fate, hmm?" Tom laid the bowl of his spoon on the table, pinned it in place with a finger, and flicked the handle. He watched the handle spin in wobbly circles. "Round and round it goes, where it stops only fate knows."

"Look, all I'm tryin' t' say is, whether we acknowledge it or not, our lives are guided by invisible hands."

Eddie had a sense of being led most of his life. It went deeper than that actually. Though he'd never been able to adequately describe it, the feeling was never far away. Several times in his life, Eddie knew that fate, if that's what Tom wanted to call it, had laid its hand upon him.

"So you think these invisible hands are around all the time, pushing us into the choices we make?" The tone of Tom's voice indicated that, for the first time, he might actually be interested in exploring the notion.

"It's far more subtle. Nobody but you decided whether ya'd put grape jelly or marmalade on your English muffin this mornin'. Typically, ya only see it lookin' back on your life."

"For example?"

"When did you develop this newfound interest in the mysterious ways of the universe?"

"Call it intellectual curiosity."

"Okay, I'll give ya an example. One time my car broke down in Peoria. They had to order the part, so I stayed over. The next morning the dealer sent a car to pick me up. On the way in, I just happened to look out at the Illinois River 'n' saw two guys in a canoe. In early March, the water's still cold in that part of the world."

Eddie held his empty cup for a passing waitress to refill and tilted the white bag toward Tom. He shook his head. Eddie pulled out another donut, took a bite and brushed sugar from his beard.

"So, I'm watchin' 'em paddle along nice as can be when all of sudden their canoe flips over, dumpin' 'em both into the river. Nobody on the bridge can see these two little specks in the water wavin' for help. I told the driver 'n' he called it in. A minute or two later a rescue boat fished 'em out."

"So something *bad* happened to you so something *good* could happen to them?"

"What other explanation is there? Everything happens for the greater good. Unfortunately, we don't always have the perspective to appreciate it."

Fate made a rude and violent intrusion into Eddie's life in Vietnam. One second the men were joking, the sun was shining, and birds were chirping. Everything felt good. The next instant, the air was full of rocks and leaves, dirt and dust. Two men were injured, one fatally, and everything felt bad, really bad.

Tom motioned toward Eddie's leg. "Even..."

His laughter sounded ragged and forced. "Yeah even the leg, although I'm still tryin' t' develop an appreciation for that one."

"Have you ever asked yourself what happens if you ignore these invisible hands?"

"Ya can't. They're *invisible* hands, remember? How can ya ignore somethin' ya don't know is there?"

"But that leads us back to co-incidence."

"Maybe, maybe not. Was it co-incidence that you saw the For Sale ad for your newspaper almost 25 years ago?"

Tom chuckled wistfully. "You should have seen the place. They suspended the paper's publication when the former owner died. His widow was in a nursing home and their only son, a Seattle attorney, had no desire to operate a small town newspaper. A local Realtor convinced him to place the ad before liquidating it. It drew a single response...me. If I wasn't interested, the Realtor was going to bring in the auctioneer. The remarkable thing is they advertised it as a *going concern*."

"More like a going-out-of-business concern, if ya ask me."

At the time, Tom was the youngest Business Section Editor at the Cleveland Plain Dealer. Management had their eye on him. If he worked hard and didn't make any big mistakes, he was on his way to the top. But then, as now, he had little tolerance for bureaucracy.

He shrugged. "The price was right, and I wanted to get out of Cleveland and run my own shop. You know how it is when you're young."

"I know invisible hands guided ya to Pine Crest."

"How can we ever be sure it's not co-incidence?"

"Easy. There ain't no such thing, remember? Look at it this way. I once worked in a shipping department with more chutes and conveyors than Los Angeles has freeways."

Eddie raised his cup over the table, "Now imagine this is an electronic scanner and somebody drops a package onto the belt." He took hold of his napkin and slowly tugged his half-eaten donut under the cup.

"It passes under the scanner and heads on down the line. Away it goes, never knowin' where it's headed." Eddie looked across the room imagining the package moving through a maze of conveyors. "Pretty soon, the package gets shuttled off in one direction or another, zips to the left 'n' zips to the right. It goes here, goes there, until it finally scoots down a chute right into the truck waiting t' get it where it's goin'."

He dropped his elbows on the table and leaned forward. "You and me, Sarge, we're like the little box. We don't know where life's gonna to take us. Every choice we make precludes a hundred others." He rolled his eyes toward the ceiling. "You gotta believe He's got a plan back of all this cause the trip we're on only makes sense once we get there."

Pine Crest, Oregon had been Eddie's destination even though he returned to his native Oklahoma when the VA released him. He married, later divorced, and then drifted. He moved across the country restlessly searching for his niche. One winter day in Chicago, finding himself with more month than money, he stopped in at the Pacific Garden Mission on State Street. They still operated their Servicemen's Center then. Eddie went in looking for something warm to eat and found a whole lot more.

To pass the time, he picked up an old, yellowed newspaper and flipped through it. Ignoring its sad condition, he spread the paper out on the table beside him. He dropped his fork and shoved the plate aside when he stumbled upon a familiar face. He smoothed out the crinkled page and read the bio at the end of the article: *Thomas Jenkins, Wall Street Journal contributor and syndicated columnist is Editor and Publisher of the Pine Crest Courier in Pine Crest, Oregon.*

Fate called with a kinder, gentler voice this time.

He tore out the article, stuffed it into his shirt pocket and hunted down an Oregon map. Pine Crest was near the coast. It had mild weather. What'd he have to lose? Just about anywhere was better than Chicago in the winter.

Pine Crest had been Eddie's home ever since. He eventually bought a few acres outside of town and built a log home. He supplemented his disability pension sawing lumber on his portable mini-sawmill and raising cattle. His demons still returned now and then, but for the most part he remained as placid as a mountain lake at sunset.

SIX

Delhi, India—*June, 1997*

Dwarakananth Maheshwari sipped the cool drink and absentmindedly watched his son, Tanveer, working with his pigeons. The boy removed them from their coops one at a time, lovingly checking them over while speaking to them in reassuring tones.

I shall miss moments such as this, he thought, listening to their soothing coos.

In his eagerness to have a flock of birds the young boy scavenged lumber from broken and discarded packing crates to construct his coops. When he completed the framing he proudly showed them to his father.

Tanveer moved his hand over the framing after his father praised his industriousness. "I shall, of course, need to cover these open spaces with metal fabric before they can house my doves. I have already priced it with a merchant. Can you advance me 1,800 rupees?" He raised his hand, stifling any resistance. "I am only requesting a loan, Pitajee. Once I have the loft and establish my name, I can sell the birds I raise. With the income they provide, I will return your funds to you."

At the time it hadn't occurred to Tanveer that he would also require bedding and nest boxes, ground grains for the feeders and, last but not least, the birds themselves. He returned to his Pitajee hat in hand, increasing his indebtedness several times over before completing the project.

He looked at Tanveer's coops precisely arranged under the heart-shaped leaves of a gajahanda tree and smiled when he recalled the tree had been covered with cup-shaped flowers. Though fading, the remaining flowers still retained their color.

Once the boy had his birds, he joined a club of racing enthusiasts and surprised his parents by sustaining what they had assumed would be merely a passing fancy. He now kept multiple breeding pairs in his loft. Pictures of doves papered the walls of his bedroom like pinups in a dorm and a small trophy for a third-place finish in the most recent Chennai-Delhi race gleamed on his dresser.

Dwarakananth felt a gentle touch on his shoulder. He turned to see his wife, Bhairavi, standing behind him. Her dark eyes sparkled as she watched their son work. "He certainly enjoys those doves of his, doesn't he?"

He seconded her observation with a nod, scooted to one side, and patted the space next to him.

She rounded the rattan settee and sat beside him. A bulbous pitcher, beaded with moisture and half full of ice cubes, sliced lemons and sweet Darjeeling tea waited on the table in front of them. She turned over a fresh glass, gave the pitcher a quick swirl, and poured. After she'd filled hers, he lifted his and she topped it off.

Bhairavi settled back, took a long sip, and sighed. "I believe the cool of the evening is my favorite part of the day. It is so peaceful."

He ran his eyes over her approvingly. "You look lovely this evening. The yellows enhance your natural coloring."

She'd chosen a citrus yellow *salwar kameez* with a flowered print. The light cotton pants fit loosely and her *kameez*, a long tunic shirt, ended just above the knee. It had open side seams below the waist and lovely *resham* embroidery at its hemline. Her *dupatta*, a matching sheer scarf, draped loosely around her shoulders and diagonally across her chest.

Bhairavi smiled and took his hand in hers. "There is something on your mind. You have been distant and distracted for nearly a week now. What is it, my husband?"

Dwarakananth smiled. "Ah Beebee, you can read me like a book. You are correct; it is time we talked."

"Is this about your work, the many secret processes that you refuse to share with me?"

"That and more. The work itself goes well. With RCI's

funding we've relocated our lab from the dingy basement to a clean, airy building." He chuckled. "I think I enjoy the new environment as much or more than Kaur's rabbits."

Bhairavi made designs on her frosty glass with a finger as she listened. "If it is not your work, what then is bothering you?"

"Last week I had a call from Mr. Winston Ridgely. He was pleased with my most recent progress report." He turned away and sighed. "He requested I relocate my work to the RCI headquarters in the United States."

The iced tea glass nearly slipped through his wife's fingers. "You told him it was out the question, correct?"

He hung his head. "I told him I would think about it."

"Think about it?" she said, her voice rising. "There is nothing to think about. I will answer for you. I say 'No, Mr. Ridgely.'"

"It is not a matter on which to make a snap decision."

"And why not? Your place is here with your wife and children. Your long hours and trips to the many conferences you must attend keep us apart enough already. You have a wife, three children, a home, and a position at the University. Do you want your children growing up not knowing who their father is?"

"You are exaggerating the situation, constructing elephants out of shrews. It is not the disaster you imagine it to be. Once you arrive there you will see that California can be quite lovely."

"I have seen the pictures. I know all I need to know about California, USA. I will not have my Tanveer associating with movie starlets who do not bother to put on their underwear. And what about the young men? Do you wish for your daughters to become involved with some surfer dude who is only looking for good vibrations?"

"There are many, many Indians in the United States of America. I am sure they will both find nice boys. The kind of boy who will please their Maamah."

Bhairavi's ire continued to grow. "You have a position which provides dignity, respect and a secure income. What else do you require? We managed fine before this Mr. Winston Ridgely stuck his nose in our affairs."

"Yes, we have managed well, and I am running like a mouse inside a wheel. Since I am the developer of this process, I can negotiate a share of the proceeds. This is our window of opportunity. It will provide us security for the rest of our lives. You can remain here in India if that is your preference."

"So now you are going to America alone by yourself." Her eyes narrowed. She poked a finger into his chest. "What has this Mr. Winston Ridgely suggested? Has he offered you women? Is that it? You plan to go to California and use their lax laws to divorce me and cavort with these loose women?"

Dwarakananth motioned with his hands. "You must lower your voice. The girls are upstairs in their room. I do not want them overhearing such wild speculations about their father."

She crossed her arms. "You do not wish for them to hear my accusations, but you have not denied them."

"They do not merit a denial." He reached for her hand, but she pulled it away. "You are not giving this a chance. I have hooked a very great fish here. Are you telling me I should not reel him in now I have him?"

"What about the man who hooked the greatest fish of his life. Then it pulled him into the water and gobbled him for dinner instead of the other way around?" Lowering her voice, she whispered her plea. "We could see a marriage counselor if you've grown displeased with me. India's strength, our strength, is the family unit. While other societies deteriorate into divorce and debauchery, the family remains the center of life for Indians. Without you we will be like a wheel with no hub nut. What will become us?"

He put his hand on her cheek. Leaning over, he softly kissed her. "I love you, Beebee. I always have and always will. I feel as if my entire life has been a prelude to this moment. If you feel better doing it, remain here with the children while I go prepare a place for you. There will be time to visit once I have found a home. It is an easy trip; Air India makes it every day."

"It is all the way around the globe. Do you remember when Hemadri went to visit her son last year? She stopped at airports she didn't even know existed. It took her over a full day just to get there." She rolled her eyes. "And the tales she told about the customs inspectors would scandalize you."

"This represents a once in a lifetime opportunity, not just for me, but for all of us. Whether we stay in America or return, we will have a better life. Let me at least see what Mr. Ridgely has in mind. You can decide once I am settled."

"My mother warned me about marrying a scientist whose work would be more important to him than his family." She shook her head. "Why could I not have met a postal worker? Delivering letters is a useful and honest occupation. He would go to work every day and come home every night." Her shoulders slumped and her chin dipped to her chest. "Very well, go if you must. Never let it be said Bhairavi stood in the way of her husband's dreams."

SEVEN

Pine Crest, Oregon—*May, 1998*

The first blush of a Saturday sun crept over the peak of Oregon's Coast Range, painting a thin orange band above the mountain's blue-gray silhouettes. Its warmth heated the cool morning air causing fog in the foothills to rise in plumes like smoke from Indian campfires.

The sun fell onto a two-story, shingled house and tinted the bedroom's white mini-blinds soft saffron. Tom Jenkins stirred, pushed back the blanket, and tiptoed into the bathroom. He smoothed his sleep-tangled gray hair while he waited for the water to warm. As he shaved, thoughts of Henry Mancini brought a smile to his face. For years his wife, Marty, kept a Mancini cassette beside their bed. During their Saturday morning lovemaking, she'd play it softly so the kids wouldn't overhear them. Was he the only one who found *The Pink Panther Theme* or *Baby Elephant Walk* arousing?

Returning to the bedroom, Tom eased into bed and cuddled against his wife.

"Oooo, you're cold." Her sleepy voice floated out of the pillow as she tugged the warm blanket around her.

"Why don't you warm me up?" He slid tighter making them spoons.

"What do you have in mind?"

"You've forgotten already?"

"I swear, Tom, you're incorrigible."

He chuckled. "What I am is insatiable."

"My lady's magazines say once a week is enough for a man in his fifties. You need to tell your friend there the honeymoon is over."

"He has a mind of his own."

She wiggled away from him when he kissed her neck.

"Maybe you should go back on those heart pills. They sure took the wind out of your sails."

"Yeah, those beta-blockers blocked more than betas. I'd rather let you handle things."

Marty gave him several lingering kisses then rested her head on his shoulder. "Fortunately, I know what's called for in a situation like this."

Afterwards they snuggled around each other savoring the lingering warmth of lovemaking. They shared the unspoken wish that this morning, these feelings, might never end. Meanwhile, the sun crested the mountains and rose higher in the sky, bathing the room in a warm, ethereal glow.

Marty stretched. "You amaze me. Shouldn't you be slowing down, at least a little bit?"

"My grandfather wouldn't want to hear you say that."

"Oh dear, here comes Grampy Jenkins again. Do you really believe that story?"

"You can't argue with hard facts."

She studied him as he spoke. He'd told this story myriad times and always with the same innocent twinkle in his eyes. Eyes that reminded her of the ocean on a cloudy day and made her weak in the knees the first time she saw them. She was standing in the doorway, Tom glanced up and smiled, and life was never the same.

"Honestly, the thought of the horny old goat bothering your grandmother *three* times a week. And they were both nearly seventy."

"They were a loving couple doing what comes naturally."

"Well, I feel sorry for the poor woman."

"Is it possible that maybe, just maybe, Grams enjoyed it too? Besides, Grampy wasn't a horny old goat. He was a virile man exercising his marital prerogatives. He's my hero."

"He's your hero if it's true."

"I've told you a hundred times, it came straight from the horse's mouth. Grams told Mom after his funeral, Mom told Sis and Sis told me." He clucked his tongue. "For some reason, Sis thought it was funny. Personally, I found it inspiring."

She patted his leg. "Your grandmother should have put Grampy on the same heart pills the doctor gave you."

An unsettled look swept over Tom's face. He pulled her close. "Hold me," he whispered.

Marty ran her fingers through his hair, smoothing it and kissed him with lips soft as rose petals. "I'm always with you. You know love transcends time and space." She touched his cheek and kissed him again. "Is there something I should know? Is it your heart?"

"This has nothing to do with my health. I had a fleeting sense of gloom and sadness." He took a deep, cleansing breath, released it, and smiled. "Forget about it. I'm fine."

As they talked, the rhythm of the day snatched them up and carried them along like driftwood in a stream. Birds chirped. Bees buzzed. Teeth needed brushing and the dog had to go out. Despite their best efforts, life overtook the moment.

"You haven't forgotten Karen's coming to stay the weekend, have you?" Marty asked over breakfast.

"I saw it on the calendar. Too bad you couldn't get John and Arlene to come too. With Tommy and Beth still living here in town, we'd have all the kids together for once." He glanced back over his shoulder at the clock on the stove. "I was planning on running down to the office for a little while. When do you think they'll get here?"

She mentally calculated the drive time from Portland. "I wouldn't expect them before noon, maybe later."

While Marty cleared away the breakfast dishes, Tom pulled down his favorite mug and filled it with coffee. On his way back to the table, he reached into the refrigerator and removed a small cardboard carton. He gave it a hard shake, carefully folded back its peak, and popped out the spout.

He was about to pour some into his coffee when Marty snatched it out of his hand. She examined the carton and scowled. "Heavy cream? Do you know how much fat and cholesterol are in one drop of this stuff? I can feel my arteries clogging up just holding the carton. The doctor told you to watch your diet. Why can't you use the nonfat powdered creamer I bought?"

"I only use a dribble." He took the carton back. "Besides, the powdered stuff makes my coffee taste funny."

The phone cut off Marty's rebuttal.

Tom read her face as she spoke. It was serious.

She hung up and sighed. "That was George Saltzman. The Hospice Nurse says Virginia has only a short time left. Both of their children live out of town. He asked me to come over. I don't know how long I'll be."

She crossed the kitchen, grabbed a pan of cinnamon rolls and quickly covered them with plastic wrap. "I'll take these with me. Don't forget about Karen," she called as she rushed out the door.

EIGHT

The Saltzmann's lived on small acreage several miles outside of Pine Crest. Marty turned off the paved highway onto a gravel lane and followed it a mile and a half before coming to their drive. The gate was pulled back and latched open.

George Saltzmann had made his living in the forest. For nearly 40 years he lugged ropes, an ax, wedges and a heavy chainsaw up mountains and down valleys in all kinds of weather to support Virginia and their two children. Quiet and soft-spoken, at six foot four and over 200 pounds, George was once as tall and rugged as the old-growth Douglas firs he felled. But now, at nearly eighty, the years had sapped away his youthful vitality.

The strain of caring for a dying wife and coping with his own health problems left George tired, weak, and sometimes confused. At times he was little more than a shuffling stick figure of a man. He'd become a faint shadow of his former self, wearing the same gray cardigan day in and day out with hands quivering from Parkinson's disease. Despite his problems, George was determined to be there for Virginia until the end.

Marty parked beside a gray Toyota belonging to Virginia's Hospice Nurse, Sally Hampton. Marty had served as a Hospice volunteer for a number of years and they'd worked together on other cases.

Rascal, George's beagle, came running when he heard the car door. Marty bent down to pet him. "Hi Rascal, I bet you can smell my dog, Charlie, on me," she said as he eagerly sniffed.

George opened the door before she knocked. Marty saw how slow he moved and noted his red-rimmed eyes. It'd been another tough night.

"I brought a pan of cinnamon rolls. I'll sit them on the counter." She put them down, turned and opened her arms to George. It shocked her to feel how frail he felt when she hugged him. "How have you been, George?"

He responded with a noncommittal shrug.

"You have to take care of yourself, too. How about a cinnamon roll? I'll warm it in the microwave and fix some coffee."

"That'd be nice." George opened a cupboard door and took out a plate. His hand wavered when he held it out to her.

"How do you take your coffee?" she asked while she set the microwave. When he didn't reply, she turned to look.

George was standing at the sink gazing out the window.

Marty wished she had more to offer than a warm cinnamon roll. She put it on the table, guided him into a chair. and left to visit with Sally.

A hospital bed surrounded by other medical equipment dominated the Saltzmann's living room. Against one wall was a recliner with a rumpled afghan where George spent most nights. The whoosh and click of the oxygen pump kept a steady pace like a metronome ticking off the waning minutes of Virginia's life. Braced up by pillows, she looked as fragile as a newborn robin.

Virginia was nearly comatose and didn't respond when Sally adjusted the IVs and checked her vital signs. Once she finished, they moved to the far side of the room away from the bed and the kitchen.

"She's fading fast," Sally whispered. "She's begun exhibiting apnea."

Apnea, Marty knew, was a physical response to decreased circulation. When dying, people often experienced these gaps between breaths. They ranged from a few seconds to as long as fifteen. It marked the beginning of the end, a dying body clinging to life one labored breath at a time.

In the kitchen, George was finishing the last bits of cinnamon roll. Marty looked from Virginia to Sally.

She nodded. It was time.

Marty crossed the room and accompanied him to Virginia's bed. George reached out and took his dying wife's hand. Marty leaned over the bed and spoke to her.

"Virginia, this is Marty. It won't be much longer. George is holding your hand. I'm going to read you some of your favorite Psalms." She brushed back feathery wisps of Virginia's thin white hair. "God bless you, Dear."

Marty opened Virginia's Bible and began reading. The woman in the bed didn't respond. She forced herself to concentrate on the reading and ignored the whirr of the pump, the apnea, and Sally, who timed each pause.

Marty finished a reading and glanced down at Virginia. The dying woman gasped. Her face took on a radiant glow. For an instant, she looked almost healthy. Then, as fast as it came, it was gone. Virginia sank into the pillows and never drew another breath.

Marty glanced across the bed at George. He'd seen it too.

She closed the Bible and put it away.

Sally turned off the oxygen and began disconnecting the monitors and removing the IVs, quietly gathering her equipment.

George gently laid his wife's hand across her body. He watched Sally roll the oxygen machine aside and turned to Marty. "I hated that thing when they brought it in. It made such an awful clatter. The first few weeks, it kept me awake all night. Eventually I came to rely on it. It told me Ginny was still here. I never knew quiet could be such an awful sound." Tears rolled down his cheeks.

Sally had packed her gear and left by the time the people from the mortuary arrived. Marty met them at the door, made sure everything was in order and then asked them to wait until she and George left the house. He sat at the kitchen table staring into his empty coffee cup.

She put her arm on his shoulder and leaned down close. "George, the people from the mortuary are here. Why don't you and I take Rascal for a walk? They only need a few minutes."

Reaching for his cane, he slowly rose and followed her out the door. Marty paused on the porch and took a deep breath.

After being in the house, it felt good to be outside where the air was clear and fresh. But even outside, sadness crowded around them like thick fog on a cool morning.

"Where does this path go?"

"It leads down to the garden, but it's pretty well overgrown. Since Ginny took sick I've let everything go."

The garden was still recognizable despite the encroachment of weeds and wildlife. Marty asked questions about this plant or that variety and played fetch with Rascal. It helped George to have other things to concentrate on.

The mortuary van finally pulled away and disappeared down the drive.

"We can head back now if you'd like," Marty said.

As they walked back to the house, she tried to determine how well George would cope during the coming days. Once they were inside, Marty called neighbors and notified them of Virginia's death. A couple who lived nearby promised to come right over. She also notified George's church. The pastor assured her several people from the congregation would drop by once they learned of Virginia's passing. The Saltzmann's two children were also due home from out of state.

Marty stayed until the neighbors arrived.

"These first days are never easy. One of the Hospice bereavement counselors will be in touch and you can call me if there's anything you need." She hugged George good-bye.

Marty stood by her car and brushed back tears. Her faith told her this shouldn't be a time of mourning, but one of celebration. Virginia had gone to her heavenly home.

She looked up at the sun filtering through the trees and whispered, "Godspeed, Virginia," as she opened her car door.

NINE

Charlie barked ferociously at the first crunch of tires on the gravel driveway. Tom glanced out the window at the dark blue minivan, put his book aside, and walked into the laundry room. The dog stood beside the washing machine, his tail thumping it like a bass drum, as he continued barking.

"Quiet down, Charlie. It's Ellie, Mark and Karen." Tom put his hand on the doorknob. "Stay on the porch."

The dog recognized the familiar vehicle and whined in anticipation.

"Stay, Charlie." Tom released the dog when Karen shut off the engine. The big Lab-Malamute mix shot off the porch and ran to the car, his feathered tail happily wagging.

Five-year-old Ellie climbed out and Charlie began dancing circles around her. Halfway to the house, Ellie stopped to acknowledge him. When he saw her hand reach out to pet him, he leaped into the air.

"Charlie, sit!"

On her command, the big dog planted his rump in the grass. His tail swept back and forth as the little girl rewarded him with pats on the head.

As soon as the dog saw Karen he ran to greet her. Having successfully defended his house and greeted his visitors, Charlie treated himself to several victory laps around the yard. Then he leaped back onto the porch and settled into the corner with a lolling tongue.

Ellie ran toward Tom with arms extended for a hug. "Hi, Grandpa!"

He scooped her up, held her close for a long moment, kissing her on the cheek and nuzzling her neck. The little girl wiggled and giggled much to her grandfather's delight. Putting her down, he turned to hug his daughter.

"Good to see you, Sweetheart."

"Good to see you too, Dad. Have you been feeling okay?"

Tom rubbed the arthritic knuckles of his right hand. "Oh, old Arthur and I have a tussle now and then, but that's part of getting older."

"You *know* what I meant." She tapped the left side of her chest.

"Hey, if I was any better I couldn't stand it."

He laughed and started up the porch steps. So what if he wasn't telling the whole truth and nothing but the truth; he wasn't on the witness stand. Besides, this was his daughter. His *daughter*. The decision to stop taking those heart pills wasn't any of her business.

What did she expect him to say? "*Well, the truth is I stopped taking those heart pills. I'll spare you the details. Impotency is one of Mother Nature's gifts that, like hemorrhoids and kidney stones, can only be truly appreciated when experienced firsthand. Oh sure, I have a little angina now and then, but that's why I hired the kid down the block to mow the yard.*"

Yeah, right!

Tom opened the door and stepped aside, letting Karen enter first. Ellie, who had run back to the car for her backpack, was next in line followed by Charlie.

"Mark didn't come with you?"

"I thought Mom would tell you. He's working this weekend. Something about meeting deadlines for the Spring catalogs. You're stuck with just me and Ellie, I guess."

Karen looked around, and grinned. The home where she grew up held many happy memories. She now lived in a two-story Colonial in the suburban Portland neighborhood of Raleigh Hills, but always found it comforting to return to Pine Crest. She did sense one thing missing though.

"Where's Mom?"

"Hospice. She got a call just after breakfast. She'll be back soon."

"Virginia Saltzmann?"

Tom nodded.

"It must be hard. I don't understand how Mom can go through this time and time again. I don't think I could stand all those people dying."

"You're young, Sweetie. You may feel differently when you're older. Your Mother isn't usually able to be with the family at the time of death. She's always honored to be invited to share such a deeply personal moment."

After settling into his favorite easy chair, he motioned for Ellie to come to him. As her tiny hands disappeared into his, he looked at her with a serious expression. "So, how's my favorite granddaughter today?"

He'd fed her the line as smoothly as Costello asking Abbott, "Who's on first?"

"Grandpa, you *know* I'm your *only* granddaughter." She replied with mock seriousness.

He thought for a moment. "Yes, of course you are. And that's what makes you extra special."

Tom and Ellie relished this lighthearted game and practiced their routine each time they were together. Ellie, a natural foil, slipped into her role effortlessly, embellishing and polishing her performance with each rendition.

"So, if I'm extra special, it must mean I'm your bestest grandkid."

He raised his right hand. "I can truthfully say that of all the grandchildren visiting this weekend, Ellie is definitely the bestest...so help me God."

"Grandpa, I'm the *only* grandkid visiting this weekend," she hollered.

Tom chuckled and scooped her into his arms.

Karen came into the room carrying a tray with two coffee

cups and a glass of milk.

Ellie's eyes suddenly widened as she sipped her milk. She put down the glass and ran for the guestroom.

"Grandpa, I've got something to show you," she yelled over her shoulder as she dashed away. She rummaged through her backpack, pulled out a rectangular box about six inches long and hurried back down the hall. "Guess what? I know where you live."

"Well, of course you do, Honey. You've been staying over with Grandma and Grandpa ever since you were just a little thing."

"No, that's not what I mean. I know your numbers."

Tom's forehead wrinkled as he struggled to decipher what she'd said. "You mean our house numbers?"

Ellie shook her head.

If Tom hadn't seen Ellie's frustration, he might have thought this was another comedy routine. "Tell me one more time. I'll listen extra hard."

Leaving nothing to chance, Ellie thrust out the box. "Look at the neat watch Daddy got me. It gives location numbers."

"Wow! That's really cool." Inviting her back into his lap, he examined the watch with all the seriousness it deserved.

Ellie pushed a button on the side of the watch. "When you press this button the time goes away and location numbers show up. See."

Karen came to his rescue. "It's a product Mark found at the National Electronics Show a few weeks ago. The watch has a built in Global Positioning Satellite locator chip. It automatically tracks and stores your position. Whenever Ellie pushes the selector button it replaces the time and date with her most recent Longitude and Latitude. Show Grandpa how it works again."

Knowing what he was looking at made understanding a lot easier. With a sigh of relief, Tom let Ellie swap the display back and forth to her heart's content. She loved showing it off and couldn't have found a more receptive audience.

TEN

Marty gathered her things off the car seat, closed the door and slowly walked to the house. She remained lost in thought and kept her eyes on the ground. Karen was right; it *was* hard when your clients died.

Tom and Charlie waited on the porch. He took her in his arms as soon as she came up the steps. "I'm sorry, Babe. Are you okay?"

She reached in her pocket for a tissue.

Charlie stood at Tom's side waiting for Marty to pet him.

She blotted her eyes, and reached down to scratch behind his ear. "I'm going to sit in the rocker by the window for a little while. Okay?"

"Take as much time as you need. I'll ask Karen to fix some of your chamomile tea."

After putting her things on the bed, Marty hugged Karen and Ellie and went into the living room. She sat in the big blue rocker-recliner next to the stone fireplace. Folding her hands in her lap, she silently stared out at the mountains framing the horizon. Geologists said they'd been standing there for eons. Before there was a Pine Crest, an Oregon...or even a United States, there were those mountains. Right now, she craved their permanence.

Charlie padded over and lay down beside her chair. He let out a big sigh as his head dropped onto his paws. It suited her mood.

A few minutes later, Ellie tiptoed over. "Hi Grandma, can I sit with you?"

"Sure Kiddo, come on up."

Marty lifted Ellie into the big chair. She nestled in beside her grandmother and Marty slipped an arm around her. The two of them enjoyed the view as they slowly rocked.

After several minutes, Ellie glanced up at her. "We're being sad, aren't we, Grandma?"

"Yes we are, Sweetheart."

Ellie refolded her hands in her lap as they rocked. After a period of silence, she asked, "How come we're being sad?"

"A lady I knew, Virginia Saltzman, died this morning."

"Was Ginya Sallman a nice lady?"

Marty nodded and brushed aside fresh tears.

Ellie gently patted her grandmother's hand. "It's sad when somebody dies, isn't it? I had a hamster named Pokey who died." Ellie studied her fingers as she remembered. "Daddy dug a hole in the backyard. We put Pokey in a little box and put him in the hole. Then Daddy covered him up."

"I remember Pokey. He lived in your bedroom in a cage with a wheel."

"Is that what will happen to Ginya Sallman? Will they put her in a hole like Pokey?"

"Sort of. When people die we don't put them in the backyard. We have special places called cemeteries where we bury them. Usually they put a marker on the place where someone's buried so we can visit it and remember them."

Satisfied to continue rocking, Ellie lapsed into silence.

Tom brought a small tray. He sat the cup of tea and the cookies he'd brought on the table beside Marty and slipped away.

She held the plate out to Ellie. "Want a cookie?"

After she took one, Charlie's head raised expectantly.

"I know, I know, you're nothing but an old cookie hound." Marty flipped one to the dog. It disappeared in a flash.

"Can I have another one, Grandma?

"Just one more, we don't want to spoil lunch."

Ellie gave her grandmother a quizzical look. "What makes people die?"

"Oh, there are lots of reasons. Sometimes people have accidents and get hurt real, real bad and die. Or sometimes people get very, very sick and sometimes they just grow old and their body wears out."

"Why did Ginya Sallman die?"

"She had a disease called cancer. It made her very sick and she couldn't get better, so she died."

Ellie had a serious expression on her face as she processed this information. "Mommy said she didn't know why Pokey died. What happens to make people die?"

Marty hesitated, searching for the right words. "Well, we believe people are made of two parts, a body and a soul. The soul is what makes the body come alive. When the soul leaves, the body isn't alive anymore."

Ellie frowned as she struggled to understand. "Can you tell it to me again?"

"Okay. Think about it like this, what comes out of the wall when you plug in the toaster?"

"Lektrizzty!"

"Right. Now if I unplug the toaster, will it work?"

Ellie shook her head. So far, she understood what Grandma was saying.

"For the toaster to work, it has to have electricity. If I take the electricity away, the toaster looks just the same, but it doesn't work anymore. Our soul's like the electricity. Without it, the body won't work. Does that make sense?"

"If you've been good, I know where you go when you die." Ellie brushed the sugar off her fingers and pointed up at the ceiling. "You go straight to heaven to live with God." She gave a decisive nod. "They taught us that in Sunday school."

Marty smiled and patted her hand.

A sudden movement in a bush outside the window caught Marty's eye. She brought her mouth close to Ellie's ear. "Look," she whispered, "on that bush eating berries, it's a Cedar Waxwing." She pointed to the tan crested bird with a yellow-tipped tail. "Isn't he the prettiest thing you've ever seen?"

ELEVEN

RCI Corp. Headquarters, Palo Alto, California

Winston Ridgely rubbed his hands together and grinned. He eyed the men gathered in the Board Room. "This is a big day, gentlemen." He checked his watch. "Yoblanski's picking him up at the airport now. This afternoon you'll meet the man who will make the Navy happy and us as rich as rajas."

Business magazines hailed Winston Ridgely as the quintessential self-made man, but like most of his country club cronies he acquired his wealth the old-fashioned way; he'd inherited it.

A native Californian, he was the only child of a wealthy industrialist by the same name. He had his father's sandy-blond hair and his mother's green eyes. Tall, tan and ruggedly handsome, he spent his adolescence in the vigorous pursuit of pleasure and personal fulfillment. Immersed in the rarefied environment of private schools, palatial homes and exotic vacations young Winston, Win to his friends, grew accustomed to having the better things in life, even came to expect them as his just due.

After prep school, he completed his undergraduate work at Princeton, came home to Stanford for an MBA and followed it up with a carefree summer in Europe. When he returned, he went to work for his father's company. Being the boss's son meant he skipped the work-your-way-up-from-the-mailroom routine and went directly into a vice-presidency. He didn't have to pass Go and he collected considerably more than $200.

San Francisco International Airport

The young Asian woman hurried through the parking garage carrying a large, hand-lettered sign and two mouse-eared helium filled balloons.

The elevator chimed.

Shiri Yoblanski's heels clicked on the rough concrete as she dashed for it. The elevator's lone passenger saw her coming and extended his arm to bar the door. Nodding a breathless thank you, she shortened the line on her balloons and stepped to the rear of the car.

The passenger, a man in his early forties, cast her appreciative sidelong glances as the elevator began to descend. He guessed her to be five to ten years younger than he was. And, strangely enough, perfectly at ease running through airports with helium balloons and a hand-lettered sign that read: *Dr. Maheshwari*.

For her part, Shiri concentrated on the floors clicking by.

He contemplated asking who Dr. Maheshwari was. It'd be a great conversation starter.

She checked her watch.

He took a second, longer look. She was petite and attractive, probably Japanese and wearing a wedding ring. He sighed...just his luck.

The doors opened and she hurried away toward the British Airways gates, balloons trailing in her wake.

Shiri Yoblanski, the newly-promoted Director of Executive Recruiting at RCI Corp., had a well-defined and straightforward mission. Her orders came down from the top. She'd meet Dr. Dwarakananth Maheshwari at the airport and convince him to move to the United States to work at RCI. It would mean taking an extended sabbatical from his University Professorship, severing connections with his research team, and leaving his wife and children behind in India.

She had already developed her battle plan. It helped that Dr. Maheshwari had an existing relationship with RCI. Leveraging this relationship, Shiri planned to establish a personal connection over lunch and nurture this bond into a friendship.

Most men found her attractive and she wasn't above flattery and a little harmless flirting, if that's what it took to get the job done. There'd also be limo rides around the Greater Bay Area to help him get a feel for the terrain, dinners at expensive restaurants, and use of the company's penthouse condo.

And last, but not least, she had the corporate checkbook. She was prepared to offer Dr. Maheshwari a very handsome compensation package. If very handsome didn't get the job done, she'd replace it with extremely generous. If that didn't do the trick, she'd raise it some more, all the way to flat-out ridiculous. This was, after all, defense work. RCI could bury Maheshwari's cost somewhere among the $100 hammers and $250 toilet seats.

She arrived at the gate early and spent the time attaching a stick to her sign and tying her balloons to it. She positioned herself well back from the gate so she had a good view of everyone coming up the ramp. After a few minutes, her nervous energy kicked in and she began pacing back and forth.

Her mother's voice echoed in her ears. *Shiri, stand still. Why must you always fidget? It's not ladylike.* She'd heard it a million times. She rolled her eyes, came to a stop, and softly whispered, "Yes, Mama."

She had no trouble identifying Dr. Maheshwari.

Seeing her sign, he smiled and gave a short wave of hello as he approached her.

He was several yards away and closing when she called to him. "Doctor Maheshwari, it's good to finally meet you. After all the phone calls, I feel as if we're old friends."

He appeared taken aback by her boisterous welcome, but reached for the hand she extended.

"Everyone here at RCI has been looking forward to your arrival. I'm Shiri Yoblanski, of course." She gave a nervous laugh and pumped his hand. "But then, you knew that, didn't you?"

He glanced up at her balloons. "It was very kind of you and Mickey to greet me, Mrs. Yoblanski."

Shiri had an unusually firm grip for a woman. She'd worked hard to perfect her strong handshake and coupled it with prolonged and frequent eye contact. She felt it important to make a memorable first impression when recruiting high profile applicants. Most men remembered her friendly, confident attitude and good looks. Those from Asia, accustomed to more subservient behavior in their women, sometimes found her style harsh and abrasive, pushy. So be it; she was who she was.

She read his perplexed expression. "I know, I know. My appearance surprised you. I get that all the time. With a name like Yoblanski everyone expects a steroid-enhanced gal who's built like a member of the old East German Women's Olympic team."

She lifted her arms slightly and rocked from foot to foot, suggesting the bulk of a Sumo wrestler. She grinned at Dr. Maheshwari's startled expression. She often had this effect on applicants.

"You'll be staying at RCI's condo until you find a place of your own. I've made reservations for lunch. I thought it would give us a chance to become better acquainted. After lunch we'll swing by and tour the offices and research facilities."

Maheshwari glanced up at a terminal clock. "Is that the correct time?"

Shiri grew solicitous, almost motherly. "Are you tired from the long flight, suffering from jet lag?"

"No, I am not lagging; I simply wished to adjust my watch."

"I think it was wise to break your trip into two parts," Shiri said as they walked. "Straight through from Delhi to San Francisco is a grueling flight."

"So you know of my stopover in London?"

"Our Travel Department always cc's me on—"

Dr. Maheshwari's look cut her off.

"Pardon me for interrupting, Mrs. Yoblanski. I believe these young people here are coveting your Mickeys." He pointed to a pair of youngsters staring longingly at Shiri's bright balloons.

"Perhaps they should have them."

Shiri undid the strings and handed them to the children. "Did you sightsee while you were in London? Buckingham Palace...Westminster Abbey...Big Ben and the whole routine?"

"It had what I believe you Americans call a working holiday."

"Really, what did you do?"

"I was a guest lecturer at Cambridge University. Professor Hawking and I made a joint presentation at the Isaac Newton Institute."

"You know Stephen Hawking?"

The surprise in her voice drew a chuckle from Maheshwari. "Yes, our work throws us together several times a year. Professor Hawking and I regularly attend Strings Conferences.

She came to a halt and gave him a hard stare. "You're telling me you have conferences about *string*?"

His dark eyes sparkled. "Most certainly. Various attendees present their papers on kite string, packaging twine, why one even did a study on shoe strings."

"You're pulling my leg, aren't you?"

His eyes widened. "I think not. We just met and I am a happily married man."

"I meant you were joking with me."

Maheshwari could not hide his delight. "Yes, Mrs. Yoblanski, I suppose I am indeed tugging your leg. Not string, *String Theory*."

"What's String Theory?"

"String Theory is the future of physics. It unites all elementary particles...electrons, photons, neutrinos and quarks as well as gravity, electromagnetism and weak and strong nuclear interaction. It mathematically combines Quantum Theory and Einstein's General Theory of Relativity, thereby allowing us to calculate all of matter's ten dimensions."

"If there are ten dimensions why did my science teacher

tell me there were three? Well, four if you include time." She lowered her eyebrows. "Sounds to me like something funny's going on here."

"You learned the dimensions of Newtonian Physics, the dimensions of our everyday world. Dr. Hawking and I, along with other scientists pursue a relativistic universe where time expands or contracts. It has ten dimensions, allowing us to unify the fundamental forces operating among the particles of matter."

Noting her startled expression, he added, "There is no cause for alarm. The other six dimensions are contracted into such a small size they can never be observed. The ruler in your desk drawer remains quite secure."

"I attended Dr. Hawking's address at Cal Tech," Shiri said as they entered the baggage handling area. "He's sort of like Albert Einstein; everyone's heard of him."

"Besides being blessed with a towering intellect, Stephen has the gift of expressing his lofty thoughts in understandable ways. It's a unique combination. Few of us do it as well."

"It took me a few minutes to get used to his speech synthesizer," Shiri admitted. "He hasn't let ALS stop him. He's amazing."

"The world needs holy men to explain God. Just as we require men like Professor Hawking to explain our world. Outward appearances and physical limitations should not define a person. The human spirit is invincible."

"He sure has it all figured out, doesn't he?"

"Are you familiar with the parable of the blind men and the Indian elephant?"

"Sure. One was touching the elephant's leg and said it was like a tree; another had his tail and said it was like a rope, the third had his trunk and said it was like a hose."

"Likewise, we physicists play a game of blind man's bluff." He pulled the first suitcase off the luggage carousel and set it aside. "The final answer, it seems, is always just beyond our grasp. Forcing us to remain *Theoretical* Physicists."

TWELVE

They collected Maheshwari's baggage, left the San Francisco International airport, and drove to Shiri's favorite restaurant.

"What does your husband do for a living?" Maheshwari asked while they waited for the maitre d'.

"Yoblanski, of course, is my married name. My family's third generation Japanese-American. My husband, Jared, was a lineman for the 49'ers. Six foot four. Big guy, really, really big guy." Shiri waved her hand high above her head for effect. "Since he retired from the game, he's working with them as an Offensive Line Coach."

The maitre d' recognized Shiri immediately. He grabbed two bound menus and led them to their table. As they crossed the room, she paused briefly at several tables. At each stop, she laid her arm across a person's shoulder, conferred with them in exaggerated whispers and quiet chuckles, before moving on.

Maheshwari, meanwhile, wondered what, or who, the 49'ers were and what it was that made her husband's work so offensive. From there, his mind went to the petite Shiri with a man nearly six and a half feet tall. He was still pondering those implications when she resumed her monologue.

She took the menu offered her and slid into a chair beside the window. "There's enough of Jared to make at least three of me with parts left over."

Dr. Maheshwari took the chair opposite her. As he listened to her chatter on and on, he realized she'd entertained many other prospects with these same stories.

The two diners were a study in opposites. The man quiet, unassuming and soft-spoken, the woman expressive and animated. Throughout the meal, Shiri maintained a nearly constant stream of comments, questions, and observations while Maheshwari quietly sipped his tea, smiled and politely nodded.

An observer might have concluded he was not enjoying himself. While the subject of their conversation held little interest for him, despite her exuberant personality, he found Shiri quite charming.

Gradually, the thin, dark-skinned man's gaze strayed to the window. He focused his attention on a flock of birds scavenging around the dumpster.

Shiri continued her monologue unaware she'd lost her audience. "Don't you agree, Dr. Maheshwari?"

He ignored her.

She asked again, louder. "I said, don't you agree, Dr. Maheshwari?"

He jerked at the sound of his name. He turned to face her with a sheepish smile. "I must apologize, Mrs. Yoblanski. It seems I have failed to pay attention to our conversation." He pointed toward the dumpster. "I am afraid my concentration was diverted to those lovely Rock Doves just beyond our window."

Cupping her chin, she appeared confused. "I don't see any doves. There's nothing out there but a few scruffy pigeons milling around in the trash."

"Beauty resides in the eye of the beholder. These humble birds that populate our cities, both yours and mine, are *Columba livia,* the European Rock Dove...commonly known as the feral pigeon. They have, however, an illustrious history extending all the way back to the time of the Pharaohs in ancient Egypt."

Shiri watched the birds with newfound interest. "Their purple and green feathers are sorta pretty, I guess."

"Most everyone admires their hackles."

"Their what?"

"Hackles. That is the ornithological term for the iridescent feathers on their neck. You were referencing them, were you not?"

"Yeah, I suppose I was."

He pointed out the window at the ground below. "You may find it interesting to know that those birds have neither green nor purple feathers. The colors you see are the result of iridescence; it results from the diffraction of light."

For the first time since they'd left the airport, Shiri grew quiet and he became animated. An astute observer of body language, Shiri immediately understood she'd inadvertently pushed one of his hot buttons. She allowed the conversation to continue, and in the process, learned more about pigeon feathers than she ever wanted to know.

"You seem to know an awful lot about birds," she said when he finished. "I thought you were a physicist, not an ornithologist."

"Indeed I *am* a physicist. But there is an entire branch of physics devoted to the properties of light."

Maheshwari noticed a beam of sunlight streaking through the window and thrust his hand into its path. The bright circle of light on their table vanished. "Light, you see, interacts with matter in a variety of ways. At times it behaves as a particle, at other times as a wave. It bounces and reflects, causing things to appear shiny or dull. It passes through certain materials and bends...refraction. It goes through narrow slits and splits into its constituent parts...diffraction. The spectroscopic diffraction produced by the bird's feathers created the iridescence you admired."

He leaned back in his chair and interlocked his fingers. "Light, of course, does many other things as well, but we don't usually cover them in our introductory course." His voice dropped to a confidential whisper. "Among other things, my potential contributions to RCI center on the properties of light and electromagnetic forces."

"And the birds?"

"My interest in birds comes by way of my son, Tanveer. He

is the bird fancier in our family. He started down this delightful path several years ago when he acquired a pair of Indian fantail pigeons. Most recently, he has chosen to pursue his hobby with racing pigeons."

"Do they look anything like those birds?"

"There is a resemblance. A racing pigeon is a cross of several breeds, including the carrier dove."

"Are they anything like a carrier pigeon?"

"One and the same. Throughout the world people know them by many names. For instance, the Dutch use the term *postduiven,* or messenger-dove."

"How old is your son, Dr. Maheshwari?"

"He will celebrate his fourteenth birthday quite soon. In just a few days, actually." He sighed. "Unfortunately, I shall not be there to share the occasion with him."

Rather than dwell on his absence, Shiri suggested they leave.

Her high-energy personality re-asserted itself on the trip from the restaurant to RCI's Palo Alto headquarters. Once the RCI campus came into view, she regaled Maheshwari with a host of information relating to its construction.

She quoted all sorts of statistics about their energy-efficient architecture. Told him how they'd sited the buildings to minimize solar heat gain during the summer months, used natural and recyclable materials when and wherever possible, and much, much more.

Winston Ridgely was waiting in the lobby when they arrived. He rushed forward and grasped Maheshwari's hand. Ignoring Shiri, he swung an arm around his shoulder and led him away. "Come upstairs, Dr. Maheshwari, there are some people I want you to meet."

Maheshwari noticed Shiri left behind and looking bereft. He walked back to her. Taking both of her hands in his, he gave her a respectful nod. "Thank you for a wonderful morning, Mrs. Shiri Yoblanski. You and I will accomplish great things together."

THIRTEEN

Annapolis Maryland,—*August, 1998*

Claudia Monet rose early and tip-toed out of the bedroom and down the hall. She reached the guest bath, paused to glance up and down the hall, then slipped in.

Everyone is still asleep, so far so good.

She'd begun easing the door closed when a furry brown paw suddenly appeared around the edge. Claudia knew Mousse well enough to know he'd start meowing if she didn't let him in. She pulled the door back a bit and he padded through the opening.

After noiselessly closing and locking the door, she picked up the cat and held him at eye level. "You better behave yourself and keep quiet. Give me away, Mr. Kitty, and you'll go back out so fast you won't know what hit you."

Mousse circled the unfamiliar room, nosing around and quietly meowing.

Claudia opened the lowest drawer of the linen cabinet and stretched to reach in. She kept her stash all the way in back, hidden beneath a pile of towels. She chose one of three boxes and sat it on the vanity. Next, she removed a cellophane-wrapped disposable cup from the medicine cabinet, placing it on the counter beside the toilet.

She frowned. This whole process reminded her of high school chemistry class. The only things missing were the slate sinks and the periodic table.

The vanity became her work area. She smoothed a hand towel over the counter and put the receptacle and eye dropper on it. After washing her hands, she unwrapped the new cup and filled it with urine. She sat it on the towel and washed her hands again.

Curious, Mousse leaped onto the counter to investigate. He sauntered over and sniffed the cup.

She spun around and scooped him up in one quick motion

and deposited him in the bathtub.

The directions in the box said this was an easy process. And it might have been if her hand wasn't shaking so badly. After several false starts she got the pregnancy test started. She marked the time and rechecked the directions to be certain.

Her nervousness seemed to be contagious. Mousse left the bathtub and walked back and forth along the window sill. His coppery eyes followed her as she paced the room. When sufficient time elapsed, she noted the result and then decided to do the whole thing all over again just to be sure.

Claudia skipped back to the bedroom with a wide grin. Snuggling up beside Jeremy, she smoothed his hair and kissed his cheek. "Time to wake up, Daddy."

He blinked several times then checked the clock. "It's Saturday, why are you up so early?"

"Oh, I had something I needed to do."

He yawned and stretched. "That's nice. What's important enough to wake me up early?"

"I thought you might want to know you're going to be a father...again."

"How did that happen?"

She poked him in the ribs. "Didn't they explain about the birds and the bees in med school?"

"I just..." he pulled her into his arms and kissed her. It was several minutes before either of them spoke.

"I meant are you absolutely sure?" he said softly.

"You can take it to the bank. I used two different tests and they both had the same result." She giggled."Well, actually that's not true. One had a blue bar and the other one had a plus sign." Eyes sparkling, she let out a whoop and slapped the mattress. "But they both mean the same thing. We're going to have a baby."

Her eyes widened. "What am I doing here with you? There's someone I have to tell."

Jeremy expected her to reach for the phone to call her Aunt Wheezie, or her best friend Stephanie, or perhaps one of her brothers. Instead, she leaped off the bed and headed for the door.

"Where are you going?"

"I just told you. I'll be back in a minute or two."

Her nightgown billowed as she raced down the hall. Reaching Trevor's room, she went in and sat on the bed. She placed a hand on his shoulder and gently rocked him awake.

The little boy opened his eyes and stared up at her in amazement. "What are you doing here, Mommy?"

"I have some news and I wanted you to be the first to hear it." She couldn't stop happy tears from trickling down her checks.

He reached up and touched one. "What's wrong?" he asked, rubbing his damp thumb and forefinger together. "Why are you sad?"

She shook her head and swallowed the lump in her throat. "I'm not sad. Ladies cry when they're happy too. And I'm happier than I've ever been. I wanted you to know you're going to have a brother or sister." She pulled her six-year-old stepson into her arms and kissed the top of his head. "I'm going to have a baby, Trevor."

FOURTEEN

Pine Crest, Oregon

"You haven't forgotten the Mothers of Song are going to Chadwick's Nursing Home this afternoon, have you?" Marty asked.

They were on their way home from church with Karen and Ellie in the backseat.

Tom kept his eyes on the road. "Saw your note on the calendar this morning."

Leaning forward, Karen rested her hand on the back of her mother's seat. "Chadwick's is where Angela Kelley's mom went after her stroke, isn't it?"

"Yes. That was eight years ago; she was there five years."

"Gee, that sounds awful. Nursing homes always seem so dreary."

"Those are the exact words Angela used." Marty said as much to herself as to Karen.

"It's just so dreary there. The place exudes loneliness and isolation," Angela Kelley had told Marty shortly after they admitted Angela's mother to the Care Center.

"Why couldn't a group of us go over to the Center and lead the patients in song?" Marty had wondered aloud.

Angela cleared the idea with the Center's Director; they recruited a few more friends and nervously drove over to the nursing home on a rainy spring day. They met with resounding success. Casting about for a name, they'd settled on the Mothers of Song.

The mothers, mostly grandmothers now, spent the next several years polishing their act. Several of the women played musical instruments, and their repertoire consisted of old favorites interspersed with a few *newer* numbers from the 70's. They served up a winning combination of pleasing harmonies, moderate tempo and a sing-along format.

Ellie rocked in her seat. "Can I go with you to sing, Grandma? Please...I'll behave, honest."

Marty glanced over the seat at her. "You might get bored."

"I want to see the ladies...please...ple-e-e-ez."

"Okay, but no complaining about how long it lasts."

As they grew more confident, the Mothers of Song branched out. They continued making regular visits to local nursing homes, but also performed at charity fundraisers. A little over a year ago, they'd taken another big step and begun doing paid performances. They developed several comedy skits and punctuated each with well-placed double entendres.

They were pleasantly surprised to see how well received they were by various business groups. Every month or so the Mothers of Song traveled to a regional sales conference, a district meeting of the Grange, or a 4-H Banquet. Commercial performances were especially welcome because of the income they produced. The Mothers of Song adopted their local Hospice organization and donated the money to them.

They rolled to a stop on the crest of the big hill at the four-way intersection of Coos Bay-Pine Crest Road. A wide valley spread out in front of them for several miles on each side. Nestled in that valley floor, surrounded by forest and protected by mountains, was Pine Crest. Marty smiled; they were nearly home.

Tom and Karen were enjoying a lazy Sunday afternoon when they heard Ellie's excited chatter on the porch. Tom opened the door and Ellie burst into the house waving a handful of brochures.

"Grandpa! Mommy! Look at the big boat Grandma's going to ride on. Look Mommy, look!"

When Marty came into the room, Tom greeted her with a look that said, *What is Ellie talking about?*

Marty walked across the room and kissed his cheek. "Just give it a chance." She caught Ellie as she whirled by. "Sweetheart, give those to Grandma for now. I'll let you take some home with you when you leave."

Tom grew increasingly anxious by the minute. *Big boat Grandma's gonna ride?* What was going on here?

"I know you've got questions. Let me get out of these clothes and freshen up a bit. I'll be back to tell you all about it."

"Boy do I have news for you guys," Marty said as she took a seat on the couch. Smiling broadly, she picked up one of the brochures.

Ellie tried to jump back into the conversation, but Karen pulled her into her lap and wrapped her up in her arms. "Let Grandma talk."

"After we finished at the nursing home today, Melody said she had an idea to share with us. Somehow, she'd found out about a cruise line that's looking for entertainers."

Tom felt a sudden sense of foreboding. Though he had no idea why, he somehow knew he wasn't going to like hearing what Marty had to say. It was silly to feel apprehensive, he told himself. He didn't even know what she planned to say.

Yet he couldn't shake the persistent and overpowering feeling of trepidation. He sensed his life, their life, was poised to undergo a wrenching change. How he knew this, he couldn't say. He just did.

Marty unfolded the brochure. "It's a really terrific opportunity. Most of the time is our own, they provide free room and board, plus you get paid for the work. Isn't that just about the greatest thing you've ever heard?"

No, Tom thought, that's not the greatest thing I've ever heard. He didn't like it one bit. Through sheer power of will he forced himself to sit quietly even though every fiber of his being urged him to scream, "No! No! NO!"

A sudden chill caused a shiver.

What was he frightened of?

He couldn't say, exactly. It wasn't anything solid he could get his hands around; it was more like a, a...a gut feeling. They were heading towards certain disaster as surely as if they were racing downhill in a runaway car with no brakes. But how could he convey these feelings to Marty?

She leaned forward and fanned out the brochures across the tabletop. "Now, I know what you're thinking."

Oh, no you don't!

Marty arched an eyebrow and gave him a surprised look.

Could she have somehow read his mind? Did she sense his inner turmoil?

Her eyes softened and she reached for his hand. When their fingers touched, she pulled away. "Your hands are like ice. Is something wrong; do you need a sweater?"

"I'll be alright." He shifted in his chair. "There must be a draft in here or... or something."

"You're probably wondering why any cruise line would be interested in the Mothers of Song," Marty said, returning to her narrative. "One of those big outfits with thousands upon thousands of passengers wouldn't be. They hire some pretty big names, famous singers, Las Vegas acts and so forth. But Melody found a company that operates smaller ships, so it's no problem."

They knew nothing about this outfit. Who could say if they were reliable? What kind of a crew did they have? Were their boats even seaworthy? Tom imagined a rusty scow wheezing its way through the waves. Fantastic! She wants to book passage on the *African Queen*.

"The cruise goes to Alaska, all the way to the Bering Sea. The ship's called the *Paradise Voyager* and it sails out of San Francisco. This time of year, there will be whale watching too."

Karen smiled. "It really sounds great, Mom."

Excitement danced in Ellie's eyes. "I wish I could go, Grandma." She hopped down and ran over to the table. She grabbed a brochure and waved it in the air.

Marty looked to her left. "Tom, you haven't said a word. What do you think?"

Did she want the truth? No, not really. What she wanted was his approval and support. But he wasn't ready to give them, not yet anyway. "The truth is I need time to think this over. I'm, I'm just not sure."

His reluctance did nothing to diminish Marty's enthusiasm. "Well, I think it's a perfectly splendid opportunity. Melody says most of the passengers are either retirees or honeymooners. You know our act goes over big with the older folks and as for the honeymooners," Marty winked at Karen, "they'll mostly be spending the time in their cabin anyway."

"How long does the cruise last Mom?"

"They call it a two-week cruise. We leave on a Sunday and return on a Friday. That works out to 13 days and 12 nights. I suppose they must clean the ship on Saturday. Then they're ready to start the next cruise again on Sunday."

Tom snapped up in his chair. "The next cruise? How long do you plan on doing this?"

"It's a one-shot deal, but Melody says if they like us we might get the chance to do it again sometime."

Tom picked up a brochure and began thumbing through it.

"Oh, I almost forgot the best part," Marty said. "Besides free room and board, we get a transportation allowance back and forth to San Francisco and $500. There are eight of us going, so we'll have $4,000 for Hospice when we get back."

Marty glanced at her watch and dropped the brochures onto the table. "Look at the time. Karen, can you help me get supper started?" The two of them went into the kitchen and continued an excited conversation about the upcoming cruise.

FIFTEEN

Ellie and Tom remained in the living room while the women prepared supper. She picked up one of the brochures and crawled into his lap. "Wanna look at the pictures with me some more, Grandpa?"

He didn't, but for Ellie's sake said he would.

She rooted around until she was comfortable and began carefully opening the brochure on her lap for him to see. Ellie pointed to each picture, explaining them as she went. When she opened to its centerfold, there was a photograph of the Directors seated around a table along with a short letter they'd supposedly written to prospective passengers.

"Who are these people, Grandpa?"

"They're the men who run the cruise line."

"What about this pretty lady in the middle?"

Tom had somehow overlooked the beautiful blond at the head of the table. Taking the brochure from Ellie, he brought it closer and squinted at the list of names. "She's Claudia Monet. It's says she's the Company's Chairperson. That means she's the boss."

Ellie flipped over the woman's magazine on the coffee table. "What's she doing on the back of Grandma's magazine?"

Seeing the ad reminded Tom of the commercials he'd seen for the cruise line on cable TV. He'd assumed she was merely window dressing for the ads. *Since when did supermodels start running cruise lines?*

Ellie pointed to a man's portrait. "What about him?"

With his friendly smile, mane of white hair, and ruddy complexion, he looked every bit the archetypal English gentleman. He wore a navy blazer with an insignia embroidered on the pocket and had one hand resting on a ship's wheel. The line beneath the photo identified him as Admiral (Ret.) Reginald Schoonover, President and Chief Operating Officer of the company.

After Tom explained Schoonover's position, Ellie returned to her narrative extolling the various amenities available onboard the ship.

He pretended to listen, but his mind was on other things. There was no justification for the Mothers of Song to be taking off on an Alaskan Cruise, he thought. If they wanted to go to Eugene or Salem for an afternoon or evening, okay, but Alaska? Alaska was out of the question. What came next, a worldwide concert tour? Who did they think they were, the Charlie Daniels Band? A bunch of naïve women from Pine Crest, Oregon had no business getting involved in something like this.

Karen and Ellie left right after dinner for the long drive back to Portland.

Tom, meanwhile, had said little ever since Marty came home with cruise brochures. She could read the signs and knew he was upset over something. They sat across from each other in the living room, she sewing and he reading.

Marty put her needlepoint aside and cleared her throat. "Why don't you tell me what's bothering you?"

"You wouldn't like what I'd say."

"How do you know, if you don't tell me?"

"I know. Believe me, I know."

"Very well, if that's how you want it." She picked up her sewing again.

He hated it when she did that. Women never fought fair. She'd wait until he'd built up a full head of steam and then become reasonable and placating. He wanted her to fume and holler and maybe even throw in a curse word or two. That way he could yell right back and feel good about doing it.

"Very well, I'll tell you. I don't think you have any business running off on some cruise ship for two weeks. It's a crazy idea and you don't have my permission to go."

Marty's hand was poised above her work. Instead of adding another stitch, she stopped and calmly slipped the needle through the edge of material. "So I'm crazy now?"

"I didn't say *you* were crazy; I said the *idea* was crazy." She already had him defining terms. Why did their arguments always go like this?

"You're splitting hairs. We're trying to do something a little ambitious, something to help the community. What's wrong with that? Can't you take care of yourself for two lousy weeks? Are you afraid I'll meet someone on the ship, run off with them, and never come back?"

"Yes!"

Marty's eyebrows shot up.

"I mean, no."

"There's your problem; you don't know what you mean. And you say I'm the crazy one? This is a good thing. It's for a good cause and I'm damned well going to go whether you like it or not."

She rose and walked to the window. As soon as her back was turned, she reached up to wipe away tears. After a moment, she took a deep, cleansing breath and spun around. "You haven't even given this a chance. That's not like you. There's something else, isn't there?"

"It's hard to talk about. Something just doesn't feel right. This whole idea has bothered me since the minute you walked in the door."

"Why?"

"I don't know."

"You're being ridiculous."

"I don't care if I am; you're getting in over your head."

"What about the other women?"

"What about them? If they want to go, let 'em."

"Two things, Tom." Her hand shook when she raised it to tick off the points. "One, it's already been decided; I *am* going. And two, you need to do a lot better than *it doesn't feel right* before I'll reconsider."

Marty turned and headed for their bedroom. When she reached the hallway, she looked back. "One other thing. As for your permission, I don't need it. In case you didn't get the word, Lincoln freed the slaves over a hundred years ago." She slammed the bedroom door behind her.

Tom sat alone in the living room, replaying their argument in his mind. She'd even thrown in a curse word, not that it made things any better. He seemed to have a knack for saying the wrong thing.

He hadn't realized it before, but he truly was afraid she wouldn't come back. Why? He knew she'd never run off with someone else; that was preposterous. So, why did he answer yes? He wasn't referring to her meeting someone on the ship. He was...he was answering the last part of her question, the *never come back* part.

Tom gave Marty sufficient time to get ready for bed. Normally, he enjoyed watching her undress, but after an argument, he knew from experience she'd go into the bathroom, lock the door, and come out in her long, flannel nightgown. She'd punch her pillow a few times to fluff it up, probably wishing it was him, pull the covers up to her chin and turn her back to him.

He hated the whole routine. Why couldn't he learn to keep his mouth shut?

Tom let the dog out, brought in the cat and locked the doors before going into the bedroom. As expected, the lights were off and Marty had burrowed down in the blankets and turned toward the wall. When he got into bed he tried to make peace by patting her hip.

"Don't even think about it, Buster."

Tom turned his back to her and straightened the blanket. He hadn't been thinking about *IT*.

SIXTEEN

RCI Corp Headquarters, Palo Alto, California

"Mrs. Yoblanski, finding you here is an unexpected pleasure I did not anticipate. May I join you?"

Shiri looked up from her book and smiled. She hadn't seen Dr. Maheshwari since they'd finished the *getting the new employee settled-in phase* of his employment. Evidently he'd been kept too busy with his research work to even get out of the lab long enough to make the short walk to the employee cafeteria.

"It's good to see you. I'd be happy to have your company." She directed him to a chair opposite hers and slipped the book into her purse.

He sat his tray down and smiled across the table at her "Lest I forget, I must tell you I have now chosen a new name. Henceforth, you are to address me as Derek."

Shiri seemed surprised. "Derek? You've changed your name to Derek?"

He chuckled. "Oh no, no, no, Mrs. Yoblanski, you misunderstand. I have found most Westerners prefer something easier on the tongue, a bit more manageable and several syllables shorter than Dwarakananth. So I adopted a new moniker, a nickname, an alias if you will. I have become Derek. It rolls off the tongue quite nicely, don't you think?"

"Derek. Derek?"

He leaned across the small table to speak in a conspiratorial whisper. "I gave this a lot of thought. You will notice I have learned good lessons from Hollywood. My new name is short with many hard consonants." He leaned back in the chair like John Wayne and hooked his thumb though a belt loop. "It has a rather macho ring to it, don't you think?"

"Derek." She said again and smiled. "It will take some getting used to, but I'll adapt. I guess you could say our friendship has progressed to a first name basis."

"That would indeed be a true statement, Mrs. Yoblanski." Derek surveyed his tray with satisfaction. "They provide such a wealth of choices here at RCI. You failed to mention your cafeteria menu includes a vegetarian entrée each and every day. Had I only known, I would not have waited so long to visit your establishment. This is a considerate concession to those of us who are Hindus."

"Here in the Bay Area, you'll find there are many more vegetarians than Hindus."

"Regardless, the benefit still accrues to me. When I saw you sitting here it brought doves to my mind. Have I ever shared the story of the doves from the Panchatantra?"

"You've told me several tales, but I don't recall anything about doves."

His eyes danced in anticipation. "Then prepare to be entertained." He rubbed his hands together. "It seems that once upon a time a flock of doves flew in search of food. They looked all day, but could find nary a thing to eat. Due to lack of sustenance, many of them grew tired and wanted to quit, but their wise leader encouraged them to persevere. And then, quite fortuitously, they spotted some rice grains scattered under a banyan tree."

He paused for a bite of noodles and washed them down with a sip of iced tea. "The doves landed and began to eat the grain, all the while congratulating themselves on their good fortune. Then a large net descended from the tree trapping them. The doves fluttered their wings trying to escape, but it was to no avail. Looking up, they saw a hunter coming with a gleeful look upon his face."

He leaned toward her. "A dire situation if ever there was one, don't you agree?"

Shiri nodded.

"Well, their wise leader refused to let the hunter outsmart him. He advised the other doves to each clutch a portion of the net in their beaks and, on his command, rise into the air as a group. It worked. Each dove picked up a piece of the net and they rose up taking the hunter's net with them. He ran after them, but could not catch them."

"That's all well and good," said Shiri, "but the poor doves were still tangled up in the net."

Derek gave her a sly smile. "So it would seem at first glance. However, their wise leader then led his flock to the home of a friendly mouse. The mouse nibbled through the net allowing them to escape."

"I'll have to remember that one. I'm sure there's some great moral hidden in it somewhere. Are you getting settled in?"

"I have found accommodations, quite satisfactory accommodations. Thanks in no small part to the assistance of the rental agency you recommended." He shook his finger, pretending to chide her. "I have found you are very well known in certain circles. The name Yoblanski opens doors in this city."

"That's because everyone thinks you're referring to my husband."

"Oh no, I have made it very clear I am referencing the pretty one."

Shiri blushed and mumbled her thanks.

"Speaking of your husband, perhaps I will be able to meet the famous *Mister* Yoblanski. I feel he should know his wife tells everyone he is offensive."

"Maybe we could have you over some weekend soon."

Derek shook his head. "Since I have begun establishing my home, putting down roots as some would say, I unpacked my spice tins. You know an Indian never travels very far without his spice cupboard. I would like to repay your kindness by cooking an authentic Indian meal for you and your husband.

"That sounds great, but Jared's traveling a lot right now. I can mention it to him."

"I am also very close to convincing my wife that she and the children should join me here in the good old US of A," he said with a sly grin.

"Do you have a timetable? My department can assist in their transportation and moving arrangements."

"No timelines yet. The worst thing I could do is try to push her into a quick decision. Like a mahout, I must move with extreme caution. Overuse of the ankus can result in the elephant crushing its trainer."

Shiri appeared startled.

Derek's eyes darted about nervously. "I was only utilizing a metaphor like...like a large quantity of straw can sometimes injure a camel's back. I never intended in any way to imply my wife is a large woman or that I must manage her with a metal hook. She is quite petite, small boned if you know what I mean, quite a lovely creature actually..." Derek's voice trailed off and he focused on his plate.

"I believe you'll find American women are less inclined to allow their husbands to dominate them."

He winked. "Just as many Indian wives rule the roost by pecking at their husbands like an angry hen."

"Just let me know when you're ready."

"Like your Jared, I too shall be away for a period of time." He put a finger to his lips. "I would love to share more details, you understand, but I am afraid it is not permitted."

Shiri nodded. A number of RCI's government projects were highly classified. And, based on the amount of money the company expended recruiting him, she guessed he was working on one of them. She'd learned early on to stay away from things that didn't concern her.

"Maybe when you get back," she said.

He raised his right hand. "You have my solemn promise. Curry and rice, when I return."

SEVENTEEN

Pine Crest, Oregon

The droplets, which had begun as a tentative pitter-pat on the windows, grew into a full-blown rainstorm. After the mail arrived, Tom rose from his desk, threw on his jacket and pulled the hood up. He peeled a newspaper off the stack of mail and stuffed it inside his jacket. "I'm going over to the Sugar Shack for a break."

As often happened, Eddie Beltzer moseyed in a short time later. "Mornin', Sarge, feelin' okay? Ya look a little green around the gills."

"I'm tired, that's all. I haven't been sleeping well the last few nights."

"You 'n' the missus have a little spat, did ya? Those sofa-beds can be hard on the back."

Tom looked like a deer in the headlights. How could Eddie tell he and Marty had been arguing? Was he that transparent, or was it just an educated guess? "It's nothing I want to talk about."

"My, ain't we in a mood this mornin'. Did ya spend the night on the floor instead of the sofa-bed?"

"I did not spend the night on the floor or the sofa-bed."

"Well, somethin' must really be eatin' at ya. Spit it out before ya choke on it."

Tom shifted in his seat. "You're right about the spat. Things haven't been right between us since Marty came home talking about going to Alaska."

"I heard the buzz around town. A group of ladies goin' off t' entertain on a cruise ship. So what's the problem?"

"I have a bad feeling about this. Something just doesn't feel right."

"Tell her how ya feel."

"I've tried, but she doesn't understand. Why should she? It doesn't even make sense to me. She thinks I'm standing in her way, holding her back. The last couple of nights, we've hardly said two words to each other. She's even stopped coming into the office."

"You're blowin' this all out of proportion. Ya can't direct someone else's life. Most of us don't do such a grand job with our own. She's your wife, you're supposed to be cheerin' her on, not holdin' her back."

"When did you become such a guru?"

"I've earned myself an advanced degree in the school of hard knocks. Remember? Ya need t' try bein' the box, not the conveyor."

"I'm not sure I can do that. This is a special situation."

"It's always a special situation." Eddie kept his line taut, refusing to let Tom slip the hook. "Look, I can't tell ya what to do. Nobody can. But don't let this thing get bigger than it oughta be. We're only talkin' a coupla weeks. It ain't like it's a matter of life and death."

After Eddie left, Tom jammed the paper back into his jacket and headed toward the newspaper office. He hadn't resolved his internal conflicts, but was glad for Eddie's insight. He felt marginally better about things.

He came to a corner. As he waited for a car to clear the intersection he ran his eyes around the town's compact business district. *Had invisible hands really guided him to Pine Crest?* He'd never regretted the decision to relocate. This was where they belonged.

The newspaper office, a tan building with shingled overhang and board and batten façade, stood at the end of the block. Tom smiled when he saw *Pine Crest Courier* flowing in gold, banklike script across the center of the building's plate glass window. He crossed the street and entered the business he loved.

"Welcome back, Mr. J. How are you liking this liquid sunshine?" Darlene asked when he walked in.

"The radio said they got six inches of new snow in the Cascades last night. They'll be lining up at the ski lifts," Tom replied.

The newspaper office was neither expansive nor plush. An L -shaped, Formica-topped counter divided the front room, creating a small entry foyer. Several sturdy oak chairs scavenged at a Post Office surplus auction waited opposite the counter anticipating an overflow of customers yet to materialize.

Darlene's desk sat in the small square formed between the short arm of the counter and the front wall. A low rail and a swinging door with a frayed *Employees Only* sign guarded entry to the back half of the room, which they jokingly referred to as the executive suite.

In the rear of the building, behind a partition wall, were a small lunch area, a restroom, and a darkroom where Tom's oldest son, Tommy, developed and printed news photos. The layout and paste-up area and the mailroom were also in the back.

Tom waved an arm at Tommy.

He crossed the room to his father's desk and sat in an oak chair matching those in the entryway.

"Heard what your Mother's up to?"

"Yeah, Mom's called Beth several times. They were on the phone last night for a long time. Sounds like she's really excited."

"I wish I was."

He normally wouldn't have discussed his marital problems with his son, but he had no one else. He hoped talking to Tommy would help him resolve his internal conflicts.

"I know this sounds silly, but ever since your Mother brought up this cruise idea I've had these...uh, misgivings. I checked the cruise line's website and everything appears legit, but..."

"What sort of misgivings are we talking about?"

"Intuition, I guess you'd call it."

"Intuition?"

"Yeah, intuition. The power of knowing things without conscious reasoning."

"I *know* what it means. I just don't recall intuition ever being considered much of a guy thing." Tommy crossed his arms and leaned back in the chair. "So, what's your intuition telling you?"

"I'm almost afraid to talk about it. Remember when you were a kid and afraid to say something bad for fear it'd come true?"

Tommy took a deep breath. His expression reflected the concern he felt for his father. "You don't believe that, do you?"

"I don't know what to believe. I've never had such strong feelings before. We've all heard stories of people refusing to board airplanes because of a premonition and then the plane crashed."

"You're having premonitions, too?"

"I don't know if that's the right word. I just know I don't want your Mother going on this trip."

"Have you talked to anyone about these feelings? Maybe you should see a counselor."

Tom regretted ever starting the discussion. He kicked himself for not seeing it for the bad idea it was. He'd said too much already and now risked losing credibility and upsetting his son. He set about repairing the damage. "Forget it. I'm not making sense. The real truth is I don't want to be alone while your Mother's away."

He was grateful he hadn't mentioned the dreams, nightmares actually. They weren't the full-blown kind that left you so afraid of going back to sleep you sneaked into the living room and read a book with all the lights on. No, these jarred him awake and left him feeling uneasy, unsettled...bothered.

He grabbed some papers he'd clipped together and handed

them to Tommy. "Here's a hard copy of next week's column. After you've looked it over, ask Darlene to fax it to them."

Tommy reached for the papers.

Tom pulled them back. "One more thing. I'd appreciate it if you kept this intuition stuff between you and me. Okay?"

Darlene swept in as Tommy rose. She dropped a pile of invoices on his desk "Need your autograph, Mr. J."

She'd clipped an unsigned, three-part check to each bill. Tom grabbed a pen and, after a quick review, scribbled his name on the checks one at a time. It provided a pleasant diversion and he hummed to himself as he signed his way through the stack.

In the early years while they struggled to make the paper a viable enterprise, the strength of Tom's editorial personality carried it forward. There were few ambiguities in his thinking and he knew where he stood on most issues. He frequently wrapped his nuggets of wisdom in self-depreciating humor and established a reputation for honesty, fairness, and forthrightness.

Readers came to look forward to his columns. Eventually, people living up and down the Oregon Coast, and even some in the inland valleys, subscribed to hear what Tom had to say. The Pine Crest Courier's paid circulation increased. Increasing circulation meant additional ad revenue. Increased revenue resulted in a better bottom line. To their surprise and delight, he and Marty found themselves actually making a living from the dilapidated little paper they'd bought.

In the ensuing years they'd built a home, raised their kids and expanded the paper. In so doing, they gradually achieved a modest level of financial stability. Life as a small town newspaperman would never be easy. From time to time, there were still financial struggles and probably always would be.

Tom was still signing checks when Billy Nevins arrived. He was his usual exuberant self despite the torrents of gusting rain outside.

"Good morning, everybody," Billy hollered in a voice several decibels louder than necessary. He took off his jacket and shook it out, spraying water droplets throughout the room.

"It's raining real hard. Did you know that, Mr. J?"

Tom nodded and continued scanning invoices.

"Hey Darlene, Mrs. Johnson's cat is going to have kittens. She said I could have one. I could get one for you too."

Darlene told him she'd have to get back to him on it.

Accepting her answer, he headed to the back of the building to start work.

As the parent of a son with Down syndrome, Kate Nevins had grown distressed seeing how few employment opportunities existed for people with special needs. "The State should do more to sponsor sheltered workshops, life skills training, and so on," she told Tom, "and the *Courier* ought to spearhead the effort."

"Everything you say is true, Kate. Unfortunately, the current economy makes it difficult to motivate the legislature on spending issues. I'll do some research and see what I turn up."

Tom eventually wrote several columns highlighting the problem. He'd done his part by making people aware of the situation. That's what newspapers did.

Kate's visit, however, resulted in immediate changes for her son, Billy. Each week the Courier delivered several 4-color, folded advertising inserts along with the paper. This created a dilemma. They welcomed the added income, but the work of stuffing those inserts bogged down their mailing process.

Tom solved the problem by hiring Billy to collate and stuff the inserts. Billy reigned over a kingdom of two large tables made from 2x4's and plywood. Every Monday, he laid out the week's inserts on his table and combined them into a single piece. Later in the week, when they mailed the paper, Billy returned to merge the inserts into the *Courier* before it went to the Post Office.

Fringe benefits included a shelf for Billy's radio, the title of *Advertising Coordinator* and, each Thursday after they'd stuffed and addressed the papers, the *Courier* staff sent out for pizza and sodas. Life suddenly became very good for Billy.

EIGHTEEN

Annapolis, Maryland

Claudia raised her eyes from the computer screen when she heard a light tap on the office door.

Six-year-old Trevor leaned his head in. "Mommy, can I talk to you? It's real important."

She glanced at the screen to check the time then waved him in. "We'll have to make it quick, it's close to your bedtime."

Already dressed in his pajamas, Trevor tiptoed in with Teddy Bumpkins under his arm. He sat the bear aside long enough to ease the paneled oak door closed and silently release the knob. Once the latch slipped into its mortise, he threw the lock.

"Why don't we sit by the fireplace?" Claudia sat on a couch and Trevor scooted in beside her. She patted the chubby Teddy in bib overalls on the head. "How's my friend, Teddy Bumpkins, tonight?"

Trevor's expression turned serious. "He's fine. I'm the one who's not so good."

She rested the back of her hand on his forehead. "Are you feeling okay? Does your stomach hurt?"

Her motherly concern brought a frown to the boy's face. "It's nothing like that."

"How's your drawing for school coming?"

"I finished it."

"I give up, what's bothering you?"

Avoiding her eyes, he traced the pattern on his pajamas with a finger. "Well...I, um...sorta overheard you and Daddy arguing yesterday."

She gave him a stern look. "Trevor, you know it's not polite to eavesdrop on other people's conversations."

"I wasn't...honest. I was in the living room watching cartoons when he started yelling."

"If you're talking about last night, neither of us was yelling. Sometimes when adults have a conversation about serious issues they raise their voices, but no one yelled. What's the matter?"

"Before you closed the door I heard Dad say, 'This is my son they're talking about.'" He raised his eyes to meet hers. "Is something awful going to happen to me?"

She gave a relieved sigh and hugged him. Pushing aside the shock of hair that'd fallen over his forehead, she kissed him. "He didn't mean you, Sweetheart. Daddy and I were talking about the new baby inside Mommy's tummy."

Trevor's eyes widened. "How come?"

Claudia sighed deeply and bit her lip.

A small hand patted hers. "It's okay, Mom."

She blinked hard and blotted a tear out of the corner of her eye. "I hadn't planned on talking to you about it yet." She gave him a reassuring smile. "It's nothing that you should have to worry about."

"I'm his big brother. You can tell me."

"I suppose whether it's sooner or later doesn't make much difference." She lifted him into her lap. "The doctors did some tests and found out your baby brother has something called Down syndrome."

"How did he get it?"

"It's a congenital condition," she said without thinking. Seeing the confused expression on the Trevor's face, she explained. "You've heard of cells, right?"

"The little things we can't see that are growing all over us?"

"Yeah." She took his hands in hers and pressed his palms together. "Let's pretend your hands are a single cell and God wants to make a baby."

"Don't the Mommies and Daddies make a baby?"

"God let's them help. The Mom and Dad contribute their

love then God works his miracle and turns that love into a new life."

"But a kid at school said—"

She put her finger to his lips, stopping him. "Believe me; none of your friends at school have any idea what they're talking about. Your Dad is not only a medical doctor he's also a doctor of science, a molecular biologist. When you're older he'll explain all about the science of life. For now, trust what your Mom tells you."

Satisfied, Trevor made a cell by pressing his palms together.

"Very good. Now God makes a baby out of just two cells — one from the Mommy and one from the Daddy. The reason I'm using your hands is because each cell in our body has two sets of chromosomes. The chromosomes job is to tell a hair cell how to be hair, and an ear cell how to be an ear, and so on until every cell in your body knows what it's supposed to do."

Trevor's nod indicated he understood.

Claudia put her palms together, mimicking his. "Now let's pretend we want to start a baby. You bring your cell over next to mine."

Trevor did as she instructed.

"Do you notice anything wrong?"

"Your hands are bigger?"

She chuckled. "Actually, the woman's egg *is* bigger than the man's cell, but that's not what I meant. Count the hands."

He quickly counted to four.

"Right, but remember what I said? Each cell can only have two sets of each chromosome. We've got twice as many thumbs as we need, and twice as many pinkies. We've got four of everything and we only want two of them. What can we do about it?"

Trevor took his hands away.

"Now we only have two hands like we're supposed to, but they're both Mommy hands. That won't work either."

Trevor separated her hands and pressed his palm against hers.

"Very Good. That's exactly what happens inside our bodies. The special baby-making cells split apart so they only have one of each chromosome. That way, a new baby gets a set from its Mom and a set from its Dad." She rested a finger from her other hand over his. "But what if when the cells were dividing they made a mistake and one pair of chromosomes got stuck together? What happens then?"

"You'd have three of one of that one instead of the two you're supposed to have."

"Exactly, and the baby would have what they call Down syndrome."

"Is it something real bad?"

She shook her head. "Not really. He's going to look a little different...not bad, just *different*. He'll be a little slower than other kids. It may take him longer to learn to walk and talk and learn to dress himself and tie his shoes. He might have trouble running real fast or throwing a baseball. And he will never be able to do some things you will like learn to drive a car or go to college." She shrugged. "Stuff like that."

Trevor quietly mulled over what she'd said for a long time. "How come you and Dad were arguing?"

"We were *discussing* what the doctor said. When the test showed the baby had Down syndrome, the doctor, well he...um, he scheduled me for an abortion."

"What's that?"

"In the olden days nobody knew what a baby was going to be like until it was born. Nowadays they have tests that can tell you if the baby has a problem like we were talking about. A lot of people don't want a baby with Down syndrome." She began to weep. "So they tell the doctor to take the baby out."

"Why?"

"They want a baby that's perfect."

"But nobody's perfect?"

"Where did you hear that?"

Trevor seemed surprised she should have to ask. "You and Dad say it all the time. Every time one of you messes something up or forgets to do something, you go like this." He gave an exaggerated shrug, rolled his eyes, and said, "Well, no one's perfect."

Claudia smiled. "Guilty as charged, Your Honor."

"So, if no one's perfect why would people think they were supposed to get a perfect baby?"

"I don't know, Sweetheart. Maybe it's because they don't stop to think about it the way you did."

"What happens to him then? I mean, after they take him out of the Mommy's tummy?"

Claudia reached for a tissue. "The little baby dies. Taking them out of their mother before they're ready kills them."

Trevor gasped.

She felt him tremble in her arms.

Tears rolled down Trevor's cheeks. "You're gonna let 'em kill our new baby before he even gets here?" He didn't wait for her to answer. "No! You can't let 'em do it."

"Let me explain."

Trevor grabbed his Teddy and shoved his way out of her arms. He retreated to the far end of the couch. "Why do they kill somebody just 'cause he's got a extra little chromy thing nobody can even see? If he can't run very fast, I'll go slow. If he can't tie his shoes, I'll tie them for him. And if he can't catch a ball, I'll roll it to him."

She stretched her arms to him. "You didn't let me explain. Scoot back over here."

He gave a wary look. "I won't sit beside you if you're gonna kill my baby brother."

"I'm not going to let anyone harm the baby."

"So Dad's the one who wants to kill him?" he asked in an incredulous whisper.

"No, Sweetheart. No, no, no. Your father would never suggest I have an abortion. He was angry with the doctor. And he became upset with me because I lost my temper and threw some papers around the doctor's office and called him a bad name."

Trevor flew into her arms. He grinned up at her. "Why didn't you punch him in the nose?"

"Adults don't go around socking each other in the nose." She squeezed him with all her might and rocked him back and forth. Leaning close, she confided, "Although, I sure wanted to pop him one."

Experiencing firsthand the joy of coming motherhood, she'd celebrated by adding maternity wear to her signature line of clothing. The press, always critical, questioned her motives. They accused her of attempting to profit from her pregnancy.

When tests indicated the child would suffer from Down syndrome someone in the doctor's office leaked the information to the press. The media attacked her because she refused to abort the infant. She suddenly found herself fodder for late night talk shows. Her image showed up on tabloid covers making an already difficult situation more so.

"Why does God let stuff like this happen to little babies?"

"We aren't given to know all of God's secrets. We have to believe that no matter what, His way is best. What we do know is one way or another, everything will be okay. For his own reasons, God housed a very gentle soul in a slightly less than perfect body. Your baby brother will have some struggles like all of us do, but he'll also have us there to help him."

Eyes misting, she hugged him to her and rocked him. "Oh, Trevor we spend such a short time on this earth. This life is merely the childhood of our immortality. God didn't make him different, he made him special. When your new brother gets to heaven there'll be a crown waiting for him and he will be just as bright and beautiful as anyone there."

NINETEEN

Pine Crest, Oregon

It didn't take long for Tom and Marty to realize they'd reached an impasse. Like opposing armies, they'd both dug in and refused to yield ground. In an effort to avoid long and fruitless arguments, they built a fence around her trip, forestalling any further discussion. They spent the weeks leading up to her departure enmeshed in a cold war of feints and quick retreats, innuendos, and truncated conversations followed by extended silences.

Meanwhile, Marty quietly went about her preparations to leave as planned.

Fall was coming on. The days had begun growing damper and Tom kept a few logs ready by the fireplace. Outside, twilight painted the yard in shadows as a cool wind ruffled through the firs and hemlocks. Inside, Tom and Marty went about their tasks. This was their last full day together before she left on the cruise and, with evening upon them, their remaining hours had dwindled to only a few.

She's spent a good portion of the day preparing for the trip. Marty began setting the table for dinner as Tom lugged the last of her suitcases out of the bedroom.

For several days, he'd struggled to write her a letter. He felt a need to spell out the negative feelings he still harbored regarding her trip. He'd started a hundred times only to discard it because it sounded at best naïve and at worst ridiculous. How could he explain to her what he couldn't understand himself?

Finding the task impossible, he eventually abandoned the idea. There was no way to put into words what he held in his heart. Instead, he bought several cards at the discount store and slipped them into her luggage for Marty to find. When she unpacked, she'd know he was thinking of her, missing her, counting the days until her return.

Tom went into the laundry room and Charlie fell in step beside him, sniffing the suitcase as they walked. The dog instinctively knew they were planning a trip. He wagged his tail in anticipation, but he could also feel the melancholy that hung heavy in the air. He sensed the unspoken tension between the two people he most loved. Charlie had spent the afternoon going back and forth between Tom and Marty seeking reassurance.

"Better wash up for dinner," Marty called.

She wanted the meal to be special and had prepared a delicious dinner. It was her way of telling him not to worry, everything will be all right. Her way of letting him know that in spite of the craziness of the last few weeks, her feelings for him hadn't changed.

Tom watched her as she ate. The way she cut her meat, buttered her roll, salted her peas. How she dabbed the corners of her mouth with her napkin, the way she automatically gave him the larger slice of pie. He wanted to gather up every nuance and seal it away in his memory. Every fiber of his being screamed for him to grab her, hold her, keep her from leaving.

But he knew he couldn't.

Marty looked up, caught him staring, and smiled.

He didn't look away and neither did she. Without a word, they both rose from the table and rushed into each other's arms. They hugged for a long, long time.

"I'm going to miss you so much, Tom," she whispered into his shoulder.

"Not as much as I'll miss you."

"We're both being silly. It's not even two full weeks. I'll be back before you have time to miss me."

He tightened his grip. "I miss you already.

When they finally released each other, Tom suggested they have a fire. Just a small one, so it wouldn't heat the room too much. He crumpled some newspaper and lit it while Marty poured coffee. They sat on the couch in the dark, drinking their coffee and watching flames dance in the fireplace.

Charlie curled up at their feet, content to share their mood.

Neither of them spoke for a long time. It was enough to sit close, hold hands and feel the moment. They'd learned over the years that words weren't always necessary for communication. They shared what was in their hearts in silence. After a time, nothing remained but the flickering glow of the ashes.

Marty patted his knee. "We'd better get ready for bed. Tomorrow will be here before we know it."

He let Charlie out and waited for him on the porch. A million stars were scattered across the night sky. Tom looked up at them wishing he could shake this constant feeling of apprehension. He was a sensible person; he'd analyzed things from every possible angle. There was no logical reason for him to feel this way.

And yet he did.

Tom struggled with the indefinable notion that a dark, malevolent force was stalking him, them. He'd first felt it the Saturday morning when they'd slept in. It was the same morning Virginia Saltzman died, but he knew this had nothing to do with Virginia and everything to do with Marty.

Like electricity in the air before a storm, anxious thoughts filled his mind. Over the weeks the fears grew and no matter how hard he tried, he couldn't shake them. Thinking about it gave him a chill. He rubbed his arms for warmth and called the dog. Maybe tomorrow, he thought. Maybe tomorrow, once they were underway, everything would settle back to normal.

While Tom was outside with the dog, Marty undressed and pulled on one of Tom's Oregon Coast tee shirts. She absentmindedly watched herself in the mirror as she brushed out her hair. She sensed Tom's uneasiness about her trip and didn't like to see him worry. As much as she looked forward to this cruise, like Tom, she had begun to develop second thoughts.

Marty smiled as she laid the brush on the counter. Tom built the vanity himself when they remodeled the bathroom. At her request, he'd slipped an extra board under each cabinet for added height. Measured from countertop to the ceramic tile floor, the vanity was several inches higher than standard.

"We're tall people," she'd told him. "Why should we break our back every time we use the bathroom sink?"

He agreed and silently thanked her every time he shaved or brushed his teeth. Tom had also run a wallpaper border around the room and arranged the mirrors so she could see her hair and makeup from all sides. Pulling the medicine chest door out a little, Marty surveyed herself in the full-length mirror on the adjacent wall.

Not too bad.

Of course, she wasn't as firm as she'd been when they'd married. But then, who was? Time and three children had rounded her curves and softened the tautness of youth. There were a few extra pounds here and there, but not enough to matter. As a mature woman with a body to match she was quite satisfied with things as they were. She rather enjoyed maturity, kids out of the nest, more time for Tom and the grandkids, and a chance to pursue her own interests.

When she finished, she turned off the bathroom light and walked into the bedroom. Tom was already in bed and a small lamp by the bed lit the way. She walked over to the window, parted the curtains, and stared out.

"Anything out there?" Tom asked from the bed.

"I'm just enjoying the stars and the moon rising over the mountains. It's so beautiful here at night. I've always loved this view."

Tom chuckled. "Yeah, so do I."

As Marty came over to the bed, she raised her arms and pulled the shirt over her head. She tossed it aside and removed her slippers. She clicked off the light, and climbed under the covers.

"My side of the bed's cold."

He slipped his arm under her head, pulled her close and kissed her several times.

She stretched in the bed, easing away the tensions of the day. "We had a really great evening, but it always feels so-o-o good to lie down."

Tom's hands traced her body. After nearly three decades of marriage, her supple femaleness continued to tantalize him. He knew he could never get enough of her, never touch her too many times, never hold her close enough, never make love to her often enough.

True, lovemaking was different now than it had been in their younger years. Ardent, pressing need had given way to tender familiarity. To Tom, Marty's body was like a secret garden, a primeval place ever new, ever fascinating. A place where they could mingle and refresh their spirits, share their triumphs, solace their hurts. He knew his way around the paths and the secret delights hidden here and there. He visited them all.

As the afterglow ebbed, they curled around each other as they had done on so many other occasions. The rift between them disappeared as they drifted into the night.

TWENTY

The jangling phone jarred them awake.

Tom snapped up in the bed. Bad news, he'd learned over the years, most often comes at night. He mentally ran through his personal checklist as he groped for the receiver. First, he thought of the children Tommy, John and, finally, Karen. She was alone with five-year-old Ellie in Portland more often than he liked. Her husband, Mark, traveled a lot. Too much in Tom's estimation.

"I'm calling for Tom Jenkins."

"You got him." Tom's chest tightened. A call from a stranger in the middle of the night couldn't be anything good. He swung his feet to the floor and sat up on the side of the bed. "This is Art Briscoe down at the Golden Lantern. I'm sorry to bother you, Tom, but I didn't know who else to call."

He glanced over at the clock. It was 1:25. Tom sat on the bed, silhouetted in the moonlight.

Marty lay behind him in the dark, her fears growing as she waited for him to finish. She, too, had done a mental inventory of people and possibilities.

"It's almost closing time and Eddie Beltzer's down here. He's had a few too many and not showing any inclination to leave. Can you help me out? I'd hate to have to call the cops."

Why now, why him? He'd finally patched things up with Marty. The last thing Tom wanted to do was go drag Eddie out of a bar. There had to be another alternative, although he couldn't think of one.

Marty sat up in bed and turned on a lamp. She tugged the covers and, when Tom turned, shot him a questioning look. He shook his hand, indicating it wasn't one of the kids.

He sighed. "I'll come down, Art. Give me a few minutes."

He could feel Marty's stare in the dimly lit room. She wouldn't be keen on him going out in the middle of the night. He began addressing her unspoken questions as he gathered his clothes.

"Eddie's having a little trouble and they asked me to come get him. It shouldn't take very long. There's really no one else they could call." He leaned over to tie his shoes.

She shook her head. "No, Tom, not tonight. You're not his Guardian Angel. We have to drive to Eugene tomorrow morning. We deserve this time together. Let them get someone else."

"There isn't anybody else. He has no local family. Why do you think Art called me?"

"I don't care. Call him back and tell him you aren't coming."

Tom sat down on the bed, took her hands in his. "Look, I know the timing's awful, but something's very wrong. This isn't like Eddie. Can't you cut me a little slack here?"

She jerked her hands away. "Cut you a little slack? What do you think I've been doing these last few weeks? I've cut you enough slack to string a line from here to China."

"Please, let's not argue. Things were just starting to get better between us."

"Right, things are getting better and now you're running out the door. Wham, bam, thank you, Ma'am! Don't wake me up when you come back to bed." Marty jerked the covers up around her neck and snapped off the light.

Tom walked to the closet to get a jacket. He bent to kiss her goodbye, but she turned away before he could.

"I'll open the Dutch door so Charlie can sleep at the end of the bed if you want him to," he said as he tiptoed out.

A country tune from a jukebox in the corner met Tom as he walked into the Golden Lantern. At the far end of the room, Art stood behind the brightly lit bar. Tom cautiously inched his way across the dark barroom, trying to avoid an unseen chair.

Empty tables sat around the room with equally empty booths along one wall. Other than a few hangers-on strung along the bar, the place was deserted.

A flash of recognition crossed Art's face as Tom approached. He put down the glass he was washing, walked out from behind the bar, and led him to a dark corner. Pulling out a chair for Tom, Art removed an empty glass and beer bottle. He dropped a towel on the table and wiped it with a single, practiced sweep.

"I'll bring over some coffee."

Eddie lay face down on the table, his head resting on folded arms.

The lingering smell of stale beer enveloped Tom as he sat down. "Eddie?" He gave him a hard shake. "Wake up, Eddie."

Eddie's head sluggishly lifted off the table. He blinked.

Art sat some coffee cups and a pot of strong coffee on the next table and slipped away.

"Hiya, Sarge. Whatcha doing here?" He dipped his head, glanced side to side, and whispered, "Better lay low, man. We've been takin' some heavy fire."

The lights at the bar blinked and Art shouted, "Last call for alcohol."

By the time Art locked the door, Eddie was leaning back in his chair drinking his second cup of coffee. "Know what today is?"

"No, what is today?"

"Today's the 5th. It's my anniversary."

A pained look filled Tom's eyes. "I've been so busy that I didn't think about it. I'm sorry, I really am."

Eddie lifted his coffee cup. "A toast to my leg, may it rest in pieces." He gave a harsh laugh and took a long sip. The strong, bitter coffee matched his mood. He continued sipping the coffee with a faraway look in his eyes.

Tom wondered what he was remembering, but knew better than to ask.

Eddie clanked the cup down and stared at him. "Know what the hardest part was?"

Tom shook his head. There were a lot of things he didn't know, thank God.

"The lack of respect hurt more than losin' six legs. After my stump healed, the folks at the VA said I could go out for the afternoon. I was still getting' around on crutches, but I put my uniform on and caught a bus into town. Wouldn't ya know, I got off the bus right in the middle of a war protest."

Looking afar off, Eddie swung his arm in a wide arc. "There was a whole bunch of 'em carryin' signs, shoutin' and cussin'." He took a deep breath. "Anyways, when I came down the steps of the bus, they took after me callin' me names. A girl spit on me. Why? She didn't know me from Adam."

"Those were turbulent times," Tom said softly.

"I tried to get away from 'em by goin' the other way. Then my crutch jammed in a crack in the sidewalk and I fell down. God it hurt. I was down there strugglin' to get up. All I wanted to do was get the hell away from 'em. Those little pukes circled round me 'n' started laughin'."

With all the chairs turned over, Art moved around the room with a push broom. He passed them without glancing up.

"I remember layin' there on the sidewalk, my face scraped 'n' bleedin'. I had spit runnin' off me and my uniform was torn. I thought, *they took my leg, what more do they want*?"

Tom gave a wry nod.

Eddie's voice became the growl of a tormented animal. "I was scrufflin' around on the sidewalk like some half-squished bug. Every time I'd get started up, my crutch'd slip and back down I'd go. Finally a cop came over and helped me up, God bless him. I crossed the street, took a bus back to the VA Hospital and never told a soul."

He sighed and shook his head. "Those kids'll never know

what it's like to wake up in the middle of the night with your toes achin' when ya ain't even got toes. When that mine went off I knew I was gonna leave my leg in 'Nam, but I didn't count on leavin' my dignity there, too."

Eddie slammed his cup down on the table, looked away and bit his lip. He sat quietly for a time , then he continued.

"Course, no matter how ya slice it, I came out a helluva lot better than Jim Kershaw. We were side by side when that mine went up. I lost my leg; he lost his life.

For a while, I told myself I musta been the one who stepped on it, but that made me responsible for Jim's death. I didn't much care for that idea so I decided he was the one who stepped on it." He shook his head. "There's no way anyone could ever tell. I finally realized it doesn't make a bit of difference. Either way he's just as dead and my leg's still gone."

Tom refilled Eddie's cup and returned the half-empty pot to the table behind him.

"You didn't know Jim, did ya, Sarge?"

"No. This is an awful thing to say, but all I remember about him is his terrible injuries."

"He was a tall, skinny kid with bright red hair and a face full of freckles. He came from upstate New York. Never knew a gentler soul. When he wasn't on duty, you'd find him writin' letters home...real salt of the earth."

Eddie took a long sip of coffee. "He used t' carry these little bags of candy with him all the time. He'd toss 'em to the kids in the villages. The last time I saw him, he was layin' there ripped to pieces 'n' bleedin' like a stuck pig, with M & M's scattered all over hell's half-acre. I still can't look at those damned things without thinkin' of him."

The cup quivered in Eddie's hand. Coffee splashed against the sides and over the rim, ran down the cup and pooled in his saucer. He folded a paper napkin and laid it in the puddle. When he put the cup down a dark, wet stain wicked across the white paper.

"His daddy was a carpenter, don't ya know. Jim always talked about how they'd build houses together someday. After they released me at the VA hospital, I went to see his parents. They were hard-working, God-fearing folk. Met his aunts 'n' uncles...even the little gal he hoped to marry. You'd a thought the President had come to visit."

He shook his head. "They took it hard. Ya see, Jim was an only child. At supper one night, his Momma started asking me about 'Nam. What it was like, how Jim lived. Eventually we got around to the day Jim died. She wanted to know what happened. Course, I couldn't tell her. There are things a Mother shouldn't have to hear. Jim's daddy fought in World War II. He knew. I saw it the minute I looked across the table at him."

"It was kind of you to go see them."

"I went to New York for a day and ended up stayin' a week." Eddie stretched. "After that, we kept in touch. Mostly cards at first, then letters, eventually phone calls. One summer we got together in Washington to visit that long black wall."

Eddie turned to face him. "Guess I filled a little bit of the hole losing Jim put in their life. Jim's daddy passed about eight years ago. Judy, his Momma, went into a nursing home coupla years later. I've thought about goin' t' see her, but when I call, the nurses tell me she wouldn't even know me."

Art had cleaned the bar and was waiting on them so he could leave.

Eddie was talked out and sobered up.

Outside, the eastern sky glowed with the first pink hints of daybreak.

The two men stood facing each other beside Eddie's truck. Art drove by, honked, and roared onto the highway.

Eddie looked down, pushing gravel around with the toe of his boot. He took a deep breath and held out his hand. "Thanks Buddy. I owe ya one. I'm sorry my troubles messed up your night's sleep. Tell Marty I'm awful sorry 'n' tell her I'll do somethin' nice to make up for it."

TWENTY-ONE

Tom came in the back door as quietly as possible and tiptoed into the kitchen.

Marty was up, dressed, and putting breakfast on the table. *Her* breakfast, he noticed.

She turned. "Do you have any idea what time it is? I have to be in Eugene in less than four hours. I was about to call Tommy and see if he'd take me to the airport. Where have you been all night?"

"I wasn't gone all night; Art didn't call until almost 1:30."

"Silly me, how could I have overlooked such important details?"

"I'm sorry, Babe. I really am. Eddie needed to talk. I'll explain it another time."

Marty got up from the table and shoved her plate over to Tom. "Sit down and eat."

"But those were your eggs."

"An egg's an egg. Is my toast okay, or do you want an English muffin?"

He sat down at the table and picked up a fork. "Toast is fine."

"And don't dawdle, you've still got to shower and shave."

Marty pulled two more eggs out of the refrigerator, shoved a couple of slices of bread into the toaster and grabbed the skillet. A moment later, she turned away from the stove. "Oh, that was all the bacon we had, save me a couple of—"

Tom froze. The last slice of bacon was in his fingers on its way to his mouth. He gave her a weak smile and dropped it back on the plate.

"You don't need all the cholesterol." She viciously attacked the eggs with her spatula.

Marty brought a big mug of coffee to the table and clunked

it down in front of Tom. "Here, I poured you some coffee. You look like you'll need more than this, but we don't have any half-gallon sized mugs." She smiled for the first time since he'd returned home.

Tom was staring at the creamer when Marty walked over beside him. She rested a hand on his shoulder. "I wish you wouldn't worry so."

Was it merely intuition, or could she somehow read his mind?

She squeezed his shoulder.

Placing his hand over hers, Tom turned and lightly kissed her fingertips. "Everything will be fine," he said, as much for himself as for Marty. He tilted the creamer over his cup and to his surprise white powder spilled out of its mouth. Marty's contribution to the war on cholesterol.

The drive to Eugene meandered through the Umpqua River valley. The river steamed with patchy, morning fog. Traffic was light, the scenery beautiful. On Highway 38 east of Reedsport, they passed a large herd of elk.

Charlie popped his head up in the back seat when Marty called them to Tom's attention. The dog scrutinized the large animals, gave a soft woof then settled back to resume his nap.

They rode most of the way in silence. Lost in their private musings, they held hands and enjoyed the scenery.

Chaos replaced solitude when they entered the airport. The other six Mothers of Song were in the lounge area along with their husbands and families. Excited about the upcoming trip, everyone spoke at once and Marty quickly joined the conversation.

Seven women swapping stories, comparing notes and giving

last minute instructions was more than Tom needed. To get away from the chatter, he discretely distanced himself from the boisterous crowd. Standing near the last row of seats, he heard the familiar shout of "Grandpa!" echo down the concourse. He turned to see Ellie walking between Mark and Karen.

She danced with excitement and waved.

No one could have predicted Jennifer's husband would fall off a ladder at the hardware store and break his leg. She and Marty were sharing a room, but Jennifer could hardly take off on a cruise leaving a broken-legged husband behind. Marty explained the problem to the cruise line and they agreed to let her granddaughter fill the vacancy.

Ellie shouted to him again then broke into a run. Wisps of blond hair fluttered in the air and her eyes sparkled. A fuzzy, red Elmo arm poked out of her small backpack, threatening escape. She leaped into Tom's arms and hugged his neck.

"I'm going on the big boat with Grandma," Ellie shouted.

Her enthusiasm was contagious. Tom grinned and squeezed her tightly. He continued holding her until she wiggled to be put down.

Ellie unzipped her pink windbreaker and pulled it open. "Hey Grandpa, look what I'm wearing."

The cruise line's Passenger Services Department sent each woman a colorful tee shirt with the Paradise logo on the front. Some considerate individual at the home office mailed Ellie a child-sized shirt when she replaced Jennifer.

Tom grinned and admired her shirt.

"I'm gonna fly in an airplane too." She extended her arms and flew around the small waiting area in big, swooping circles. As she zoomed past, Marty scooped her up for a hug and carried her over to the windows overlooking the tarmac. Together they watched planes landing and taxiing to the terminal.

Soon it was time for good-byes. Tom hugged Marty and whispered in her ear, "You haven't left yet, there's still time to back out."

She stepped back, staring at him like he was someone she didn't know. Her words came quickly and quietly, meant for his ears only. "Are you crazy? We're standing in the airport. The plane leaves in a few minutes. These people are counting on me; I can't back out now."

"Jennifer did."

"Jennifer's husband broke his leg," Marty muttered under her breath.

"All I'm trying to say is you can still change your mind."

"You just won't give up, will you?"

"Blame it on me if you have to. Just back out now and we can drive home."

"That's a splendid idea. I'll tell my friends I have to stay behind because my husband's lost his mind."

Tom felt her anger and disappointment. He didn't care; this was his last chance. He reached for her.

She shoved him away. "Drive carefully on the way home," she said as she turned away.

Marty took Ellie's hand and together they began walking towards the gate. She never looked back.

Tom stood in the waiting area and watched her go down the ramp. Minutes later their plane lifted off and disappeared into the gray Oregon sky.

Marty and Ellie were in San Francisco by the time Tom returned to Pine Crest. He fixed a TV dinner and wondered if they'd boarded the ship yet. He wished he had a way of knowing where they were and what they were doing every minute of every day until they returned.

As he ate, Tom's fears grew to become a ghoulish voice inside his head. Unseen, it was never far away. Coming without warning, it articulated his deepest fears in a voice as dark as the blackest night and as cold as death itself. Tom felt its presence as surely as a blind man knows when someone enters the room.

He'd been a fool to let her go, he thought. And now it was too late. Marty was gone.

Tom took Charlie out in the yard, but his fears were waiting there.

You should have done more...something, anything.

His head pounded. He brought the cat in, locked the door and put the animals to bed. Then he took some aspirins and headed to bed himself.

When he pulled back the covers, a yellow envelope fluttered free and settled onto the floor at his feet. He recognized Marty's handwriting and smiled. He removed the small card and opened it.

> *Tom, I love you with all my heart.*
> *Be happy and safe while we're apart.*
> *And never forget I am always with you.*
> *Love transcends time and space.*

He carried the card into the kitchen and taped it to the refrigerator door. It looked out of place among the jumble of Ellie's drawings, notes, clippings and assorted reminders.

When he finished Tom lifted its flap and peeked in. Her words were still there, he hadn't imagined them. He reread them again and again, letting his soul feast on them and savoring the comfort they brought.

TWENTY-TWO

Aboard the *Paradise Voyager*, 9 September 1998

Marty, Ellie and the Mothers of Song left San Francisco Sunday afternoon. They sailed north and docked in Vancouver, British Columbia Tuesday morning. Passengers went ashore to sightsee while the ship took on fuel and supplies.

Bright and early the following morning, with several additional passengers aboard, they retraced their path, threading their way past the San Juan Islands.

They encountered heavy commercial traffic in the Strait of Juan de Fuca. They saw tugs shepherding barges and passed a grain ship full of Northwest white wheat heading to the Orient. Crabbers, their decks stacked so full of traps they scarcely left room to walk, trawlers with big nets suspended above their stern, and salmon boats came and went.

Passengers clustered along the railings watching the parade, Marty and Ellie among them. The group marveled at a Hyundai container ship carrying a multi-colored mountain of shipping containers bound for the Port of Tacoma.

For a time they shadowed a Daio Paper ship on its return voyage to Japan. With its holds full, it rode low in the water. A young woman standing beside Marty gaped up at the giant, black vessel. She raised her hand to shade her eyes, stepped back and bumped into Marty.

She turned and smiled apologetically. "I'm sorry. I didn't realize you were so close. It's crowded with everyone trying to see." She extended her hand. "My name's Jeanine Baker and—" She reached behind her. Finding nothing, she swiveled her head.

She grinned and pointed to a group of men. "There's my husband Ted. We're on our honeymoon. He's the handsome one," she added in a whisper.

Marty shook her hand. "My name's Marty Jenkins." She took Ellie's shoulders and spun her away from the railing. "And this is my granddaughter, Ellie Grant."

Jeanine pointed up at the *Daio Journey*. "That's such a giant ship. I wonder what's in it."

"It's full of wood chips," Marty replied.

"Wood chips, what in the world for?"

"They cook them to make paper; it's headed for Japan."

"You seem to know a lot about this stuff."

"We're from Pine Crest, Oregon. Daio Paper ships regularly dock at Coos Bay to load chips. Any time we see one, Ellie and I usually stop to watch."

Ellie raised an arm at a 45 degree angle. "They lift the big trucks way up like this, open their back door, and, whoosh, the chips pour out."

"We're from Kansas City. Ted and I have never seen the ocean before."

The sun had begun its slow descent to the western horizon by the time the *Voyager* crossed the bar and returned to Pacific waters. The harbor pilot who'd guided them through the Strait returned control of the ship to Captain Werner and boarded a waiting helicopter. The Captain laid in a westerly heading at 14 knots and prepared to leave the bridge.

After a short rest, Werner went to the dining room. Once he'd completed his meal, he rose and tapped his spoon against the side of his water glass.

The room stilled as everyone turned in his direction.

He surveyed the room with a smile. A retired navy skipper, Werner was the *Voyager*'s first Master. Everything had proceeded according to plan and they were right on schedule, just the way he liked. "Did everyone enjoy Vancouver?"

Positive responses and scattered applause filled the room.

"Well, the best is yet to come." Werner paused to let the

moment build. "I want everyone to know we'll be in the Gulf of Alaska tomorrow."

Excitement rippled around the room and a sense of expectation gripped the passengers. The following day promised to be an exciting one.

The *Voyager* had made her maiden run the previous spring. Not surprisingly, there'd been a few bugs on her first few outings. The last time, the *Voyager's* guidance systems had given them some trouble, causing the ship to gradually stray off course. Not so far as to become a problem, but still annoying.

First Officer Malcolm Hunter likened it to driving a car with the wheels misaligned; you had to aim a little to one side to go straight. He made the necessary compensations to keep them on course and had technicians examine the problem when they docked in San Francisco. Both he and Werner anticipated an uneventful trip.

The Captain moved from table to table, pausing to answer questions and visit with the passengers. Outside, moonlight glinted off the sleek white ship as it sliced through the dark water. The *Voyager* was alone now. Vancouver and Seattle lay far behind and the Alaskan Peninsula dead ahead.

Winter came early to the north Pacific. This would be the *Voyager's* last northern cruise of the season. The crew would take a short furlough when they returned to port and, after some refitting, the *Voyager* would join her sister ship the *Paradise Explorer* on the southern routes to Mexico. Mexico, however, still lay in the future. For the time being, the *Voyager* would continue steaming west.

Aboard RCI Vessel, *Tango, 9 September 1998*

A loud crack reverberated off the small room's metal walls when Winston Ridgely smacked his hands together.

"Maheshwari, you're a genius." He lifted the glass of champagne he'd carried into the room. "Until I saw it for myself,

I never truly believed this scheme of yours would work." He offered Derek a paper cup and the champagne bottle. "Care for a glass of bubbly?"

"No, thank you. I do not consume the bubbly, Mr. Ridgely."

Ridgely took another gulp. "Suit yourself, leaves more for me."

Derek stopped typing for a moment and took a deep breath. "Just for the record, I do not consider my work to be some sort of scheme. I am not a magician relying on prestidigitation, but a scientist putting a series of well-researched hypotheses to a practical application."

Ridgely refused to have his enthusiasm diminished. "Well, I have to tell you, seeing that wretched tub of a ship we towed out here vanish right in front of my eyes was one unbelievable experience."

"By the way, you may call me Derek, if you prefer. Most westerners find it considerably easier to pronounce than Maheshwari."

"Derek, Schmerek. Why aren't you celebrating? Everyone topside is dancing circles around the deck."

"I am delighted to hear your associates are so elated. There are, however, still many things to learn about the process. We have additional data to gather, results to correlate, outcomes to map. That is, after all, why we are here, is it not?"

"Don't be such a party pooper. If any of those hotshot Admirals at the Pentagon saw what I just saw, they'd be reaching for their checkbooks and lacing up their dancing shoes."

Derek finished inputting the data, swung his chair around and directed Ridgely into a nearby chair. "Sit. We have things to discuss."

Ridgely tossed back the remainder of his champagne and crumpled the cup. "What's the matter? Is something wrong? Aren't you pleased with the experiments so far?"

"Pleased is perhaps too strong a word. At this point, one could say I am cautiously optimistic. The project is proceeding as planned and the results encourage me. However, the night is still young. What you, what everyone has become so excited about are close range, extremely low intensity efforts. Yes, it went well and that is gratifying, but much work remains to be done."

"Well, that hulk is riding pretty low in the water. How would you know if it sank in the middle of a test?"

"Our process is built around *visual* stealth, Mr. Ridgely. Whether it is visible or not, the mass of the test ship remains constant. My team anticipated this possibility, which is why we are towing it with a detachable tether. Should it sink or capsize, our connection to it will automatically be severed, notifying us of the event. And, visible or not, its sinking would still generate a visible wake."

"You'll have everything you need by morning, right?"

"We have accumulated a vast amount of data. It will be weeks, perhaps months, before all of the results are thoroughly analyzed."

Ridgely started to reply but the sudden whine of machinery in the adjoining room drowned him out.

At the sound, Derek spun around and began rotating a dial on the console beside him as he monitored its progress on his main screen.

Ridgely watched him work for a moment, then shrugged and left the room. They had more champagne topside.

TWENTY-THREE

Paradise Getaways Offices, London, *10 September 1998*

Ten time zones and thousands of miles from the *Paradise Voyager*, Jerry Delaney's workday was just beginning. Though he and the *Voyager's* crew worked for the same company, they'd never so much as heard each other's name.

Delaney entered Paradise Getaway's home offices in London a little before three in the afternoon. He nodded a passing hello to the receptionist and went straight to the Tracking Center.

He carried a plastic box with his lunch tucked inside and had his jacket, damp from a light drizzle, thrown over his arm. He wore the wind breaker more for protection from the rain than warmth, although it promised to be in mid 50s by the time he clocked out at the end of his shift.

The Tracking Center served as the company's communications hub, channeling all electronic transmissions between the home office and their ships at sea. Delaney provided IS support for the company's intranet, which circled the globe continuously bouncing messages off multiple satellite relays.

He maintained the servers and corrected the occasional glitch. Each day he came on at three and clocked out again at half past midnight. He made his way to the underground station in pitch darkness, took the tube home, and tiptoed into their flat so as not to wake the baby.

A major portion of his time was spent monitored the reporting screens. He likened it to overseeing a nuclear reactor. You were there to catch a problem, if and when one occurred. Meanwhile, you prayed you never found one. Rather boring, actually, but it paid the bills.

Delaney sat down, logged on, and scanned the screens. He smiled. It promised to be another uneventful evening.

Aboard the *Paradise Voyager, 10 September 1998*

Noticing the first hints of dawn over the eastern horizon, Malcolm Hunter, the Officer in Charge, stretched and checked his watch. He looked forward to the end of his shift. And what a shift it'd been.

First, there were the lights. Mac McCloskey caught sight of them and alerted everyone on the bridge. An intermittent shimmering glow on the horizon appeared for several moments then winked out. When Mac checked a short time later, it had returned. Strangely enough, none of their instruments detected anything out of the ordinary.

Several passengers on their way to their rooms after a nightcap noticed it as well. One couple stopped in at the bridge wanting to know if they were seeing the *aurora borealis*.

"No, it pulses in the sky." Hunter motioned with his right hand. "You'll see them on the starboard side. The light you saw was off the port bow."

"If it wasn't the *aurora*, what is it?"

He had no answer for them.

As a precaution, they began monitoring the emergency frequencies. The radio was deathly quiet all night. Unlike the radio, the radar screen remained active. For a time, Mac thought he detected two ships in the area.

They broadcast the standard request to identify but got no reply.

When Mac turned back to his screen, there was only one ship.

After sending a note to Engineering asking them to check the radar system, Hunter broke out the binoculars. Sometimes the old-fashioned way worked better. And if there was something out there, he wanted to know it. Mac peered into the darkness for hours and never saw a thing.

Hunter gave the bridge to McCloskey and walked out onto the surrounding deck. Framed by shiny black railings, the barrow deck had stairs on both sides.

He buttoned his jacket, folded up the collar, and gripped his coffee mug with both hands. This is the *Voyager's* last northern trek of the season, he thought. Hunter looked forward to Mazatlan, Puerto Vallarta, and Acapulco. He preferred girls in bikinis to moose and glaciers any day.

He listened to the dark water splash against the bow as he rehashed the night's strange occurrences. He was a pragmatist who held no superstitions and didn't believe in omens. He'd duly noted the previous night's anomalies in the ship's log as stipulated. He doubted they'd hear any more about it.

Life aboard the *Paradise Voyager* had settled into a predictable, albeit somewhat dull, routine. They carted passengers from San Francisco to Alaska's Prince William Sound, on to the Bering Sea and back again. They'd been sailing this same route week in and week out, month after mind-numbing month. At times, he felt like a glorified bus driver.

Turning east, he squinted at the looming brightness taking shape along the horizon before returning to the bridge. The *Paradise Voyager* continued on its southwesterly course, leaving gentle, V-shaped ripples in her wake...ripples that quickly disappeared in the frigid water masking any trace of her passing.

"Wake up, Grandma." Ellie tapped her shoulder again. "It's time to get up."

Marty groaned and cracked one eye to check the clock. "It's still early. The alarm hasn't even gone off yet. Can't you go back to sleep until it buzzes?"

Ellie shook her head. "I'm not sleepy. I wanna get dressed and go see the fishies."

Unlike Ellie who had nothing to do but play, the Mothers of Song had rehearsals scheduled all morning and shows to do that evening.

Ellie paced between the beds, impatiently rocking from one foot to the other.

Why had she ever let her choose the bed by the wall? Marty would have made a different choice if she'd only known that the morning sun poured in through the porthole. Oh well, too late now, she thought with a sigh. Who could have guessed the sea air would turn a sleepy little girl into an early riser?

Ellie cupped her hands around her grandmother's ear, leaned down, and, like a drill sergeant, yelled "C'mon. Rise and shine. Chop! Chop!"

Marty gave a startled jerk. Her eyes popped open. "Where did you learn to do that?" she asked, rubbing her ear.

"That's what Mommy does when I don't get out of bed for kindergarten."

"Well, I need to have a talk with your Mommy when we get back home." Marty tossed the covers aside and reluctantly sat up on the edge of the bed.

Ellie grinned and clapped.

"Everything ready?"

"Yes, Sir. Tables are set and waiting. The coffee's brewing."

One deck below the bridge the dining room and kitchen were in a state of controlled frenzy as breakfast preparations drew to a close. Miguel Diego, the *Voyager's* Chief Chef lingered near the back of the room watching the morning unfold. On his left, white-coated servers hurriedly finished stocking the steam tables.

The doors opened at the chime of a bell and the early risers began drifting in. Busboys poured water and juice, waitresses circulated with carafes of coffee, and his assistant chef began cooking eggs to order on a small grill next to the buffet line.

Diego glanced around and smiled. It all seemed routine, beautifully routine, just the way he wanted it. "Carry on."

The head waiter acknowledged with a nod.

Diego returned to the kitchen to prepare his own breakfast. He usually ate his morning meal in his office while reviewing menus and inventory reports. The menu seldom varied: sliced fruit, melon, or a tall glass of juice, *frijoles refritos, huevos rancheros* with *chorizo, queso fresco* and *salsa verde* washed down with several cups of strong, black coffee.

He opened the big stainless steel refrigerator door and rummaged in his personal larder. With the ingredients in hand, he scattered several skillets across the stove and set to work.

He slid out a saran covered fruit plate to nibble on while he cooked, and sat a container of tomatillo-based *salsa verde*, his mother's recipe, on the worktable. Beside it went a bowl of cooked pinto beans he'd prepared the evening before.

He carefully slit the casing on a length of *chorizo* sausage and crumbled the meat into a skillet with his fingers. The sausage released its familiar spicy aroma as it sizzled. Diego's dark eyes crinkled when he grinned. It smelled like home. Laying a spatula across the cooked meat, he pressed out the grease into an adjoining skillet.

The sausage drippings enhanced the flavor of his refried beans, but he still missed the *epasote* his mother added. It was one of many things he missed. He'd left a part of himself behind when he chose to forsake his home village, he thought, patiently mashing the soft beans with a fork.

This was their last Alaskan cruise of the season and he was glad for it. He looked forward to the southern routes. Passengers expected a different cuisine when sailing to Mexico. Goodbye grilled salmon and halibut, hello Chile Rellenos, Chimichangas, Quesdillas, and Guacamole.

Diego planned to fly home while they refit the *Voyager* for the southern run. His smile faded. It would not be an easy visit.

He and his father had been enjoying cold bottles of *Negra Modelo* when Diego said, "A woman has moved in with me. Her name is Kathleen."

His father had clinked beer bottles with him and grinned.

"I'll bring her with me on my next visit."

His father nodded.

He wanted to add, *We're planning to be married*, but didn't because he worried about his family's reaction to Kathleen. His father wasn't a problem and his mother, if she was disappointed with his choice, would hide it well. It was *Abuelita*, little Granny, who concerned him. To her, the old ways were the only ways. She'd been opposed to him going to Mexico City to study cooking. What would she think of his intended?

Thoughts of Kathleen lifted his mood and Diego's smile returned. What a pair they made, he tall and ruggedly handsome with dark eyes, black hair and mustache; Kathleen fair with auburn hair and as Irish as a shamrock on St. Patty's Day.

"Everything will be all right," she'd told him, modeling the lace mantilla she'd bought for Mass in the village church. She showed him the tag. "See it's even made in Mexico."

Diego knew his family would love Kathleen just as he did if they would only take the time to get to know her. He cracked two eggs into a skillet. Despite his concerns, he looked forward to the trip home.

And today? Ah, today would be a fine day.

While his eggs cooked, Diego quickly fried a couple of corn tortillas until they were soft, not crispy, and slid his eggs out on top of them. At this point, when cooking for passengers, he sprinkled on shredded Jack cheese and quickly ran the plate under the broiler.

Instead, he added on *queso fresco*, white farmer's cheese, just as his Mother had. He spread the hot sausage over the cheese, and topped it with *salsa verde*. He completed the plate by spooning on some of the beans and garnished it with slices of avocado.

TWENTY-FOUR

Aboard the *Paradise Voyager*, 10 September, 1998

Captain Werner arrived on the Bridge at 0600. Though he'd left the Navy several years prior, Ian Werner's bearing still revealed traces of time spent at the Naval Academy. His presence on the bridge laid a veneer of formality over everyone's demeanor.

He grabbed a stack of overnight faxes and began flipping through them. "How goes it, Hunter?"

"A-OK, Captain."

"That's what I like to hear." Werner tossed the papers aside and headed towards his office door. "Carry on. I've got morning reports to file. You know where to find me."

Hunter interrupted Werner's exit. "Uh, Captain...there is one little thing...probably nothing. We had some problems with the radar last night. I've noted everything in the log, but I thought you might want details."

Werner spun a chair around, straddled it, and gave him an expectant look.

"Mac picked up a couple of unknown vessels in the area. Off and on, that is."

"Off and on?"

"Yeah, they were there and then one wasn't. It's probably just the equipment. I've put in a request to have maintenance check it out."

"But you're not completely confident it *was* an equipment problem, is that what I'm reading here?"

"I don't know, Sir. Mac thought at first it might be fishermen, but we're too far out for trawlers and factory ships don't fish these waters this time of year. We're beyond regular shipping lanes, which pretty much rules out freighters. We monitored all the marine band frequencies and came up empty-handed there, too."

"But you're still not convinced, hmm?"

"Well, there was also the light."

"Light?" Werner stroked his chin for a moment. "Maybe that's what those passengers meant when asked me about the *aurora*. He brushed his hand through his short, gray hair. "What about these lights?"

"I feel a little silly talking about it. There was this strange bluish glow over the horizon. Not all the time, just now and then. You know, off and on."

"Sounds like Mac's radar. Did they correlate?"

"Now that you mention it, they did."

"Keep monitoring the radio. Until we know different, let's assume the radar's fully operational. If someone's out there, they may not have much in the way of electronics or, for all we know, they're running contraband. If they are, that's their business, not mine."

Werner rose and crossed the room to his office. A high-backed, totally adjustable, black leather office chair with full lumbar support awaited him in front of his desk. Like all the furnishings and appointments in his office, the *Voyager's* Interior Decor Team specified it and Central Supply purchased it.

His contribution to the office was limited to three items: a bank of family photos on the left wall, a Plexiglas case on a table with a replica of the Navy destroyer he'd commanded and an ancient wooden-beaded back support. He'd had it so long the finish had worn off the beads and he'd re-threaded it twice. He carried it on his first day aboard ship. The Captain had an aversion to sweaty backs and sticky shirts.

He powered up his computer and, in the process, initiated a stream of chatter back and forth between the ship, a stationary satellite in synchronous orbit miles above the earth and the home office in London.

Quickly running down the familiar decision tree, he clicked and toggled his way onto Paradise Getaways' intranet site. His wife's initials and birth date became a line of asterisks in the password box. Another click and he'd logged on. Werner opened an email from his wife.

"Sean, their youngest, passed his entrance exam and their daughter-in-law had a sonogram; it would be another boy. The car was making a funny noise, but he mustn't worry about it. She hoped he looked forward to his upcoming furlough as much as she did. Love and kisses."

Werner moved on to other work. Recalling his discussion with Hunter, he decided to manually recheck the ship's position. It took him only minutes to determine that they hadn't corrected steering problem in San Francisco. In fact, they'd made it worse. The ship was dangerously off course.

All night long they'd been sending erroneous position reports to the home office. Such a breach of operating procedures would undermine rescue efforts in the event of an emergency.

In room 321, honeymooners Ted and Jeanine Baker opted to sleep in. Afterwards, as Jeanine luxuriated in the afterglow of lovemaking, she found herself wondering if life would always be as wonderful as the last few days had been. Would they, could they, build the fulfilling life she dreamed of?

Jeanine mapped out their future, imagining shady streets, well-manicured lawns, and a white house with powder blue trim. She pictured excited children opening presents around the tree and a big dog greeting them at the door.

A sudden chill rippled through her causing an involuntary shiver.

Ted lifted his head off the pillow. "Hey, you okay?"

She assured him it was nothing to worry about and snuggled against him. He put his arm around her and drifted back to sleep.

She'd had these sudden shivers for as long as she could

remember. Once, after a particularly bad incident, her mother told her such shudders occurred when someone walked across your grave.

"That can't be," Jeanine had replied. They were clearly sitting on their front porch. "In order to feel the chill, I'd have to be in my grave."

"Of course you're not in your grave *now*. But all of us will be someday, and that spot, *your spot*, is already known to the spirits. When it's tread upon, the spirits pull us into the grave for just a split-second and the cold chill of death wraps itself around us."

Her mother picked up a pack of cigarettes and struck a match. The flame bathed her face in flickering yellow light as she touched the tip and inhaled deeply. She held it for a moment then let it slowly escape into the Kansas night. She took another puff and closed her eyes, savoring the nicotine's effect.

With her mother's raspy words echoing in her ears, Jeanine had imagined herself in the grave, trapped inside a dark coffin. The heat grew oppressive, the air rank with the peaty smell of soil and humus. Sweat dripped off of her body as she clawed and kicked to get free. She reached up through the strands of shredded shroud and pushed the curved lid with all her might.

The end of her mother's cigarette glowed red as she took another puff. She smiled and leaned close. "Every year we all celebrate our birthdays. Yet each year another day passes unnoticed. Like our birthday, it's a special day, a more important day...the date of our death. And the spirits know," her mother whispered. "Trust me, Jeannie girl, they know."

Jeanine pictured herself on the front porch of her childhood home. She dabbed her tongue along her lips, checking for the tart remnants of lemonade. Fireflies blinked in the dark woods. Crickets chirped and the croaking of bullfrogs reverberated around her. She saw the porch floor with its worn gray paint, heard the floorboards creak in time with her mother's rocker and felt the terror of that night all over again.

Why was she remembering these things now, on her

honeymoon? Her mother's stories were nothing but old wives' tales. The phrase rolled around in Jeanine's mind.

Would she ever be an old wife?

Down the hall, in Room 327, Ellie dressed quickly. After carefully closing the Velcro clasp on each shoe, she hopped off the bed and skipped through the open bathroom door.

"Look, Grandma, I'm all dressed. Do I look like a princess?" She spun on the rug while Marty continued blow-drying her hair.

Ellie held up two pink barrettes embossed with fairy princesses. "Will you put my barrettes in?"

Marty sat the hair dryer aside and picked up her hairbrush. "You're going to have to hold still if you want me to do this."

Ellie froze in place while Marty drew the brush through her fine blond hair. After separating and clamping two wispy tufts for her wannabe Princess, Marty took the little girl by the shoulders and turned her to the mirror.

"Okey, dokey?"

Ellie straightened her shirt and gave a happy nod. She ran for the door. "I'm going upstairs to see the fishies, Grandma."

"Not so fast there, Missy. Before you leave, tell me all the rules."

Ellie straightened, dutifully repeating each and every one of her grandmother's instructions and admonitions.

Satisfied, Marty pulled the top of her robe together and knelt down in front of the youngster. "Remember, we're going to have breakfast with the other ladies at nine o'clock. Do you know what that looks like on your watch?"

Ellie assured her she did.

"Give me a kiss and be careful." Marty headed back to the bathroom, as the door slammed shut.

This trip had been very educational for Ellie. As soon as the

Paradise Voyager left San Francisco, they began sighting California Gray Whales shepherding their young calves on their northern migration. She and her grandmother waited along the railing, watching for the whale's telltale spouts.

They'd spotted pods of Orcas when the *Voyager* passed the San Juan Islands, and once the ship returned to open water, they saw the California Grays again along with Pacific white-sided dolphins. Small pods of 8-10 dolphins frequently shadowed the ship, riding its bow waves.

Marty pointed out the identifying characteristics of each species, but to Ellie they all remained *fishies*.

Ellie opted for the nearby stairs instead of the elevator at the other end of the ship. The steep angle of the narrow stairway made it a difficult and unnerving climb for a five-year-old. She took them one at a time, pausing frequently to adjust her grip on the thin metal rail welded to the adjoining bulkhead. The ship's rocking motion reinforced her belief that disaster lurked on every step.

An inset steel door with rounded corners waited at the top of the stairway. Ellie put her shoulder against it to force it open. The stiff hinges gradually responded to her strident pushes and the open edge of the door glowed as sunlight oozed into the passageway. The door finally swung full back. Fresh sea air swept across Ellie's face and ruffled her hair.

She took a deep breath, smiled, and stepped across the threshold. She paused long enough to close the door as Grandma taught her.

A man's voice startled her. "And how are you this fine day, M'lady?" asked the Purser.

Ellie turned.

The smiling Purser made a slight bow and gave her an informal salute.

Drawing herself up to her full height, Ellie returned his salute with all the military precision she could muster.

TWENTY-FIVE

Aboard the RCI Vessel, *Tango, 10 September 1998*

Derek and Ridgely stood side-by-side on the deck of the *Tango* as they began the final experiment. The tether was at maximum extension, making it difficult to see the test ship without binoculars. Throughout the night, the gutted carcass they'd outfitted for their tests had been gradually taking on water. It now rode only a few feet above the water. In the morning light, the dark hulk of the test ship appeared as nothing more than a distant speck.

"It's been a long night, hasn't it Derek?" Ridgely asked with a yawn. "Satisfied?"

Derek strained to keep the test ship in sight as it bobbed and dipped behind the waves. "Long, but fruitful, Mr. Ridgely."

Ridgely's champagne glass accidentally slipped through his fingers. "Oops. Man overboard!" He giggled as it disappeared into the ocean.

"Perhaps it is just as well. You have had more than enough bubbly for one person."

"You sound like my wife. She's always harping about my drinking." He aimed his binoculars northward. "I didn't think the old tub would make it, but it's still out there. I hope you're not planning on hauling it back to San Francisco."

"We've placed charges in the bulkheads. When remotely detonated, they will breach the hold causing the ship to sink."

Below deck, generators sprang to life. The ship vibrated as their familiar whine grew in intensity. A steel panel rolled aside and a bluish beam arced out toward the intended target.

Ridgely slapped him on the back. "Here we go, my man. The final test has officially begun."

Derek started to answer him, but stopped when a movement in his peripheral vision caused him to jerk his binoculars to the east. A shiver crawled up his spine when he noticed the approaching ship. It would enter the test zone any moment.

"We must abort the test," Derek shouted. "There is a ship approaching from the east." He let the binoculars drop to his chest. Spinning away from the rail, he prepared to head down a nearby stairwell.

"Not so fast, Professor." Ridgely reached out and snagged the collar of Derek's jacket, nearly yanking him off his feet. "Let's not get carried away here. We won't be able to do another test from this range."

Derek was close to hysterics. "That matters not at all. There is a ship out there entering our test zone. We must power down the beam while there is still time."

"Stop the test and say what? 'Hi fellas, great morning isn't it? Sorry about the mix-up. You see we're out here testing some top secret gizmo. Just be on your way now and pretend you didn't see a thing. Oh, and be sure to keep this hush, hush. Okay?'"

"There are innocent people aboard that ship. They could be harmed." Derek pulled free of his grip.

Ridgely motioned to a security guard. "Grab him before he does something foolish."

The burly man caught Derek and wrestled him back to Ridgely's side.

Derek's voice grew shrill with fright. "We must stop it, I tell you. I beg you; please do not let this proceed."

Ridgely gave him a bemused smile. "You said the system would eventually have to be tested on human subjects. Here's your opportunity."

Derek thrashed against the security guard's hold. "Not yet. You have consumed too much alcohol. You are not thinking with a straight mind."

"I don't remember it hurting the bunnies."

"You witnessed a controlled laboratory experiment. There

are many things you do not understand. This is different, completely different. The bubbly has clouded you brain. You must abandon this course of action."

"This technology is worth hundreds of billions and you want me to toss it all overboard because these fools bumbled in on our test? I don't think so, Dr. Derek. For all we know it's a competitor checking up on us." He turned to the guard. "Take him below and keep him away from the computers."

Derek glanced back over his shoulder as the guard shoved him toward the stairway. His eyes widened in horror, as a shimmering blue light danced along the *Paradise Voyager's* bow.

Aboard the *Paradise Voyager, 10 September 1998*

Werner stared at his calculations. He started to rise from his chair and return to the bridge when the ship shuddered.

It reminded him of the hull thumping against the pier when they docked. He instinctively looked out the porthole expecting to see the dock they'd bumped against. There was only ocean.

Out on the bridge, Hunter felt it too. He looked up and locked eyes with Mac McCloskey.

Something was wrong and Hunter didn't like it, not one bit. "Check the radar," he said, scanning his instrument panel.

McCloskey watched one of the blips on his screen slowly vanish.

Hunter raised his head and stared out the bow windows. A shimmering blue light was coming toward them. Or were they sailing into it?

Could it be fog?

He didn't know. His eyes no longer focused.

Marty finished dressing with time to spare and decided to

go up on deck to check on Ellie. As she reached into the closet for her jacket, the ship gave a momentary shudder. Dismissing it as nothing important, she grabbed the jacket and hurried toward the door.

Meanwhile in room 321, Jeanine was still sorting out her feelings when the bed began to sway. At first she thought Ted had rolled over. She smiled to herself. There were things a married woman had to get accustomed to. Then she realized Ted hadn't moved.

Jeanine shivered again.

And down in the kitchen, Diego felt the shudder ripple through the ship. He froze in place for a moment. The movement ended as quickly as it'd begun. He picked up the breakfast plate with a shrug and went into his office.

Offices of Paradise Getaways, London *1858 GMT*

The office windows reflected the overhead lights and bank of computer screens, making the small room appear twice as large as it was. These ghostly images, superimposed over London's dark night sky gave everything a surreal quality. Jerry Delaney found it unnerving to see his tall, lanky reflection floating multiple stories above the London streets. He watched his eyes blink back at him, but the image in the glass wasn't clear enough for him to discern his red hair and freckles.

He put his sandwich down and cautiously toggled back to the reporting screen. The blank column continued to lengthen. He checked the clock. It'd been an hour since they'd lost contact with the *Paradise Voyager*.

TWENTY-SIX

Aboard the *Paradise Voyager*

Ellie spotted the black-edged, hook shaped dorsal fins of a pod of white-sides as soon as she reached the rail. Several sleek bodies materialized below her as they surfed in the ship's wake. Tiring of that, they began squealing and leaping out of the water in pairs. She giggled and clapped her hands in delight. Engrossed in watching the dolphins, she didn't notice the jolt.

The dolphins, however, reacted immediately. They peeled away from the ship and regrouped. Mothers with youngsters began emitting high-pitched whistles to their calves. A large male circled the pod, aggressively slapping his tail against the water.

Ellie sought out her friend the Purser. "Are the fishies scared?"

He walked to the railing and glanced down. They were behaving as if they sensed danger. Could it be a predator? He scanned the horizon, but didn't see any. "I don't know what's upsetting them."

Ellie and the Purser watched the dolphin's actions become increasingly frenzied. Without warning, they formed a tight group and quickly swam away. Once they were a significant distance from the ship, they paused and stared back.

The Purser watched and wondered. The white-sides were clearly reacting to some threat. A threat they could perceive, but he could not. Were only the dolphins at risk, or was there more to it than that?

Moments later, the school of dolphins disappeared beneath the water.

"They sure looked scared," Ellie said as the last dorsal fin slipped from sight.

A low rumble drowned out her words. She put her hands on the railing for support then jerked them back to cover her ears.

She moved away from the railing and ran to a chair. Ellie curled up in a ball. Covering her ears, she began to quietly sob.

Why couldn't she get away like the fishies did?

After the second jolt, Diego leaped up and ran out of his office. He hurried across the dining room, pushing his way between panicked passengers.

An elderly woman snagged his sleeve. "You're part of the staff on this ship, aren't you?"

"I'm the ship's Chief Chef."

"Shouldn't we be going to the lifeboats?"

"I, I don't know. I'll try and find out."

Perhaps she was right, he thought. What if they had to abandon ship? There'd been no announcements, no warnings... nothing. He needed to get above deck to assist with evacuation procedures. He jerked away from her and ran across the room praying he remembered what they taught him in the safety drills.

"You're going to leave us here, aren't you?" the woman yelled after him. "That's what always happens. The Captain and crew get in the lifeboats and leave the passengers to fend for themselves."

Ignoring the woman's words, Diego jogged down the hallway. A low, rumbling moan enveloped the ship. His pulse hammered. He reached the service stairs and thought of Kathleen. He took them two at a time, making desperate deals with God as he climbed.

He felt himself growing weaker by the second as the rumbling continued. Each step became harder than the last. He gathered strength from his love for Kathleen. He couldn't die. Not now, not here. He had too much to live for.

Marty was on her way to find Ellie when the rumbling

began. Everything around her groaned and reverberated. The sound seemed to bounce back and forth between the walls causing her temples to throb. Her field of vision narrowed.

Where was Ellie?

She hadn't worried when Ellie wanted to go up and watch the dolphins. The space between the railings was fenced; a child couldn't fall through. It was safe, wasn't it? Well, wasn't it?

Marty knew she had to get out of the stairwell while there was still time. If she stayed there much longer, she might not have the strength. Taking a deep breath, she threw herself against the bulkhead door.

Ellie! Where are you Ellie?

The noise woke Ted. "What's happening?"

Jeanine's her eyes grew wide with fear. "I'll never be an old wife, Ted."

Taking her in his arms, he pushed her bangs aside and kissed her forehead. "Don't be silly, Babe. We're going to grow old together. We'll have matching rockers, his and hers. I'll wear suspenders and walk with a cane. You'll put on a flowered apron and bake cookies for our grandkids."

Jeanine nestled into his arms, but never acknowledged him.

Putting his hand on her chin, he lifted her face. "Talk to me, Jeannie. Tell me what's been going on."

"Mama was wrong."

"Wrong? Wrong about what? I meant what's been going on with the ship." He blinked several times. Things were getting fuzzy around the edges.

Jeanine seemed to be in some kind of trance. Her voice sounded different, far off. "Today's the day, Ted. Mark it on your calendar."

"Day, what day? You're not making sense."

Jeanine turned to face her new husband. Tears glistened in her unblinking eyes. "No one will ever walk on our graves. Mama said the spirits knew, but they don't."

"What on earth are you talking about?"

"It's very simple. We're all going to die and the ocean will become our grave. Even Mama's spirits can't walk on water."

Werner snatched the calculations off his desk and headed for the door. The low, rumbling sound reminded him of someone moaning in deep pain. It came from the ship's bulkheads, plating, floorboards...everywhere.

He rubbed his eyes. Why couldn't he see? Werner staggered toward where the door had been moments earlier, but his legs didn't want to work. He felt like he was slogging through knee-deep mud.

"*Keep going,*" he told himself. "*You're the Captain. You have to send an SOS.*" Their emergency satellite phone lay on the other side of the door. He had to make it. People were counting on him.

On the other side of the door, Hunter struggled to make his mind work. Whatever this, this blue stuff was; it wasn't fog. It'd come through the windows, into the bridge and surrounded them. His vision was just about gone.

He heard McCloskey's voice. It sounded faint and far away. Mac gestured and yelled something that Hunter couldn't make out.

The switch to activate the emergency beacon was in front of him on the instrument panel. All he had to do was flip the switch and turn it on.

Hunter's hand weighed a ton. He groaned as he tried to lift his fingers.

Offices of Paradise Getaways, London

Jerry Delaney attempted to contact the *Voyager* yet another time. He couldn't think of anything else to do.

His hands shook as he typed the short message. A click of his mouse sent his urgent plea on its way. While he waited for a response, he picked up the ship-to-shore phone and punched in some numbers.

An automated female voice asked for his employee ID.

He gave it to her.

Next, she wanted his security code.

He tapped out the baby's birth date.

Once he secured a line, Jerry put in the *Voyager's* emergency contact number. Holding his breath, he listened to the intermittent static and electronic chatter as he silently pleaded.

Please. Please. Please, let them pick up.

After a short while, a recording informed him his transmission hadn't gone through. He still had the phone to his ear when a window opened on the computer screen. His message had bounced...again.

Something had happened to the *Paradise Voyager*, the newest ship in the line. He could feel it in his bones. He'd come to work every day for the last four years knowing something like this could happen. This was the day he never wanted to see.

Then it occurred to him, the fate of all those people now rested in his hands. They were depending on him. Their families depended upon him. The company depended on him.

He needed to sound the alarm.

TWENTY-SEVEN

Jerry Delaney left the console and raced down the corridor. He needed someone to verify what he already knew but was afraid to accept. Reaching his destination, he threw open the door and stepped into the room's inky blackness.

"Davey, are you down there? How do you see where you're going without the overhead lights?"

"I'm here, Jerry. The light switch is on the wall, same place it's always been." Meredith heard a click and rows of fluorescent tubes flashed and hummed, giving off a dim glow that quickly grew brighter.

He squinted at Delaney. "Jeez man, you look like you've seen a ghost."

The big redheaded computer tech was wide-eyed with concern. He carried several bulky day logs under his arm. Grabbing a chair from a neighboring cubicle, he dragged it in and sat down. He balanced the pressboard-covered logs on his knees.

"Something bad is happening, Davey." He tapped his chest. "Something real bad; I can feel it inside."

"Don't go making a bloody fool of yourself. What is it we're talking about here?"

"A ship's not reporting that's what we're talking about here. I didn't notice at first cause everything else kept coming in right like it should. Then one minute I looked over at my screen and I noticed those blank spaces. It's the *Paradise Voyager*. They've gone and blinked off on me."

David Meredith laughed. "You worry too much. Somebody probably plugged in an electric razor and fried their electrical system." He turned back to his screen.

Delaney grabbed the arm of Meredith's chair and spun him back around. "Don't you be making light of this, Mate. I helped design the system myself. It's all new hardware, top notch. We've heard nothing from them for over an hour now."

Delaney's hand shook when he tapped the logbooks in his lap. "There's a year's worth of reports in each one of these logs and nary a day can I find when a ship skipped more than one scheduled report. This is serious. It's been over an hour."

"What do you expect me to do about it?"

"Drop what you're doing and rerun the diagnostics with me. I don't trust myself anymore. I need your help, man."

"I was updating the inventory program when you came in."

"Well, this is more important."

Delaney picked up his day logs and trudged out of the cubicle. Meredith followed him down the hall, muttering about his quiet evening being shot to hell.

An open Coke can, a half-eaten tuna sandwich, and a crumpled potato crisp bag sat in the middle of Delany's desk. He swept it all into the wastebasket as he sat down.

He pointed to a workstation on his left. "You can use Garrison's console." He flipped Meredith a pad. "There'll be a pencil or a pen in one of those drawers. Why don't you run down the checklist? That way, I can re-verify everything I've done."

"First off, when was their last position report?" Meredith asked.

"It came through at 5:45 this evening."

"Was that the *last* contact?"

"No, I've found a perpetual inventory re-supply requisition for hand soap and toilet paper at 5:53."

"And you've tried to contact them?"

Delaney signed. "I used computer lines *and* satellite phone. Over and over, but I'm getting nothing. It's like they're not there anymore."

The two men continued the question and answer session,

retracing each step of Delaney's work. After that, they rechecked the integrity of all the COM links and then they pulled up the reporting screen. Additional blanks had accumulated in the *Paradise Voyager*'s column.

Finally, the two men sat in their chairs staring at each other. They'd been at it 20 minutes and had nothing left to check.

Meredith spoke first. "End of the line, Jerry. You'd better call Schoonover and tell him what you've got here." He flipped the pencil onto the desk. "I'm going to grab something to eat. I'll be down at the vending machines if you need me."

Delaney's palms grew sweaty as he rummaged in his desk drawer for the confidential phone directory. He'd never had to use if before. He didn't even know if it was up to date.

He found Schoonover's home number and quickly rang it up. *Why me, why me?* He asked, counting each ring.

Around the office they referred to Reginald Schoonover, the company's Chief Operating Officer, as the Admiral. Tall and ruggedly handsome with his white hair combed straight back, he commanded immediate respect.

As a manager, he demanded excellence of his employees and ran the far-flung divisions of Paradise Getaways as if they were his own. Schoonover's office was one floor up in the Executive Suite. Delaney had never even spoken to him. He could count on one hand the number of times they'd passed in the hall. He dreaded being the one to bring bad news.

A maid answered. "The Admiral and Mrs. Schoonover are having dinner and can't be disturbed. Please call back later."

Delaney panicked. "I'm calling from the office. There's an emergency. I *must* speak with him now."

The maid asked him to hold.

Moments later he heard the Admiral's deep voice. "Schoonover here."

Delaney began to shake. He tried to convey his message, but it came out as unintelligible stammering.

"Get hold of yourself, man. Start again slowly, from the beginning."

Delaney did better on his second try due in a large part to the Admiral's coaching. Schoonover began punctuating their conversation with well-timed *I see's* and *Tell me more's* which helped Delaney's delivery immensely.

Once he finished, Delaney took a deep breath and awaited further instructions.

"Is there anything else?" Assured there wasn't, Schoonover ended their conversation. "Stay close at hand. I'll contact the proper authorities and ring you back shortly for an update."

Delaney began to move the handset away from his ear.

"Oh, and by the way."

He pressed the phone to his ear again.

"That was good work, Delaney. Continue to monitor the situation."

Jerry Delaney cradled the phone and returned to his computer with a satisfied smile. The Admiral said he'd done a good job. Maybe he wouldn't lose his job over this after all.

New York City

It was early afternoon on the East Coast and Claudia Monet was in New York for a photo shoot. Schoonover caught up with her via cell phone.

"Good day Mrs. Tilden, this is Reginald Schoonover. Sorry to bother you, but I've just received troubling news from the office. I thought you'd want to know."

"What is it?"

"It seems one of our ships, the *Paradise Voyager*, is unaccounted for. It apparently blinked off the computer screen for no apparent reason. It's coming up on two hours since their last report and they haven't been able to raise them by sat phone or computer. Could be nothing of consequence, of course, but it's been my experience that these things seldom are. It's better to meet them straight on."

"Have you notified the authorities?"

"I wanted to apprise you of our situation first. I plan to ring the office back as soon as we hang up. That Delaney chap may have new information. If not, I'll contact the United States Coast Guard so they can initiate search and rescue procedures."

"Better to file a false alarm than ignore a potentially dangerous situation. I'll wrap things up here and wait to hear from you. I can be in London tomorrow."

"At this point, I don't care to speculate on what's happened, but the least we can do is act in an expedient manner. We owe the passengers that much."

"I agree. Let me know once you've spoken to the authorities so we can arrange a press conference."

"I'll issue a press release this evening," Schoonover said. "We can schedule a news conference in the morning when we have better information. The best way to deal with unpleasantness is forthrightly. We're well insured. I'll contact Lloyd's in the morning. We're in agreement on this course of action then?"

"Absolutely, I'll do anything necessary to assist you."

By the time the call ended Claudia felt a headache coming on. There were 250 souls aboard the *Voyager*. Whatever she and Schoonover did, it had to be right. She also knew their handling of this situation would have a lasting impact on the company's standing.

She selected Brian's name from the contacts list on her phone. He'd always been her first line of defense in any legal situation. She chewed her lip as she waited for her call to go through.

TWENTY-EIGHT

Pine Crest, Oregon

It was mailing day at the Pine Crest Courier. Billy Nevins showed up at eight on the dot and began stuffing and collating his way through the stacks of papers. As soon as Billy completed a paper, Tom took it from him and ran it through the addressing machine. Tommy got it next. He sorted them by zip code and bundled them with crisscrossed strips of yellow plastic strapping. Then the bundles of newspapers went into mailing bags, the bags into the van, and the van to the Post Office.

Shortly after they'd finished the papers the man from Domino's Pizza tapped on the back door. Billy let him in and arranged the lunch table before popping his head around the partition and hollering, "Pizza time!"

As the crew ate their pizza, the talk turned to the Mother Singers. Everyone around the table speculated on where the cruise ship might be and what those aboard were doing at that very moment.

Through threads of mozzarella, Billy said they must be whale watching. In his mind, all whales looked like the Geppetto-swallowing Monstro he'd seen at Disneyland. He imagined friendly leviathans bobbing alongside the ship playfully entertaining the passengers with their umbrella-shaped spouts. The thought of missing it all disappointed him.

Tom started to speak, but a sharp knock at the door interrupted him.

Billy's expression soured. "Don't they know it's Pizza Time?"

Tom wiped his lips on a paper napkin and dropped his slice onto his plate. "I'll get it."

He looked through the front window as he walked to the door and saw a uniformed man. At first he thought it was a policeman, but quickly recognized it as a military uniform.

The man was in his mid 30's, a shade over six feet tall and stood ramrod straight. He looked directly at Tom when the door swung back. "Mr. Jenkins, Thomas Jenkins?"

His pulse began to race. Fear tightened his stomach. "Yeah, I'm Tom Jenkins."

The man removed his hat and slipped it under his left arm. "Sir, I'm Coast Guard Lieutenant Albert Darrow from Coast Guard Air Station North Bend, may I come in?"

Tom's imagination raced. In the split second needed for his response dozens of scenarios cascaded through his mind. He felt as if his worst fears were about to be confirmed.

"Okay...sure, I guess so." He opened the door wide and re-locked it behind the Lieutenant. "What's this about?"

"Sir, the United States Coast Guard received notification earlier today from the executive offices of Paradise Getaways. They've lost communication with one of their ships, the *Paradise Voyager*." His eyes went down to a scrap of paper in his hand. "I understand your wife, Martha, was aboard."

Tom felt like he'd been hit by a truck. He grabbed the counter for support when the room began to spin. Seconds ticked by in slow motion as fearful apprehension welled up within him. The room grew cold, deathly cold.

"What exactly does that mean?"

"They aren't sure. That's why they contacted the Coast Guard. You see—"

Tom's raised hand stopped him in mid-sentence.

"There are some other people who need to hear what you're going to say." He pointed the way to the rear of the building. "Come on back."

Darrow followed him around the partition and over to the lunch table where everyone sat laughing. The air was heavy with the smell of spices and pepperoni. While Tom was away, Billy had opened a container of his mother's oatmeal cookies and put them in the middle of the table for dessert.

All talk ceased at the sight of the uniformed man.

The Lieutenant politely nodded to the group and remained standing.

"I'm sorry; let me get you a chair." Tom disappeared for a moment and returned rolling the chair from his desk. "Sit here."

After Tom introduced him, Darrow unbuttoned his jacket and sat down in the black office chair. He transferred his hat from under his arm to his lap. His hands, pale white against the dark blue of his uniform, rested on his thighs. A crisp crease dropped straight off of each knee to cuffs that angled out above highly polished shoes. He glanced around the room as Tom repeated what Darrow had told him.

An eerie silence settled over the group. One by one, everyone at the table put down their partially eaten slices of pizza. The sudden quiet magnified even the slightest sounds; a faint car horn on the street outside, the hum of the refrigerator. Darrow's sudden appearance had ruined Pizza Day.

Implications that were obvious to the rest of the group came slower for Billy. Deep in thought, he kept his head bowed. He stared down at his hands and picked at the ragged cuticle framing his uneven fingernails. If the ship was gone, where did the people go? He began wringing his hands to alleviate his rising tension. Try as he might, Billy could come to only one conclusion.

Billy's head snapped up. He glared at Darrow. "What did you do to Mrs. Jenkins?"

The Lieutenant recoiled at this unexpected attack.

Billy allowed him no time to respond. "She's dead isn't she? They're *all* dead!"

The outburst ended as suddenly as it started. Billy sank back in the chair, rocking and wringing his hands as he sobbed. "Oh no," in a barely audible voice.

Tom caught Darlene's eyes and nodded in the direction of

the phone.

She excused herself and called Billy's mother.

Mrs. Nevins came right over. Looking deeply saddened, she approached her distraught son. "Billy, I think you'd better come home early today." She reached for his jacket.

"Mom, Mrs. Jenkins is dead." Billy pointed a finger at Darrow. "And he's the one who did it."

Darrow visibly straightened in the chair.

Kate Nevins blushed. Try as she might, there were times when Billy's behavior embarrassed her. She turned to face the group. Her hands fluttered in little circles like frightened birds as her mind searched for words she couldn't find.

"I'm, I'm so sorry," she said with a sigh. She turned to face her son and spoke with surprising firmness. "Billy, we don't know what's happened. Besides, it's none of *our* business. Put your jacket on. It's time for us to go."

Billy sniffed and swiped his nose with the cuff of his sleeve. Taking the jacket from her, he shoved in his arm.

"Billy, there's leftover pizza. Wanna take it with you for a snack?" Darlene asked.

He gave a noncommittal shrug and Beth quickly gathered the uneaten slices into one box. She gave it to him along with his container of cookies. With his mother by his side, Billy silently headed out the door.

Tom put his hand on Kate Nevin's shoulder and squeezed. "Thanks for coming so quickly. I'll try to call you later when we get things sorted out."

"Sorry about the delay," Tom said when he returned to the table. "Can we pick it up near the beginning?"

Tommy was the first to speak. "You said they'd lost communication with Mom's ship. What exactly do they mean? Did someone on the ship forget to check in on time or something?"

"The home office in London maintains a nearly continuous line of communication with each of their ships. It's computerized, of course, but it's still unprecedented to have a ship just blink off like this."

"How do they know it wasn't a computer glitch?" Tom asked.

"It very well could be. You have to understand, however, we're not talking about just one computer talking to one other computer. There's a whole net of communication links. For instance, there's a constant interface to the bridge. There are multiple email conduits, perpetual inventories kept of supplies, food and fuel tracked on multiple platforms. In some cases, the ship transmits data directly to suppliers rather than through the corporate office. The redundancies built into a system like this pretty much preclude a total blackout."

"But still, in the event of a complete power failure isn't that exactly what would happen?"

What would cause a total power failure? Tom wondered in the short time it took Darrow to answer. The engines must generate electrical power just like a car. So, if the engines shut down could that cause a power failure? What would shut the engines down? Running out of fuel...a collision...a fire...sinking. None of those possibilities sounded like anything he wanted to explore in depth.

"Yes, that *would* happen in the event of a power failure, were it not for a couple of things," Darrow said. "First, the ship's computers have a UPS, an Uninterruptible Power Supply. The system automatically switches to battery back-up in the event of an electrical outage. This keeps the essential systems running for several hours, more than sufficient time to report an emergency. And, secondly, there were several satellite phones aboard. They pack their own power source and bounce signals off other satellites besides the home office relays."

"When did you hear about this?" asked Beth.

Darrow unbuttoned a pocket flap and pulled out a small notebook. He folded the black leatherette cover over and scrutinized his notes. "Coast Guard offices in Washington, DC received the notification today, Thursday, at 1435 hours, Eastern Time."

"If that's when you were notified, when did whatever happened happen?" Tommy asked.

Darrow frowned as he ran through his list. "Now things get a little stickier. Keep in mind Thursday, 1435 Hours in Washington converts to 1935 in London. That's well beyond their normal business day. We don't know how heavily they staff their second shift. We can only guess at how much time elapsed between the actual event and when someone noticed the lines were down."

Great, really great, Tom thought. Everybody goes home to dinner leaving Marty and Ellie to fend for themselves. How long did it take them to notice something was wrong? What were they doing in the meantime?

"So you're saying ships just blink off the computer screen and nobody gives a damn?" The pencil in Tom's hand shook. He slapped it down on the tabletop to keep from dropping it.

"No Sir, that *isn't* what I said. They monitor 24-7. As soon as they noticed, they back-tracked the logs to determine when the last report came in. The last communication from the ship was received at," he paused to check the book again. "Here it is. It came in to London at 1753. Overlaying that on a 15 minute reporting cycle places the event somewhere between 1745 and 1800 hours."

"What did the Coast Guard do once you were notified? Did you send out those little orange helicopters we always see flying around?" Tommy asked.

"Washington immediately relayed the Ship Missing Status to all stations from North Bend to Air Station Kodiak. They also alerted commercial shipping in the North Pacific to the existence of a possible emergency situation. Then they formed a Unified Response Team. As for the helicopters, no, we didn't send them out."

Seeing their wide-eyed reaction, Darrow raised his hand.

"The *little orange helicopters* you referred to are HH65A Dolphins. They can fly up to 150 miles off shore, hover for about 20 minutes and return. Reaching the *Paradise Voyager* is beyond their operational capability. Instead, they launched two fixed-wing aircraft, HC130's, to initiate the search and rescue. A cutter is standing by to provide support once the incident site is located."

"How did your planes know where to begin looking," asked Darlene.

"Paradise Getaways provided the ship's last reported position."

"When did they last report their position?" asked Beth.

"As I was about to say earlier, their system does this automatically. The last position report, the coordinates where the Coast Guard initiated its search sequence, came in at 1745, London time, of course. The final contact with the ship occurred at 1753. It was a perpetual inventory restock request ordering more hand soap and toilet paper when they docked."

Tom's voice grew thick with sarcasm. "Wonderful! At least we know all the *important* things are taken care of"

"That tells us more than you may realize," Darrow said. "Inventory requests are normal, day-to-day procedure, certainly not something done during a perceived emergency. It's a strong indication that whatever overtook the *Paradise Voyager* was quick and unexpected."

Tommy asked the question on everyone's mind. "What did your planes find?"

Darrow frowned. "So far, nothing."

"Nothing?"

"That's correct. There's no sign of the ship, nothing on radar, no oil slick, no flotsam." Darrow took a deep breath. "And no lifeboats. I'm sorry."

The little group fell silent.

Darrow rolled his chair back and rose. "Here's my card. I'm one of the Public Information Officers at the base. You can call me anytime; it'll roll over to voicemail if I'm not there. I'll let you know of any new developments. I'm sorry to rush away, but I have other families in town to contact."

Before Lieutenant Darrow left the newspaper office, Tom suggested he or Tommy should be the ones to contact Karen. They were, after all, family.

Darrow happily complied. Although he never said so, he appeared to already have more than enough on his plate for one day. He and another Officer from the North Bend Station had rounds to make. Between them, these two Coast Guard Lieutenants met with all the families of The Mothers of Song.

TWENTY-NINE

Tom closed the newspaper office immediately after Darrow left; There seemed no point in staying there.

Beth noticed an eerie stillness when they stepped outside. "What's going on?" she asked in a voice tinged with fright.

Even the dogs weren't barking. Flocks of gulls and other seabirds who'd abandoned the shore clustered in nearby trees seeking safety.

Darlene rested her hand on Tom's arm and pointed to the sky. "Look."

The group stared up in awe. Ignoring the intermittent spattering of rain and the wind rippling their jackets and ruffling their hair, they silently contemplated the ominous gray-green sky.

That afternoon the year's first storm of the season blew in off the Pacific with unexpected fury. The Coast Guard issued small craft advisories. Radio stations broadcast high wind warnings and cautioned people to stay off the jetties and away from low-lying beaches.

In small towns along the southern Oregon coast, groups of storm watchers began suiting up. "So early this year. How exciting to have a storm like this in September," they said as they tugged yellow slickers over thermal underwear and down jackets.

Those who went to Shore Acres State Park got what they came for, maybe more. The wind whipped the incoming tide into frothy whitecaps and sent waves smashing against the cliffs with the chest thumping intensity of summer fireworks. Huge plumes of water roared up the sides of the steep, rocky ledges leaping a hundred feet into the air before crashing down on the storm watchers. Farther north, gusts swept across the dunes turning sand into buckshot and bowing solitary shore pines till they threatened to snap.

Awe quickly turned to worry, and worry to fear. People

wondered if they were in for something akin to the storied Columbus Day storm of 1962. The *Big Blow*, as it'd come to be called, was the most powerful storm to hit the Pacific Northwest in the 20th century. The storm wreaked havoc across the western half of the state. The anemometer at Cape Blanco lighthouse read 145 mph when the wind tore the unit apart. The one at the Mount Hebo Air Force Station in the Oregon Coast Range held steady at 130 mph. The wind eventually damaged their radar dome, sending 200 pound chunks of tile careening down the mountainside and tearing through trees. Inland, they clocked 70 mph winds throughout the Willamette Valley.

This freak September storm vented its fury on Pine Crest, Oregon too. All around town, the tops of tall firs and hemlocks shuddered in the wind. Trashcan lids clattered across dark streets, and the rain beat on the rooftops like a thousand drums.

The storm watchers were right about one thing; it turned out to be a day to remember. But their memories would have nothing at all to do with the weather. A much bigger event shoved this uncharacteristically violent storm aside. Instead, they'd recall where they were and what they were doing the moment they heard the news of the *Voyager's* disappearance.

Tom sat at home alone, brooding as he listened to rain pound the roof and ping against the windows. Everything his instincts told him had proven out. Marty should never have gone on the cruise. No one should have. He'd been right all along, but no one listened.

Vindication came with a bitter aftertaste.

He heard a rapping. Tom hesitated before going to the door. Was it a knock or merely the storm door shivering in the wind?

He found Eddie waiting in the amber glow of the porch light, water dripping from the brim of his cap. The short jog from his truck to the stoop had turned his normally light tan Carhartt jacket a dark chestnut brown. He stepped in and dried his face with a shirt sleeve.

He looked Tom in the eye. "Came soon as I heard."

THIRTY

RCI Corp Headquarters, Palo Alto, California

Brandon Steele scanned the horizon from the window of RCI's boardroom. The pen between his fingers bounced against the tabletop like a jazz drummer beating out a solo. Extending his arm, he shoved back his cuff and checked the time, again. He flipped the pen down onto the table and punched a button on the intercom.

"Yes Sir."

"Any word on where he is?"

"On his way. A company helicopter picked him up on the ship. He's aboard and headed to Corporate Center, ETA two minutes. They should be visible any second now."

Steele glanced out the window again. A small, fast-moving dot appeared on the horizon and rapidly grew in size as it approached the building. In a few seconds it became recognizable as a blue and silver helicopter heading straight towards him.

As it approached the building, the chopper vanished over the upper edge of his window. It was, he knew, landing on RCI's rooftop heliport. The day they left, Steele watched them load case after case of champagne onto the *Tango*. He was pretty sure it wasn't required for Maheshwari's experiment.

A short time later, the door swung open. Tired and unshaven with bloodshot eyes, Winston Ridgely strode across the large room.

"What happened out there, Win?"

He ignored the question, choosing to pace instead. He stared out the window with his hands jammed into the pockets of his blue and silver windbreaker. Ridgely wore leather deck shoes, cotton slacks and a tan RCI ball cap. Stress lines eroded his usually handsome face and hidden fear clouded his gray eyes.

"What you said on the phone, did it really happen?"

Ridgely sank into a chair and planted his elbows on the large conference table. He made a fist. Wrapping the fist with his left hand, he rested his chin on his hands without ever acknowledging Steele's presence.

He'd be damned if he'd let one stupid mistake wipe out years of work, Ridgely thought. It was all over the TV. They were going to have to keep a low profile. Wait until it dropped out of the news, as it sooner or later would. If they stayed under the radar, they could wait this thing out.

Reaching for a notepad, Ridgely dug into the pocket of his windbreaker and extracted a gold-plated pen. He glanced over at Steele, with hand poised above the pad. "We need to plan our response. We have to be ready with damage control."

"Damage control? There's no damage control for what you did. How could you let several hundred people wander into the test zone and not stop them? You've single-handedly created the greatest public relations disaster of the century. This makes Three Mile Island look like a walk in the park. How much did you have to drink?"

Ridgely grunted in reply.

"What in God's name were you thinking?"

"I'll tell you what in God's name I was thinking. I was thinking the Navy would love to get their hands on this project. I was thinking that if we played our cards right they could slip the initial contract into the budget without going back to Congress for approval."

Ridgely rose from the table and resumed pacing as he spoke. "I was thinking the announcement of a major contract would goose RCI's stock price. Stock on which you and I both hold options due to expire soon. Pulling a few extra million out of a rising market sounded pretty good to me. That's what, in God's name, I was thinking."

Most of the energy had gone out of him by the time he finished. He slumped back into his chair and stared down at the monogrammed pen in his hand He flung it across the room. The pen smacked the wall and exploded in spring-loaded frenzy, scattering parts across the light carpet. If Ridgely was concerned about the potential for ink stains, he gave no sign of it.

Steele jumped up. Leaning forward, he planted his outstretched palms on the tabletop. "What about the people?"

"The system had to be tested on human subjects sooner or later."

"You've stranded several hundred people in the middle of the ocean. Turn on the TV. Every channel is full of it. We've got to do something."

"Why? Even the technicians conducting the test and the Captain of the ship hardly know anything about what we were doing."

"It's only a matter of time before they put two and two together."

"Maybe, maybe not. In the meantime no one has any reason to link RCI with the *Paradise Voyager*."

"Don't kid yourself. Someone's going to connect the dots."

"I'm not sure anyone ever will. Yes, it's gotten a little messy. Big deal, it's not the end of the world. We've worked ourselves out of tight situations before. We need to approach this calmly. It's not unmanageable and with risk comes reward."

"With risk also comes disaster. Whether you want to admit it or not, we're sitting on a time-bomb here. We need to develop a coherent strategy and do it in a hurry."

"Jacobson should be part of this discussion," Ridgely said.

"I'll call down to Legal and get him up here. Have you eaten? I can order lunch for three."

"Make it four."

"Four? Who else is coming?"

"Maheshwari."

"Why Maheshwari?"

"He and I had a difference of opinion about who was in

charge of this test. I brought him back in the chopper with me. He's down in security right now, why don't you go retrieve him?"

Steele returned a few minutes later accompanied by Derek.

Ridgely immediately rose from his seat when the two men entered. He crossed the room and extended his hand. "Dr. Maheshwari, I'd like to apologize for our earlier disagreement. Please, sit down and join us for lunch. This is Ben Jacobson, the company's lead attorney." He spun a chair aside. "Sit here. We can talk while we eat."

The meal progressed politely. Their guest said nothing and everyone else restricted themselves to comments on the weather. When he'd finished eating, Steele took a sip of iced tea and gazed across the table at Derek.

"Dr. Maheshwari, I'm given to understand you and Mr. Ridgely had a minor misunderstanding during the recent tests."

His dark eyes blazed with anger. "If being restrained by armed guards and bound up in ropes is considered a minor misunderstanding in your circle, then yes, that is what we had."

Jacobson judged this to be an attorney moment and inserted himself into the conversation. "Aren't we being a little harsh in our judgments here? After all, you're only the Chief Project Consultant. Mr. Ridgely, by virtue of his position within the company, is the ultimate decision maker in all matters."

The attorney raised his hand to stifle any rebuttal. "You have no enemies here. RCI generously enabled you to come to this country and has facilitated your prolonged residence in the United States by continuing to extend your employment."

He glanced at his yellow legal pad as he spoke. "I see we also paid your travel expenses and provided a very lucrative employment contract. Your remuneration, I daresay, greatly exceeds what one might expect to receive in your native country."

"Are you threatening to rescind my employment?"

Ridgely elbowed Jacobsen aside. "Of course not, you've been an exemplary member of our team. Jacobson here is merely establishing the facts relevant to our discussion. There's no need for anyone to feel intimidated. We don't deal in manipulation or blackmail here at RCI."

"This is becoming much too adversarial," Steele said. "Forget everything Jacobson said." He flicked a finger at the other two men. "Perhaps Dr. Maheshwari and I should discuss this matter alone."

Taking their cue, Ridgely and Jacobsen left the room.

"Would you care for anything to drink?" Steele asked once they were alone. After pouring his guest a glass of water, he directed him to a corner of the room "Why don't we sit over here? The sofa is more comfortable than those straight chairs."

Derek did as he suggested and Steele settled into a love seat opposite him.

"I understand a passing ship unfortunately blundered into the test zone and became enmeshed in the test."

Derek stared straight ahead, his face a mask of stone.

"It's been my experience that most disputes arise when two parties develop differing interpretations of the same facts. Why don't you tell me what occurred between you and Mr. Ridgely?"

"The facts are as you stated them. Our disagreement arose over the morality of proceeding with the test knowing full well innocent people might be harmed."

Derek related all of the details of their confrontation aboard ship as well as the facts surrounding the disappearance of the *Paradise Voyager*. When he finished, he quietly awaited a response.

Steele leaned on the arm of the love seat letting his hand dangle down. He lowered his voice. "Just between you and me, I was as shocked by Win's behavior as you were. I didn't realize he was capable of such things. However, as much as we'd both like to change what happened, we can't. Can you reverse the effects and bring the ship and its passengers back?"

"I believe I can, given time and resources."

"I'll see that you have whatever you need. I'd like you to keep me personally apprised of your progress. My Administrative Assistant can reach me day or night. Communicate your needs through her," Steele said, rising from the sofa.

The two men walked to the door. Steele rested his hand on Derek's shoulder. "I'm glad we had this talk. We seem to be in complete agreement on the course of action required here."

Derek smiled and extended his hand.

Steele took it in his. "There's, uh, just one other thing. I'm sure you understand that prematurely disclosing the company's involvement in this could have a negative impact on all concerned. That serves no one's purposes. Our focus here needs to be on fixing the problem, not on fixing the blame. Holding press conferences to rehash old facts only wastes precious time. We must hold this...uh, problem in strictest confidence. Do you agree?"

Derek nodded.

"Fantastic. If there's anything you need, don't hesitate to let me know." Steele held the door for him. "Together I'm confident we can bring this whole affair to a swift and successful conclusion. After all, it's the least we can do for those unfortunate souls aboard that ship."

"I can't believe you," Steele said when Ridgely returned to the room. "Foreign nationals are neither slaves nor indentured servants. No matter how much you'd like to do it, you can't bind someone to the rail of a ship. Such behavior is generally frowned upon in most courts. There are other, more effective, ways to accomplish our goals."

"Such as?"

"I was able to soothe him with heartfelt expressions of concern. Is he a critical component in getting this problem solved?"

"We can do without him if we're forced to."

"Good. And by the way, Maheshwari thinks he's reporting to me now. So don't be surprised if you notice a change in attitude. It usually happens whenever a disgruntled employee finds support for their insubordination. Let him act anyway he pleases, just don't upset the apple cart."

"What are you going to do with him?"

"Give him a private lab and let him conduct experiments to his heart's content. We just have to make certain no one knows what he's up to."

"How long do you expect to maintain this charade?"

"It's been my experience that these touchy-feely routines have an unpredictable shelf life. He could wake up tomorrow morning and rethink his decision."

Ridgely bit his lower lip. "Regardless of how long this lasts, Maheshwari's days are numbered. But you're right; so long as he thinks he's fighting the good fight he's controllable.

"I'll assign someone to keep an eye on him," Steele said.

"As far as he is concerned, recovering the ship will be our highest priority." Ridgely chuckled. "Who knows? He might even solve this thing before he disappears too."

"Anything else?"

"Develop a list of all possible scenarios...the good, the bad and the ugly. We'll review them together and craft a response to each one. We can't risk getting caught flat-footed."

Steele's eyebrows lowered when he smirked. His tongue darted across his lips like a snake. "Silence and time are our allies. If we can keep this thing on ice long enough, we'll be free to do whatever we please with Maheshwari and that ship."

THIRTY-ONE

Pine Crest, Oregon

For an instant Tom thrashed in the mist between dreams and reality. He jerked awake in the darkness, sweat-drenched and shaking, his eyes full of tears. He sat on the edge of the bed, grabbed his pillow off the floor, and tossed it onto the damp, wrinkled sheets.

Not yet ready to trust his shaky legs, he remained on the bed with his head in his hands. Had their ship sunk? Did Marty and Ellie find themselves adrift in the frigid ocean? Did they have time to react, to slip on a lifejacket? The uncertainty increased his turmoil. He'd never felt so helpless in all his life.

He lifted his head and sat up straight. He wouldn't accomplish anything this way. Rather than become a prisoner to fear and uncertainty, he must focus on finding out what happened.

Putting on his robe and slippers, he went into the living room. Charlie walked over and nudged his hand. A shaft of moonlight stole through the blinds and pooled at his feet in the dark room. He scratched Charlie's head for a time then the big dog curled up at his feet.

Tom clicked on a lamp and opened a book. He didn't know how long he read before falling asleep in his chair.

Tom held up his Styrofoam cup. "Can I take this in?" He stood at the entrance to Coast Guard Air Station North Bend.

"Coffee's fine, Sir. Identify yourself and indicate the purpose of your visit, please."

He handed the guard a business card. "My name's Thomas Jenkins. I have an appointment with Captain Harrison."

The guard scanned the day log, found his name and picked

up the phone to notify them of his arrival.

Tom waited hoping his visit wouldn't be a futile one. It beat doing nothing.

"Someone will be out to escort you into the building."

The sudden high-pitched whine of a jet engine precluded further conversation. On the other side of a high fence, one of the Coast Guard's HH65A Dolphin helicopters revved its engines in preparation for takeoff.

Tom stepped to the fence to watch.

The red-orange HH65A slowly rose into the air. It hovered a few feet above the tarmac for several long moments, rocking as if suspended by an invisible wire. Then its nose swung around and the craft quickly lifted up and away from the base in a northwesterly direction. Once it attained sufficient altitude, the copter leveled out, swept across the bay, and vanished over the crest of the dunes.

Lieutenant Darrow escorted Tom in to see the base's commanding officer. The three men discussed the status of the *Paradise Voyager* for over an hour. Tom left the meeting knowing no more than when he arrived. He drove back to Pine Crest burdened with an overwhelming sense of disappointment. He looked forward to returning to the newspaper office and the comfort of established routines.

Even though puddles from the previous night's rain still glistened along Main Street, Tom enjoyed feeling a light mist as he walked from the parking lot to the newspaper's front door. He and Marty had always looked forward to the gray, rainy days of winter. To them, winter on the coast meant watching fierce storms at Shore Acres State Park followed by bowls of clam chowder, warm fires in the evening, and snuggling in bed with raindrops pitter-pattering on the roof.

Tommy, Beth and Darlene were rehashing yesterday's events when Tom entered the office. They saw him and stopped.

He felt ill at ease being the center of attention. Giving them an uncertain smile, he walked to his desk. "I called Karen last night."

Three expectant looks urged him to continue.

"Mark's in Europe, which doesn't help matters. He won't be able to get home right away."

"How's she dealing with things?" Beth's voice was full of concern for her sister-in-law.

"She took it as well as can be expected, I suppose. She stayed with John and Arlene last night."

"Thank goodness she has family close by," Tommy said.

The three of them inched forward as Tom continued speaking. When they reached him, the group spontaneously wrapped their arms around each other and hugged. Beth and Darlene sobbed. Tommy reached out and squeezed his Dad's arm. The warm touch of others who shared their pain gave them all temporary solace.

"You don't look like you slept very well," Tommy said.

"I got in a few hours before a nightmare woke me up. I dozed off in my chair with a book sometime later. How's everybody here?"

Their vague, mumbled replies indicated they hadn't done much better.

"I stopped at the Coast Guard station this morning," Tom said. "None of the news is good; they still haven't spotted anything from the air. They're sending them out on a regular basis, still hoping for some sign of the *Voyager*.

The room grew deathly still. Nothing Tom said was unexpected, but hearing it made it all the more real.

"Captain Harrison says a person can only survive in those waters for about 30 minutes or so, an hour max. It's already been...over...at least...26 hours...since..." Tom stopped trying to speak.

After a pause, Tommy asked, "Don't ships such as the

Voyager have an emergency transponder like airplanes?"

"They have what's called a Locating Beacon, technically, an Emergency Position Indicating Radio Beacon or EPIRB. It transmits to a SarSat, a Search and Rescue Satellite, using multiple frequencies. It's quite a bit different from what they put in a plane. When it comes to aircraft, they want them to stay put so they bolt 'em down."

"But a Beacon wouldn't do much good if it sank along with the ship," Tommy said, nodding.

"They're designed to float free. The way I understand it, the Beacon sits outside in a bucket-like contraption. If, and when, a ship goes down, the Beacon floats away and stays there to mark the spot."

"Wouldn't it get tossed around by the waves and move away from the spot it was supposed to mark?"

"They must work, at least well enough to get a search started," Darlene said. "Maybe the SarSat thing records their position when the Beacon begins transmitting."

"So, what did the Beacon from the Paradise Voyager tell them?" Beth asked.

"If it's out there, the Coast Guard hasn't been able to locate its signal. Honestly, I think Harrison and the search team are as befuddled as we are. Nothing about this seems to make sense."

With no more to add to the conversation, the women went back to work.

Tom motioned Tommy over. "If you've got a couple of minutes, I need to talk."

In the midst of personal tragedy, Tom was poised to become extremely busy. When a spokesman for the National Transportation Safety Board announced the ship's disappearance at a Washington press conference, newspapers began contacting him for commentary. They wanted his insight on a major angle in a big story, the loss of seven women from the same town. At least they did today. Tom knew how fickle the reading public could be. Today's headline became tomorrow's birdcage liner.

He could have declined their requests. No one would have blamed him if he did. His instincts told him there was more here than met the eye. What, he didn't know, but he needed the leverage of national exposure to pry it out.

Understanding that his window of opportunity could snap shut at any time, Tom made the gut-wrenching decision to provide the media coverage. This decision would exact a tremendous psychological cost, perhaps more than he could handle. Yet it was the only way he could steer the direction the unfolding story took.

He didn't want to relinquish this opportunity to strangers. Out-of-town reporters focused only on the negative. Like TV crews, they took advantage of people in their weakest moments, exposing their most private pain to public scrutiny.

Marty and the others deserved better. So, knowing it would be the hardest thing he'd ever done in his life, Tom took the assignment.

He owed her that much.

Tommy could tell his Dad had something on his mind. "What's up?"

"I know this is going to seem a little sudden, but I've given it a lot of thought. I want to do some investigative work and see what I can ferret out. The wire service has already contacted me and so has the newspaper syndicate. I've agreed to do a series on the *Voyager*."

"How can I help?"

"I need to hand off the day-to-day operation of the paper to you for a while." Tom looked across the table and gave his son a self-depreciating smile. "What am I saying? You already handle most of the day-to-day stuff. My sixth sense tells me there's more going on here than meets the eye. I want to be free to follow this story wherever the trail leads. "

It was a bittersweet moment that neither of them wanted to acknowledge. Tom knew someday he'd hand over the paper to Tommy. The whole family did. It was the unspoken commitment he'd made when Tommy came to work.

His oldest son had worked hard the last few years to help the paper grow. It was no longer Tom's paper; it was now their paper, and the time had come to acknowledge that fact.

"Of course, I'll still be around," Tom said. "I can always pitch in if you need help. This is just something I need to do for your Mother."

"I understand, Dad. Go and do whatever you need to. The paper will be here when you come back."

Tom reached his hand across the table and laid it on top of Tommy's. "I knew I could count on you. I'm booked on a flight to London tonight."

"Wow, that's fast."

He gave a wry chuckle. "Is it? Between changing planes and the time differences, it'll be Saturday night when I arrive. Since Ellie's father is already in Europe, Mark and I are going to get together on Sunday before he heads home. I'll be at Paradise Getaways' offices bright and early Monday morning."

"How long will you be gone?"

"I should be back in time to help wrap-up the next edition."

THIRTY-TWO

Heathrow Airport, London

Tom returned to Heathrow Airport on Sunday to meet with his son-in-law, Mark Grant.

Glad to see a friendly face, Mark embraced him tightly. "Hi Dad, how was your flight?"

Tom assured him it'd been fine. "Do you have time to visit?"

"Sure. We could discuss things privately in the Club." As a Frequent Flyer, Mark had access to the airline's Executive Lounge at the airport. They found a small meeting room and sat across from one another.

"How has it been with you?" Tom asked.

"Since your call I've just been going through the motions. I keep waiting for someone to shake me and tell me it's all a bad dream or a tasteless joke, that they're not really gone."

Mark rose and walked to the window, pretending to be interested in looking out at planes coming and going. After a few moments, he sighed. He sat his laptop in the center of the table and sat beside Tom. "Am I the only one who finds it hard to believe that a ship can just disappear without a trace?"

"You're hardly the Lone Ranger. I think everyone finds it slightly incredulous. Sudden tragic loses are a fact of life, but unexplained disappearances? Well, it's another thing altogether."

"Since the accident, I've been at loose ends. I just couldn't get it out of mind, yet here I was thousands of miles from home. Since I wasn't sleeping, I had plenty of time on my hands. I decided to see what I could find out."

"Find out about what?"

"The accident, the sinking, the disappearance...whatever you want to call it. I can't imagine such a thing happening in this day and age. Spanish Galleons, sure, but this is the 20th century. So I began doing some research. It was a way to feel useful. And you won't believe what I found."

Mark reached over, tapped a few keys and began scrolling down the screen. "Now here's an interesting statistic. Did you know the world's oceans, on average, claim one ship every week?"

"Put that way, it sounds almost like some sort of macabre tithe."

"That's bad enough, all by itself, but they're mostly ships we know about. Like the New Carissa running aground off the Coos Bay jetty, fishing boats getting into trouble in a storm, the Exxon Valdez in Alaska and so forth. Then I tried researching what you might call *mysterious circumstances*; ships that just up and vanish without a trace."

"But you didn't find any, right?"

"The heck I didn't. Every so often, a ship routinely reports its position then disappears. Lloyd's of London posts them missing and, after a short time, declares them lost. What fate overtook their passengers and crew is anyone's guess."

"Are you sure about this, Mark? This isn't coming from some kind of conspiracy theory website, is it? You know, UFO's, alien abductions, and that kind of thing."

Mark raised his right hand. "Swear to God, this is the straight stuff. It happens to all kinds of ships. It doesn't seem to matter if they're big or small, powerful or not so powerful. Some of them were equipped with all sorts of electronic gizmos; others had the minimum navigational array. Some of the skippers were young and inexperienced, others seasoned veterans. Weather sometimes appears to be a contributing factor, but in other cases the skies were clear, the weather mild, and the sea calm."

Tom couldn't believe what he was hearing. "Can I see some of that?"

"We can look at it together." Mark angled the computer in Tom's direction. "Here are the solitary disappearances."

"Solitary? You mean there are multiple disappearances, as well?"

"Yeah, they're coming next. You probably remember the

Edmund Fitzgerald."

"You bet I do. Marty and I lived on Lake Erie then."

"All I remember is the Gordon Lightfoot song," Mark confessed. "When the *Fitzgerald* vanished beneath Lake Superior she was within eight miles of her destination," Mark tapped the table, "*eight* miles. She was 729 feet long, the largest vessel on the Great Lakes at the time and her sister ship was a few miles away tracking them on radar."

Tom nodded his head as Mark recounted the fate of the *Edmund Fitzgerald.*

"You probably know all this stuff, but it was news to me. In 1980, Jacques Cousteau's ship, the *Calypso,* mounted an expedition to search for the wreckage using a 2-man sub. They found the ship, but never determined what sank her."

Tom raised his eyes from the screen and glanced across the room. He hadn't thought about the *Edmund Fitzgerald* in years. "I remember it as if it were yesterday. I interviewed Jacques and his son, Felipe, after their mission. It was shortly before we moved to Pine Crest."

He'd always liked being around the water. So did Marty. They rented an apartment that allowed them to see a little piece of Lake Erie from their front window. It wasn't in the best of neighborhoods. The building was growing old, the radiators clanged and banged in the winter, and there was a perpetual coating of fine dust from a nearby foundry on the windowsill, but they didn't care. On winter weekends, they pulled back the curtains on the big French windows and watched snow squalls come in off the lake. And in summer they opened those windows wide to gather the evening breeze as sailboats slid across the water.

Tom thought about the *Edmund Fitzgerald* at 700 plus feet. Much larger than the *Paradise Voyager* yet they still weren't exactly sure what happened to it. Swallowing hard, he glanced over at his son-in-law and signaled him to continue.

"Here are some I bet you don't know." Mark clicked open

another window. "The *Sandra*, a 340-ton coastal freighter, with a crew of 11 left Savannah, Georgia bound for Puerto Cabello, Venezuela. She signaled her position off the Florida coast and then vanished."

Mark scrolled down. "Look at this one. The *El Caribe*, was a 339-foot freighter. She set out with a crew of 28 from Barranquilla, Venezuela headed for the Dominican Republic. The Captain radioed he'd arrive in two days. No one saw or heard from the ship again. The *El Caribe* had an EPIRB, an Emergency Position Indicating Radio Beacon. A 36,000 square mile search found no trace of the *El Caribe*, or the EPIRB."

"The *Voyager* had an EPIRB, too," Tom said softly.

Mark frowned, but didn't comment. "There was a Norwegian ship, the *Anita*...a 541-foot long 13,000-ton vessel. It left Norfolk, Virginia manned by a crew of 32. Without ever sending a position update or transmitting an SOS, the *Anita* vanished."

Tom watched him scroll down the screen. "This list of yours goes on and on, doesn't it?"

"It sure does. These incidents aren't limited to only cargo ships; passenger liners have disappeared as well. I found a bunch of 'em."

Tom shook his head. "No more. Not now. It hits a little too close to home."

"I wish you'd take a look."

"Why are you doing this, Mark?" Tom's tone made it sound like an accusation rather than a question. "Aren't we all hurting enough? Is this some strange reaction to your grief?"

"Can't you see I had no choice? My baby was on that boat; I wanted, needed, to know if this really could happen."

The two men stared at each other then both turned aside. Tom cleared his throat after several moments of strained silence. "Let's skip the cruise ships. What else do you have?"

"Here are incidents involving multiple ships." Mark opened another file. "One April day a large fleet of Norwegian ships headed into the cold waters above Greenland to hunt seal." He paused. "We're not talking dinky ships here. They were well-powered and ranged from 150 to over 400 tons.

They got caught in a storm and, when they regrouped, five ships were gone." Mark read the list. "The *Buskøy*, the *Brattind*, the *Pels*, the *Varrglint* and the *Ringsel* had disappeared. An air search by 17 planes from the U.S., Iceland and Norway never found a trace of them." He spread the fingers of his left hand. "We're talking five ships and 77 men."

Mark studied a note he'd added to his file. "Oh, you might find this interesting. The widow of one of the men aboard the *Buskøy*, reported a strange experience the night her husband's ship disappeared. She was alone in the living room and the kids were asleep. Here's what she said...

'...all of a sudden it seemed as if Elling came into the hallway. Whether I felt it or heard it I cannot say. The whole room was filled with a strange peace, like reconciliation after a struggle. First, I looked around to see if anything had moved. Nothing had changed. As I opened the outer door, I was met by an uncomfortable and sad silence. Inside there was peace...My thoughts seemed to no longer work. In the morning, they told me.'"

"What do you make of it?"

"I think I'd want to do a little more research before I formed an opinion. I've never been a big believer in visitations by the departed."

Mark shrugged. "Yeah, I kinda felt the same way, but for some reason it stuck with me."

He glanced up from the screen. "This next one concerns six French fishing vessels. They all vanished inside of two weeks. Seventy men," Mark snapped his fingers, "just like that. There was only one message. The *Pierre Nelly*, a 73-ton trawler, only six months old when it left port, radioed they were on their way to fish. Less than a month after the first ship left port, Lloyd's announced they were all lost."

Mark glanced down at his watch. "We don't have much time left before my flight, but there's one more story I want to share with you. It's another strange occurrence on a passenger liner, the *Waratah*. Okay?"

Tom reluctantly agreed.

"Actually, it concerns Claude Sawyer, a director of the company that owned the liner. He began his trip in Melbourne and began having frightening dreams and premonitions of disaster. After three nights of this, he forfeited his ticket and disembarked at Durbin, the *Waratah's* last port of call before she left Australia for London. The officers and other passengers laughed at him when he walked down the gangplank. They never heard from the ship again. It was only her second voyage."

Mark closed the laptop with a sigh. "People have premonitions about things sometimes, I suppose."

The two men hugged each other as Mark prepared to leave for the boarding gate.

"It's been good to see you. Thanks for taking care of things at home while I was away."

"It's a shame you were over here when this happened."

"All this traveling is not a good thing." Mark shook his head. "I'm away too much of the time."

"Learn from my mistakes. I spent my todays like I had a bushel basket of tomorrows. Figure out what's important in your life and grab hold of it while you can."

Mark stared at his feet. "Uh, I've been offered another job. Financially, it would be a nice step up and I'd be sleeping in my own bed most nights."

Tom grinned.

"But the position is on the East Coast."

Tom's smile quickly faded. "I suppose you and Karen will decide this together. I wouldn't be in a hurry to change anything right away. You can't run away from your pain. It'll find you no matter where you go."

Mark adjusted the shoulder strap of his bag and nervously cleared his throat.

"I know you need to leave. Have a good flight and give my love to Karen when you get home."

Mark handed him a flash drive. "This is for you. It's everything I found. Review them when you can. We'll talk again."

Tom slipped it into his pocket. He had no desire to know any more than he'd already heard. He felt as if he and Mark had been peering into open graves. Is that what Marty, Ellie and the rest were destined to become? Statistics, footnotes, curiosities?

Tom vowed then and there not to let that be their fate.

THIRTY-THREE

Offices of Paradise Getaways, London

Early the following morning Tom took a taxi to Paradise Getaways' offices. He arrived for his appointment and, after checking in at the front desk, took an express elevator to the Executive Suite.

Amid the paneled walls, marbled foyers, plush furnishings and carpets so thick they threatened to swallow your foot, a beautiful blond woman waited to greet him. She looked smart, tailored and businesslike in her cashmere-wool blend suit and contrasting blouse. Her hair was perfectly coiffed, her make-up perfect, her jewelry tastefully understated.

Claudia's welcoming smile masked inner turmoil. She took a calming breath and gathered her thoughts as she approached Tom. Over the years she'd come to respect the power of the pen. A little bit of negative publicity went a long way and she knew millions of people would read the columns Tom wrote. This meeting could play a critical role in forming the public's perception of Paradise Getaways.

Giving him her best smile, Claudia offered him her hand. "Good morning, Mr. Jenkins, I'm Claudia Monet. Admiral Reginald Schoonover planned to be here, but an urgent phone call drew him away. He'll join us as soon as possible. Meanwhile, let me show you to a conference room."

Architects placed the large conference room at the corner of the building. With rows of windows on two sides, it offered breath-taking views of London's commercial district. In the center of the room was a boat-shaped table with teak inlays surrounded by high-backed leather chairs.

"Sit anywhere you like," she said, adjusting the lighting. "Would you care for something to eat or drink?" She inventoried the refrigerator. "It looks like we have various juices, coffee and tea, fruit, croissants, muffins and sweet rolls."

Tom settled for coffee.

She prepared it for him and carried the china cup and saucer to the table. As she reached around him to place it on the table, Claudia rested a hand on his shoulder. "Tom, I hope you don't mind me calling you that, I know this can't be an easy task. I want you to know how much we regret the pain the *Voyager's* disappearance has caused you. We'll facilitate your work in any way we can."

"Thank you for your concern." He found this sudden intimacy unexpected and somewhat unnerving. His reportorial instincts made him question whether it was genuine or a well-rehearsed act.

Claudia sat across the table from him and opened an embossed leather folder. "While we wait for the Admiral perhaps I can provide you with some background information."

Tom nodded and took his notebook out of his briefcase.

"I had this material prepared for you. It details some key points in the company's decision to begin offering Alaskan cruises. It also contains details of my acquisition of the company three years ago, along with recent financial reports and information about the *Paradise Voyager*." She closed the folder and slid it across the table.

Tom pushed it to one side.

She hesitated for a moment, ordering her thoughts. "It's a bitter irony that your wife, Martha, and granddaughter, Ellen, were not paying passengers aboard the *Voyager*. My legal advisors tell me her position as an entertainer brings your wife and her friends under the blanket insurance policy we provide for all employees. We will, of course, extend that same coverage to your granddaughter as well. These benefits would be in addition to the provisions we make for all passengers under Maritime Law."

Tom's demeanor hardened. "I didn't come here to negotiate

their insurance settlement."

"I never imagined you had. Because of the potential loss of life, the company's solicitors are driving some of what I say. There is no hurry. The last thing we want to do is pressure you. My brother and personal attorney, Brian Combs, will be handling the claims since most of the passengers and employees were American."

Schoonover's entrance cut their discussion short. The Admiral crossed the room and greeted Tom with a firm handshake. "I want to assure you this company adheres to all Maritime Rules and Regulations. The loss of the *Voyager* occurred on my watch and I accept full responsibility."

Tom felt good hearing him say that, but like Claudia, there was little the Admiral could do besides express his regrets.

Although Schoonover remained cordial throughout their meeting, it was clear the strain of the previous days wore heavily on him, particularly when the discussion turned to the loss of the *Paradise Voyager*.

Schoonover drew a deep breath and cleared his throat. "I am afraid I have some rather unpleasant news to share with you. I've just gotten off the phone with the Leader of the United States Coast Guard's Unified Response Team."

Tom lifted out of his chair slightly. "Have they found something?"

"No, I'm afraid not. And that is the problem. The following fax from the United States Coast Guard was waiting when I arrived this morning. His eyes dipped to the single sheet of paper in his hand. "Those in charge of the recent incident involving the disappearance of the cruise ship, *Paradise Voyager*, have reached the conclusion that hope is no longer a viable option. Following an examination of the facts, we no longer believe there is a chance of finding anyone alive.

Searchers have scoured 50,000 square miles of ocean for

three days without finding any sign of survivors. The United States Coast Guard weighed the exhaustive search, the absence of identifiable wreckage, the nature of the disappearance, the temperature of the water, and the time elapsed. Based on these factors they have chosen to call off the rescue effort. The order will go into effect as soon as the planes involved in the search return."

Tom's hands began to shake. He bit his lip, swallowed hard, then turned aside.

Claudia touched his hand. "I'm so sorry. I know this isn't what you hoped to hear when you came to London. Would you be more comfortable if we left you alone for a few minutes?"

He swallowed hard and nodded.

She and the Admiral quietly left the room.

After a time, Claudia knocked and opened the door a crack. She found Tom by the windows silently gazing at the cityscape.

"May I come in?"

He motioned her in. He seemed to have aged in the short time they were apart. His face looked thin and drawn. His eyes were red-rimmed.

"Is there anything I can do?"

"Yeah, find the ship." He gave a bitter laugh and shrugged "Apparently there's nothing anyone can do. What is, is."

"I arranged to have all the people involved available for you to interview. If you like, you can meet with the head of our Cruise Division as well as the individual who was on duty the night the ship vanished. They will be happy to address any questions you may have about company procedures and so on."

Tom seemed distracted. It took him several moments to respond. "Yes, that would be helpful information to have for my articles."

"As you probably know, each of our ships makes a regular

check-in. I've ordered copies made of the *Voyager's* reports for the 24 hours preceding her disappearance. You can take them with you to examine at a later date. You'll also be given copies of our communiqués to the US Coast Guard, Lloyd's of London and the British Maritime Board."

"That's kind of you."

"Why don't you follow me and I'll take you to meet some of these people. Spend as much time with them as you wish."

It was mid-afternoon by the time Tom completed his meetings.

"Can we offer you lunch," Claudia asked as Tom packed his briefcase.

"I'll pass. I have to get back to the airport for the flight home. Before I leave there is one question I'd like to ask."

"Certainly, what is it?"

"The financial reports, the operating data, and all the other information, you're exposing everything. Most companies would have clammed up. You didn't. Why?"

"Do you really want to know?"

"Yes, of course I do."

Claudia hesitated then sighed deeply. "I'm willing to put everything at risk because, like you, I have a personal stake in this. I want this resolved almost as much as you do. You see, adding these cruise ships marked a big step for the company. I'm also the one who suggested we ought to have entertainers to celebrate the last cruise of the season. I'm sorry."

When they reached the lift, she took his hand in hers. "I want to express my condolences again. Let the Admiral know if there's anything else you need. You'll find it is our intention to be as honest and forthright as we can about all aspects relating to the *Voyager* situation. There's a limousine waiting downstairs to take you anywhere you want to go."

THIRTY-FOUR

Pine Crest, Oregon

Tom wrote his first syndicated article on the flight home. In it, he recapped the pain felt by the people of Pine Crest, Oregon. He wove short bios of each member of the Mothers of Song into his story, traced the group's growth, and talked about their desires to benefit Hospice. Poignant and heartbreaking, it tugged at readers' heartstrings.

His next article zeroed in on Paradise Getaways. Without making direct accusations, Tom questioned various aspects of their operations, highlighted previous lapses, and questioned the sincerity of their reaction to the sinking.

"Well, what do you think?"

"Give me a minute, I'm rereading." Tommy raised his eyes from the pages in his hand. "Do you know how difficult it is to concentrate when someone's badgering you to hurry up and finish?"

"The article isn't that long."

"You're hovering again. You know I can't read with someone looking over my shoulder. Why don't you get a cup of coffee or go to the john or...or something?"

Tom sagged back in his chair. The heel of his right foot bounced up and down never touching the floor. He picked up a pencil and twirled it in his fingers before jamming it back in the mug that served as his pencil holder.

Tommy turned the last page and flipped the stack over.

"So?"

"It's good, very good. It's well-written and thoroughly researched. It's an excellent column." Tommy kept his eyes on the article, pushing it around the desktop as he spoke.

"But? I hear a *but* lurking in there somewhere. What's the problem?"

Tommy ran his fingers through his hair and frowned. "Dad, this is not your style. It's gotcha journalism. It's like chasing an executive with a microphone in your hand and a camera running all the while. Is attacking the cruise line really the best way to find out what happened to Mom and Ellie?"

"It's the only way. The Coast Guard has ended their search. Lloyds of London declared the ship lost and closed the file. Everyone's treating this as business as usual. If I don't keep a spotlight aimed on the *Paradise Voyager*, it'll slip from public awareness and whoever's responsible will get away."

"I think you're losing your objectivity."

"What are you talking about? I did my research." Tom tapped his finger on the paper-clipped pages neatly stacked on the corner of the desk. "These are hard facts; I didn't make that stuff up."

"I certainly hope not."

"I plan to send documentation to the newspaper syndicate along with the article." Tom snatched the pages off the desktop. Folding the first page back, he pointed to a paragraph and rattled the article in Tommy's face. "Look at this. Did you see this list of violations noted by the Maritime inspectors?"

"Most of those have little or no impact on the Cruise Division. Besides, they're old news. You're implying Claudia Monet is somehow at fault, yet you admit in the article that these things occurred under previous ownership."

"The Cruise Line was also cited for lapses in maintenance and sloppy record-keeping."

Tommy shrugged. "It's a human organization. There are oversights and foul-ups in every business. Remember the time we printed the lumber yard's ad upside down? These inspectors always find something. That's what they're paid to do."

Tom folded his arms across his chest. "But they still found them."

"Four years ago. Every time there's a plane crash, the media goes wild with supposed faulty maintenance. You know as well as

I do that ninety-nine out of a hundred times its inconsequential."

Tom pounded his fist on the desk. "Why are you defending Paradise Getaways? These people killed your mother."

"Calm down, you're going to give yourself a heart attack. I'm not defending anyone. I'm only saying a handful of old citations and a few sloppy records didn't sink the *Paradise Voyager*. It's also certainly not anything Claudia Monet did."

"Well, I'm going with it," Tom lifted his chin and hugged the pages to his chest, "whether you like it or not."

"That's your prerogative."

"I have lots more stuff I didn't even mention in the article. Things like this don't just happen, there's a reason behind this disappearance and I intend to find it."

"The woman went out of her way to cooperate with you. Would she do that if they had something to hide?"

"People lie all the time. There's a villain hiding in the bushes somewhere."

Tommy leaned forward and rested his hand on his father's knee. "I don't doubt that, Dad. But how can you be so certain Claudia Monet is your villain?"

Tom shoved his hand away. "She'll do until someone better comes along."

RCI Corp Headquarters, Palo Alto, California

"Did you see this?" Ridgely tossed a newspaper across his desk with a satisfied grin. "I told you there was nothing to worry about."

The bold headline caught Brandon Steele's eyes as he scanned the page. Tom's column had merited placement above the fold. A few paragraphs in he glanced up. "Man this Jenkins is one nasty SOB, isn't he? He's painted a huge bulls-eye on Paradise Getaway's back."

When he finished, Steele dropped the newspaper on the desktop and shook his head. "I warned you about this. It's not good, not good at all."

Wadding the paper, Ridgely tossed it into the wastebasket. "Not good? What's not good about it? They've already declared the ship lost. Lloyd's of London is starting to pay off on their policy. Meanwhile there's not a word about RCI anywhere in the article."

"You're missing the larger point. Look at the headline. *What Really Happened to the Paradise Voyager?* We don't need someone poking around and digging into things. This guy Jenkins could become our worst nightmare. We've got to do something about him."

"Don't get your undies in a knot. He's focusing on the cruise line and its ownership, not us. He doesn't even know RCI exists."

"What happens if and when he learns about us? By the time he gets finished reaming us out what he's doing to the Cruise Line will look like a picnic in the park."

Ridgely leaned back in his chair. Folding an arm across his chest, he stroked his chin. "Who says he'll ever find out about our part in this thing?"

"What guarantee do we have that he won't?"

"You can count on one hand the number of people who know what really happened. No one at the Pentagon is aware the technology even exists. This situation could benefit from benign neglect. If we tip our hand, Jenkins will be on us like a lion on a wildebeest."

"We've got to keep a close eye on him," Steele said. "I want a team ready in case this heats up."

Ridgely nodded in agreement. "It won't take long to go back up there and scuttle the ship."

Steele asked the question on both their minds. "What about Maheshwari?"

"I've got someone watching him. deal with the professor from India when the time is right."

THIRTY-FIVE

"That's some vanishing act you've got there, Doctor Houdini. If I didn't know better, I'd think you were avoiding me." Chuckling, Shiri sat her lunch tray on the table and took a seat opposite Derek.

He hadn't seen her coming and her boisterous greeting startled him. He slammed down the cover of the folder in which he'd been making notes, flipped it over, and rested his arm across it protectively.

"Good day, Mrs. Yoblanski. I did not see you approaching my table."

"Regardless, here I am. What have you been up to?"

"Shh!" Derek fanned his left hand closer and closer to the tabletop as Shiri spoke, desperately trying to coax her into lowering her voice. His right arm remained across the blue-covered report folder.

"I have been up to work, Mrs. Yoblanski." Derek's eyes swept the room as he spoke. "Nothing else, simply the diligent pursuit of my work."

Shiri leaned closer, practically whispering. "You've got to come up for air once in a while. You look, um...well, awful."

"I am grateful for your concern and thank you for it. However, there are times in life when one must push forward regardless of the personal cost."

It became Shiri's turn to glance around the room. She reached for his hand.

Derek detected the movement and jerked the report back out of her reach. As he whipped it across the table and into his lap, the corner smacked the salt shaker and toppled it over.

Shiri righted the shaker and brushed the spilled salt off of the tabletop. "You know, I don't care what's in that folder."

"I do not wish to have your fingerprints accidentally appear upon it. It is better if innocent parties such as Mrs. Shiri Yoblanski not become involved."

"Fingerprints?" Shiri scoffed. "It's just a job. You're blowing this way out of proportion. Don't let them put you under so much pressure. This place isn't worth it."

"I am afraid you lack an understanding of the situation. The project has moved to a much higher plane. It is no longer about just RCI any longer."

Shiri didn't know how to respond. She looked down at her tray, realizing she hadn't touched her lunch. She plucked a few stray croutons from the edge of her salad plate, tossed them into her mouth and slowly crunched them as she mulled over Derek's comment. She decided it best not to press for answers he didn't want to give.

"I have an idea. Jared has some time off coming up, why don't we plan a little get together. It will give you a chance to unwind, decompress."

"I appreciate your offer of hospitality. Unfortunately I will be unable to attend."

"But I haven't even given you a date."

"It does not matter. I am no longer available for unwinding and decompressing."

"What about your spice tins? You promised to cook for us. Remember the curry and rice?" she asked, teasingly. "Are you telling me you can't make curry and rice for us?"

"Yes, I cannot. Curry and rice is no longer possible."

"I don't understand."

"Perhaps a story from the Panchatantra will help clarify matters. Once upon a time there were a large number of fish in a pond. Among them were three fish who were friends. Their names were Anagatavidhata, Pratyutpannamati, and Yadbhavishya. Some passing fishermen noticed the pond was full of fish and made plans to come the following morning with nets. Anagatavidhata, whose name means the one who foresees danger in time, overheard and called a meeting of all the fish. He told them, 'The fishermen will come tomorrow. We should not stay here in this pond for even a moment longer.'"

"Derek, these stories of yours may offer a good moral lesson for young children, but I don't see why you're telling them to me."

"Patience, Mrs. Yoblanski, patience. If the story does not make sense now, it will very soon. Where was I?" His brow knit as he retraced the story in his mind. "Ah, yes. I remember now. You see Anagatavidhata knew of a canal which led to another pond and he suggested they use it for their escape.

"'I endorse your suggestion,' said Pratyutpannamati. 'Let us go where it is safe." Yadbhavishya laughed loudly. He said, 'Your plans are no good. So what if the fishermen have evil intentions? All is determined by kismet, we cannot escape our fate no matter where we go.' Unable to convince the others, the two fish left the pond. The next day, the fishermen took a big catch of fish. Yadbhavishya was among them."

"And?"

"And you will eventually understand what the Panchatantra is telling you." Derek shoved his chair back and quickly rose. "It is better we not be seen together. Please give my regrets to your husband." He dipped his head. "Have a pleasant day."

He tucked the blue folder under his arm and scurried away.

Shiri watched him execute a zigzag path across the lunch room, glancing from side to side as if someone were in hot pursuit.

Something had clearly frightened him. But what...or who? And why all the concern about the project? She hadn't heard about any problems. Of course, she didn't even know what his project was. And on top of that he insisted on telling that strange story. Shiri crunched another crouton.

THIRTY-SIX

Pine Crest, Oregon

With Marty gone, every day at the newspaper office became Bring-Your-Dog-to-Work-Day. Charlie was lying in his usual spot next to Tom's desk on a small rug beside the file cabinets. The dog opened his eyes when Beth appeared behind Tom's chair. His tail slowly swept back and forth as Beth rested her hand on Tom's shoulder and leaned forward.

"Why don't you come over and have supper with us tonight, Dad?"

Tom placed his hand over hers. "Thanks, Sweetie, it's kind of you to ask, but you and Tommy need time to yourselves. Besides, Charlie would leave hair all over your carpet."

The dog stood up and walked over at the mention of his name.

"Don't be silly, we're always glad to have our step-dog visit." She reached down and patted Charlie's head. Beth kissed Tom on the cheek. "It's no trouble to set an extra place."

"I was just getting ready to call for take-out. Thanks anyway."

The others left, leaving Tom and Charlie alone in the office. As the setting sun whittled away the last slivers of daylight, Tom absentmindedly arranged pencils and straightened sheets of paper on his desk. The gold script letters on the office's plate glass window darkened in the red-orange sunset and his thoughts turned to Marty.

Most of the day, she lingered in the recesses of his mind. Now, as he killed time sorting and stacking, Marty filled his thoughts. Charlie walked over, sat down beside him and nudged his hand.

"You miss her too, don't you boy?" Tom ruffled Charlie's mane. When they looked into each other's eyes, Tom knew without a doubt that Charlie understood. He sighed and reached for the phone to order dinner.

"Got your order right here, Tom." Chou pulled a bag out from under the warming lights. Sitting it on the counter, he glanced in and double-checked the contents. When he finished, he raised his eyes to meet Tom's.

"Kim and I were awfully sorry to hear the news about Marty's cruise ship." Chou packed fried rice into a cardboard carton as he spoke. "Words can't change what's happened, but I wanted you to know your whole family's been in our prayers."

Tom thanked him for his concern and paid for the order.

He was about to pick up the bag when Chou stopped him. "Wait, almost forgot your fortune cookies."

He tossed two cookies into the bag and pushed it across the counter with a smile.

Charlie popped up in the back seat as soon as the car door closed. He poked his head between the front seats to see what smelled so wonderful.

Tom covered the open top of the bag with his hand. "Hey, you snoop, get away from that."

Charlie sniffed the air and retreated to the back seat. Tom talked to the dog as he traced the familiar route home. "Don't worry; you'll get your share. I even got a fortune cookie for you. Maybe we'll both find out what's going to be happening in our lives. How does that sound?"

Tom glanced into the mirror. The dog smiled at him from the back seat.

When they got home, Tom removed two dinner plates from the cupboard. He studied them sitting on the counter then looked down at Charlie.

"You know Mommy never liked it when I fed you off a china plate. But then, I guess that doesn't matter much anymore, does it?"

Tom leaned against the island bar and hung his head. He never knew what word or phrase would bring on these feelings. His life had become a minefield of grief. To a casual observer, he appeared to be coping well. But he knew better. With no one else in the house, Tom spent many evenings sharing his pain with Charlie.

"What say we both have some of everything?"

Charlie's wide grin signaled his concurrence.

Tom dished up both plates, cut Charlie's egg roll into bite-sized pieces, and placed the plate on the floor in front of him. "Have at it, Chum," he said, pulling a stool up to the island bar.

When they finished, Tom picked up the fortune cookies and walked into the living room. Charlie followed close at his heels. Tom had several articles waiting to be edited on the table beside the blue recliner. Cookies first and then he'd get to the editing.

He broke the first one open. "This one will be yours, Charlie."

He tossed half of the cookie in the dog's direction. The dog snatched it out of the air. Tom unfolded the little paper strip. After reading it, he furrowed his brow then read the fortune to Charlie.

"*Only the truth solves a mystery*. Not great, but at least you've still got half a cookie coming." He flipped the remaining piece in the dog's direction.

Tom smoothed out the little strip of paper and laid it on the table beside his chair. It seemed like a rather odd fortune. He picked up the other cookie and, as soon as he ripped the cellophane wrap, Charlie nudged his elbow begging for more.

"Hey, this one's mine," he said with a chuckle. Tom cracked the cookie apart. He popped a piece of cookie into his mouth and unfolded the second slip.

Shed no tears until seeing the coffin.

"Jeez, those cookie guys need to hire some new writers.

Whatever happened to *Everyone respects your wisdom, Unexpected wealth is headed your way* or *Happy thoughts make a happy life?*"

He slipped the dog the remaining piece. "After that, I don't feel much like eating."

Tom sat the second strip aside on the table with the first and reached for his stack of articles. The dog curled up at his feet. Pages in his lap and red pencil in his right hand, he leaned the recliner back with a sigh.

He had trouble reconciling himself to the strange fortunes tucked inside their cookies. He shook his head, attempting to rid himself of the negative feelings they generated, and set to work.

He'd finished several paragraphs when his eyes returned to the table. Stretching out a finger, he nudged the strips around. Interestingly, they made sense regardless of their order. He switched them back and forth several times, silently rereading them.

Shed no tears until seeing the coffin. Only the truth solves a mystery.

Tom rested his chin in his hand. The strips of paper seemed to possess an indefinable power. They were trying to tell him something, but what?

After a minute or so, he returned to the pages in his lap. He read through several pages, marking them up as he went. Outside, the sky was clear and black, speckled with a million stars. He heard a faint meow at the back door and put his work aside to let Arnold in. Charlie padded after him and went out when the sleek black cat came in.

Tom followed the dog out the door and waited on the porch. A passing car slowed to turn the corner and, as it did, its headlights swept across the side yard. Tom watched the wind raise tufts of fur on Charlie's back. It promised to be a chilly night.

A strong gust whipped around the corner of the house as he shooed the dog back in. Tom hurried in behind him, closed the door, and double locked it. Although he was never truly afraid of being alone in the house, the combination of Marty's absence, the sharp wind and his recurring nightmares, left him feeling, at best, unsettled.

As soon as they were back inside, Charlie headed over to his bed and settled down for the night. Arnold hopped into a living room window seat, curled up on a cotton throw and began cleaning up for bedtime.

Tom returned to his chair rubbing his arms for warmth. When he reached for his pencil, his eye caught the two fortune strips.

Shed no tears until seeing the coffin. Only the truth solves a mystery.

Though he tried to work, his mind kept returning to the two little fortune strips on the table beside him. Why? They meant nothing. They were only random pieces of paper. Finding them tonight was just a coincidence.

Before the last remnants of that thought faded away, Tom heard Eddie's voice echo in the back of his mind.

"Ya know, Sarge, there ain't no such thing as coincidence."

Tom jerked around, half expecting to see Eddie peering over his shoulder. He put the editing aside and stared up at the ceiling. Their meaning was so clear and unambiguous, why should they create such a sense of mystery? Sure, he hadn't seen any coffin. So what?

So, how did he know Marty was dead? Well he didn't, really. Like everyone else, he'd accepted that conclusion without any proof.

Without seeing the coffin!

Having an analytic personality comes with unique drawbacks. Tom, like his apostolic namesake, remained a bit of a skeptic. He typically demanded proof positive. He had to see things with his own eyes, touch them with his own hands in order to believe. Or did he?

There were, after all, only two possibilities, dead or alive.

And he couldn't absolutely eliminate either one.

Shed no tears until seeing the coffin. Only the truth solves a mystery.

Tom knew one thing for certain; he didn't want to lose those two strips of paper. He snatched them off the table and carried them into the kitchen. He'd put them where all the important papers went. He'd tape them to the refrigerator.

Tom stepped back and let his eyes drift over to the freezer door. There, surrounded by Ellie's drawings, was the card Marty had tucked under his pillow the morning she left. Love truly does transcend time and distance, he thought, remembering her words.

The room suddenly changed. The chill he'd felt earlier vanished, replaced by glowing warmth. He felt like he was sitting in the sun on a summer afternoon. He knew immediately it was Marty.

Whether he understood it or not, he realized Marty was right there in the room with him communicating her presence to him, wrapping him in her loving warmth.

Tom threw his head back and laughed for joy. He raised his arms into the air, letting the love flow down, around and through him. He turned slow circles, reveling in this new, wondrously delicious freedom.

Charlie rose from his bed and came to join him. He cocked his head and looked up at Tom with a peculiar expression. After a moment, he began whining softly, wagging his tail and dancing circles around Tom.

Tom knelt and hugged Charlie's thick mane. "You feel it too, don't you, Boy? Mommy's thinking about us right now just like we're thinking of her. She's sending us her love."

Suddenly everything became subject to re-examination. Not just the things he'd always believed to be true, but also the things he held to be false. He'd stepped through a door and locked it behind him. A new reality would direct his life from now on.

Somehow, someway, somewhere, Marty still lived.

THIRTY-SEVEN

Tom awoke early the next day, refreshed and invigorated. It was the first good night's sleep he'd gotten since receiving the news about the *Paradise Voyager*. He swung his legs out of bed and planted his feet on the floor with a firm thump. He felt like himself again.

Even Charlie, who'd been moping ever since Tom got the bad news, was peppy as a pup. At the sound of Tom's feet hitting the floor, Charlie jumped up from his spot at the foot of the bed and bounded over to him. He ran up, gave him a poke, and then jumped back, grinning. He wanted to play.

Tom reached down and hugged his neck. The dog's sudden exuberance validated his feelings. He needed someone to share this newfound happiness and who better than Charlie? He was there last night. He'd sensed Marty's presence. He knew.

Tom whistled a happy tune as he showered and dressed. When he stared into the mirror to comb his hair, the reflected image surprised him. The gaunt, gloomy stranger who'd taken up residence there was gone.

In the closet, Tom pulled a shirt off of a hanger and brushed one of Marty's blouses. Remnants of her perfume wafted around him. He closed his eyes and breathed it in, delighting in her scent.

Then, without warning, a cloud of doubt appeared. It wasn't much, just one teensy cloud in an otherwise clear sky. But it was enough.

What if last night was nothing more than a product of an overactive imagination, of loneliness and desperation, the pathetic fantasies of an overwrought mind?

No! She was here, he thought. She communicated with me. Even the dog sensed her presence. It was real.

Reality is subjective, experiential. Are memories real? What about hopes, or dreams, fears? Saying something is real is like saying something is true. What is truth?

Tom ran out of the closet. This needed to be resolved. He had to tell someone about it. If he didn't, his doubts would surely grow and Marty would slip away again. He had to maintain his belief; everything depended on it.

Eddie waited while the waitress filled Tom's cup. "Ya seemed kinda upset when ya called. What's up?"

"I *was* upset when I called. I am upset *now*. There's something I need to talk to you about."

"I imagine you've had a lot on your mind lately, let's have at it."

Tom struggled to find a way to say what he'd come to say. Over the years, he'd written thousands of news articles, editorials and columns, the words should have come easily, but they wouldn't.

He dropped his head in frustration. "I can't seem to get started."

Eddie scanned the small coffee shop. "Maybe ya'd do better if people weren't packed in around ya so close."

"What do you have in mind?"

"Got any plans for the day?"

Tom shook his head. "Not really."

"What say we head out t' the beach? Call it a mental health day. There's no rain in the forecast. Low tide is comin' up in about an hour, so we won't have to keep an eye on the waves. We could even pick up some smoked tuna and crackers on the way."

"Sounds like a plan. What if we swung by the house and picked up Charlie?"

Eddie didn't mind.

They settled on the Seven Devils Wayside. It was the middle of the week and the two men had the beach pretty much to themselves. The air was clear and crisp under a partly cloudy sky and, as promised, the tide was on its way out. As it receded, it left behind a wide expanse of firm, damp sand for them to walk on.

Eddie carried a bag with sodas, crackers and a smoked fillet of albacore tuna they'd bought at a fish market on the way. The two men strode along the beach with the dog trailing behind.

Without warning, Charlie broke away and streaked toward a group of seagulls near the water's edge. Barking, he raced into the center of them, sending gulls in every direction. Satisfied he'd showed them who was king of the beach, he turned and trotted back. The gulls circled indignantly squawking insults.

After they'd walked a while, Tom noticed a large drift log partially buried in the sand, an impromptu picnic table. Logs such as this sometimes snapped their cables and escaped over the sides of ships during winter storms. Once set free, they drifted with the currents as the salty ocean water sucked away their resins. Eventually, they were tossed up on the beach to bleach gray in the sun.

The men straddled the log facing each other and unwrapped their lunch. Despite a steady breeze coming off the water, the air around them filled with the smell of the cured and smoked fish. Charlie moved closer, sniffing as he approached. He sat down in front of Eddie and licked his chops. Ignoring the dog, Eddie gave Tom an expectant look.

"Well I really don't know where to start."

"Go ahead and jump right in. If there's somethin' stuck in your craw, spit it out."

Tom wanted to explain about the previous evening, but it was hard to talk about. It didn't exactly square with most people's beliefs. The last thing he wanted to do was appear silly or foolish.

"Let me ask you a question. Just a simple Yes or No, is all I need."

Eddie nodded.

"Do you believe in the paranormal?" There. He'd gotten the ball rolling. Now they could sit on the log, eat their tuna and talk.

Tom broke off a piece of fish.

"Whoa pardner, that's way too big a subject for any Yes or No answer. Let's try whittlin' it down some. There are lotsa phonies and weirdoes runnin' round out there."

Tom nervously nibbled small bites of tuna as he waited for Eddie to continue.

"OK, one step at a time. Do I believe Uri Geller can bend spoons with his mind? No way. Has Shirley MacLaine lived a whole bunch of different lives? Naw! But it doesn't make much difference to me one way or the other." Eddie shook his head and chuckled. "Is that fella on TV gettin' messages from people on the other side? I don't think so."

Eddie picked up a piece of fish and carefully split it in two, handing the larger piece to Tom.

Tom split it again, tossed a piece to Charlie, and popped the remainder into his mouth. "So far, you've been talking about the lunatic fringe. What about more, um, conventional concepts?"

Eddie shrugged. His nonjudgmental attitude indicated he was open to anything Tom wanted to suggest.

"What about unexplained phenomena of one kind or another, communication across distances?" Tom quickly added, "Just for instance."

Eddie smiled. He finally understood what Tom was trying to say. He decided he'd nudge the conversation along a bit. "I think there's a special connection between some people. People joined by deep love. Sometimes, and I don't claim to know how or why, these people are able to know things, feel things, even though they're separated by time and space."

Eddie's words unleashed a flood of emotion for Tom. He thought of Marty's card taped to the refrigerator door. She'd written: *Love transcends time and space.* He couldn't remain silent a moment longer. The words poured out.

"Marty talked to me, Eddie. She really did. Well, not really *talked*. It wasn't out loud; it was in my mind. And not with words, exactly...more like a feeling, a presence."

Tom avoided Eddie's eyes, fearing what he might see in them.

"How long did it last?"

"I can't really say. Time seemed to stand still. When I finally looked at a clock, hours had gone by."

Eddie listened thoughtfully, occasionally nodding his head to indicate his understanding. "Doesn't surprise me."

"It doesn't?"

"Course not."

Tom never imagined it would be this easy.

"Why are ya lookin' at me like that? Everybody in town knows you and that woman of yours got somethin' pretty special going on between ya. If the two of you ain't kindred spirits, who is?" Eddie took a sip of soda.

"Then you don't think I'm losing my mind?"

Eddie chuckled. He coughed several times and then began choking. When he finally regained control, he wiped the tears from his eyes and shook his head. "Warn me next time, I coulda choked to death. Look, I've seen crazy and you ain't it. You're still a good twenty miles from the border." He took another sip of soda. "Viktor Frankl had the same experience."

"Is he someone you knew in Oklahoma?"

"Never met him. I read his books." Eddie slipped the dog another piece of tuna. "Actually, it was Dr. Frankl. He was an Austrian psychiatrist. After the Nazis annexed Austria, he was taken away to the concentration camps. He managed t' live through it and wrote a book of his experiences called *Man's Search for Meaning.*

"One winter day Frankl and another prisoner were on a work detail. It was cold 'n' icy; they weren't wearin' much more than rags and he felt like he was comin' t' the end of the line. Well, all of a sudden, his wife's presence came to him. Sorta like what you were sayin' happened last night."

Wrapped in a warm glow of contentment, Tom listened

spellbound. The salty smell of the ocean, the sound of the waves, the cool wind rushing past his cheek, even the screech of passing gulls faded. He wasn't losing his mind, he hadn't been dreaming, and he wasn't alone. Someone else had a similar experience. Tom urged him to continue.

"He said that in his mind's eye, she was more luminous than the risin' sun. Her presence brought him a warmth and peace that wrapped itself around him. She stayed with him for a long, long time. He said one other thing, too."

"What was that?"

"He said for first time he felt he understood the ultimate truths of life. Love is the highest goal to which man can aspire; love exists beyond the physical realm, it's spiritual. And love is the strongest force in the universe."

Tom took a deep, cleansing breath. "Lately, there were times when I was sure I was losing my mind. And the nightmares I've been having are unbelievable. The odd thing is since I had those feelings about Marty I feel at peace. I slept like a baby last night."

Tom detailed the experience of the previous evening. He talked about the fortune cookies and their strange, mystical message. Eddie's quiet acceptance gave him the courage and support he needed to reveal his innermost feelings.

"She's alive. I know she is."

Tom swiveled on the log, stood up and gazed out at the surf. The sky had cleared. A brilliant afternoon sun sparkled off whitecaps in the incredibly blue water. The breeze ruffled across the sleeve of his jacket when he raised his arm and pointed toward the ocean. "She's alive, Eddie. She's out there waiting for me. Don't ask me how I know, I just do."

He turned and, in a firm, resolute voice, said, "I've let this go on too long. It's time for me to act."

THIRTY-EIGHT

RCI Corp. Headquarters, Palo Alto, California

Shiri heard the commotion from her office. Even though there'd been no alarms sounded, her instincts told her a crisis had occurred. She stepped out of her office to investigate just as a pair of men zipped around the corner. One of them bumped into her. She staggered back flailing at the doorframe for support.

He grabbed her by the elbow, arresting her fall. "I'm sorry, I didn't see you."

Shiri straightened her jacket and smoothed her blouse. "Maybe you should try looking where you're going next time. Didn't your teacher ever tell you not to run in the hallway?"

A light of recognition flashed in the man's eyes. "You're the Executive Recruiter...umm, Shiri Yoblanski, right?"

"First, why don't you tell me who you are?"

He tapped the picture ID dangling from the pocket of his dark suit. "Glynn, FBI. Can I talk to you for a few minutes?"

"What the heck's going on?"

Ignoring her question, Glynn turned to the man who'd been running alongside him. He was older and heavier and flushed from the sprint. He paced as nervously as a racehorse in the starting gate and gulped for breath. Like his partner, he had a picture ID dangling from his pocket.

"Go over to the Research Center without me." Glynn tilted his head in Shiri's direction. "I'm going to spend a few minutes here."

The other man jogged away.

Glynn eased the door back and ushered Shiri into her office. As the door snapped shut, she heard more running in the hallway then Steele's voice. "He can't have gotten away, keep looking."

Shiri stared at him. "I demand to know what's going on."

Glynn didn't respond to her, but instead he circled the room examining the knick knacks in her bookcase and photos on her desk. He walked over to the window and paused to glance down at the parking lot.

He looks as if he's expecting to see someone, Shiri thought.

Glynn turned and smiled. He approached the small table where she conducted private interviews and patted the tweed fabric on the back of a chair. "You can sit here."

"And you can tell me what the FBI is doing running up and down the halls."

A cell phone buzzed. Glynn raised his hand to Shiri, snapped it open and listened. "Did you check the computer? Well, secure his office until our lab guys get there."

Glynn smiled at Shiri as he took a seat opposite her. "I'm going to need all of your files on Maheshwari."

"Why?"

He removed a folded piece of paper and snapped it open. "Because I have a warrant."

Shiri struggled to make sense out of the chaos surrounding her. "All my files are confidential. I can't release anything until the Legal Department authorizes it. If this is about some sort of immigration issue, I'm sure it can easily be straightened out."

Glynn looked at her with a derisive smirk. "You and Maheshwari were friends, weren't you?"

"I recruited him to the company, if that's what you mean. I found him interesting. What's he done?"

"He's disappeared!"

"Derek, gone?"

"Derek...Maheshwari, call him whatever you want to, the sonofabitch slipped away."

"What in the world are you saying? You make it sound like he's a criminal or...or something."

"I'm afraid, Mrs. Yoblanski, your Dr. Maheshwari wasn't who he appeared to be."

"Oh, and who was he?"

Shiri listened as Glynn described a man she didn't know. One who'd hidden his true identity and was, in fact, a sleeper agent...a member of a Pakistani terrorist cell. He'd hacked into RCI's computers and downloaded classified research data. He'd stolen military secrets. She found it impossible to believe.

"Who told you these things?"

"Everything's on a need to know basis. I can tell you, however, that he's absconded with classified research data, sensitive information that could be used to facilitate a terrorist attack."

Glynn smiled when he noticed the shocked look on her face. His little speech had its intended effect. "I understand your concern, Mrs. Yoblanski. There's no cause for worry, everything's under control."

After receiving authorization from the Legal Department, Shiri turned over all her files to Glynn. He handed her a receipt before tucking them under his arm.

"I'll want to talk with you again after I review this material. Are you planning to leave the city?"

"Am I under surveillance, too?"

"Of course not, I simply wanted to determine your future availability. You do travel for the company, don't you?"

"At times," Shiri said, "but I have no trips planned."

"Then I'll be back tomorrow."

As the door closed, Shiri remembered the last time she'd seen Derek in the lunchroom and his odd tale about The Three Fish. She smiled to herself. Someone *was* lying, just like Agent Glynn said. But it sure wasn't Derek.

THIRTY-NINE

Pine Crest, Oregon

Charlie beat Tom to the door when someone knocked. To Tom's surprise, he found Claudia Monet on his front porch. Sensing that she offered no threat, Charlie pushed past and ran to greet her with his tail wagging.

"Hello, Claudia. What brings you—"

Instead of waiting for him to finish, she marched toward him waving a newspaper. As she drew closer he began to give ground.

When she reached Tom, she put her hand on his chest and pushed him the rest of the way inside. "Cut the 'Hello, Claudia,' crap." She pointed into the living room. "Get in there, sit down, and shut up. I've got something to say to you."

Tom did as he was told, taking a seat on the couch. He motioned toward a chair.

"I'll stand."

"You came all the way from London?"

"I don't live in London; I live in Annapolis, Maryland."

"It's still a long way," Tom said meekly.

"I was in LA on business so it seemed like an opportune time to get this off my chest." She stared daggers at him. "I'm so mad at you, Tom Jenkins; I'd like to wring your bloody neck."

She extracted a wad of newspaper clippings from her pocket and rattled them in his face. "I offered you unfettered access to company records, answered all your questions, even provided a channel to the British regulatory officials, and this is how you repay me?"

"What do you mean?"

"Don't be coy. I know biased coverage when I see it. Most of the violations you cite occurred long before I took over the company."

"But you retained a majority of the former employees. How can anyone be certain this wasn't a continuing pattern of behavior?"

"Because I wouldn't stand for it and neither would Schoonover. If you'd done your homework you would have found out that the company has an impeccable record since the change of ownership. We've cooperated any way we could to unravel the mystery of what happened to the *Voyager*. Meanwhile, you paint us as a couple of two-bit criminals."

"If there's no merit to the articles I wrote, why didn't you just sue me?"

The muscles in her jaw tightened. "I should have, I really should have. Instead, I decided to cut you a little slack. You've lost your wife and granddaughter. I understand you're still hurting, grieving...maybe more than a little angry. But that doesn't give you the right to strike out at anyone who crosses your path."

She gave a sigh and stared down at him with her hands on her hips. "Has it ever occurred to you that you might not be the best person to write these articles?"

"My son said the same thing."

"For all the good it did." She tossed the clippings at him like so much confetti. "Those Alaskan cruises were my idea. Do you honestly believe I'd sabotage my own enterprise? Don't you think those employees and passengers meant something to me? If I hadn't brought up the idea, none of this would have happened. How do you think that makes me feel?"

Tom had no reply.

"Well, I'll tell you. I can't sleep at night thinking about it."

"I never held you personally responsible for anything."

"No, instead you portrayed me as a figurehead. Some dumb blond with a pretty face they drag out whenever they want to divert the press's attention. Well, let me tell you something, Buster. I'm a senior advisor to the President of Souvanée America and I sit on the Board of their parent company. I'm also

Chairman of the Board and the majority stockholder of Paradise Getaways. I stopped doing pretty a long, long time ago."

"Okay, you've had your rant. What do you want from me?"

"Give me my reputation back. My sleazeball of an ex-husband lied, cheated, and cut corners everywhere. Since I took the company away from him, we've played by the rules, paid our bills on time, and treated people fairly. Now you come along loaded for bear and begin the character assassinations and innuendoes all over again."

Exhausted, Claudia dropped into the chair and fell silent. Her breath came in shallow gulps. Panic lines furrowed her brow as she stared at the carpet. Her hand discretely inched up to rest across her stomach.

Lost in deep concentration, she ignored Tom and focused on the roiling in her abdomen. She gulped and swallowed hard. Her hand rose to cover her mouth as color flooded into her cheeks.

Swallowing again, she glanced up at him. "I'm sorry. I'm going to have to use your bathroom."

Tom pointed the way.

She raced down the hall and disappeared inside. The sound of her heaving and retching could be heard all the way into the living room.

Charlie, who'd followed her down the hall, paced nervously in front of the door.

Claudia emerged several minutes later pale and weak. She supported herself by leaning against the wall as she made her way to the living room.

When she sagged into her chair, Charlie curled up at her feet. She blotted her lips with a tissue and gave Tom an apologetic smile. "I'm sorry to make a spectacle of myself."

Her eyebrows arched with surprise when she noticed a plate on the table beside her. It contained a dish of soda crackers, a cup of warm tea, and a glass of what looked like water with ice.

"It's flat 7-Up and spearmint tea," Tom said. "It used to help Marty when she had nausea."

She nodded her thanks and began alternating bites of cracker with tiny sips of the 7-Up.

"Feeling better?" Tom asked after several minutes of silence.

Claudia absentmindedly twisted a lock of blond hair around her finger as she spoke. "I'm really sorry about this. It comes on like gang busters and there's not much I can do to control it."

"Stress does that to people."

She lowered her eyes for a moment, wondering how much of her life she wanted to reveal. "Believe me, I'm under plenty of stress, but it didn't cause my nausea. My *morning sickness* seems to last all day."

"You're pregnant?"

She smiled for the first time. "Why are men always surprised when a woman says she's going to have a baby? That's what we do."

"No, I just meant…"

"You couldn't believe that beneath this persona of a successful businesswoman lies a real flesh and blood human being?"

"I was surprised that the stories I've seen in the tabloids are apparently true."

She sighed. "Read those things do you?"

"Just the headlines while I'm waiting in the grocery line. Need more 7-Up? Anything else I can do?"

"Yeah, admit you've behaved like a disingenuous jerk."

The tension in the room dissipated when they both laughed.

"So much for my righteous indignation, huh?" Her voice softened. "Seriously Tom, what did you hope to accomplish?"

He lowered his head and massaged his forehead. "You're right. I was frustrated and had no one else to go after so I picked on you. I thought if I stirred the pot hard enough something would rise to the surface."

"In other words, when you didn't have an enemy handy you picked on your friends instead. Is this what they mean when they say someone was hit by friendly fire? So, where did it get you?"

"Truthfully, nowhere."

"Then why don't we declare a truce." She handed him the glass. "I think I will take a little more 7-Up."

"Where are you headed from here?" Tom asked when he returned with the glass.

"I'm picking up a youngster in Portland tomorrow. We're going to ferry him to Memphis for cancer surgery. After that, I'm headed home to Maryland."

"So you're staying over tonight?"

"I planned to fly up tonight and stay somewhere near PDX."

"Could you stay on the Coast instead?"

"Why?"

"Because I want you to come to the newspaper office." He smiled. "My vicious watchdog will be there too. Take a chance. You'll be glad you did."

FORTY

Claudia arrived at the newspaper office the following morning wearing a tan, single-breasted corduroy jacket over a cornflower blue silk blouse with tailored navy slacks.

Tom held the door for her. "C'mon in, there's someone I'd like you to meet."

After introducing her to Tommy, Beth and Darlene, he asked her to wait while he went to the back.

Billy Nevins stood with his back to the door happily collating inserts. Hearing footsteps, he turned. "How are you this morning, Mr. J?" Billy asked with his usual boisterous enthusiasm.

"I'm great, Billy. I have someone I'd like you to meet." Tom stepped aside and Claudia entered.

Billy gasped. He fingers gripped the edge of the table. "Do, do you know who she is, Mr. J?"

"Yeah, do you?"

Billy grinned. "I sure do." He held up one of the inserts. "She's the lady whose picture is on this week's coupon booklet. What's she doing here?"

"I came to meet you, Billy." Claudia crossed the room and took his hand in hers. "Hi, I'm Claudia." She gave him a reassuring smile. "Mr. J told me about the great job you do here."

Tom slipped away, leaving them alone.

Unlike most young men, her good looks didn't seem to faze Billy. "Wow! Mr. J really said I do a great job?"

"He sure did." Claudia ran her eyes around the mail room. "So this is where you work, huh? Can you show me around?"

Billy gave her the grand tour of the back room saving the best for last. "And these are my tables where I stuff the inserts," he said proudly.

She pointed to an empty table beside them. "Would you

teach me how to do it?"

"You want to learn how to stuff inserts?'

She chuckled. "Of course I do."

Billy grabbed a denim apron off a hook. "You better put this on first. Mr. J bought 'em when I went home with ink all over my clothes."

Claudia draped her jacket over the back of a chair, rolled up her sleeves and donned the apron. She tied it in back and did a little pirouette. "Am I ready for work, Boss?"

Billy grinned and nodded. Reaching under the table, he started grabbing bundles of inserts and tossing them onto the tabletop. When he had one of each, he set about tutoring her in the fine art of insert stuffing.

"These bundles don't all have the same number of inserts." He tapped a stack of sale books from a discount store. "See how thick these are. They run out real fast and you have to keep getting more." He tapped a pizza chain's insert. "This one is a single page so they last and last."

He stepped aside giving her access to the table. "Okay, the first thing you have to do is open all your bundles."

Claudia gave the strapping a tug, but couldn't open it. "Do you have a pair of scissors?"

Billy grinned. "You don't need scissors. See where the strap's joined?"

"Yep."

"Now watch me close and I'll show you what to do." Billy twisted the strap over. "You grab this tab here on the bottom, and yank it. It'll open real easy." He stepped back. "Go ahead, you do it."

Claudia gripped the tab and pulled, freeing the bundle.

Grabbing the long end, Billy jerked it out and wadded it into a ball. "They go in here." He dropped it into a trash can half full of plastic strapping.

"I already arranged the bundles for you. All the folded sides have to go the same way, otherwise the pages fall out when you put it in the paper. It's better if you start with the thin ones and stack them inside a big one."

"Mr. J was right. You really do know your stuff."

Billy beamed. He motioned her up to the table and repeated what Tom said to him the day he started. "Try one or two and see how you like it."

She ran through the routine and began a new stack for the ones she finished.

Billy returned to his table and resumed stuffing. His hand flew across the stacks with practiced ease. He glanced over at Claudia's slower effort. "It's okay if you're not very fast at first. I was pretty slow when I started too."

He finished a bundle and paused to re-supply his table. He popped the strap and gave her a quizzical look. "How come your picture's on the front of the coupon insert?"

"The coupons down at the bottom are for money off on Souvanée cosmetics. I work for them. It's my job."

"They pay you to take your picture?"

"Yeah, sounds kind of silly, doesn't it?"

"I thought maybe they put you on there because you're so pretty."

Her cheeks colored. "Well, maybe that too."

They worked together for about an hour, talking as they stuffed. She told him a little about her life and Billy told her a lot about his. When it grew close to the time for her to leave, she cleaned the ink off her fingers with mechanic's soap from a dispenser.

"Do they have someone here at the newspaper who takes pictures?"

"Tommy takes most of the pictures. He's Mr. J's son."

"Well, I was thinking it might be fun to have him get a picture of us in our aprons? What do you think?"

Billy went into the front room and returned with Tommy.

Claudia placed Billy in front of the tables. Stepping beside him, she rested an arm on his shoulder.

Tommy snapped several and promised they'd run in the next week's edition.

Grabbing a scrap of paper, she wrote her email address and gave it to Tommy, asking him to forward her a copy. Before she left she signed the cover of two of the coupon inserts with her picture on the cover, one for Billy to take home to show his Mom, and another for him to post above his work table. On both she wrote—

To Billy Nevins—

The best Advertising Coordinator I've ever met. Thanks for teaching me the tricks of the trade.

Love, Claudia Monet

Billy escorted her out to the front office. He tapped Tom on the shoulder. "I told her if she came back on Thursday she could have pizza with us."

"I'd like to do that some time, Billy." She put her arms around him and hugged him. "Thanks for teaching me how to stuff inserts." Leaning close, she kissed him on the cheek and whispered, "I'll never forget the morning I spent working with you."

Billy returned to the back room rubbing the spot on his cheek where she'd kissed him.

She turned to Tom with a grin and opened her arms. "Come here, Tom Jenkins, you scalawag. Give me a hug. You're forgiven."

FORTY-ONE

San Francisco, California—

The entire office had been in turmoil ever since Derek vanished. Ridgely used his government connections to turn Derek's absence into a terrorism issue and an army of agents descended upon RCI like hungry locusts on a wheat field.

White-coated technicians in rubber gloves examined every nook and cranny of Derek's office. They sifted and sorted their way through his files and impounded his computer. Rumor had it they planned to reconstruct his deleted files and dissect them for hidden meanings and coded messages.

Shiri wondered why Derek's work demanded such scrutiny.

The men in dark suits appeared after the technicians left. They interviewed and re-interviewed everyone at RCI who had any contact with Derek. And, since Shiri was his first corporate contact, they spent an inordinate amount of time with her. Most mornings she found the dour-faced Agent Glynn waiting when she arrived.

It'd been a stressful week and Shiri was happy to see Friday come. After changing into jeans and her 49er's tee shirt, she tied on an apron and began chopping vegetables for a stir-fry. Her husband, Jared, was a meat and potatoes kind of guy and she seldom had an opportunity to fix the dishes she liked. But with football season well underway for the next several months he'd be away a lot of the time.

Jared was off scouting college linemen in Indiana or Iowa or maybe Illinois. Why did it matter, Shiri thought, they were all one big cornfield anyway. Following Saturday's collegiate game, he'd fly to Seattle to join the team for Sunday's game with the Seahawks.

Shiri slipped in a CD and hummed along with the music as she sliced and diced her way through the vegetables. She'd begun trimming a stalk of Bok Choy when the phone rang. Expecting it to be Jared, she ran to grab it with a smile.

The sound of breathing followed her *Hello* instead of Jared's familiar voice. It never failed. Somehow the oddballs always knew when he was out of town.

"Look Buddy, I don't have time to play sicko games." She jerked the phone away from her ear, but for some reason hesitated. Instinct told her to slam it down, but a tiny voice in the back of her head whispered, *"Don't hang up."*

She returned the phone to her ear. "I can't wait forever."

A tentative voice quietly said, "Please do not disconnect the phone line, Mrs. Yoblanski."

A shiver of recognition shot through her.

"Dr.... Derek? Is that you? What's happened? Where have you been? How are you?"

Derek chuckled at her excited response. "As usual, you are full of questions. My, how I have missed your company."

"Are you well?"

"I am fine. I have, however, gone into hiding. I have become a fugitive from injustice."

After wiping her hands on her apron, she pulled back a chair, sat down and crossed her legs. Her foot bobbed restlessly as she listened. "Why did you call?"

"I need your help. I would not trouble you were I not in trouble myself. There is no one else I can go to for assistance. You, Shiri Yoblanski, are my only hope."

Shiri nestled the receiver in the crook of her shoulder and reached for the plastic wrap. After covering the chicken, she turned off the stove. Gathering her vegetables, she tossed them in a bowl and covered it with wrap too. "Winston Ridgely told everyone you're a terrorist. He says you came to work at RCI to steal our research.

The roar of a passing truck drowned out Derek's reply.

Realizing he was in an open phone booth, she strained to pick up clues as to his whereabouts. She heard the thumping beat of salsa music in the background. It rose in intensity and then drifted away in the distance.

"I must apologize for the noise." Derek cupped his hand over the receiver. "My phone is in a very lively area. You were telling me what Winston Ridgely has been up to in my absence."

"All sorts of government agents have been in your office looking for clues."

He exhaled in frustration and waited while a siren passed. "I deny those charges, but we both know what I say makes scant difference. A person's beliefs ultimately guide their actions. Tell me, Mrs. Yoblanski, do you believe I am a terrorist?"

"No, I know you're not a terrorist."

In her interviews, she'd repeatedly insisted that this whole affair must be a huge misunderstanding. The men in dark suits smiled at each other, shook their heads, and scribbled notes.

"I thank you for saying so. Regardless of what you choose to do, knowing someone believes in me strengthens my resolve. That said, I must now ask for your assistance."

Shiri's mind raced. What would Jared think? She could lose her job, possibly even be arrested. None of it made any difference. In reality, her decision had been made years earlier.

Her grandparents were flower-growers in the San Fernando Valley prior to World War II. Though innocent farmers, they were removed to an Internment Camp after the bombing of Pearl Harbor. Many Japanese-Americans lost everything they owned while in such camps.

Her grandparents would have too except for the kindly intervention of caring neighbors. Their neighbors, all Caucasians, stepped in and maintained their land, preserving their livelihood.

Her grandparents never forgot the kindness. Shiri heard the stories over and over at her grandmother's knee. She understood the importance of doing what was right and of standing up for those who were unjustly accused. Some situations demanded action regardless of the risk.

"What do you need?"

"I must establish my hideout, a safe place with Internet access."

"You can stay in our guest room." She'd work out the details with Jared when he got home.

"Thank you, Mrs. Yoblanski, you are very kind."

Shiri began to give him directions to their condo, but Derek stopped her. "Unfortunately, I am no longer in possession of an automobile. It occurred to me that RCI would surely give its description and license plate numbers to whomever they sent to search for me."

"I'm sure they did. Federal agents have been running around the office like ants at a picnic.

"Once I arrived at this understanding, I realized I must distance myself from my vehicle. So I drove to the Los Angeles airport and abandoned it in the long-term parking area."

He made sure to leave plenty of fingerprints. Derek also left a rumpled Chicago street map on the seat along with a printout of his flight itinerary from LAX to O'Hare. He locked the doors, deposited the keys in an airport trashcan and boarded a flight to Chicago. As soon as he landed, he took a bus back to San Francisco.

"You must come and retrieve me. Taking a cab will leave a record of my presence."

"Where are you now?" She was shocked when he gave her his location. "Derek, that's in the barrio. It's...it's not safe there."

He laughed. "At the present time nowhere is safe for Dr. Maheshwari."

Shiri swallowed her fears and made arrangements to meet him.

"I shall be awaiting your arrival at our rendezvous spot."

"I'll leave right away."

Shiri squinted down at the map book on the seat beside

her. The neon glow from the shops and bars on both sides of the
street painted a rainbow across the hood of her car. Friday night
traffic was heavy and navigating the bewildering maze of
unfamiliar streets grew increasingly difficult.

The surrounding streets and sidewalks pulsed with activity.
Young people clustered around light poles talking and laughing
with friends. A caravan of low-riders cruised the block with
speakers thumping. Shiri found herself boxed in, an unwitting
participant in their parade.

She stopped at a light and glanced down at the map. She
was so engrossed in it that she failed to notice a car roll to a stop
beside her. A young man crawled halfway out of the window and
shouted something in Spanish to a girl on the sidewalk.

Shiri jumped and reflexively hit the automatic lock switch.

Her cheeks flushed when she realized everyone nearby had
heard the locks thunk down. Resisting the urge to look in his
direction, Shiri rigidly stared straight ahead.

When the light changed, she drove to the next corner,
turned right and pulled over to the curb. Derek was nowhere in
sight. The old building beside her housed a small restaurant on
the ground floor and several floors of cramped apartments above.
Even with the windows rolled up, spicy cooking odors seeped in
to surround her.

The street slowly rose for several blocks and then became
quite steep. The sidewalks ahead were deserted. She scrutinized
the empty street. Where was Derek?

Shiri became aware of movement beside her and turned.
She hadn't noticed the young couple in the shadows when she'd
parked. Momentarily forgetting about Derek, she sat in the dark
car observing the lovers.

The girl leaned against the brick wall under the flaking
residue of an old, nearly unreadable soft drink sign. Her male
companion slipped his arms around her, pressed himself against
her and kissed her deeply several times.

They were either unaware of Shiri's presence or didn't care.

The young man ground against her as his hands traced the curve of her hips. He kissed his way up her neck, whispering sweet nothings in Spanish.

The girl giggled.

He whispered something else.

She shoved him away and smacked him on the chest.

They kissed again. Smiling, he took her hand and they disappeared into the building together.

When Shiri's attention returned to the street she saw something white moving in the shadow of a burned-out streetlight, Squinting, she eventually identified it as a man's white cowboy hat.

He entered a shaft of light spilling out of an open doorway giving her a better look. He had a drooping mustache and wore Western boots with loose jeans and a cotton jacket that hung below his waist. He carried a cloth rucksack over one shoulder and a large metallic case in his other hand.

Her eyes remained on the case as the man moved in and out of the shadows. It seemed odd, out of character. When he drew nearly even with her, he stepped off the curb and began to cross the street in front of her car. Halfway across, he changed direction and stopped beside her window.

"Mrs. Yoblanski. You are a sight for tired eyes."

"Derek? Is that you?" She lowered the window an inch for a better look.

"Si, Amigo." He pushed up the wide brim of his hat and grinned.

"You look like—."

"A Mexican?"

"Yeah, in a strange sort of way."

"You did not recognize me. That is good. Engage your mechanical trunk-opening device and I will deposit my goods."

Shiri pushed the button and watched as he walked to the back of the car. He deposited his luggage, closed the trunk lid, and moved to the passenger side of the car.

"I can't believe this...you," she said as he took a seat beside her. Shiri eased the car away from the curb and waved her hand over him. "What is this?"

"It is my disguise, of course. You mistook me for a Mexican, did you not?" He grinned with satisfaction. "Go ahead, you must admit it. I am telling the truth. Go ahead and say so."

"Well, maybe you look like a Mexican from a distance, a very, very long distance."

"It was not for nothing that I chose to masquerade this way. I am making good use of my natural skin coloration. There are many more Mexicans in California than Indians. I considered impersonating Juan Valdez, but was unable to procure a burro."

Shiri glanced over at him.

Derek winked.

She'd never seen him so happy. "What is in the metal suitcase you were carrying?"

"Computer disks, programs. I have written, notes, research materials...all of my work."

"So you took it all with you?"

"At this moment it is the most precious possession I have."

Shiri nodded as they turned onto the freeway ramp.

Like a seasoned cowpoke, Derek leaned the seat back, tilted his hat down until it concealed his face, and interlocked his fingers across his stomach.

FORTY-TWO

Pine Crest, Oregon—

Twilight cast long shadows across the yard and lamps blinked on in windows up and down the street. At the foot of Tom's back steps a sleek black cat extended its front legs, arched its back and stretched. Looking around, Arnold spied a small beetle and leapt onto the step to pursue it.

The back door opened. "Here kitty, kitty, kitty. Time to come in, Arnold. Look, I have soft cat food, the kind you like."

The bug was much more interesting than Tom's offer of supper. Arnold tentatively poked a paw at the bug and jumped aside when it skittered away.

"Arnold, are you paying attention?"

The bug retreated under the step and the cat bent over, poking its head between the open stair treads to see where it'd gone.

"I'm speaking to you, Arnold."

Tom always felt like an idiot standing on the porch making cutesy kitty noises. Despite his best efforts, this 10-pound ball of fluff played him like a fiddle. Night after night, it was the same game, Tom begging and coaxing, Arnold having nothing to do with it.

Arnold tired of chasing the bug and wandered aimlessly around the side yard. He remained sublimely aloof, ignoring Tom's inducements and pleas. Cats, being cats, he had his own agenda and his first priority wasn't going inside just now, thank you very much.

"This is your last chance, Arnold. Come in now!"

The cat ignored him.

"Okay, you can stay out here all night. Maybe a bear will eat you. See if I care." He slammed the door.

A few minutes later, someone knocked.

It was their next-door neighbor, Margaret, with Arnold nestled in her arms. The little traitor was purring and snuggling against her. Before she could say anything, Arnold rolled over for a tummy rub.

"Look what I found," Margaret said. "And just for the record, I wouldn't come in either if you yelled at me like that."

"Do you want to step in for a minute?"

She carried the cat into the room and Tom closed the door behind her. He pointed to a small throw rug in the corner. "You can put him down over there. I have some canned cat food for him."

He sat the bowl in front of Arnold and motioned Margaret into the living room.

"How have you been, Tom?"

"No good." He swept his arm in a wide circle. "Look around you. I forgot to water the houseplants before I went to London and half of them dried up. Now the ones that didn't turn brown are yellowing because I over-watered them. Have you seen Marty's rose bushes? I think I've killed them all."

Margaret had the understanding look of one who'd been there. "Don't expect so much of yourself. I know how overwhelming things can seem. It was this way for me when Alex died."

"He was a good man. It hurt me to see him linger the way he did."

"Can I share something with you?"

Tom nodded.

"You're not the first one to say you regret Alex lingering. I heard it a lot, especially at his funeral. The funny thing is neither Alex nor I ever felt that way."

"You didn't?"

"No, we didn't. Oh, it hurt me to see him suffer and it embarrassed him when he got to the place where I had to help him with everything."

Margaret shook her head when the flood of memories brought tears to her eyes. She dabbed at her eyes and took a deep breath. "It was a privilege to be with him until the end. Some days, I still expect him to walk in the front door. I've imagined myself being upset, demanding to know where he's been. He just laughs and gives me that smile of his."

Tom shifted uneasily in his seat and handed her a box of tissues.

"I lied." Margaret said as she wiped her eyes. "You never really get over it; you just learn to live with the pain."

Tom wondered why she was telling him this. Marty was still alive. She was coming home.

"Although many people view a terminal illness as some kind of curse, in reality it's a blessing. We had time to come to terms with our life and his death. We talked late into the night, reminisced, laughed, held each other and cried."

Tom recalled lying in bed with Marty looking out at the stars and talking about how things would someday be. They planned to turn the paper over to Tommy, retire, and make time to travel. Time stretched out like an endless highway then, or so it seemed.

"I wouldn't take a million dollars for even one of those minutes. Don't you see, the real curse is losing someone you love without having the chance to say goodbye." Margaret caught Tom's eyes and held them. "There's something I've been meaning to talk to you about."

"What is it?"

"I heard you went to the City Council and protested the construction of a memorial garden."

"You heard right."

"That Memory Garden represents the love this town had for those who were lost. Everyone wants it, little children, moms and dads, grandmas and grandpas. They're your friends and neighbors. Don't turn your back on them. This isn't what Marty would want."

"What *would* Marty want?"

"She'd want you to get on with your life. It hurts. Believe me, I know how much it hurts. But there's no other way; you've got to do the hard stuff. Clean out the closets, put away the knick-knacks, take down the pictures and start over."

"Start acting like she's dead, in other words."

"She is dead, Tom."

He glared at her. "I thought you, of all people, might understand. I thought you'd be on my side, but you're not."

"Your side? There are no sides here."

"You've written her off like everyone else."

Margaret tried to respond, but Tom didn't let her.

"Go ahead and say it. Everyone else has. You think I'm crazy." He was practically shouting now. "I've heard it all before: *Come on Tom, face reality. She's gone and that's that. In time, you'll get over it.* But you're wrong. You, the people of this town, the Coast Guard, Lloyd's of London, you're all wrong."

Tom's anger quickly dissipated. When he spoke again his voice was calm and controlled, frighteningly so. "I'm sorry. I know you were trying to help, but you have to understand that whether you want to believe it or not, Marty's coming back."

What Tom did next disturbed Margaret more than she could have imagined. He walked into the kitchen and pointed to the refrigerator door. "These slips were in my fortune cookies a few nights after Marty disappeared. Its proof she's still alive."

An unbridgeable chasm opened between them.

"This whole town can scoff if they like. I know what I know, and all the naysayers in the world won't dissuade me."

"It's time for me to go." Margaret rose, gave him a brief hug and hurried out the door.

FORTY-THREE

San Francisco, California—

"Mrs. Yoblanski, you have returned just as you said you would."

"Well, of course I did." Shiri sat her bag of groceries on the kitchen counter. "You didn't think I'd left forever, did you?"

"No, I meant you are right on time." He tapped his watch. "I have been waiting impatiently for your return."

Shiri passed the island bar where Derek had newspaper pages scattered all over it. "What's this?"

"I found something very exciting in today's newspaper. I could not wait to tell you about it."

Shiri opened the closet door and reached in for a hanger. "Oh yeah, what was it?"

"Hope, Mrs. Yoblanski. Today in your daily newspaper, the most unlikely of places, I found hope. I am not alone. Here, let me show you."

"Okay, show away."

Derek grabbed a cutout square of newsprint and proudly held it up for her to see. "I removed it from the page with a scissors."

"So I see."

His face fell. "I should have waited until you read the paper first. In my excitement I am afraid I threw caution into the wind. I usually do not act so impulsively." He fit the square back into the hole and smoothed its corners. "If you wish to read the other side, we can reattach the article with a roll of clear cellophane tape."

"Forget about the paper, silly. Tell me what has gotten you so excited."

"It is an article concerning the disappearance of the *Paradise Voyager*."

"Oh yeah, I've seen a few of those."

"There are more? I should like to read them all."

"Um, well okay."

"The article was written by a Mr. Thomas Jenkins from Pine Crest, Oregon." Light danced in Derek's eyes. He rocked from foot to foot with excitement as he spoke. "If it was part of a series, I must have the others Please tell me you have not destroyed your newspapers."

"I have a recycling pile in the closet. Let's go through them, I'm sure they'll all be there."

Derek was in the living room studying the papers from the recycling pile when Shiri put supper on the island bar. "What do think?" she asked as Derek sat down.

"Mr. Jenkins appears to be a very sincere individual and highly motivated in his search for the truth." He lowered his eyes. "I have learned his wife and granddaughter were aboard the ship when it disappeared."

"No wonder he's writing the articles, he has a vested interest in finding out what happened."

Derek toyed with his food, eating little of the meal Shiri prepared. He sat at the table with his head down, apparently lost in thought.

"Not hungry?" Shiri removed the plate when he nodded. "What happened to the excited scientist who met me at the door?" The sound of the garbage disposal nearly drowned out her words.

"It is quite a sobering experience to encounter a person actually touched by the tragedy of the *Paradise Voyager*."

"It's unfortunate, but why should it mean so much to you? It's not like you had anything to do with the ship's disappearance."

Derek rested his elbows on the table and buried his face in his hands.

Alarmed, Shiri touched his shoulder. "What is it Derek?"

He kept his head bowed, avoiding her eyes. "You will understand as soon as I make you privy to several carefully guarded secrets. You see, Mrs. Yoblanski, rather than not having anything to do with the *Paradise Voyager's* disappearance, I had everything to do with it. I am the dastardly scoundrel who inflicted this suffering upon so many people."

The dishtowel in her hand slipped through her fingers and landed in a clump at her feet. She numbly walked into the living room and collapsed into a chair. For the first time in her life, Shiri didn't know what to say.

Derek followed, hovering near her, pacing and wringing his hands.

She lifted her eyes and stared at him in disbelief. "You're saying you can actually make things appear and disappear at will?"

"In a manner of speaking, yes, that would be a true statement."

"How?"

He smiled for the first time. "I do it with delicacy, finesse, and the laws of physics."

"So you discombobulate all the atoms, convert them into an energy beam and transport them into an alternate universe through a wormhole like they do on the Sci-Fi channel?"

He shook his head. "Sorry to disappoint you, but I used no transporter beams." He sighed. "Dr. Hawking would easily understand the physics behind what I did. It becomes more difficult to explain it to a layperson such as yourself."

Shiri understood. "So where did the ship go."

"Nowhere." He shrugged. "We are playing an elaborate game of blind man's bluff here. Only in this case, everyone else is blindfolded and the central participant remains clear-eyed."

"Why did you leave RCI and go into hiding?"

"Do you not recall the story of *The Three Fish*?"

"I understand that you ran away, but I don't know why."

"We did not intend for the *Paradise Voyager* to disappear. It was an unfortunate accident. And now, rather than confess to his part in it, Winston Ridgely has successfully camouflaged his evil deed. It seems he was correct when he said, 'In a short while, everyone will forget there ever was a *Paradise Voyager*.' It gradually became clear to me that rather than admit an involvement in the ship's disappearance it would be more expedient for him to arrange for Dr. Maheshwari's disappearance."

"What about Jenkins, he hasn't forgotten."

"True, but Mr. Thomas Jenkins blames the wrong party. He believes the owners of the cruise line are the ones with guilty hands. He does not know the true state of the affair."

Shiri folded her hands in her lap and glanced across at Derek. "And you intend to correct the problem."

"I must."

"What are you proposing to do?"

"I am proposing to go to Oregon and meet with him. He must know the truth."

Shiri shook her head. "I'm not sure that would be a good idea. Your life could be at risk. What if you are arrested?"

"It is a risk I must undertake before, as Winston Ridgely said, the world forgets."

"There's plenty of time. Let's not do something rash."

"You do not understand. It is the people on the cruise who may not have *plenty of time*, Mrs. Yoblanski."

"You have an open receiver; are you blind?" Shiri shouted at the television set when the receiver crossed into the end zone untouched and empty-handed. "What are those guys doing? Where's their offense?"

It was Sunday afternoon and she and Derek were spending it watching television. It was Derek's first exposure to American football. Shiri did her best to explain the game without much success. Derek's respect for Jared, however, increased the longer he watched the game's progress.

On the next series of downs, they sacked her quarterback in his own end zone. She threw her hands in the air and shook her head in disbelief. "Can you believe it? A safety."

"I believe very little of what I am seeing and understand even less of it. However, I believe you are mistaken on this point. I have been watching closely and there appears to be no safety anywhere on the playing field. In fact, they sometimes chase each other beyond the boundaries."

A key turned in the front door lock interrupting Shiri's explanation. She muted the television, put a finger to her lips and tiptoed out of the living room. She was in the hallway when the door opened.

Her eyes widened in surprise. "Jared, what are you doing here? I wasn't expecting you until late tonight. Why aren't you in Seattle?"

The big man tossed his suitcase aside and kicked the door closed with a heel. Without a word, he scooped Shiri up and hugged her tightly.

"Jared, put me down."

"But I'm your incredible hunk, remember? You like it when I pick you up."

She tried to wiggle away. "Well, I don't like it right now."

"Is this how you greet a man you haven't seen in almost a week, especially one who's about to fulfill your wildest fantasies?"

"But Jared—."

He cut her off with a kiss. Shiri stretched her eyes to see past the foyer and into the living room as he continued pressing his lips against hers.

"My connecting flight out of Minneapolis was delayed because of snow. Coach suggested I come home early and maybe get a little R & R." He gave her a knowing wink. "I could sure use some R & R, what about you?"

"Jared, we need to talk."

"We can talk later. Right now I've got something else on my mind."

"Can't it wait?"

He carried her into the kitchen. Sitting her down on the island bar, he nuzzled her neck. "I've *really* missed you, Babe."

Shiri couldn't extricate herself from his strong grasp.

"Wanna go for a horsey ride little girl?" Jared pushed her legs around him and began undoing the buttons on her blouse.

Shiri's cheeks flushed. She smacked his hand.

He jerked it away in mock pain. "Hey, that hurt! Why are you beating on me?" His fingers quickly returned to her buttons. "Whatcha got hidden away in here? Daddy Bear's gonna gobble up your little—"

"Jar-ED, we have company!"

He snapped back like a 300-pound tackle had plowed into him. He glanced into the living room.

The slight, dark-skinned man sitting on the sofa gave him an anxious smile.

Jared looked from him back to Shiri who shrugged nervously and hurriedly re-buttoned her blouse.

"I...I can explain," she said, hopping down from the island bar.

"You'd better have a good explanation." Jared glared at Derek. A look of understanding slowly crossed his face. "You're the hackles guy. The one everybody's hunting for."

"Indeed, and you would be her offensive husband." Derek rose and extended his hand. "It's so nice to make your acquaintance, Mr. Yoblanski. I have heard many interesting things about you."

Once the three of them recovered from the shock of Jared's early return and the presence of a stranger in the living room, the conversation turned to Derek.

"Why is he here?" Jared asked.

"He needed a place to hide."

"And so you turned our apartment into a safe house?"

"I couldn't just turn my back. The FBI's hunting for him."

"Well that's dandy. If they find him here, we'll all go to jail."

"I am willing to reveal the truth of my affairs," Derek said. "But I fear that if I am arrested, I will not have the opportunity. Mr. Winston Ridgely has very powerful connections."

"So I hear." Jared rotated his chair and stared out the window, ignoring both Shiri and Derek. A minute later he spun the chair back around and gazed over at Shiri sitting on the corner of the couch hugging a pillow. "Okay, he can stay, but only temporarily. And the two of you had better come up with a plan before we all end up behind bars."

Shiri smiled.

"I've got another recruiting trip next week. When I get back, one way or another, you'd better be gone," Jared told Derek.

The plan Shiri devised provided a safe and effective way for Derek to contact Tom Jenkins.

"Left to my own devices I would have assumed my disguise and gone directly to the offices of the *Pine Crest Courier*. Your idea is much better, I am fortunate you are my co-conspirator."

"Going to Pine Crest would not have been wise. Your disguise would only make you stand out. Besides, I'd bet someone is watching our Mr. Jenkins."

"I am becoming quite excited by this idea of yours. You would make a bang-up spy."

"In your dreams," Shiri licked the envelope, "but our card should pique his curiosity."

FORTY-FOUR

Pine Crest, Oregon—

Tom and Charlie went to Tommy's house after work. Beth had promised a roast for dinner with apple pie for desert. Tom looked forward to a home-cooked meal and spending time with them away from the office.

They'd finished grace and dished up their plates when Tommy reached into his pocket and removed a small envelope. He passed it across the table to Tom. "You were out when the mail came. I stuck this in my pocket and forgot to give it to you."

Tom turned the small envelope in his hand then held it up for everyone to see. "No return address. Looks like a woman's handwriting and has a San Francisco postmark."

"It's addressed to you. You're allowed to open it," Beth said.

Tom slipped his finger under the flap and ripped it across the top. The envelope contained a 3 x 5 card.

"Blank," Tom said as he slipped the card out. "What do you make of it?"

"Turn it over. There's some writing on the other side.

Tom flipped it over. It contained a reference, *Jeremiah 33:3.* "Is this someone's idea of a joke?"

"Let's find out." Tommy sent one of the boys after a Bible. When they returned with it, he started flipping through it. "What book and chapter again?"

Tom held up the card for him to see. "Jeremiah."

Tommy worked his way back. 1 Kings... 2 Chronicles... Nehemiah... Psalms... more Psalms... Proverbs... Isaiah... Jeremiah. His progress slowed as he inched his way ahead, page by page. Finally, there it was. He looked at it for a long time before passing the book to his father. "Here, I'll let you read it."

"Call to me and I will answer you, and will tell you great and hidden things which you have not known."

Tom eased the Bible closed and stared across at Tommy and Beth. They appeared as baffled as he was.

Tom stayed longer at Tommy and Beth's than he intended. Though it had gotten late, he wasn't anxious to go home.

Reminders of Marty surrounded him there. Knick-knacks she'd bought on trips to the beach sat on end tables. A half-read book still lay on the nightstand, recipes stuck to the refrigerator, notes she'd made on the calendar. Marty was everywhere and yet nowhere.

Since her disappearance, Tom's relationship with Charlie had inexplicably deepened. He counted on the dog for moral support. They also shared a bond Tom had with no one else. Charlie had been with him the night he'd felt Marty's love wrap itself around them. Though the dog had no way of expressing it, like Tom, he knew and believed.

Charlie leaped out of the car as soon as Tom opened the back door. He circled the yard, discovered a fascinating scent, and followed it around the corner of the house.

"I'm going in, Charlie. You can push the door open when you've done your business."

Over the years, it had become part of their routine. If Tom tired of waiting, he'd push the back door closed without letting it latch. When the dog finished, he'd nose his way in and woof. One thing Charlie had never learned was to close and lock the door behind him. But then Rin Tin Tin and Lassie didn't either.

Tom stepped into the house, set the door for Charlie, and flipped the light switch.

Nothing happened.

He decided the bulb must have burned out and started down the dark hallway, groping his way to the kitchen doorway. In the dark the laundry room seemed larger and longer. At last his fingers found the corner and he turned into the kitchen. The light switch lay mere inches from his fingertips, but he never turned it on.

The kitchen's darkness masked a fist flying toward him. Caught off guard, Tom absorbed the full force of its blow. Stars sparkled in his left eye as his head snapped back. His hand grasped for support that wasn't there. His fingernails scraped across the wall as he toppled backward and landed on the floor with a thud.

Someone was in the house!

Before he could react, his assailant kicked him in the side. Tom grunted in pain and gasped for breath. The man gave a coarse laugh and kicked him again.

Knowing he had to fight back, Tom anticipated the next kick. He rolled away from it and grabbed the man's foot. He twisted his leg and jerked the man off his feet.

Ignoring the ache in his ribcage, Tom leapt at his attacker. He struck his assailant several times as they grappled on the floor, but the other man still held the advantage. Unlike Tom, his attacker wasn't in shock and struggling for breath.

The man's fist slammed into Tom's ribs. Searing hot pain arced across his chest. He momentarily loosened his grip.

The man shoved him aside. Grabbing him by the shirt, the man slammed him against the side of the doorway.

The metal corner bead split the back of Tom's scalp. Warm blood oozed into his hair and dripped onto his collar.

The intruder leaned close. He stank of booze and old perspiration. His voice was hard and full of malice. "It's over, Jenkins. You'll never write another story when I'm done with you."

Still holding him by the shirt, his attacker backhanded him across the face to drive home his point.

Tom's head rocked back and forth like a rag doll. He struggled to make sense out of what was happening.

The man hit him again and everything grew fuzzy.

Now Tom had to fight unconsciousness as well as the attacker. He knew he wouldn't last much longer.

Charlie finished outside and bounded up the steps, tail wagging. In an instant he sensed danger on the other side of the door and flung himself against it.

The door slammed back against the wall. At the sound of the door flying open, the man let go of Tom's shirt and jerked up.

Tom rolled against the cabinet, drew into a fetal position and cradled his throbbing head between his hands.

Charlie saw the intruder as soon as the man stepped into the hallway. His ears flattened and the hair on his shoulders rose. He lowered himself for attack. His instinctual wolf heritage asserted itself. He inched forward, baring his teeth and making a low, guttural growl.

The man backed away. Keeping his eyes on the dog, he rooted in his pocket for his knife.

Charlie's white mane briefly glowed silver in the dim light then he became a dark blur flying toward the intruder.

The man collapsed when the big dog hit him. He thrashed on the floor trying to avoid Charlie's snarling fangs, and slashed wildly with his knife.

Charlie ignored the blade's thrusts and fought on. The knife spun out of the man's hand and skittered down the hall.

Left with no defense, Tom's attacker pulled his arms up to protect his face as the dog tore into him. Charlie shredded the man's leather jacket like a wolf peeling flesh from its prey. His claws etched deep, bloody tracks across the man's arms.

When the stranger reached up, Charlie clamped his arm in his mouth. He bit down hard and, for the first time, tasted the man's blood. The warm, salty liquid ignited deep, primal instincts in his canine brain. The dog would have killed the man if Tom hadn't called.

When he heard Tom's voice, Charlie abruptly released the man and hurried to his master. Their assailant, now torn and bleeding crawled into the laundry room. He pulled himself to his feet with the aid of the washer and staggered out the open door.

Tommy was reading when the phone rang. He picked it up and heard his father gasp, "Need help."

Charlie whined in the background before the phone clattered onto the floor. Tommy tossed the receiver in Beth's direction and ran for the door. "Call 911," he hollered over his shoulder. "Get somebody over to Dad's. Tell them it's a possible heart attack."

Tommy ran out the door, hopped in his car, and headed for his father's house. There was no one else on the road and he sped across town at twice the posted limit. He heard a siren wailing in the distance as he leaped up the porch steps.

Inside, Tom drifted in and out of consciousness. He awoke and found Charlie lying beside him licking his face. Fighting the pounding in his head and the overwhelming desire to drift back to sleep, he reached out and petted him.

Charlie whimpered.

"Good boy, good boy." He stoked the dog's side. "You're wet, Charlie. What have you been doing?"

The dog licked Tom's face as he sank back into oblivion.

"Its okay, Charlie. It's only me," Tommy yelled at the doorway. He expected him to bark, but everything remained still, deathly quiet. He took a deep breath and stepped in. An ambulance swung around the corner bathing the street in flashes of red light.

When the light switch didn't work, Tommy opened the circuit panel beside the back door and felt for the main breaker. He flipped it and the lights flickered on.

Nothing could have prepared him for what he saw.

There was blood everywhere...splattered on the walls, streaked down the door. The floor was wet and slippery with it and covered with red footprints, some human and some canine.

The house was in shambles. Strips of black leather lay scattered around the hallway and what he guessed to be remnants of a denim shirt covered the kitchen floor.

Tommy found Tom, bruised, bleeding and semi-conscious with Charlie lying protectively beside him. The dog looked up and whimpered when Tommy knelt beside his father.

Behind him, Tommy heard the EMT's coming into the house. He picked the phone up off the floor, hung it up, and stepped aside so they could work on Tom.

"Looks like the dog's in bad shape too," an EMT said.

Charlie lay on the floor in a puddle of blood, panting.

Tommy slipped his arms under him. "You take care of Dad; I'll take care of the dog." He glanced around the room as he carried Charlie to his car. This couldn't be the house where he'd grown up. Not with all this blood. He felt like he'd walked onto the set of a Slasher movie.

FORTY-FIVE

Tom's head throbbed even with his eyes closed. He pressed it against the pillow trying to force the cobwebs from his brain. His confrontation with the intruder remained a distorted blur, so many grainy, out-of-focus images.

"Good morning, how are you feeling today?" a cheery female voice asked.

Tom opened his eyes a crack.

A nurse stood beside his bed. "Can you tell me your name?"

"Yeah, Tom Jenkins."

"And where do you live?"

It hurt to think, but he managed to give the nurse his address.

"Very good, Mr. Jenkins. You're improving. Last night you didn't even know your name."

Some improvement. His head felt like it was going to break into a million pieces.

"Do you know where you are?"

He ran his eyes around the room. "How many guesses do I get?"

The nurse chuckled. "Based on the way you look, you had a pretty rough evening. You're in Bay Area Hospital in Coos Bay. Could you handle some breakfast?"

"Coffee sounds good."

"No caffeine...possible concussion."

"Whatever, I'm not picky."

"They just delivered the cart. I'll see what they have for you. Are you up to a visitor? Your son's waiting."

"Sure, send him in."

Tommy crossed the room to sit beside the bed. He spent the first few minutes assessing the bruises and swelling that marked

Tom's face. "How much do you remember about last night?"

Tom thought for a minute. "I recall thinking the light bulb had burned out. Then someone punched me and I tried to fight back. Charlie growled at something and I told him to be quiet. He licked my face to wake me up then they put me in an ambulance."

"Do you remember calling me and saying you needed help?"

"No, but I'll take your word for it."

"You've got the general idea. You were attacked last night and Charlie came to your rescue. He probably saved your life."

Of that much, Tom was certain.

The nurse returned. She put his breakfast on the tray-table and rolled it over to him. After raising the head of the bed slightly and helping Tom sit up, she tiptoed away.

"We know your attacker wore a black leather jacket and a denim shirt. The shredded jacket was in the hallway along with pieces of his shirt. That must have been where he and Charlie had it out. There was blood all over the wall and on the back door. Since you were hit in the kitchen, I'm guessing it belonged to the man who attacked you."

Tom lifted the cover on his breakfast plate and surveyed its contents. He picked up a crispy slice of bacon and took a small bite while he waited for Tommy to continue.

"There was also blood on the corner of the doorway. You must have banged your head when you fell. In case you haven't figured it out yet, you've got stitches in the back of your head."

Tom cornered some scrambled eggs with his toast and brought the fork to his mouth. As he chewed, he reached up to explore the back of his head. Underneath the bandage it remained sore to the touch.

Tommy leaned over the bed and examined his father's eye. "You've got a real shiner there. The doctor told us you're lucky your cheekbone wasn't broken. Several ribs are fractured; it's going to hurt for a while when you laugh."

Tom gave him a wry look. "Not much potential there."

"Don't worry about the house. The police asked us not to touch anything until they look things over. Once they've finished, Beth will straighten everything up before you get home."

Tom tried to protest, but Tommy cut him off. "The police are convinced you walked in on a burglary in progress. You must have startled the thief and he attacked you."

An unexpected flash of memory came back to him. He'd let Tommy believe what he wanted. Let everyone think it'd been a burglar if they wished, but burglars don't yell *No more stories* in your face.

"They're going to discharge you tomorrow morning. I think you ought to stay with us until you get back on your feet."

Tom was too weak to argue.

Tommy checked his watch. "I'd better be going. I just wanted to see how you were doing."

When he stood up to go, Tom stopped him. ""Why didn't you bring Charlie with you?"

Tommy paused and sighed deeply. "I, I couldn't."

"Sure you could. They let dogs come into the hospital, I've seen them. Charlie's very well behaved; he wouldn't cause any trouble."

"I know, Dad."

"Speaking of Charlie, when I was lying on the floor last night, I reached out to pet Charlie and his fur was damp. Wet, actually. Why?"

"It was blood."

Tom stared down at his hand half expecting it to be red. He looked up, caught Tommy's eyes and held them. "Why was Charlie bleeding?"

"The attacker had a knife, a large knife. It was lying on the floor in the kitchen." Tommy looked away.

"Well, how's Charlie doing? He's going to be alright, isn't he?"

After a long silence, Tommy raised his head. "I couldn't

bring Charlie, Dad. When Charlie attacked the man, he stabbed him several times. I took him to the vet right away. They've done everything they can, but it's still too soon to say. I'm sorry."

The color drained from Tom's face. He turned away, burying his face in the pillow.

Tommy placed his hand on his father's shoulder and felt it quiver as he sobbed. He patted his shoulder, turned, and tiptoed away.

It was afternoon when Tom awoke. The blinds had been pulled, darkening the room. His door was cracked, letting in a thin shaft of light from the hallway. Outside the door he heard hospital sounds, carts rolling down the hallway, nurses talking, an occasional laugh, passing footsteps.

He gradually became aware of someone's presence in the semi-dark room. At first he thought his mind was playing tricks on him. But as his eyes adapted to the shadows, he picked out their shape.

His heart began to race. Had he been sent to finish the job?

Tom searched for a way to defend himself. He scanned his tray-table looking for something to use as a weapon.

Whoever lurked in the darkness seemed aware of his search.

He could not allow them to catch him unprepared again. He walked his fingers around the bed searching for the call button. He found the cord and his fingers closed around it.

He felt more secure having it in his hand even though he knew he couldn't use it. If he pressed the button, it would light up. Whoever was in the room would know he'd called for help. They could be gone before the nurse answered.

The chair squeaked.

Tom froze.

"You awake, Sarge?"

He let out a huge sigh of relief. "Yeah, I'm awake. I was afraid you were somebody come to do me harm."

Even in the dim light, Tom read the concern in Eddie's eyes. "How ya feelin', friend?"

"Better knowing it's you sitting there. How long have you been here?"

"A while."

"Charlie's badly hurt, worse than I am."

Eddie nodded. He'd talked to Tommy.

"He saved my life and it may cost him his." Tom's voice quivered. There was so much more he wanted to say, but the words wouldn't come.

When he regained his composure, he motioned Eddie closer. "I want to tell you something. I haven't told anyone else, not Tommy, not the police, not anyone."

He spent the next several minutes explaining the previous night and what his assailant said. "Don't you see, this wasn't a burglary and assault. It was attempted murder. It's somehow about the newspaper articles I've been writing."

"Sounds like ya got somebody's cream churned into butter."

"The crazy thing is, they're worried enough to kill me and I don't even know who they are."

"How's that make ya feel?"

"It only strengthens my resolve."

Eddie gave him an understanding smile. *"Was mich nicht umbringt, macht mich stärker."*

"What did you just say?"

"It was German, Nietzsche. *That which does not kill me, makes me stronger.*"

"My jacket's around here somewhere, see if you can find it." When Eddie handed it to him, Tom shoved his hand into the pocket. He smiled when his fingers brushed the corner of a small file card.

FORTY-SIX

RCI Corp. Headquarters, Palo Alto, California

Brandon Steele cast a sidelong glance at Arturo Ricetti as the elevator rose. He cleaned up pretty good, he thought, checking out Ricetti's off-the-rack suit, wingtips and pinstripe shirt.

He was trying hard to look the part, but his cheap suit wouldn't fool anyone. It screamed ex-con trying to go straight.

Steele glanced down at the business card in his hand and smiled. *Ricetti and Associates, Special Investigations*. You always added *Associates* when you had a one-man office.

The elevator doors parted. Exiting, Steele led him around and past redwood-paneled conference rooms with names like *Yosemite*, *Sequoia* and *Big Sur*.

Between a wall of windows, original paintings and greenery, they crossed the softest beige carpet Ricetti had ever felt beneath his feet. He glanced into an open office door and gave a low whistle. "Nice digs. So this is how the other half lives."

"Watch it. You haven't been hired yet."

They followed the hallway into yet another expansive room. A secretary glanced up from her computer as they approached and smiled. "Mr. Ridgely is expecting you."

Winston Ridgely leaned back in his chair as they entered, appraising the candidate. "Arturo Ricetti. That's Italian, isn't it?"

Ricetti watched him bring his fingertips together making a little tent out of them the way the prison psychologist sometimes did. "Ridgely. That's WASP, isn't it?"

Settling back, Ricetti crossed his legs, smiling when Ridgely's jaw dropped. He didn't care how much money Ridgely had; he wasn't about to let the SOB intimidate him. "So I'm a Wop and you're a WASP. What else do we have to talk about?"

Ridgely scanned his notes. "You have a criminal record,

correct?"

Ricetti lowered his eyes and examined his fingernails for a moment. "Yes sir," he said, humbly. "During the pre-release orientation they advised us to never try and cover it up when applying for employment. A thorough background check usually turns it up, providing an employer with sufficient reason not to hire us." He smiled. "I always say, honesty is the best policy."

Clearly agitated, Ridgely shuffled and reshuffled the papers spread out on the desk. A person sitting in the chair across from him usually groveled.

Seeing that he had him off balance, Ricetti decided to take control of the conversation. He jerked a thumb at the man beside him. "Steele here tells me you want someone to do surveillance. You're offering pretty good money just to have somebody sit in a car and drink coffee all day."

"We need someone who can be discrete."

"Discretion is my middle name and my bladder is as strong as anyone's. What else are you looking for?"

"I don't understand. I thought Mr. Steele provided you with a job description along with a complete outline of our expectations."

"He did. If that's all you want, I'm your boy."

"You sound as if you think there's something we're not telling you."

"There always is." Ricetti picked up the single sheet of paper he'd gotten from Steele and snapped it with his finger. He turned it over and waved the blank side in Ridgely's direction. "Where's the rest? I want to know what's not on this page."

"I don't understand what you mean."

"Something's missing. What has this Jenkins guy got on you? Did he catch you with your hand in the till or in some hooker's underpants?"

Ridgely bristled. "We're not talking about one of your hoodlum friends. Mr. Jenkins happens to be a newspaper publisher, a respected member of his community and a successful businessman."

"Someone just like you in other words."

The muscles in Ridgely's jaw tightened.

Ricetti glanced over at Steele. "Bit touchy, ain't he."

Returning his attention to Ridgely, Ricetti said, "So this Jenkins guy is a pillar of the community, but you need someone to keep tabs on him just in case he goes a bit crazy and takes up jaywalking."

Ridgely pushed the papers to one side, rose, and extended his hand across the desk. "Thank you for your time, Mr. Ricetti. I'd like to confer privately with Mr. Steele for a few moments. You can wait here, if you don't mind."

Ricetti nodded.

The conference room door had barely closed behind them when Ridgely snarled, "I don't like him."

"Calm down, Win. You don't have to like him. I'm asking you to hire him, not marry him."

"I don't want him working on this project. It's too sensitive. He'll get us in trouble, I can feel it."

Steele took a deep breath. "He's a two-bit mobster, so what? You severely limited our options when you decided to take the *Paradise Voyager* hostage. Once Ricetti figures out why we're interested in Jenkins—."

"Keep him on a need-to-know basis."

Brandon Steele looked across the conference table and shook his head. "The man's not the fool you'd like to believe he is. Trust me, he *will* figure it out. And when he does, he won't go running to the authorities like some misguided Boy Scout."

"That doesn't make me like him."

"I promise you, he'll leave here today and go about the work we want him to do. You never have to interact with him again."

Ricetti watched the two men file back into the room. "You don't look so happy, Mr. Ridgely."

"You're an astute observer of human nature."

"Let me guess. You and Mr. Steele have been disagreeing about the advisability of contracting with Ricetti and Associates, am I right?"

"Yes you are."

"You said that I lacked," he rocked his hand in the air, "uh, polish...finesse."

"You do."

Ricetti leaned forward. Resting his forearm on Ridgley's desk, he looked him straight in the eye. "I didn't try to impress the warden at Lompoc Prison and I'm sure as hell not going to try to brown nose you."

"In other words, you're saying you're not interested?"

"Interested? Of course, I'm interested. I wouldn't have come all the way from LA if I wasn't interested."

"We haven't offered you the job yet."

"Steele made that decision when he picked up the phone and called me. The last Bozo you hired dropped the ball and you want me to go in and pick up the pieces."

"You have no idea what you're talking about."

"Don't I? You know, Mr. Ridgely...Win, I don't have any fancy degrees from some high-priced college. I don't have a big house, or a yacht, or much else for that matter. I'm just a workin' stiff trying to get by. But there is one thing I do have."

"And what would that be?"

"An inquisitive mind. The last guy you hired didn't. He was supposed to kill Jenkins, but he wasn't smart enough to check ahead and find out about the dog. Fortunately for him, the dog didn't have him for dinner, at least not all of him. By the way, how's his recovery coming along?"

"I don't know who you're referring to."

Ricetti studied him for a minute then grinned. "Let me give you a piece of advice. Don't ever get on the witness stand, you don't lie so good. I did some more checking. Jenkins' wife and granddaughter were aboard a cruise ship that mysteriously disappeared. Interesting co-incidence, don't you think?"

"It's just more speculation on your part."

"Most likely there's no connection," Ricetti said, nodding. "Then there are these newspaper articles Jenkins has been writing. Just another co-incidence, I'm sure, but what if I shared those speculations with the authorities?"

Ridgely's face went slack. His mouth opened a little as if he was going to speak, but no words came out.

Ricetti looked from Ridgely to Steele and back again. "I can read people and what I read here is that you want me in the worst way. Matter of fact, you *need* me."

"What on earth would make you say that?"

"As I said, I can read people's faces. I'm not exactly sure what you and Steele are up to yet, but somebody's got you by the short hairs. You've had your hands in the cookie jar and you don't want to get caught with crumbs on your fingers."

"None of what you've said makes sense."

Ricetti uncrossed his legs and sat up straight. "Doesn't it? Then tell me why didn't you call a reputable agency? There are plenty of them in the Yellow Pages. Or could it be that they draw the line at becoming an accessory after the fact?"

"I recommended you for this job," Steele said. "I...uh, I felt it was an opportunity for rehabilitation that you would welcome. However, if you're not interested..."

"I said I was interested, already. I just want to know what's expected." Ricetti picked up the single-sheet outline and shook it again.

"Everything is on a need-to-know basis," Ridgely said.

"Fine. I need to know, why me? Maybe it's because down

the road you're going to want a little persuasion applied, although you haven't said so. Or is it because this Jenkins character isn't the upstanding citizen you've portrayed him to be? Or perhaps you just like working on a cash basis with no records? Now why would that be?"

Ridgely slammed his hand down on the desk. "Do you want the job or not?"

"Sure. Now let's get to the important part. I can and will do whatever you want done. But I'm cock of the walk right now and I don't come cheap. Understand?"

Ridgely jerked open his desk drawer. He pulled out an envelope and threw it onto the desktop. The fat envelope spun in circles as it slid over the highly polished surface.

Ricetti watched its progress with apparent disinterest. Just before it dropped off the edge, his finger flew out and pinned it. He opened his suit coat and slipped the envelope of cash into his breast pocket. When he removed his hand, he patted the left side of his chest and smiled at Ridgely. He rose and extended his hand across the desk.

"Thank you for choosing Ricetti and Associates, you won't regret it."

"Jenkins will be your primary concern," Ridgely said, "but there's someone else we'd like you to watch for."

"No problem, who is it?"

"A Dr. Maheshwari. If he were to show up in Pine Crest, I'd want to know immediately."

"I'll keep my eyes open. Maheshwari? Is this guy like a raghead, or something?"

"No, he's not a raghead," Steele said. "He's a former RCI employee. I'll provide you with a photo."

"What's he done? No, never mind." Ricetti spread his hands in front of his chest and waved them back and forth. "I know, I know, it's all on a need-to-know basis. He must be another one of those upstanding citizens you keep running into."

FORTY-SEVEN

Pine Crest, Oregon

After one day's rest at Tommy's, Tom returned to the office. The questions surrounding the card with the Jeremiah quote remained unresolved. And, though Beth had done an excellent job of cleaning up the laundry room and kitchen, he was too restless to remain at home.

The Vet continued to tell him it was still too soon to know what Charlie's condition would be when, and if, he recovered.

"Tommy's out on ad calls," Darlene said when Tom walked in. "Guess it's just you and me this morning, Mr. J."

Tom crossed the small lobby and shoved the swinging gate aside without replying.

He sat down at his desk, looked around and shrugged. He hardly knew what was going on here anymore. He picked up a stack of notes he'd made for future articles, rifled through them and tossed them into the wastebasket. He checked his pencils, sharpening any that needed it. He was aligning his In-Basket with the edge of his computer when Darlene interrupted him.

"Sorry to bother you. I know you're busy and all, but the UPS lady is here with a package. She says you have to sign for it."

A woman in a brown uniform waited behind Darlene with a small box in one hand and a brown, rectangular pad in the other.

"The box isn't ticking, is it?" Tom asked.

The driver smiled and shook her head. After scanning the package's barcode with her register, she put it in front of Tom for an electronic signature. "Just use the stylus there on top."

He scrawled his signature in the designated box. "What is this thing?"

"It's my DIAD. That's an acronym for Delivery Information Acquisition Device. It tracks the package and confirms delivery."

"Neat!" Darlene said. "That's what lets me go online and

check the status of a package."

"Yep. When I get back in my truck, I'll plug it in and it automatically uploads your information to the company's mainframe via satellite. A little while later, it's on the website for the whole world to see." She handed him the small box. "Gotta run, have a good day."

"What do you think it is?" Darlene asked.

Tom shook the box. "It doesn't rattle, that's a good sign."

"Who is it from?"

Tom spun the package around and examined the label. "No name. It came from one of those mailbox and shipping centers in San Francisco."

His hand began to tremble. Jeremiah's card was also postmarked San Francisco. He grabbed a letter opener and slit the tape. The box contained a cheap cell phone along with a note.

The phone's charged. Turn it on. I'll call as soon as
I know you have it.   Jeremiah.

Tom turned the phone on, sat it on the corner of his desk and went into the back to pour some coffee. When he returned, he looked from the phone to Darlene.

"Did it ring?

"Not yet."

"Well let's see, the driver said she uploads the data real time." He checked his watch. "It's 9:25 now. A nickel says it doesn't ring before 9:30."

"You're on."

The deadline passed in silence. "What say we make it double or nothing? It rings by 9:35 or I owe you a dime."

For the next hour, Tom and Darlene took turns making penny ante wagers on what the phone was going to do. Both of them consistently bet *ring* and both of them consistently lost.

Finally Tom reached in his wallet and took out a ten-dollar

bill. "It's an elaborate practical joke. Ten bucks says it sits there until the battery dies."

He slapped the bill down on the corner of his desk, leaned back in his chair and put his feet up on the desk. He'd barely gotten comfortable when the little phone chirped.

He swung his feet off the desk. "Why didn't I look to see how this thing worked?" He snatched the phone off the desk, studied it for a moment, and punched a button.

"Hello."

Darlene tiptoed over and lifted the ten off the desk. After precisely folding the bill several times, she smiled and slipped it into her pocket.

"Thomas Jenkins?" a woman's voice asked.

"This is Tom. Who's calling?"

"For now, let's just say it's Jeremiah."

"Funny, you don't sound like a Jeremiah ought to sound. You seem to lack the...how can I put it, the hormones? Isn't it some kind of a sin to impersonate a prophet?"

"The card was designed to pique your interest. If this is going to work, you're going to have to trust me."

"Sorry to disappoint you, Sister, but my supply of trust is pretty well tapped out. You sound awfully young. Does your Mother know what you do when she's at work?"

It never occurred to Shiri that she might have trouble making Tom believe her. She glanced over at Derek.

He smiled and tentatively raised a thumb in the air.

She shook her head and his smile wilted.

"Why the cell phone?"

"I needed a secure line. I didn't want to risk using your home or office phone. You know, Mr. Jenkins, Paradise Getaways had nothing to do with the disappearance of the *Voyager*."

"I know that all too well. But how do *you* know they didn't?"

"The man who knows what happened is sitting right beside

me."

"Who are you, what do you want?"

"We want what you want: your wife and granddaughter safely back home."

"How do I know this isn't an elaborate prank?" he asked, praying it wasn't.

"I don't have time for pranks and neither do you. Please don't make this any harder than it already is." Shiri's tone made Tom want to believe her. "The two of you have a lot to talk about."

"Fine, put him on. I have all morning."

"Not yet. Let me explain our situation. My friend wants to meet with you face-to-face. Believe me when I say his life is in danger. Your meeting entails great risk for you both. Exercise extreme caution at all times. Most likely, someone is watching you. Assume they're also following you. If they learn of this, it will jeopardize not only my friend's life, but your wife and granddaughter's safety."

"They? Who are they? Why do you have to use this cloak and dagger routine?"

"We wouldn't be doing it this way if we didn't think it was necessary."

Tom ran his fingers along his ribcage. "How do I know this isn't some kind of a trap?"

"You're cautious, Mr. Jenkins. That's good. Trust, however, is also necessary."

"What is it you want from me?"

"I've already told you, the only thing I want from you is your cooperation."

"You say that as if I had a choice."

"Of course you do. Your wife is the one without a choice. She's counting on you. You, in turn, must count on us. It's hard to solve a puzzle when you don't have all the pieces."

The words of Jeremiah 33:3 echoed in Tom's mind. "What

pieces do you have to add to the puzzle, Jeremiah? What is it that I knowest not?"

Shiri chuckled. It wasn't a derisive or condescending laugh. Rather, it was the happy acknowledgement that he was beginning to come around.

Tom desperately wished he shared her confidence.

Shiri gave Derek a big thumbs-up. "A few more details, my friend will require a safe place to stay. Not your house, it's too obvious, and clearly not a motel. Is this a problem?"

"No, I have someone who can put him up. He lives out in the country. When do you want to meet?"

"How about tonight...say around midnight?"

Tom reached for a pencil and paper. "Where?"

"We'll be coming up from San Francisco. The Lakeshead Rest Area off of I-5 at Mt. Shasta is about halfway between. How's that?"

"I'll be there."

"There's an auto-adapter for the phone in the box I sent. Plug it in and keep the phone turned on while you're driving. If anything changes, you'll hear from me. And Mr. Jenkins, may I suggest it would be best to leave Pine Crest in the daylight? It will be easier to tell if you're being followed."

When asked, Tom gave her the make, model, color and license number of his car. Shiri, in return, provided the same information. There seemed to be little left to do.

"Thank you, Mr. Jenkins. I promise you won't regret it. My friend thanks you too. Have a safe trip."

Tom stared at the phone in his hand for several minutes after she hung up. Returning the phone to its box, he picked up his jacket and crossed the office.

With his hand on the doorknob, he glanced back at Darlene. "I'm going to be out for the rest of the day. Don't expect me tomorrow either."

FORTY-EIGHT

Lakehead Rest Area, Shasta County, California

Following Shiri's suggestion, Tom left Pine Crest in the afternoon. He circled aimlessly for a time making certain he wasn't followed then drove to Eddie's. They ate an early supper and made arrangements for Derek's stay. Facing a five-hour drive, Tom headed south towards Roseburg and I-5 around six. Other than the usual log trucks and chip haulers he encountered very little traffic.

Tom pulled into the rest area, parked in the middle of a group of empty slots and shut the engine off. Despite the late hour, the rest stop remained busy. Big rigs with loads scheduled for deliveries in Portland the following morning jockeyed in and out continuously. He reclined his seat slightly and cracked the window for fresh air while he waited.

Derek and Shiri arrived about 30 minutes later. Once they established each other's identity, the transfer went quickly and without incident. After Derek stowed his luggage into the back of Tom's van, he and Shiri talked quietly.

She reached up and hugged him. "Be very careful. Let me know how things are going. You can call me on the cell phone I sent to Mr. Jenkins. Good luck."

Derek thanked her and walked around to the passenger's door. He climbed into the van with Tom and extended his hand. "Mr. Jenkins, I trust you had a satisfactory trip. It is so good of you to come this long way. Hopefully, you will not feel it is time wasted."

"I am Dwarakananth Maheshwari," he said, as they shook hands, "but everyone calls me Derek." He clasped Tom's hand tightly with both of his. "I have been looking forward to our meeting with great anticipation."

Tom checked the traffic and slowly backed out. "By the way, Derek, it isn't necessary to call me Mister. Most people call me Tom."

Derek smiled broadly, flashing white teeth. "Excuse me. Of course no such formality is necessary, Thomas."

"You seem to know something about me, so tell me about yourself."

"Where to start, where to start," Derek wondered aloud as they drove north. "As you can tell, I am clearly Indian. My wife and children still reside there, in fact. My training is in theoretical physics. I held a university post prior to being hired by RCI in Palo Alto, California."

"And you're still working for RCI?"

"No, our paths have diverged. Mr. Winston Ridgely and I had a serious falling out, a disagreement on a...a very important subject."

"So you quit."

"More than that, I must confess to you that I am a wanted fugitive, pursued as a criminal and hunted as a terrorist, if you can believe it. *Me*. But that is a story for another time. Are you at all familiar with RCI?"

Tom wasn't.

Derek spent the next hour giving Tom details about RCI's operations. When he finished, both men retreated into their own thoughts. Several miles later Derek broke the silence.

"I congratulate you on the articles you have written. I read them all. The pen can indeed prove mightier than the sword."

"How do you know all this?"

"I have followed your exploits with great interest, cheering you on from the bench, as it were. You know, regardless of how it may feel or appear at the time, we seldom act alone in this world."

"I appreciate your interest, but my efforts haven't gotten me any closer to my ultimate goal."

"Ah yes, the supreme goal, the restoration of your lovely wife and precious granddaughter."

Tom nodded. "Yet throughout it all, I've had a nearly

indescribable sense of expectation. I've felt as if something of great significance is about to happen."

The headlights of an approaching truck illuminated the van's interior. As the semi drew closer, it swung into the adjacent lane to pass. Tom glanced over at his passenger.

Derek held up two crossed fingers. Despite the roar of the passing semi, the car became eerily quiet. "Your feelings are correct, Thomas. It could be no other way. It was our destiny, our Karma...Kismet. That is why the universe has brought us together on this night. Your fate and mine, you see, are as closely intertwined as mating cobras."

Beltzer Property, Rural Pine Crest, Oregon

Tom followed I-5 north back into Oregon. Exiting at Roseburg, he headed north and west to the Old Wagon Road. The sun broke over the horizon as they wound through the foothills.

"Here comes Eddie's place." Tom lifted his foot off of the accelerator, letting the rise of the road slow the car's progress. When an opening in the trees appeared, he applied the brake and quickly turned onto a gravel drive.

It was indistinguishable from any of a dozen abandoned logging roads they'd passed. Only the presence of a rusting mailbox on a weather-beaten post gave the faint promise that, unlike those logging roads, these well-worn ruts actually went somewhere.

Salal, huckleberry, Oregon grape, and holly competed for space on both sides of the drive. They extended long tendrils into the sunlight like prisoners stretching their arms out between their cell bars. Further back, ferns grew luxuriantly in the shade of tall firs, hemlocks and spruce. Here and there, a ghostly white trunk identified one of the few surviving alders in this sea of green shadows.

When they crested the hill the driveway opened onto a wide plateau. Eddie was in a fenced pasture spreading a swath of cattle feed. White-faced cows and their half-grown calves lined up, heads to the ground. Like children, some of the calves broke away from the group to play. Their mothers, preferring to eat, ignored the youngsters as they bumped and butted each other.

Hearing the sound of their wheels on the gravel, Eddie glanced back over his shoulder and waved.

"He's finishing up, let's get out and stretch our legs," Tom said.

Eddie's log home lay fifty yards ahead. He'd constructed it himself from second-growth timber logged on site. Though modest in design, the house was sturdy and well cared for. Its blue metal roof extended over a wide porch that wrapped around the front and east side. A stone chimney on the west wall vented the living room's fireplace, and matching dormers identified two upstairs bedrooms.

Being on a high plateau, Eddie had an unobstructed view of the Cascade Range. Rows of snow-capped peaks followed one after the other, marching toward the eastern horizon. Very few people in town even knew this place existed. It offered an ideal hideaway for Derek.

Tom pulled the gate back and Eddie chugged through on his ATV, rolling to a stop beside the two men. He shut it down and climbed off.

Lifting his John Deere cap, Eddie wiped his forehead on a sleeve as he approached them. He removed a leather glove and extended his hand. "How ya doin,' I'm Eddie Beltzer."

"It is a pleasure to meet you, Mr. Beltzer. Thomas speaks highly of you."

He shook his head. "Mr. Beltzer was my father."

"Indeed. If he were not, it would have no doubt proven a great embarrassment for your mother."

Eddie's mouth dropped for a moment. Then he grinned and laughed out loud.

Derek took a few steps forward and rested his hands on his hips. Slowly rocking back on heels, he studied the house and the mountains beyond. "This is a lovely homestead you have here. Quite isolated, too."

Eddie pointed to the tall trees framing the meadow. "Built it myself; cut the logs right up there in those woods."

"Alone? You did all this with no help from others?"

Eddie grinned with pride and nodded. "Yep, by myself."

"It must have been a difficult task."

"Whenever I needed somebody on the other end of a board, I'd call Tom. He and his boy, Tommy, spent more than one weekend helpin' out. But ya'd be surprised how much a body can accomplish with just a chainsaw, a come-along, and the ol' Johnny Popper."

Derek swept his eyes across the panorama while he contemplated Eddie's words. "All this, and to think you did it with just a chainsaw, a come-along, and the old Johnny Popper." After a long pause, he turned and stared at Eddie straight on. "And what, Mr. Beltzer, is a come-along and the old Johnny Popper?"

Eddie threw an arm over Derek's shoulder. "My friend, *come along* with me and I'll show ya."

Leaving Tom beside the car, he led Derek to the barn. Eddie swung the door aside and they stepped into its dark interior. The stale air trapped inside the barn rushed to greet them. It was heavy with the pungent smell of livestock and the grassy scent of hay.

When his eyes adapted to the muted light, Derek glanced around. The barn was framed with large, rough-sawn timbers. He slapped an 8 x 8 post. "Did you also cut these timbers yourself?"

Eddie answered by pointing to a large, tarp-covered lump against the wall. "That gizmo over there is a portable sawmill."

He raised the tarp and explained its operation. "See, ya skid your logs to an open area 'n' transport 'em to this mill. Then ya take your peavey," Eddie pointed to a long-handled tool with metal point and hinged hook, "'n' coax the log up onto this track. The chain drive advances the log into the saw's blade. A slab drops off and one side's square. Pull the log back, flip it over 90 degrees and run it through again. Keep it up and before ya know it, the whole log is trued up."

"It is quite an interesting process. You are very clever indeed."

"I only bought the machine. The guy who invented it was the clever one." Eddie pointed up at the beams and rafters above them. "Once your log is squared, ya can cut it down into boards or leave it as a dressed timber like those."

He scanned the barn for a moment then pointed to a post several yards away. "There's what we came to see."

"What is it?"

"Why the come-along, of course."

Derek examined it for a moment. "It resembles a hand-powered winch with a ratcheted brake."

"Yeah, small world ain't it? Hook that sucker onto something, crank the handle and I guarantee it *will* come along. There are only two things to keep in mind."

"And what would they be?"

"First, the cable has to be stout enough for the job at hand. And second, whatever you anchor it to better be bigger than what you're tryin' t' move. With a big enough come-along and somethin' t' anchor it to, I could move just about anything." Eddie thought about what he'd said and chuckled. "Kinda sound like Archimedes, don't I?"

Derek smiled. "Ah yes, Archimedes and his celebrated lever. *'Give me a place to stand and I will move the earth.'*"

"Over here is our last exhibit, the infamous Johnny Popper." Eddie walked to the other wall and tapped the hood of an old green tractor with bright yellow wheels.

"I see the words *John Deere*, but why is it called a Popper?"

"That comes from the sound it makes when it's runnin'. Here, give a listen." Eddie clambered into the driver's seat and started the engine, letting it idle for a short time.

"I heard the popping sound, but why?"

"It has a 4-stroke engine. During the course of two revolutions, the first cylinder fires at 0 degrees and the second one at 180. Then the engine coasts 540 degrees until it fires again, beginning the next cycle."

"One would be tempted to suggest you fire each cylinder at 360 degrees and even out the power stroke."

"And if one did that, one would have the crankshaft throws for both pistons on the same side of the crankshaft at the same time. It'd buck and rock like a one-cylinder. Alternatin' the pistons allows it t' run smoother."

"I sense you have a certain affection for this machine."

"I suppose I do. It's just like the one my Daddy had when I was a boy. The two of us broke it down for repairs more times than I can count. Most of what I know about mechanics I learned at his side workin' on that Model 50."

He leaned his elbow against the tractor and poked up the brim of his hat. "Tom didn't say much. Just that ya had connections to the *Paradise Voyager*. Where do ya fit into this picture?"

Derek glanced around the barn nervously. He brought his hand together, lowered his eyes and confessed, "I am the dastardly villain who made the *Paradise Voyager* disappear."

"You're jokin' with me, right? Havin' a little fun with ol' Eddie?"

Derek sadly shook his head. "How I wish that were the case, but unfortunately it is not."

FORTY-NINE

On their way back from the barn, Derek stopped at the car and removed his luggage. Once inside the house, he carried a rectangular metal container into the kitchen.

"Looks pretty important," Eddie said. "What's in there?"

"It contains my spices and teas. Do you have milk available in your home?"

When Eddie assured him he did, Derek requested a pan, measuring spoons, and a teapot.

Eddie peered over Derek's shoulder. "Whatcha gonna make there?"

Derek arranged the items on a small side counter as Eddie handed them to him. "My contribution to our breakfast will be ready in a few minutes."

Tom watched Derek pour an aromatic liquid the color of heavily creamed coffee into his cup. "What is it that you're pouring?"

"It is Chai, Indian milk tea...ambrosia to share with my new friends."

Eddie sniffed his cup. "Smells kinda spicy."

"Indeed it is. It is an old family recipe. I brought my own tea and spices with me. You know, we Indians never stray far from our spice chests."

Derek waited expectantly as the two men took their first sips.

Tom nodded in appreciation. "Very good, what spices do you use?"

"You must, of course, begin with fine Darjeeling tea. The spices are a special blend of fennel seed, green cardamom pods, cinnamon, cloves, ginger root and a hint, just a hint, of black peppercorns. Add milk, sweeten with honey and there you have it."

Derek raised his cup, took a sip and returned it to its saucer. "I will share the recipe with you both, but it must remain our little secret. Grandmother can never hear of it."

Tired from a night of driving, Tom and Derek sipped Chai while Eddie cleared the breakfast dishes. He slipped the last plate into the dishwasher and glanced over at Tom. "How come ya didn't tell me Derek was the one who made the ship disappear."

Both men's cups clattered to the tabletop. A large, tan lake formed between them.

Tom's eyes narrowed. He glared at the Indian scientist sitting across from him.

Derek's eyes skittered around the room like a frightened colt.

"Where did you hear that?" Tom asked through clenched teeth.

Eddie shrugged. "He told me out in the barn. Figured ya already knew. Now I'm guessin' ya didn't." He righted the cups and began mopping the table with a dishtowel. "Let's take it easy on the crockery, fellas. The owner of this establishment prefers not to have his dishes broken."

Tom found himself wondering if Derek's culpability was the great and mighty answer Jeremiah promised. "Why didn't this salient piece of information come up on our drive?"

Derek stared up at the open ceiling as if the words he searched for were written on the joists. He folded and refolded his hands. "Do not hate me, Thomas. I am a contemptible coward who allowed two large men with guns and ropes to overpower him."

Eddie's laughter diffused the tension in the room. "There now, aren't we all glad to have that out 'n' on the table? See, confession's good for the soul." He carried their cups back to the sink, shaking his head and chuckling.

"I'm only interested in facts," Tom said. "The facts and

bringing my family home safely."

Derek stared at the tabletop. "Before I can say the things I've come to say, I must wipe the slate clean. I have already confessed to being a fugitive, a wanted man. Mr. Beltzer is correct; I had a part in those shameful events, an unwitting part, to be sure, but a part nonetheless. In retrospect, I feel I failed to exhibit bravery equal to yours. I hope you can find it in your heart to forgive me. I haven't been able to forgive myself."

"Let's put it aside for the time being and hear what you came to say."

Derek took a deep breath and let it out slowly. "You recall on the trip I mentioned I was employed by the firm, RCI and their involvement in sensitive work for the United States Navy. Only a handful of people knew of my research. We were developing, uh, for now let's simply call it advanced stealth technology. May I diverge momentarily?"

Tom told him to take whatever path he liked so long as it led to the desired destination.

Rising, Derek began to pace the room. "Let me pose a scenario."

Eddie turned and leaned back with his elbows resting on the counter.

"Imagine you are a high official in the United States Navy. You have a number of aircraft carriers under your command. They're marvelously ingenious tools when it comes to waging war and quite adaptable. They come equipped with the latest attack aircraft which can take-off and land right on top of the deck. They have guns, missiles and who knows what else. As if that were not enough, you can also deploy them wherever and whenever circumstances warrant. As a commander this makes you feel rather secure, correct?"

Tom wasn't certain where he was going with this story, but he could agree aircraft carriers were definitely nice things to have around.

Next, Derek pointed out the downside. "All aircraft carriers share a similar weakness, their heel of Achilles, if you will. By their very nature, they are big, relatively slow moving and highly vulnerable. The Japanese learned this bitter lesson during World War II. All told, they lost 17 aircraft carriers, including the *Shinano*."

Eddie rose from the slouch he'd been in. "I remember seein' somethin' about it on the History Channel. Seems like, it was the largest carrier ever built at the time. That sucker was only in the water ten days when a single American sub sank it."

"Did your television program also say the *Shinano* had extra armor to defend against torpedoes and was considered unsinkable? Weaponry has advanced tremendously since World War II, but a laser-guided torpedo or cruise missile is not necessary. Kamikaze fighters inflicted enormous damage on American warships."

Derek sat back down. He lifted the teapot and gave Eddie an imploring look.

He took down some cups from the sideboard and sat them in front of him. "Treat 'em nice and gentle or I'm gonna start chargin' a security deposit."

Tom frowned. "First you tell us how valuable aircraft carriers are and in the very next breath you tell us they're worthless. Which is it?"

"Both. That is the conundrum," Derek said after a sip of Chai.

"This is all relevant military information, but my wife wasn't on an aircraft carrier. She and Ellie were on a somewhat smaller cruise ship with no Kamikazes in sight."

"I have one final proposition for you to consider. Suppose again you are my mythical naval commander, only now you could make your aircraft carriers disappear at will?" He made a quick sweep with his hand. "Wipe them away, mask them with stealth technology. Would this be of strategic benefit?" Derek folded his arms to await their reply.

He'd captured their full attention by suggesting aircraft

carriers could disappear. As unbelievable as it sounded, he discussed it matter-of-factly. Tom decided Derek either knew what he was talking about or he was so crazy he shouldn't be out wandering the streets. An incoherent jumble of unrelated puzzle pieces clicked together in his mind.

"So, you're telling us you can make aircraft carriers appear and disappear at will, whenever you want?"

Derek raised his hand. "That is not what I said. If you recall, this began as a theoretical discussion. I was attempting to illustrate why the United States Navy would be interested in possessing such a technology. And, if the United States Navy is interested in possessing something, RCI is equally interested in developing it for them."

"How does this stealth technology you're talkin' about work?" Eddie asked. "It's still pretty new stuff, right?"

"The specific details of my work are far beyond this morning's discussion. Its foundation rests on some of Einstein's later work. It also incorporates electromagnetic fields, particle physics, and other sophisticated concepts including advanced metallurgy and polymer science." He spread his arms in a hopeless shrug.

"As for being new," Derek's hands returned to the table, "I would say yes and I would say no. The earliest research in this area began in the 1930's. Your military saw a war coming and moved in many directions. Everyone's heard of the Manhattan Project, of course, because it yielded the atomic bomb. Some of the unsuccessful programs are, shall we say, slightly less famous."

FIFTY

"What led you to this invisibility stuff?" Tom asked

"Several years ago I was waiting to board a flight. It was early, but already intensely hot. To pass the time, I watched waves of heat shimmer above the tarmac. In the distance, I noticed the disembodied tail of a British Airways jet floating above the dry grass as it awaited take off. As a physicist, I could not help but be intrigued."

"You're describin' a mirage, right?"

"Yes. Mirages are a well-known and easily explained phenomenon. It was the mirage's ability to fool the eye that intrigued me. Throughout my long flight to Europe, I conducted what Einstein called a *Gedankenexperiment*, that is, a thought experiment."

"And what did these experiments tell you?" Tom asked.

"They told me that if the refractivity and light absorption quotient of solid materials could be controlled and manipulated, then solid objects could become invisible."

Tom and Eddie exchanged a shocked look.

Derek outlined the brief history of electronic camouflage that ultimately facilitated the B-1 stealth bomber. The B-1, he said, relied upon what he termed radar stealth. That is, the plane is essentially invisible on a radar screen. The Holy Grail would be to not only make it undetectable by radar, but also by the human eye....truly invisible.

"In a general sense, are you understanding what I am saying?"

"I guess," Tom said warily. "It seems like we're getting pretty far out there.

Derek smiled at the implied compliment. "Welcome to the frontiers of theoretical physics, gentlemen."

Tom and Eddie still had a hard time accepting what Derek

told them. "Why haven't I ever heard anything about this stuff?" Tom asked. "I'm in the newspaper business; I should know."

"None of the earliest experiments resulted in useful prototypes. No Government enjoys discussing its failures. Over a thousand sailors were lost the day the *Shinano* sank, but the military never told the Japanese people. It only came to light after the War."

Tom's skepticism placed him in a very uncomfortable position. Clearly someone considered Derek credible. If he rejected the things he said, what implications did that have for Marty? "I want to believe you, I really do. It's just that your ideas seem unbelievable."

"Suppose we approach it from a different angle. Have either of you heard of events occurring in Roswell, New Mexico in, oh say, July, 1947?"

"Of course, everyone has."

"What happened?"

Tom rubbed his chin. "Well, some people say a spacecraft crashed. Supposedly, they recovered the remains of several aliens and they're still in a deepfreeze at Wright-Patterson Air Force Base. Personally, I don't believe it."

"But you are willing to acknowledge that *something* happened in Roswell in 1947. Perhaps it was a UFO, perhaps it was a weather balloon, and perhaps it was neither. You simply don't know precisely *what* happened. Am I correct?"

Tom nodded.

"Would you also agree that it's possible for a Government to cover up events by classifying information, blurring records, conducting misinformation campaigns and so on?" Derek's raised hand stifled Tom's reply. "Keep in mind we both know these things have occurred in other circumstances."

"You're right. I can either reject something, about which I know nothing at all, or I can keep an open mind." Tom lifted his eyebrows and smiled. "Okay, you win. I won't reject the possibility of what you've been telling us, at least not yet."

Derek picked up the teapot and shook it. "I'm afraid we've exhausted our supply of Chai. Were it not for that, I would suggest we toast our breakthrough. As you have seen, one cup demands another and then another. One never overcomes their need for more Chai. You are hooked my friends. Coffee pales by comparison."

Eddie cleared his throat. "Both of ya have been up all night and I got work t' do outside. How 'bout we break it off here? You two take a nice long nap 'n' we'll pick it up this afternoon."

It seemed like a sensible idea. Tom eased himself out of the chair, yawned and stretched.

As he did, Derek touched his arm. "Thomas," he whispered, "the time to turn back has long since passed. Earlier I spoke of Chai, now I speak of life. I promise, when all is said and done, you will not regret your decision to bring me here."

FIFTY-ONE

Tom returned late that afternoon and sat a pair of large white sacks on the counter. "I brought supper."

"How did you sleep Thomas?" Derek asked as they dished up the Chinese carryout.

"Better than expected." Tom remained eager to pick-up where they'd left off. "This morning, we left an awful lot of unfinished business. You implied the test wouldn't injure anyone aboard the *Paradise Voyager*. How do you know that?"

"We performed many prior tests on small animals, carefully monitoring the effects upon living tissue. Testing it on larger life forms was a future goal, but Mr. Ridgely accelerated the research schedule without warning." Derek gave him a reassuring smile. "Regardless, I remain confident there will be no lasting biological impact."

"You're hedging."

Derek put down his chopsticks. "I certainly am not. You and I both know there are no guarantees in life. For goodness sake, Thomas, a certain amount of trust is required here."

"So you're saying no one should have been injured based on your previous research."

"And we won't know more until we attempt to reverse the process," Derek added.

Tom favored conversation over fried rice. "And the process is reversible? You've done it before?"

"Countless times. What use would the technology have if its effects could not be undone?"

"Then why didn't you just flip the reverse switch and fix everything right then and there?"

"There are two reasons it was not done, one good and one bad." Derek cut a chunk of deep fried tofu into pieces, dipped one in sauce, and ate it.

"We had previously worked with laboratory animals, rabbits, not people. I felt it would be foolhardy to risk possible injury by attempting to immediately reverse the procedure. Mr. Ridgely, on the other hand, cared nothing for the victims of his perfidy and everything for his pocketbook. To reverse it would require admitting our mistake, which he did not wish to do since it would also result in negative publicity, lawsuits, and lower stock prices."

"So the lives of those people never meant anything to him?"

Derek shrugged. "A more charitable view might conclude the company felt it better to admit their mistake *after* the problem was corrected. Either way, your hypothesis remains valid."

Tom snapped his fingers. "Of course, it makes perfect sense. Correct the problem and *then* announce its existence. Sort of like a nuclear power plant calling a press conference to say, 'We had a big problem last weekend, but don't worry it's all fixed now.'"

"And, if things do not work out as intended, you still retain the option of covering it up. We cannot be certain how much, if any, recollection the people on the ship will have of the event."

Eddie, who'd been listening quietly, said, "In a best case scenario, no one remembers a thing. Then it never even happened. So, why haven't they done that?"

"They have not done so because Mr. Winston Ridgely devised an even better strategy."

"Which is?"

"Do not awaken the dogs when they are sleeping. In spite of all the media coverage about the disappearance of the *Paradise Voyager*, RCI's part in this fiasco remains hidden. Why should he rock the boat? No pun intended."

"So, in other words, Marty was more than likely not injured. And RCI could bring her back, but Ridgely decided it'd be more beneficial for him if they didn't."

"You have summarized it very well."

"Okay, what's it like t' be sittin' in an invisibility cloud day after day?"

"We have no way of knowing. The only ones to undergo the process were Kaur's rabbits. Unfortunately, they've never been forthcoming about the details of their experiences." Derek rested his elbows on the table. "I see my words have upset you once again, Thomas."

"You've just told me my wife and granddaughter could be in excruciating pain. How can you expect me not to be upset?"

"You have posited the worst case scenario, which is highly unlikely." Derek raised three fingers. "The process can be viewed as three discrete events. Let us examine them individually. First it must be activated. This may have been stressful since the people aboard the ship had no prior warning. I said stressful, not painful. The rabbits never exhibited any physical trauma and were anesthetized to avoid stress. This portion of the process lasts only seconds, not even a minute. It may also have been disorienting; we have no way of knowing."

Tom gave a confirming nod.

"Let us now consider the reversal process. The people aboard the ship have yet to undergo this, however, it too lasts only a very short time. My guess is that it may also produce temporary confusion or disorientation. After all, people who take long flights suffer from jet lag and those taking a sea cruise must develop their sea legs and then re-orient themselves to solid ground when they dock."

"So far, you've made it seem very manageable. But their time isn't spent coming and going. You've yet to mention the prolonged period of...of, whatever you want to call it," Tom said.

"It is the most difficult to address." Derek looked from one man to the other. "Are you familiar both with what is known as the time paradox?"

"Ya mean the guys on the theoretical spaceship and the folks who stayed home?"

"I do. It is the classic example of the effects of relativity on time, of what is termed time dilation. No one can say with certainty, but my analysis leads me to conclude those aboard the ship experience time in a way that varies significantly from what we would call normal."

"Would you care to elaborate on that a bit?" Tom asked.

"Liken it to time spent sleeping. Time is a comparative function. Like motion it is measured in relation to something else. When subjects are kept in isolation their perception of time becomes distorted. That, combined with the ephemeral nature of the process, strongly suggests the individuals involved experience an artificial sense of time dilation. They go about their lives, but only at a greatly reduced pace."

Lapsing into silence, the three men concentrated on their meal.

"There's one other thing I've been wondering about," Tom said when they moved into the living room. "If Ridgely is standing pat and weighing his options, what prevents him from suddenly changing his mind?"

Derek leaned back in his chair with a contented smile. "I do." He had his metallic suitcase beside the chair. Reaching down, he stroked it as lovingly as a dowager petting her lapdog. "I have copies of all of my work inside this case. I can prove what happened to the *Paradise Voyager*. Winston Ridgley's greatest nightmare would be for me to go public with this information and thereby expose his dirty secret."

"Why haven't you done it? What are you afraid of?"

"Afraid? I am not afraid of anything, Thomas. I have Mr. Ridgely exactly where I want him."

Derek shifted on the couch. "What I have to say now is a matter of life and death. Not for you or me, although we are both in grave danger, but for the unfortunate souls trapped aboard the ship. I did not contact you in your capacity as a newsman. I do not seek publicity. You must never reveal the things I tell you."

"If Tom here doesn't blow the whistle, what chance do ya have of savin' those folks?"

"At first glance it may appear that publicity will benefit the situation, but in this case it would not." Derek's raised hand cut off any rebuttal. "Mr. Ridgely and I are in what the western movies call a Mexican standoff. So long as I do nothing, he will do nothing. However, should the public learn the truth he will have no choice but to act. If we lose our hold over him, he might sink the *Paradise Voyager* in desperation. Never forget, he retains the power to make the ship disappear forever. And if he consigns the *Paradise Voyager* to the bottom of sea, everyone aboard goes along for the ride."

Tom now understood the true nature of the threat. "Only with you gone can Ridgely destroy the *Voyager* with impunity."

"Correct. I am sure he continues to diligently search for me. Your Federal Bureau of Investigations would also like to know where I am. For the sake of safety, I entrusted the care of my wife and children to a cousin-brother in India. They are in hiding. My own life, I have put into your hands. Meanwhile, time runs out."

"You feel it's only a matter of time until Ridgely or the government catches up with you?"

Derek shook his head. "Perhaps time will run out for me or perhaps I will live to fight another day. But time is definitely running out for the individuals aboard the *Paradise Voyager*."

Tom's heart leaped into his throat. "What are you saying?"

"Our tests on small mammals indicated they suffered certain," he frowned as he searched for the correct phrase "certain *deleterious effects* related to prolonged stasis."

Derek recalled the early tests conducted in India. They repeated the experiments, gradually extending their length. They grew increasingly confident, perhaps cocky. There seemed to be no boundaries until one fateful day.

Had they grown over confident? Probably. He tried rationalizing the outcome by telling himself that if the process had limits, they needed to know it. How could they have imagined such a small amount of additional time could result in such an unexpected and horrible outcome?

Derek would never forget how Kaur's face dissolved in horror. She confidently lifted the lid, looked in and shrieked. One by one, she lifted the poor rabbits out. They were uncoordinated and incoherent, several were convulsing. Akbar, Birbal, Scheherazade and Sinbad all had to be put down. Gautama survived, but only as an invalid. Out of kindness, she eventually put him down as well.

"You never said anything about this. A minute ago you were hell-bent for leather to bring everyone back. Now you're talking about irreversible damage." Tom slammed his hand down on the arm of the chair, jumped up, and strode to the window.

He heard Derek's approaching footsteps.

Derek rested a hand on Tom's shoulder. "Ghandi once said, 'Truth is like a vast tree, which yields more and more fruit the more you nurture it.'"

Tom gave a cynical laugh. "Be sure and remind me to be patient while I wait for the fruit to ripen."

"I promised to withhold nothing, would you rather I not tell you of these things?"

"How much time do we have?"

"It is nearly impossible to say."

"So where do we go from here?"

"In any case, the prudent course of action is to act as expediently as possible." Derek sighed. "So much time has already slipped through our fingers."

Tom's back stiffened. "This is no time to let *what-ifs* weaken our resolve."

FIFTY-TWO

With the details surrounding the *Paradise Voyager* known and thoroughly discussed, the men began to develop a strategy. Colorful braided rugs were scattered over Eddie's hardwood floor. The furniture, all Mission style, was comfortable and inviting.

"Here's our situation in a nutshell," Tom said. "Derek is confident he can reverse the process. However, we have limited time and practically no resources. We need to get our hands on some computers, machinery and, last but not least, a boat."

Eddie studied the map spread out on the coffee table and shook his head. "I hate t' rain on your parade, Sarge, but the *Paradise Voyager* is one helluva long way out there. You can't go paddlin' over in your little, red, rented rowboat, especially not this time of year. This project's gonna take a real ship."

"What do you think we'll need?"

Eddie eyed the map again. He wrapped his rough fingers around his cheeks and slid them down, smoothing his neatly-trimmed beard. He continued sliding and smoothing as he thought. He propped his elbow on the arm of the chair. "It oughta be a fishin' boat."

"Why should that make any difference?" Derek asked.

"I'd bet dollars t' donuts RCI is monitorin' the area around the *Paradise Voyager*. They'd be fools not to."

"And a fishing boat, even if it was a little out of range, wouldn't alert whoever's watching things." Tom said, picking up his chain of reasoning.

"But a fishing boat cannot carry all the people aboard the *Paradise Voyager*," Derek said.

"It won't have to. Once ya bring it out, it'll be just like it went in. We can use the *Paradise Voyager* t' ferry those folks back home." Eddie looked back down at the map. "Ya want somethin' at least 80 feet long; anything else wouldn't handle the seas out there. If ya find somethin' larger, I say grab it. And steel hulled so it can take a poundin'."

"What do you think we're talking about, dollar wise? Can you ballpark it?" Tom asked.

"Might go as high as 400 hundred grand, give or take. I'll check out the engine and cooling system for ya. We don't want it breakin' down or overheatin' in the middle of nowhere. If we poke around the boatyards in Charleston Harbor, I bet we can find one that'll fit the bill."

"I also require certain specialized machinery," Derek said.

"Ya got schematics?"

Derek left the room for a moment and returned carrying a stack of CD's.

Eddie took the one he offered and popped it into his computer. "What is this stuff?" he asked, scrolling through the drawings.

"They are the engineering specifications for the housing and machinery that facilitates the process."

Eddie traced some lines with his finger. "Are these hydraulic lines?"

"Yes, all of the machinery is focused and adjusted hydraulically."

"Good. I know a fella who liquidates heavy machinery. He's got a barn full of fittings and lines." His finger moved to the left. "And this?"

"That is the pulse emitter housing. It is deck-mounted and moves in two planes, both horizontally and vertically."

"And these bolts secure it to the deck, right?"

"Correct. Will these parts be difficult to procure?"

"Piece a cake."

"What about the cost?" Tom asked.

"There's gonna be some, of course, but we'll trade and scrounge."

Derek's face clouded. "Trade and scrounge? I am afraid I do not recognize those terms."

Eddie pointed to his neatly-paneled walls. "Okay, suppose ya got a hankerin' for some madrone panelin' on your walls. Now keep in mind it's not readily available and, even if ya found it, most likely ya couldn't afford it anyhow. That's our problem."

Derek glanced around the room. "Yet you have the paneling which you could not afford."

"Exactly, 'n' here's the solution. Suppose ya find somebody who's got madrone trees scattered around their land and they're gonna do some loggin'. And suppose ya agree to do all the millin' for 'em and, instead of payin' in cash, they pay in madrone logs."

"You get what you desire and so do they," Derek said, grinning.

"There's lots of folks around the county who owe me a favor or two." He gave them a self-deprecating grin. "I've been sorta savin' 'em for the future. I say it's high time we cracked open the ol' piggy bank."

"And the scrounge?"

"Ya'd be surprised what wanderin' around the right junk yard with a shoppin' list will do. There's farm equipment, industrial equipment, 'n' loggin' machinery to choose from. Just because it didn't start out as the turret for a pulse emitter housin' doesn't mean it can't become one. 'Course when we get it all cobbled together, it'll be every color in the rainbow. That's a problem I can fix with a few cans of spray paint."

Tom picked up a pen and flipped open a notebook. "Why don't we put together a rudimentary list to budget from?"

All three men smiled. It felt good to finally be doing something.

"Perhaps I can eat some of your cake as well," Derek said. Encouraged by Eddie's description of scroungAing materials from salvage yards and junk dealers, Derek decided he too could scrounge the complex electronic components. He had contacts inside the Physics and Computer Science Departments of several universities.

Even allowing for favors, trades and scavenging, their rudimentary list easily totaled over half a million dollars. They had a problem, a big problem. Their excitement evaporated in the harsh light of reality.

Derek summed up their feelings when he said, "I should not have allowed myself to become so confident. I felt in my heart we were truly on the path to resolution. For a short while I stood at the peak of triumph and now I am again dwelling in the valley of despair. This project cannot be accomplished without a benefactor."

"I don't suppose ya could whip out a grant proposal real quick," Eddie said, chuckling.

Tom's face brightened. "Don't give up yet, I may know someone." He gathered his papers, preparing to leave. "Derek, why don't you start working the phones to see what you can find in the way of equipment. Work from our list, checking things off as you go."

Derek smiled and nodded.

Tom turned to Eddie. "We're also going to need some manpower. Do any tradesmen owe you favors? Say machinists, mechanics, electricians or boatwrights?"

"They do. What I ain't owed, I'll borrow."

"Super. Why don't you and I go boat shopping this afternoon?"

When Tom called the office of Brian Combs, they informed him Brian was in London. He waited until midnight to call. With the time difference, it was morning in London and he wanted to catch Brian as he came into the office. They put him right through.

"It's good to hear from you, Tom. You were really dragging the last time we met, how have you been?"

"Better. I've had my ups and downs, but things are on an upward trajectory."

"That's terrific, what can I do for you?"

"There's something I'd like to talk to you about. In a way it concerns the compensation you offered."

"Fire away, I'm listening."

Tom ran his fingers through his hair and stifled a yawn. "I'd rather it be face-to-face. There's someone here I want you to meet. What if we used our original agreement? Remember, ten minutes? If you like what you hear you stay, otherwise, you can leave."

Brian chuckled at Tom's suggestion. "I was standing on your doorstep when I suggested that; not thousands of miles away. You're asking me to fly halfway around the world. Have you priced jet fuel lately?"

"Why am I not crying? Fly coach."

"Why can't we discuss this over the phone?"

"Believe me, I wouldn't ask you to do this if I didn't think it was worthwhile."

"You're asking an awful lot. Can't you at least give me some inkling as to what this is about?"

"Fair enough," Tom said. "I know the party responsible for the *Paradise Voyager's* disappearance. I have proof, proof positive."

"That's a mighty big claim."

"It ain't braggin' if you can do it."

"You sound pretty darned sure of yourself."

"That's because I am."

"OK. Given what you've been through, I guess you deserve the benefit of the doubt. I'll wrap things up here and leave tonight. I'll be in North Bend tomorrow morning."

FIFTY-THREE

Pine Crest, Oregon

Brian landed in North Bend after a night flight from London. Having slept most of the trip, he arrived well-rested. But the flight crew was bushed. He piled their overnight cases into the trunk of a rental car and headed for the casino hotel. After dropping them off, he drove on to Eddie Beltzer's place following Tom's directions.

The three men conferred in the kitchen while Brian waited in the living room. Tom's eyes moved from Eddie to Derek. "Let's do our best, guys. Ten minutes and Brian could be out the door."

"He would not actually leave so quickly, would he?"

Tom shook his head and smiled. "No, I don't imagine he will, but we won't get another shot at him. Derek, you stay here until I'm ready for you. Eddie you can be my backup."

"This is your show, Sarge. I'm plannin' on tiptoein' round the room, smilin' and servin' finger sandwiches."

Brian rose when they entered. His briefcase lay open on the coffee table and he held a blank legal pad in one hand. Tom took a seat opposite him. Eddie slouched against the desk. With legs extended and arms crossed, he looked like someone killing time at the feed store.

"I've got a few questions for you, Brian," Tom said.

Brian relaxed. Leaning back in the chair, he crossed his legs and prepared for a friendly, preliminary chat.

"Is Paradise Getaways Ltd. the owner in possession of the *Paradise Voyager*?"

Brian immediately reached for his pad. "No. An offshore subsidiary owns the fleet. They're operated under a lease agreement."

"But under the terms of that agreement you have all rights of ownership other than mortgage or sale, correct?"

"It sounds like you've done some legal research."

Ignoring the comment, Tom pressed on. "Will you accept Lloyd's open form in regards to the *Voyager*?"

Brian smiled. "I didn't know you were in the salvage business."

"I am now. Can you sign off on it, or do you have to call London?"

"Only the final details require approval."

"Okay, here it is in a nutshell. I want you to accept Lloyd's open form and I want Paradise Getaways to bankroll my efforts to salvage the *Voyager*."

Brian filled a third of the page with notes to himself. "Maybe it's just the attorney in me, but I see two problems here. First, salvage is an operation undertaken to assist a vessel in danger, and said vessel must be capable of navigation. The *Paradise Voyager* has been lost."

"Set it aside for now. What's the other problem?"

Brian scribbled on the pad again. "Lloyd's open form is a no cure-no pay agreement. If we fund your work, how will we be reimbursed if you aren't successful?"

"That's easy enough. Draw up an agreement for the compensation you offered me the last time you were here. I'll and pledge it against any funds you advance on my behalf."

"Suppose you exceed the agreed upon figure?"

"I don't know. You can take a second on my house if you want it. By the time we're finished, none of this will be an issue."

"For now, I tentatively accept...at least until everything's out on the table."

Tom moved his hands like a parent settling a distraught child. "Trust, Brian. Think back to a simpler time, a time before law school. You *do* remember trust, don't you?"

Brian flipped over a fresh page.

"I have something for you." Tom reached in his wallet, removed a twenty-dollar bill, and handed it to Brian.

Brian stared at it with a quizzical expression. "I thought you wanted me to give you money."

"This has nothing to do with that. It's a retainer for your services."

Brian looked at the bill in his hand then studied Tom's face, trying to discern his motives. He learned about as much from Andrew Jackson as he did from Tom's expression.

"I, ah, usually get slightly more than this for my services," he said, waving the well-worn bill in the air.

"I once knew a guy who bought a car with two bucks down. It was all he had on him at the time."

"You want me to represent you?"

"Not me, a friend." Tom explained Derek's situation in vague terms.

"I don't practice criminal law."

Tom clucked his tongue. "I know, but you're part of that K Street gang of lawyers and lobbyists in Washington. Half of your clients are probably white-collar criminals. Besides, you've got the connections we need."

"And if I do take him on?"

"Then what we discuss today is privileged conversation."

A glimmer of understanding lit Brian's eyes. "What do you expect me to do on his behalf?"

"I want you to negotiate a peace treaty between my friend, the FBI, and Immigration and Naturalization. We're going to require their cooperation."

"I'll have to meet this mysterious friend of yours."

"He's waiting in the next room."

Derek entered the room carrying a tray with a teapot and cups. He sat it on the desk beside Eddie. Turning to face Brian, he extended his hand. "Mr. Combs, I am Dr. Dwarakananth

Maheshwari. You may call me Derek. Shall I pour you some Chai to enjoy while we discuss the *Paradise Voyager*?"

Brian sipped the Chai as he listened to what Derek had to say. Afterwards, he looked from one man to the other. "So the three of you intend to find the *Voyager* and bring her back?"

"That's our plan," Tom said. "Are you with us?"

"We are very close, Mr. Combs." Derek held up a hand, his thumb and finger less than a quarter of an inch apart.

"What if you run into trouble or need medical assistance?"

"That's another part of your job," Tom said. "After you get finished pacifying the Feds, request a Coast Guard escort."

Brian looked down at the bill Tom handed him earlier and grinned. "What a deal, and all for twenty bucks." He closed his briefcase. "I need to step outside and make a phone call."

The men paced while Brian talked.

Brian returned shaking his head. "I don't know what you did when she was here, but you've got her full support. She authorized it all and said if the money runs out to let her know."

"How soon will we have it?"

"You've already got it. She arranged a line of credit while we were on the phone."

The men stood by the window watching Brian leave.

Eddie slapped Tom on the back. "Ya did it, Sarge. Neatly folded 'n' gift wrapped. It's all over now but the shoutin'."

He glanced over at Derek. "How much time's left?"

Derek thought for a moment and frowned. "We have perhaps seven days left. I do not recommend exceeding this self-imposed time limit."

Tom slumped into a chair. After a few moments he smacked a fist into his palm. "So what? Forget the timeline. We'll just have to work as fast as we can."

"The ship we found is dry-docked in a metal shed. We can work on it night 'n' day without anyone seeing us."

"We could put Derek under a blanket in the back of the van and do a walk through this afternoon. What about the equipment?"

"I already got people combin' the salvage yards for the stuff we need. I have an electrician friend who'll run the wirin'. I can get us a mechanic and a machinist, too."

Eddie grinned and pointed to Derek. "The professor here has sweet talked his buddies at the university out of most of the computer stuff we need. By the time Brian clears things in Washington, we oughta be ready to sail."

Derek swallowed hard and lowered his head. The unexpected change in behavior unnerved Tom and Eddie. For his part, Derek developed a sudden, intense interest in his shoes.

"I don't like that look, Derek. Is there somethin' ya ain't told us?"

Tom raised two fingers in the air. "What happened to *we are very close, Mr. Combs*?"

"I fear the final piece of the puzzle, the precise location of the *Paradise Voyager*, may still remain beyond our reach."

"You were there; you must know where the ship is."

"Yes, I know where it *was*. Mr. Ridgely could have moved it. There is no way of knowing until we get there."

"So you just quietly sat there and let me make a horse's ass out of myself?" Tom glanced out the window. The dust thrown up by Brian's car hadn't completely settled. Stepping closer, he loomed over Derek. "You're telling me all of these elaborate plans we've been making are worthless?"

"The plans are definitely not worthless. Nor are they ill conceived or doomed to fail. You are taking my words out of context." Then, looking like a dog that'd just been caught peeing on the carpet, Derek mumbled, "Trust, Thomas. You *do* remember trust, don't you?"

FIFTY-FOUR

RCI Corp. Headquarter, Palo Alto, California

The office complex was dark except for lights burning in a corner office of the Executive Suite.

Arturo Ricetti extended his hand to Brandon Steele. "Brandy, my boy, how the hell are you doing, Buddy?"

"I am *not* your buddy and I've told you never to call me that. What have you got?"

"News, lots of news. The latest updates from the beautiful Oregon Coast."

When they entered Ridgely's office, Ricetti glanced across the room and smiled. "Win, it's been too long. Good to see you again, Pal. How's tricks?"

Ridgely snorted in reply and walked to a small conference table by the windows. He ignored Ricetti's outstretched hand when he passed.

Ricetti had flown back from Oregon to update Steele and Ridgely. On the phone all he would say is that he had big news. The three men began to discuss the situation, but stopped when a food service worker tapped at the door.

They'd ordered a cart from the company cafeteria when Ricetti complained of being hungry. The men's silence told the white-coated waiter he was intruding. He quickly transferred the sandwich platter to the table and distributed drinks, snacks, salads and silverware. As soon as everything was unpacked, he discretely rolled his cart out the door and closed it behind him.

Ricetti unwrapped his sandwich and lifted the top slice of bread. "Pastrami on rye. If anybody's got a roast beef or turkey on white I'll trade."

Steele tossed his unexamined sandwich across the table. "Take mine. Can't you think of anything but your stomach?"

"Since when is it a sin to be hungry? All I've had to eat since breakfast was a chintzy bag of pretzels on the plane. Toss me one of those mustard packets."

"Have you spotted Maheshwari?" Ridgely asked.

"Not a sign," Ricetti said between bites.

He opened a bag of chips, noticed Ridgely's frown, and shrugged. He'd started cruising Tom's neighborhood at five this morning. It was now ten in the evening and here he was eating a lousy deli sandwich for dinner. They'd have to cut him a little slack if they wanted to hear what he'd come to say.

"What about Jenkins?"

"Same old. He's been spending a lot of time out in the hinterlands. A friend of his from 'Nam, Eddie Beltzer, has a log cabin somewhere in the woods. The people I've talked to say they're pretty tight."

"What are they up to?"

"Damned if I know, want me to knock on the door and ask?" Ricetti grinned and pointed across the table. "Are you gonna eat that pickle?"

Ridgely shoved his whole plate at him. "This hardly qualifies as big news."

Ricetti crunched into the quarter slice of dill pickle, chewed, and blotted his lips on a napkin. "You asked. I answered. Here's something that might interest you. Know what a Cessna Citation X looks like?"

"Like a plane."

"Like a one fine plane. It's top of the line, my friend, cream of the crop."

"Not interested. I already have a corporate jet. How does this connect to Jenkins?"

"I'll tell you if you let me. I happened to pass the North Bend Airport and noticed this business jet sitting on the tarmac. It was a real beauty, desert sand with chocolate accent stripes. And from the way it sparkled, they must have just waxed it. That baby will go coast-to-coast in 4 hours. Do New York to London in under six." He winked. "Helluva rig, Win. But it looked out of place sitting there, know what I mean?"

"What was a plane like that doing in North Bend?"

"I wondered the same thing. The tail number led me to Excalibur Corporation. It's an offshore holding company. Privately owned, I checked. M. J. Tilden is the sole stockholder."

"Never heard of him."

"*Her*. Neither did I so I did some more checking. M. J. Tilden turns out to be supermodel Claudia Monet. She's also the principal stockholder of Paradise Getaways, Ltd."

The blood drained from Ridgely's face. He straightened in his chair and fumbled for a pen. "What else did you find out?"

Ricetti pried the lid off a cup of slaw. He brought the cup close to his chin and forked out a mouthful, dangling it over the container for a second to let the excess dressing drip off. He shook away the last drops, stuffed it into his mouth and chewed.

He turned the Styrofoam container in his hand. "Pretty good stuff; I like slaw when it's not too sweet."

He took a long sip of soda, stifled a belch by making a fist and tapping his chest lightly then smiled at Steele and Ridgely. "I nosed around the airport. You have to be careful doing that these days, you know. They're getting so they don't like people asking questions. Anyway, I found out the plane just arrived from London with a crew of two and one passenger, Brian Combs. He's her brother, a Washington attorney."

Ridgely began pacing the room. "We need to keep an eye on Combs. I want to know where he goes, what he does, and who he sees."

"Thought you might. He rented a car and got a hotel room. While the crew slept he went out for a drive. Care to guess where he made his first stop?"

"Jenkins' house?" Steele said.

"Close, but no cigar. He went for a ride in the country and stopped in at Beltzer's place."

"What was he doing there?"

"I have a few ideas that might help you connect the dots."

Ridgely dropped back into his chair. "Maheshwari must be staying with Beltzer." His eyes settled on Ricetti. "I have to know whether Maheshwari is there."

Ricetti studied the other half of his sandwich for a moment, took a bite, and shook his head as he slowly chewed. "You can't even see Beltzer's house from the road. It's up a long, winding drive and hidden away in the woods. If I get any closer, I'll blow my cover. There's no way unless you want to authorize a helicopter on my expense report."

"Where's Combs now?" Ridgely asked.

"After he visited Beltzer's, Combs left North Bend headed for Washington, DC. You may also be interested to know that the afternoon before Combs arrived Jenkins and Beltzer went shopping."

"So?"

"So they were shopping at the shipyards in Charleston, Oregon."

The implications of Ricetti's words hung in the air, slowly sinking in.

"Looked to me like they'd decided to become fishermen. They spent a lot of time going over a boat some guy had for sale."

Ridgely raised his eyes momentarily then dropped them again. He and Steele both examined the subtle grain of the walnut table, neither saying a word. Time ticked away, a lot of time.

Ricetti ripped open another bag of chips and munched while he waited.

They were too far down this path to turn back now, Ridgely thought. He'd spent a lifetime building this company and he wouldn't throw it all away over a bunch of stranded tourists. "Things aren't as grim as they seem."

"This from someone who thought nobody would miss

several hundred passengers and a cruise ship. What are you proposing?" Steele asked.

Ridgely stared at him across the table. His jaw was set and his eyes hard as flint. "We'll have to sink the ship."

Though both Ridgely and Steele knew the possibility had always existed, neither had given voice to it. He was recommending the cold-blooded murder of over 200 passengers plus the crew. But this wasn't the spur-of-the-minute decision it seemed to be. Ridgely had already crafted the plan for use if and when the need arose. The *Paradise Voyager* was merely a chess piece and Ridgely had been playing the game three moves ahead.

"Don't look so shocked. You always knew it could come to this. In business, you sometimes have to be ruthless."

Ricetti pushed his plate aside and scooted his chair back. "If either of you need me, I'll be back in my motel room packing. My work here is pretty well done."

"The hell it is! Sit down. You aren't going anywhere. When that ship *really* disappears I want Jenkins and Maheshwari on it."

"Hold on a minute there, Win. I don't like where this is heading." Ricetti opened his eyes wide and gestured toward his face. "My job is to watch, remember? *Watch*, as in eyeballs. You're going to have to get somebody else if you want more than that."

Ridgely ignored Ricetti's protests. "We'll snag them one at a time," he said, thinking out loud. "We'll grab Jenkins first. We need something we can use to bait the trap. We need to get him alone, alone and vulnerable. And whatever we plan has to be something a dog can't screw up."

"What about his wife?" Steele asked.

Ridgely appeared confused.

"The *Tango* still has all of Maheshwari's equipment on it. We could send it back out there and take her off the ship."

"No, it's too risky. I like the idea, but who knows if we could control her once we had her. If she escaped, we'd have even more problems."

"Here's a better idea," Ricetti said. "Use the granddaughter instead. She's just a kid. You ought to be able to handle her."

Ridgely's face broke into a broad smile. "I like it. How soon can we get it done?"

"The *Tango* came back into port the day before yesterday. The ship's taking on fuel and supplies right now. She'll be manned and ready to sail in a few hours."

"Let's move on this. We've wasted too much time already." Ridgely spun and pointed a finger at Ricetti. "And you hightail it back to Oregon and *watch* their progress on that ship."

Ricetti and Steele started for the door.

Ridgley's voice stopped them. "Wait. There's one more thing. For added insurance, while the *Tango* is out there getting the kid, tell them to move the *Voyager*. That way, even if Jenkins and Maheshwari manage to slip away, they won't find a ship waiting for them."

FIFTY-FIVE

"Grandpa, help me. I wanna come home."

Tom pressed the receiver to his ear. *Was it really Ellie?* "Ellie! Ellie? Is that you? Where are you?"

"I'm in a little room tied up in ropes. Come and get me."

"Can you see—"

A gruff voice cut him off. "That's all, Grandpa." The man barked out the terms. She would be in the picnic shelter at a small rest stop along a forested road. He should come alone. Arrive at 8:30 the following morning...if he wanted to see her again."

Tom tilted the window blind to check the weather. At five a.m. it was dark and overcast. Wet grass below told him the overnight rain had materialized as predicted. The forecast called for intermittent storms of increasing intensity throughout the morning. It wasn't the best day to be tramping through the woods, not that he had a choice.

A camouflage Ranger vest, made of a lightweight, but tough, waterproof nylon-blended fabric, lay on the bedspread. Six pockets stair-stepped their way from waist to shoulder on either side. The upper pockets had Velcro flaps; the remainder closed with zippers. A strip of shell loops crossed the middle of his chest and black clips at the waist waited to lock onto additional gear.

He lined up his equipment in a neat row beside the vest, binoculars, compass, Leatherman tool, first aid kit, buffered salt tablets, aerosol nitroglycerin dispenser, multiple pairs of plastic handcuffs, duct tape, two water bottles, and his 10-inch combat knife.

Even after all these years, the process of performing his readiness check felt familiar, comforting. As a young sergeant in Vietnam, he'd arranged his gear across his bunk this same way.

Now, as then, he was preparing for battle.

Tom turned his attention to the knife. When he finished sharpening it, he wiped the blade on a rag and returned the whetstone to its box. He was still holding it when Tommy knocked.

He cracked the door and peeked around. "I brought you some coffee, Dad. Can I come in?"

He took a step, noticed the gleaming blade in his father's hand and hesitated.

"Just in case." Tom jammed the knife into its sheath and took the cup.

Tommy surveyed the equipment spread across the bed. "Is all this stuff really necessary?"

Tom began stowing the gear in his vest. "A prepared soldier fights a better battle."

"I thought you'd want to know Karen got in late last night. I suggested she stay with us until this is over."

"Good idea. Circle the wagons."

"I also called the principal and told him we'd be pulling the boys out of school for a few days. I thought it best to keep them close. As you said, *just in case.*"

"What about John?"

"He and Arlene took the kids to her parent's place in Idaho. They should be safe there."

Tom finished lacing his boots and rose from the bed. The two men stood eye to eye.

"Dad, you don't have to go up there. It's a trap."

"Of course it is. I'm their target. Ellie's the bait."

"You'd knowingly walk into their trap?"

"I have no other choice. This is my one and only chance to get Ellie, your mother and all those people back home."

"But why you?"

"Who else? They want me, not Derek or Eddie. Besides, if I

entrusted this to someone else and they failed, I could never live with myself." Tom snapped his fingers. "One slip-up and Ellie's gone. There'll be no second chances."

"I want to go with you."

"I wish you could, but you're needed here."

"They're planning to kill you."

Tom rested his hands on his son's shoulders and looked deep into his eyes. "You can't kill a dead man, Tommy. I haven't really been alive since the day your Mother disappeared. I've got nothing to lose and everything to gain."

He took an envelope off the dresser and handed it to his son. "These are for you."

"What's in here?"

"It contains my will and a form transferring ownership of the newspaper to you."

Tommy shook his head and threw the envelope onto the bed. "No, Dad. I don't want it to be like this."

"Remember what I said, *just in case*. Your mother is the beneficiary on my life insurance with you kids as second. That pretty much takes care of it." He grabbed the vest and swung it around his shoulders.

"Will you at least have something eat?"

"If it's quick."

Beth was buttering toast when the men walked into the kitchen. Karen turned from the counter with a glass of juice. They took one look at Tom and froze. The seriousness of his undertaking immediately became apparent. After a hurried breakfast he buttoned his vest and kissed them all goodbye. Hat in hand, he headed for the door.

Tommy walked toward him. "Let me walk you out."

Once they were on the porch, he handed Tom a set of car keys. "Why don't you take my old truck? I keep it closed up in the shed. Nobody could associate it with you. It's a beater, but it'll get you where you want to go."

After they hugged Tom reached out and tapped his son's jaw with his fist. "You're a good man, Thomas Jenkins Jr. I couldn't have come this far without you. Now turn around and get back in there. I have to go the rest of the way alone."

The highway snaked up and down, around and over the hills, rising higher with every turn. Systematic logging had transformed the surrounding landscape into alternate blocks of clear cuts and tall trees. Some of the recently logged tracts still showed temporary scars from the process. Adjoining tracts, logged in prior years, were already replanted and greening.

Logging followed a repetitive, multi-staged cycle. First, loggers cut the trees. Then they de-limbed them, attached choke lines and dragged them up the surrounding slopes to a staging area. After sorting and grading, the newly-cut trees were loaded onto trucks for transport. After the trees were gone, the logging company bulldozed the slash, trash trees, brush, limbs, and stumps, into large piles and set it all ablaze. It burned for several days, reducing everything to fine, soil-enriching ash.

Replanting followed. Planting teams roamed the area poking thousands of tiny Douglas fir seedlings into the soil. A Douglas fir's growth potential in Coastal Oregon was 18 inches a year. In no time those replanted twigs became eight foot trees surrounded by lush shrubs and wild berries.

Tom had scouted out the meeting spot the previous day. It was a roadside rest built on the plateau of a ridge. He'd counted on finding a logging site nearby and did. Scattered piles of unburned slash lay waiting for the torch.

He turned onto the dirt logging road, followed it deep into the tract, and hid the truck behind a large slash pile. The mottled coloring of his camouflage outfit allowed him to blend into his surroundings. He needn't have worried. Daylight Savings Time had come and gone and any daylight saved had long since been spent.

He counted on them expecting him to drive into their trap. His plan was simple, come in the back way on foot.

Tom paused at the edge of the steep promontory. Looking west, he saw a sliver of ocean above the trees. Angry black squalls filled the horizon. Intermittent drops pelted him as he prepared to cross the valley.

Unlike their deciduous cousins, conifers shed their needles continuously throughout the year. These discarded bits eventually carpet the ground. The young trees on the hillside in front of Tom hadn't been there long enough to produce such groundcover. The falling rain gathered into rivulets and trickled down the hillside, transforming it into slippery, sticky mire. He'd be forced to make switchbacks as he descended the slope.

Tom stopped to rest near one of the bushy patches of salal scattered along the hillside. He made the mistake of grabbing one for support when he rose. Its damp, leathery leaves slid through his fingers.

The next thing he knew, he was in a face-first slide. He flailed his feet, desperately trying to get a foothold on the rain-slick slope. A lone huckleberry bush stood between him and disaster. He threw himself over onto his right side and looped his arm around its base. His newly healed ribs screamed in protest as he slammed against it and jerked to a stop.

Tom held his ribs and took small breaths. Wet dirt smeared his face and found its way into his mouth. He reflexively wiped his cheek with a dirty hand as he coughed and spit. His stomach recoiled at the musty taste of half-rotted leaves and humus. He opened a water bottle and alternately swished his mouth and spit.

He was halfway to the valley floor and the ridge loomed above him. Staring upwards, Tom watched a pair of headlights veer off the highway and onto the park's access road. They paused briefly to drop someone off then continued on to the shelter house.

Ellie was in that car.

FIFTY-SIX

Tom lowered his binoculars and smiled.

They'd dropped off a lookout near the entrance. They were clearly expecting him to drive in. He tilted his head back, staring at the overcast sky. No sun to flash off his lenses. He stepped carefully. He couldn't afford any more falls.

He crept forward and dropped to his knees behind a bushy fir. Its wet needles flicked water droplets in his face when he parted them. He rested his binoculars on a small branch and let their weight fold it down. Bending the branch in this way allowed Tom to jerk the glasses back in an instant. When he did, the branch snapped back hiding his presence.

The smell of the sap reminded him of Christmas. He thought of a younger Ellie toddling over to examine the packages under the tree. He recalled the family gathered for dinner, Marty's face flushed from the heat of the oven, the women scurrying about as they tended to last minute details.

He blinked several times to clear his eyes and scanned the ridge a second time. A tall man in a white baseball cap stepped into Tom's field of vision from behind a Sitka Spruce. He watched the man walk down to the road, check the highway and then return.

Their lookout relaxed and lit a cigarette. He smoked it fast, taking long drags. He ground the butt under his heel, looked around again, and disappeared behind the big Spruce.

Tom executed his route in quick increments, scurrying from one tree to the next. At each stop, he checked the ridge. When he saw a flash of white he froze.

The lookout emerged, lit up, and re-checked the highway.

Precious seconds ticked away as Tom knelt on the damp ground, impatiently waiting for him to go back behind his tree. Moisture wicked into the knee of his pants. He smelled Christmas trees and the scent of damp earth and waited.

He sensed movement. Looking around, he spotted the intruder. A medium-sized porcupine ambled straight towards him. It moved slowly, stopping to investigate each tree before continuing up the hill.

Tom's experience told him porcupines ranked among some of the dumbest animals God made. But, with over 3,000 barbed quills, porcupines had little need for either intelligence or bravado. Just the display of their weapons protected them against most threats. If an animal didn't respect them before an encounter, they certainly did afterwards. In the wild, tangling with a porcupine often proved fatal.

He had to find a way to divert it.

Tom carefully accumulated an arsenal of seed cones and pulled out his salt tablets. Porcupines have a love of salt that borders on insatiable. Working quickly to avoid wetting the tablet, he securely wedged one between the cone's bracts.

A moment later, a seed cone emerged from the base of the Douglas fir and rolled toward the porcupine. It turned its head, watched the cone come to a stop, and sauntered over to investigate. Once the animal discovered the hidden treat, he ripped the cone apart to get at the salt tablet.

A second cone followed with enough velocity to carry it past the porcupine. He turned and chased it, pouncing on it before it came to a full stop. Maybe he'd misjudged these guys, Tom thought, as the porcupine dug into the cone. The porcupine stared up the hill, expectantly looking for his next cone. Each toss moved it down and away from Tom's intended path.

He rechecked the ridge. The man was gone. He looked for the porcupine. Like a junkie in need of a fix, it wandered around tearing into every seed cone it could find. Tom pitched him a handful of cones

The porcupine went after them.

And Tom was on the move again.

FIFTY-SEVEN

Tommy answered the door to find Eddie waiting on the porch. Ever since the intruder attacked Tom, Eddie had kept a discreet watch on the family. These morning inquiries had become a regular routine.

"Mornin', young Tom. Wanted to check in. Everything okay?"

Tommy hesitated, wondering how much of the events of the previous twenty-four hours he should share. "Um, yeah. A-OK."

"Your mouth says *Yes*, but your eyes say *No*. Would this have anything t' do with the fact your Dad's nowhere to be seen 'n' the newspaper office is locked up tighter than a drum?"

Tommy swung the door open. "Why don't you come in. We can talk in the family room."

Eddie glanced into the living room as they passed. Tommy's young sons sat on the floor in their pajamas playing video games.

"No school today?"

"We're keeping the boys home."

Eddie followed him through the kitchen where Karen and Beth sat at the table talking in hushed tones.

Eddie touched the brim of his hat. "Mornin' ladies."

"Good morning, Eddie. How are you today?" Beth asked.

He smiled. "Think I'm 'bout t' find out."

Eddie took a seat opposite Tommy in the family room. "Sister's here too, I see."

"Just in case. We're circling the wagons, getting ready."

"Uh huh. And your brother in Portland?"

"Gone to Idaho...in-laws."

Eddie stroked his beard. "Look, Tommy, I realize I came in on the second reel. But if this is what you call A-OK, I sure don't wanna be around when you folks got real problems." His voice softened. "Why don't ya fill me in on things, son?"

Beginning with the call about Ellie, Tommy spent the next ten minutes relating everything that had happened. "What should we do?" he asked when he finished.

"Don't underestimate your old man. He led many a search and rescue mission in 'Nam. Headed off into the jungle with no more than what he could carry on his back, huntin' for lost patrols or downed aircraft. He's one tough son-of-a-gun."

"That was a long time ago."

"True, we were a mite younger then. Younger than you are now, I reckon." He shrugged. "So he's lost a half-step on his game; we all have." Eddie tapped the side of his head. "But the game's won up here and he's as sharp as he ever was."

"I wish I had your confidence."

Eddie rose and extended his hand. "Tell ya what, I'll run up there and see how things are unfoldin'."

Tom's breath came in ragged gasps. A fire burned in his chest, working its way into his left shoulder and arm.

Gotta stop, gotta stop, gotta stop, he panted, staggering forward. He was only a few feet from his goal, a broken down stump. He forced himself to keep going until he reached it.

He dropped to his knees and groped in his pocket for the nitroglycerin. Finding it, he pulled the cap and squeezed several sprays into his open mouth. He rolled off of his knees and sat in the dirt. Taking the nitroglycerin would generate a blinding headache. He didn't care. Right now he'd trade any headache for a chance to tame the beast in his chest.

Opening his jacket, Tom unbuttoned his shirt and used his undershirt to wipe his face. He continued to search between the trees for the lookout's white hat as he waited for the nitro to kick in. Leaning back against a half-rotted stump, he forced himself to take slow, even breaths.

His skin felt clammy. His hands shook. The cool breeze across his damp skin made him shiver. Tom tightened his arms around himself to contain the pain and control the shivering.

The doctor once told him stress could aggravate angina symptoms. In spite of the pain, he laughed to himself. Lately, he'd had enough stress to kill a herd of elephants. He must be immortal, or at least a hell of a lot tougher than any doctor thought he was.

Tom continued a regimen of deliberate, deep breaths along with relaxation. He forced himself to think of Marty and their good times together. He smiled to himself as the memories rolled past like scenes from an old, familiar movie.

The pain in his shoulder gradually receded. At last, the nitro was kicking in. With it came the headache. It hit him like an axe driven into his skull. Nitroglycerin works by dilating the body's blood vessels. The involuntary dilation of the blood vessels on one side of the brain caused migraines. It occurred to him that he had the unique pleasure of experiencing a migraine on both sides at once.

He shut his eyes to block out the pounding in his head. His pulse rattled in his ears. He'd never taken nitroglycerin without following it up with an analgesic. They at least made the headaches manageable. No such relief in the woods.

He'd rest a little while longer.

The pain under his breastbone remained. Better, but still there. His headache had become a dull throb. His eyes climbed the sheer hillside looming above him. Ellie was up there somewhere. Alone and afraid, she was waiting for him to come after her. His resolve overcame his pain.

He boosted himself up using the stump for support. His head began to spin. Fearing he'd fall, he waved his arms for balance. Tom stood tall and threw his shoulders back. He took another deep breath. His head cleared; his equilibrium improved.

"I'm coming, Ellie," he whispered as he started up the hill.

FIFTY-EIGHT

Tommy described the truck before Eddie left. He checked for it as he followed the rolling highway, but never truly expected to see it. Tom, he knew, was too smart to park out in the open.

Careful pacing allowed Tom to negotiate an uneasy peace with the fire in his chest. He made steady progress to the top of the ridge. The slumbering beast inside him threatened to reassert itself at the slightest provocation, but he'd made it this far and nothing else mattered.

He spotted a clump of older trees along the perimeter of the ridge. They formed the border of the cut. The loggers left them because they had little or no commercial value. From there he could cross over and approach the lookout from behind.

The skies grew darker by the minute. The earlier light drizzle had become intermittent rain. His waterproof vest continued to shed water, but cold rain trickled down the back of his neck. Branches no longer spritzed him. Each time he brushed a fir, they now dumped an accumulation of rainwater on him.

Melting into the trees, Tom promised himself another shot of nitroglycerin as soon as this was over. Legs quivering from the long climb, he stepped close to a tree trunk hoping its branches would deflect the rain.

He saw their lookout huddled against the spruce. He too was trying to avoid the rain.

Tom inched forward, taking quiet, calculated steps. He instinctively bent into a crouch like an animal stalking its prey. He drew closer, then closer still. His latent energy building with each step like a coiled spring wound tighter with each turn of the crank.

The lookout sensed Tom's footsteps too late. He lunged from his crouch with the guttural snarl of a mother grizzly come to claim a stolen cub. He struck before the man could react, driving the heel of his hand into the man's face with savage force.

His first blow flattened the man's nose. The lookout's head snapped back. Blood splattered them both. The man grasped his broken face with both hands. Blood trickled between his fingers.

Tom rammed a knee deep into the man's groin.

A look of confusion mingled with terror filled the lookout's eyes as pain surged through him. Tears streamed down his cheeks, washing over his bloody fingers. He doubled over. Gasping for breath, he vomited on his shoes.

Tom raised his arm high and crashed his elbow down on the back of the man's neck. He moaned pitifully and collapsed into the wet needles at the base of the spruce. He sprawled on the ground motionless, bubbling blood and mucus into the damp earth.

Tom dropped onto his back, pinning the semi-conscious man to the ground. His hand instinctively went to the knife in his boot. He'd been trained in hand-to-hand combat. This would be no long, drawn out affair. No repeated stabbing that left a corpse randomly poked full of holes like a well-used pincushion. Tom could slice the man's heart in two with a single thrust.

His hand lingered on the knife for another second before he pulled out a pair of plastic handcuffs. He drew the man's arms behind his back and locked them together. He put a second pair around his ankles. Tearing off a silver strip of duct tape, he slapped it across the man's mouth.

It was over.

Tom rose wincing in pain. He clutched his chest and staggered back to the trees from which he'd come.

FIFTY-NINE

The shot of nitro he'd promised himself bought additional time. Tom shook away the cobwebs and checked behind him. He couldn't stay there any longer. Surprise was his only ally and he'd lose it if someone came to check on the lookout. He must see them before they saw him.

The picnic shelter lay at the end of the entrance road a quarter of a mile ahead. It sat in the middle of a dozen or so heavily-wooded campsites. No campers this time of year. This was a one-man operation. If he needed help there wouldn't be any.

Ellie looked unnaturally peaceful sitting on the bench in her pink windbreaker. Her blue eyes scanned back and forth. Was she looking for him?

Tom wanted to shout to her, let her know he was there. But he couldn't.

Feathery wisps of blond hair rose and fell with each passing breeze. Why didn't she have her hood pulled up and tied under her chin? He would have put her in a warmer jacket, zipped it up tight, and covered her little head against the damp wind.

Tom watched Ellie's eyes plaintively searching for help. Why wasn't she struggling?

They must have drugged her.

He felt his anger rising. She was just an innocent little girl. What other unspeakable things had they done to her? If they did anything to hurt her, he'd tear them apart with his bare hands.

"I'm here baby. Just another minute or so and Grandpa will be there to get you," he whispered under his breath.

Then he saw the rope. With her hands folded in her lap, it'd been easy to miss. The rope looped from her hands to the seat of the picnic table. Drugged and bound and staked like a young goat on the Serengeti. Bait to draw the lions in for the kill. How many times had he seen footage of tiny, defenseless goats tugging at their tether and bleating helplessly while their killers circled?

In the time he'd been observing Ellie, the other person hadn't appeared. Where was he? Did he have a gun? If he could get Ellie out of the shelter quickly enough, Tom thought, he could maintain the element of surprise.

He eased the combat knife out of his boot. He took a deep breath then another and ran for the shelter as fast as he could.

Ellie glanced up at him through heavily lidded eyes. "Hi, Grandpa," she said dreamily.

"Hi, Sweetheart." Tom sliced the rope. He put his hands under her arms, lifted her up and held her tight. "C'mon Baby, let's get out of here."

Bending low, he carried her out the back of the shelter and through a campsite. He wanted to get into the brush as quickly as possible. He hadn't gone more than fifty yards when he saw a dark shape moving through the shelter in pursuit.

An inner voice screamed, "*Faster. Faster!*"

Tom ran with abandon, his afterburners fueled with pure adrenaline. He crashed headlong through the brush, snapping twigs and breaking branches as he went. Thorny vines ripped at his legs. He cursed their clinging grasp, which slowed his pace and threatened imminent demise if they tangled around his ankles.

His wheezing breath came in fiery gasps. He responded by clutching his precious cargo tighter against his heaving chest.

Ellie's stupor made her oblivious to their dangerous circumstances. She roused slightly, touched his cheek and asked, "Grandpa, do you know you're all dirty?"

Tom kept moving through the underbrush. The man was gaining on him and there wasn't a thing he could do about it. The difference in their ages alone made it an uneven match. It was only a matter of time before he overtook them. He knew it and so did the man chasing him.

He swore on Ellie's life he'd either elude him or die trying.

The man had gotten so close that Tom could hear branches popping behind him. Up ahead, a deer path crossed a small gully. Tom quickly shifted Ellie in his arms, stopped and turned.

The momentum of the chase brought his pursuer to him. Tom swung a fist at the startled man. The blow threw the man back, buying them a little more time. Leaping across the gully, he crashed down the deer path.

The younger man picked himself up. Spitting and rubbing his jaw, he re-entered the race.

The momentary advantage Tom secured for himself vanished like smoke on a windy day. His lungs were on fire. The pain in his chest had spread to his left arm with such intensity he feared he'd drop Ellie.

He needed to stop, he desperately needed a shot of nitro, but there was no way to get it. Not here. Not now. And the truck was far, far away. He longed for a jetpack, a superhero's cape, anything that would allow him to escape this nightmare.

But instead of super powers all he had was a burning in his chest and an inner voice screaming at him to stop. He veered off the path into the understory. He tucked Ellie beside a huckleberry and grabbed a hefty branch. He crouched in the brush listening to the man's footsteps drawing ever closer.

At the last instant, he stepped out and swung the branch into the man's midsection. On his best day Mickey Mantle never swung with half the intensity.

The man doubled over and collapsed in a running fall.

Tom was on him in a second. He pinned him face down, jerked out his knife and slammed its hard, square butt into the man's skull. The man went limp and Tom trussed him up in handcuffs and duct tape.

He rose clutching his chest and stumbled toward Ellie. He scooped the little girl into his arms. She was in deep slumber and making little baby snores.

Up ahead, an old, half-burned stump, bordered the narrow trail. Just as he nestled her into the curved interior of the stump, his legs buckled. Tom fell to his knees in the soft needles and rolled over, covering Ellie with his body. He talked to her as she dozed.

"You're safe now, Sweetheart," he told her as he fumbled in his vest for the nitro. "Those bad men can never hurt you again. Grandpa's a little tired right now. We'll rest here until he feels better and then go home to Mommy."

Despite the nitroglycerin, pain arced through him like lightning bolts. He coughed up bitter bile, spit it out, and struggled to get his breath.

Tom's life spread itself out before him. All the hopes, the dreams, the expectations. Would he ever see Marty again? He dropped his chin onto his chest and wrapped his arms tightly around himself. Salty tears filled his eyes as he prayed. He rocked from side to side, waiting, hoping...praying the pain would subside.

"Hey Sarge? Ya back here, Sarge?" Eddie's voice echoed through the quiet woods.

When he arrived, he'd parked his truck on the road and walked into the park. He found the lookout and surmised he'd arrived too late to be of any help. So far, the score was one to nothin', Tom's favor. Eddie went back for the truck, heaved the man into the bed, and drove up to the picnic shelter.

He found their vehicle behind the shelter, hidden by a pair of wild rhododendrons. Seeing no one, Eddie returned to the truck and yanked the man out. He groaned and muttered as he rolled off the tailgate and bounced onto the ground. Eddie grabbed him by the collar and dragged him into the shelter.

After he'd propped the lookout up against the wall, he dusted his hands and scanned the shelter. There wasn't much to see. A few stray cigarette butts and a neatly severed piece of rope tied to the picnic table.

Eddie swiveled his head scanning the adjoining campsites. There had to be at least one more of those buzzards somewhere. Leaving the man against the wall, he started down the path

He followed the trail of broken branches and smashed brush along the narrow deer path, stopping frequently to call for Tom. He rounded a bend and pushed his way between two mangled huckleberry bushes. The narrow deer path looped, twisted and sloped before leveling out in a wide flat area filled with ferns.

He saw the man on the ground first. He was lying on his side in handcuffs. Nearby, he found Tom in the curve of the stump, head slumped on his chest.

He dropped to one knee beside him. "Ya feelin' okay?" Eddie rested a hand on Tom's shoulder and gently shook him.

Tom pitched forward and hit the ground with a wooden thump.

SIXTY

With Tom on the ground, Eddie saw Ellie for the first time. She lay in the hollow of the stump, warm and dry, curled up asleep.

Eddie leaned over and examined Tom. His skin was pale and slack. Eddie pressed two fingers against Tom's neck and felt a weak, irregular pulse. His skin was cool to the touch, his breathing shallow.

"Damn it, Sarge, why'd ya have t' do it like this? I woulda helped ya. He shook his head. "There was no need for ya t' come out here alone. No need at all."

The man on the ground began wiggling and moving his lips behind the duct tape. Eddie walked over to him. Grabbing the tape, he ripped it off.

"Whaddya want?"

"Is he dead?"

"No."

"Well, I hope the sonofabitch croaks."

Eddie pounced without warning. He grabbed the man's jacket, jerked him off the ground, and slammed a fist into his face. The force of the blow threw the man's head aside. Eddie released his hold, letting him fall back onto the ground.

"Whatever he did, wasn't half what ya deserved. Say another word and I'll make sure it's the last thing you ever do."

The man nodded warily.

Returning to Tom, Eddie rolled him onto his back and began CPR. He'd been at it for several minutes when he felt a tap on his shoulder. His head snapped up and he found himself eyeball to eyeball with Ellie.

"How come you're kissing Grandpa, Mr. Beltzer?"

"I ain't kissin' your Granddaddy. He's sick 'n' I'm tryin' t' make him better." He pointed to the ground. "Sit down, I got work t' do."

Ellie sat cross legged and watched Eddie apply chest compressions. After a little while, she reached over and shook Tom's shoulder. "When's he gonna wake up?"

Eddie turned to her, out of breath and panting. "Let him rest. I told ya, he's sick." He resumed his CPR.

Ellie sat quietly while he worked. She touched her grandfather's hand and jerked away. "He's really cold. Shouldn't you put a blanket around him?"

"I would if I had one," Eddie growled.

He checked Tom's pulse. Finding it noticeably stronger and his breathing better, he pulled him to his feet. Eddie executed the same practiced motions he'd perfected in Basic Training. He lifted Tom's wrist, squatted in front of him, and let his limp body sag across his shoulders. Now all he had to do was rise to his feet. He'd had two legs the last time he tried this.

He planted his artificial leg, sucked in a deep breath and gritted his teeth. Eddie pushed with all his might. His face grew red. Sweat beaded on his forehead. His new leg wobbled and bucked, threatening to bow.

Just when he thought he'd never make it, the two of them rose into the air together. "C'mon, little Missy. We're gonna get outta here."

Eddie traced a wavering path through the forest with Ellie trailing behind. Growing bored, she picked up a stick and whacked the leaves off ferns as they made their way along the narrow trail.

At the next clearing, he stopped and gently laid Tom on the ground.

"I thought you said we were going home?"

He had no breath to spare. He ignored the girl's question and began doing compressions on Tom's chest. He worked on Tom until he'd recovered from the strain of lifting and carrying another person. Seeing a slight improvement in Tom's color, Eddie again hoisted him back across his shoulder and trudged on toward the shelter house.

They made two additional stops. Ignoring his own fatigue, Eddie spent the time taking care of Tom.

When they began to walk again, Ellie trotted around in front of him. "I'm getting tired, Mr. Beltzer," she said in a whiny voice. "It's too far. I can't walk anymore."

Eddie shot her a look. "I'm already luggin' your Granddaddy. Whaddaya expect me t' do?"

Ellie's lip quivered.

"Aw, come on. You're a big girl, ya can walk by yourself."

She began to sniff. "It's cold and rainy. Why can't you carry me too?"

Eddie's heart softened when he glanced down at her. Her clothes were covered with dirt and soaked from the rain. Her blond hair hung in wet, stringy strands. This day hadn't exactly been a picnic for her either. "Okay, okay. Can ya' touch your toes?"

Ellie bent at the waist.

"Now we're gonna play a little game. You pretend you're a sack a feed 'n' I'll be the farmer who's carryin' ya out t' my hungry piggies." Eddie slipped his free arm around her waist, heaved her up, and braced her against the side of his body. He stumbled down the trail, lurching and rocking under his load.

The rain pounded down by the time they reached the shelter. He put down his sack of feed and rolled Tom off his shoulder and onto a picnic table.

Ellie tiptoed over and studied her grandfather lying unconscious on the table. She began to cry. "He's not getting any better, Mr. Beltzer. You gotta do something real quick."

"Honey, I'm doin' all I can," Eddie said as he resumed the chest compressions.

SIXTY-ONE

Eddie alternated between the shelter and the truck, continually checking on Ellie while the EMTs worked on Tom. Deputies arrived and took the two men to the county jail. Eddie asked them to keep the arrest quiet and notify someone at the FBI immediately.

The far off thump of helicopter blades whipping the air brought back memories of Vietnam. Eddie stared into the sky, monitoring the red and white Medevac Helicopter's approach. They came in high and circled the clearing several times before selecting a landing site. The pilot flipped on two powerful landing beams and eased it into the parking area in front of the shelter. Its wheels had barely touched the ground when the EMT's raced out of the shelter with Tom on a stretcher.

Ellie pressed her nose to truck's window, watching.

Eddie removed his cap and stood at Parade Rest as the EMT's loaded Tom into the copter. Medical personnel began their work as it revved up and slowly rose into the sky. A moment later, it disappeared over the treetops on its way to Eugene. The ambulance drove off, descending the narrow gravel drive to the highway, leaving him alone with Ellie.

Eddie walked around the shelter kicking cigarette butts and stopping occasionally to tug at the piece of rope still tied to the bench. When he'd remembered all he could stand, he jammed his cap back on. After a final look around, he pulled up his collar against the wind and jogged to the truck with his head bent low.

The door squeaked when he pulled it open. "How ya feelin', Little Lady?"

"When will Grandpa wake up?"

Eddie bit his lip. "They're doin' all they can."

Her face brightened when she glanced down at her wrist. She extended her arm. "Wanna see my new watch?"

Eddie folded his rough hand around hers and looked it over

carefully. "That's a mighty pretty watch. I bet you're awful proud of it."

"My Daddy gave it to me."

"It would be a terrible thing if something happened to it, wouldn't it?"

Ellie nodded.

"Suppose I put it in my pocket? Ya know, for safe keepin'. Wouldn't want it gettin' lost or broken would we?"

The pink tip of Ellie's tongue crept out between her lips as she weighed his offer. After a few seconds, she smiled and stuck out her arm. Eddie unbuckled the band, removed the watch, and tucked it into his pocket. Reaching over, he tousled her hair and adjusted her seatbelt before starting the truck.

"I hear a car outside," Beth said.

Karen pushed the curtain aside. "It's Eddie," she hollered, and headed for the door. Karen threw a coat over her head and scrambled down the steps. She ran to the truck and stared in at Eddie with questioning eyes.

He rolled down the window. "Got a little present for ya'."

Karen leaned in and saw Ellie asleep on the seat beside him. She rushed around to the passenger's door and scooped her up, hugging her tightly. Tears of joy streaked down her face.

"Better get her in the house. She's been out in the cold rain all mornin'."

Karen tucked her daughter under the coat and raced back to the porch, not stopping to dab her eyes. Beth was waiting to hold the door open as she carried Ellie into the house.

Tommy took Ellie's place in the truck. "How was it?"

"I've had better days. Your Dad wasn't responsive when I got t' him. I'm guessin' he had a heart attack out there in the woods. I gave him CPR and managed t' get him back to the shelter and call the EMT's. He's on his way t' Eugene on a Life Flight chopper."

The two men sat in silence. Drops of cold rain pinged off the truck's metal roof and danced across its hood. Water streamed down and over the windshield obliterating the wiper's half-moons. The house, the yard and the trees blurred into a montage of colors and shapes resembling an impressionistic painting. The men's breath fogged the glass.

"Tell me about it," Tommy said, his voice cracking.

When Eddie finished, Tommy stared at the floor and shook his head. "I told him not to go. It was too much. He was bound to fail."

Eddie dropped his hand from the back of the seat to Tommy's shoulder. "He didn't fail. He had a mission. He went out there to bring a little girl home to her family 'n' that little one's snuggled up in her Mama's arms right now. As for the rest, we'll have t' wait t' see how it plays out."

"The whole family owes you a debt of gratitude."

"You don't owe me nothin'. I woulda' bled to death if your Dad hadn't gotten to me. Anybody's got debts t' pay, it's me."

Tommy gave a slight nod and opened the door.

Eddie extended his right hand. "It's gonna be okay. For the time bein' you're the man of the family, son. Go take care of those women; they need ya."

Palo Alto, California

"It's such a treat having this time together. Lately it seems like all you do is work." Marjorie Steele paused to smooth her husband's hair as she cleared the lunch dishes.

"I bought a cake. I cut us each a slice. Why don't we take our coffee out on the deck?"

Her words still hung in the air when Brandon Steele pulled out his cell phone and flipped it open. His wife paused halfway across the dining room with a cake plate in each hand.

"Steele here."

"Brandy, how the hell are you?"

He'd been expecting Ricetti's call. "Hold on a second. I need to get to another room." He pushed back from the table and left the dining room.

Marjorie sighed. She'd be drinking coffee alone again.

"What have you got?" He closed the door to his study and sank into a mahogany-colored armchair.

"Don't worry about me, Buddy. It's not what I got; it's what you got. And that's a problem, a very big problem."

"Have you found out why my people didn't report in? Did they get Jenkins?"

"I'm getting to that. I went out there to see what was up like you wanted. I found Beltzer along with two Sheriff's cars and an ambulance."

"What happened?"

"Hard to tell. The rest area is isolated. I couldn't just go waltzing in there. I circled back and forth, trying not to be too obvious about it."

"And?"

"And on my last pass I followed Beltzer back to town. He had the little girl with him."

"How did *he* get her?"

"I don't know. What I do know is that you, my friend, are in the swamp up to your armpits and the tide's coming in."

Steele walked over to the bar, poured a drink and downed it in a single gulp. "What about the two guys who were supposed to grab Jenkins when he came for the girl?"

"My guess is they got flummoxed."

"Who was the ambulance for?"

"Jenkins. A chopper went in and out while I was circling."

"Where are you?"

"I'm back at my motel room packing. My work here is pretty well done."

"You're not finished yet." Steele's voice grew low and mean. "Have you ever worked with explosives?"

"Wait a minute there, Brandy. I don't like where this is headed. Bombs are nasty things, nasty and messy. I was hired to watch. Eyeballs, remember?"

"I want you to blow up their house. We'll get rid of them all, erase every trace of that kid so no one can prove she was ever there. Understand?"

"I understand you've lost your mind. I'm out of here as soon as I snap my suitcase."

"That's your final word?"

"Not quite. You two yahoos are rank amateurs at this crime stuff. It's occurred to me that you might get the crazy idea to spill your guts to the cops, maybe even mention my name. You two may be amateurs, but I'm a pro. Unlike some people I know, when I set out to take care of someone they get taken care of. Get my drift?"

Steele didn't reply.

"I also have a suggestion for you."

"What's that?"

"You and your pal Win need to hotfoot it over to the office and fire up the paper shredder. A little bird tells me you're going to have lots of company real soon."

SIXTY-TWO

Charleston Harbor, Oregon

Eddie left Tommy's and drove to Charleston. Turning onto a small road that skirted the slough, he parked next to a metal-sided pole building. The gray, windowless building was two stories high with sliding doors front and back. Orange rust stains on its tall metal walls indicated where the gutters leaked. Oil drums, a rusting anchor, cable spools and other paraphernalia lay scattered along the side of the building.

A concrete apron sloped down to the water. Track, heavy wire cables and a winch spoke of pulling ships out of the water and into dry dock for repair. On the east, a wide wooden dock extended 30 feet out into the water.

Eddie heard voices and pounding inside. He slid the door open a crack and stepped through. He slowly approached the large blue ship filling the room. He stood with his hands in his pockets staring up at its bow.

Bright overhead lights illuminated the work area and heavy blocking and stanchions supported the ship. They'd set ladders against its sides. Equipment, parts, coils of electrical wire and toolboxes lay around the base of each ladder. Extension cords snaked across the floor and over the gunnels.

Eddie walked to a small room at the far corner of the building. He rummaged through old paint cans, found one that suited him, and sat it on a paint-spattered workbench. He opened a cupboard and removed a brush. After flexing it back and forth on his thigh to loosen its bristles, he picked up the paint and left.

Derek, who was moving equipment on the deck, watched him return carrying the brush, paint, and a stepladder. "Good day, Mr. Beltzer."

"Maybe for some folks," Eddie muttered as he opened the ladder.

"Did Thomas accompany you?"

"No."

"What are you going to paint?"

He glanced up at him from the fourth step. "I just decided on a fit and proper name for this tub and now's as good a time as any t' paint it on."

Derek picked up a computer case and carried it into the wheelhouse leaving him to his work.

Eddie completed one side, carried the ladder around, and did the other. When he finished, he stepped back and folded his arms across his chest. He'd neatly lettered *Thomas G Jenkins* on each side of the ship's bow.

Derek walked up beside him. "Very nice, it looks quite professional."

"I spent a few years paintin' signs. Eddie gave a deep sigh. "At least it's got a name now." He folded his ladder. "I gotta clean this brush. Wait for me in the office, we need t' talk."

Eddie brought Derek up to speed on the day's events.

Derek looked into Eddie's eyes. "In spite of everything, was Thomas successful?"

"He overpowered two men and the little one's back where she belongs. Ya might say the operation was a success, but the patient died."

Derek gasped. "You are saying that Thomas is dead?"

Eddie shook his head. "He barely made it outta the woods. He was hangin' by a thread last time I saw him. The EMT's said he had a bad heart attack. He's aboard a chopper on his way t' the hospital now." He shrugged. "It'll be touch 'n' go."

"This is very distressing to hear. We have a saying in my country. Whether you address the snake as cobra or Mr. Cobra, he will still bite you. Mr. Winston Ridgely is a truly evil man."

Eddie nodded in agreement.

Derek slumped in the chair. "And we came so close to defeating him."

"Whaddya mean by that?"

"I felt our path was clear, our success preordained. I allowed myself to believe that, like Thomas, we too would be successful. But I am a scientist, not a warrior. How can we go on now?"

Eddie stared down at him. "How can we *not* go on now?" He shoved a hand into his pocket. "A few days ago, ya said that the last piece of the puzzle was missin', that we didn't know the *Paradise Voyager's* current location. Well, here it is."

He laid the watch on the desk in front of Derek. "Ellie's watch has a GPS chip built into it. It'll tell ya where they picked her up. Ya got all the pieces now. So it ain't a puzzle any more, it's just you and me finishin' what a good man started."

Derek stared at the watch like it was a holy relic.

Eddie crossed the room. He jerked open the door and paused to glance back. "Remember trust? I'm goin' over t' the diner 'n' get something to eat." He pointed up at the ship. "I *trust* that by the time I get back you'll have figured out which direction we need to aim that big blue ship out there."

Eddie returned with an extra large coffee in his hand. The other workmen had cleaned up and left. The building was quiet. Derek knelt on the floor doing some last minute wiring.

He saw Eddie come in and hurried over to him. "I am glad you have returned. I have good news."

"Ya got the watch figured out?"

"Yes, but that is not my news. The FBI executed search warrants at RCI's headquarters."

"Ya don't say."

"Yes, I do say. My good friend and RCI employee, Mrs. Shiri Yoblanski, called while you were gone. The authorities were concerned Mr. Ridgely might destroy pertinent evidence and research documents. And they were correct. He was caught with red hands in the midst of shredding files when they arrived."

Eddie smirked. "Got what they deserved. Listen, I thought of somethin' while I was eatin'."

"What would that be?"

"When ya first came to the house, you told us there were only a few days left. We've passed that mark. Not only is Tom out of the equation, but the deadline's run out on us."

Eddie noticed an empty soda can on the floor and kicked it across the room. The metal wall boomed like a bass drum when the can smacked it. "We didn't act fast enough."

"True, we have been slow, but we are not at the end, but the beginning."

"Ya ain' makin' sense."

"I too have been thinking. Mr. Ridgely answered our questions. He not only demonstrated that the process can be successfully reversed, he gave us sufficient time to recover the ship and everyone aboard."

"I'm still not followin' ya."

"If the process had a biological impact, how could anyone use it? Moving back and forth is not the problem. Physiologic damage results from uninterrupted periods of stasis, hence the deadline. A live subject can be transferred an unlimited number of times with no ill effects. When they freed the granddaughter of Thomas, they ended everyone's period of confinement."

Eddie smiled for the first time. "So they reset the clock, so t' speak."

"That is precisely what they did."

Eddie was still smiling when he headed toward the back of the building. He spoke over his shoulder as he walked. "Let's crack the doors at either end of the buildin' and turn on the fans. We need to get some air movin' through here. I'm gonna fire up the engine 'n' I don't wanna fill the place with diesel fumes."

He rolled the door aside and grinned back at Derek. "We gotta get this sucker ready t' go."

SIXTY-THREE

Aboard the Thomas G. Jenkins

The regular beat of the waves splashing against the bow lulled Eddie's senses as he scanned the black ocean. Somewhere behind them, lost to the night, two Coast Guard vessels accompanied them to assist in the recovery. Derek and Eddie had sailed out of Charleston with an escort from Air Station North Bend and they picked up a second from Air Station Port Angeles in Washington en route. This small armada had been closing in on the *Paradise Voyager,* or at least the spot where Ellie's watch said she was.

Hopefully, they were one and the same. But no one could know for certain.

Approaching footsteps caused him to turn. A moment later, Derek took a position at the rail beside him. "You are still up, Mr. Beltzer."

"It ain't exactly an easy night t' sleep. How goes it down below?"

"Quite well. In truth, my work has been complete for some time now. I have run and re-run the same diagnostics many times over. As you said, it is difficult to sleep this evening."

Without time to train new technicians, Derek opted to fly two members of his original crew in from India. Ahbijay Patel and Raheel Singh remained at the controls in a small room below deck.

Eddie looked at Derek with an unspoken question in his eyes.

"I wish I could promise all will be well in the morning."

"But ya can't."

"Yes, I cannot," he said with a nod.

A stiff breeze tugged at Eddie's jacket and ruffled through his hair and beard. Both men zipped their jackets. A haunting sense of expectation rode on the night wind.

Derek sensed it as well. He drew a deep breath "Can you feel the mood, the anticipation? At times it seems to almost crackle in the air. The ocean knows we have come to reclaim what is rightfully ours. But like a pirate, it will not relinquish its ill-gotten booty without a fight."

"It's been a long, rough trip."

"That is true, so very, very true." Derek understood Eddie referred to more than the rough seas they'd encountered on their voyage.

Eddie recalled the day Tom's life had tumbled down around him, leaving a raw sore that never scabbed over. "He never wanted her t' go, ya know. Sarge had bad feelings about the trip from the very beginning. He didn't know exactly how things would play out, but he sure knew it wasn't gonna come to a good end."

"Would you care to join me in a cup of Chai?"

"Sure, why not?" Eddie's eyes returned to the water as Derek slipped away.

When Tom had first discussed his reservations about the *Paradise Voyager*, Eddie envisioned many scenarios, but nothing like the reality of the past few weeks. Life, that crazy-quilt patchwork of everyday livin', is nothin' but a peddler's sack, he thought. Tattered and torn, with its corners drawn up and tied at the top. Every mornin' Fate threw it over her shoulder and moved through the village going door-to-door distributing her wares.

Each time she opened her sack, something different spilled out. Today it could be the thick wool cloak of prosperity, the sunshine brightness of love, shiny baubles of laughter, or the sweetness of a baby's smile. Tomorrow the threadbare shirt of despair could just as easily tumble out. They all came from the same sack. Birth, death, joy and heartache were all in there just waitin' their turn.

"Here you are, Mr. Beltzer, warm Chai as ordered." Derek

handed him a steaming mug.

Derek brought his own mug close to his face. He gave it a swirl and breathed in its aroma. "Ambrosia. No other word captures its essence. A delightful aroma, a blessing for the taste buds, and warmth for the inner soul all packed into each sip." He ran his tongue across his lips.

"It's very good, thank you."

Eddie recalled how disheartened Tom had been after his trip to London. Despite Claudia's hospitality and Schoonover's efficiency, he'd returned empty handed. And then there were those jerks, Ridgely and Steele.

Derek somehow read Eddie's thoughts. "All criminals, it seems, are cut from the same cloth. They are *goonda*, bad characters. The petty thief crouching in the alleyway is not far removed from the corporate raider. At heart, they are both ruthless ruffians."

"It'd certainly appear that way. Speakin' of criminals, have you talked to your football buddy recently?"

"My friend is the football player's *wife*. She tells me things are not going well for Misters Ridgely and Steele. The company has been temporarily barred from conducting business with the government. Considering the nature of their enterprise, I would say they have rung RCI's death knell."

They saluted the bad guys' demise by clinking mugs.

Eddie leaned forward, resting his elbows on the railing. He dangled his half-empty mug and watched waves roll off the bow. A large white-side surfed their wake for several minutes. He nudged Derek and pointed. Seeing the dolphin skim along beside them momentarily relieved their apprehensions over the coming dawn.

"Whatcha gonna do when this is all over?"

"Return to India."

"That was one quick answer."

"Actually I have been giving it quite a lot of thought. It is where I belong."

"What'll ya do?"

A thin smile crossed Derek's lips. "I can, of course, return to the university. I am, after all, an honored professor. However, instead I believe I will take a long rest first. This has been a trying experience."

Eddie nodded in agreement

"Perhaps my son, Tanveer, and I will spend some time on the racing circuit."

"Ya own a racehorse, do ya?"

Derek chuckled. "No, no. Tanveer races *pigeons*."

Eddie glanced over at him and winked. "Ya must have a devil of a time gettin' them little saddles on 'em."

Derek grinned. "And what about Mr. Beltzer, what will he do?"

"Same old, I suppose." Eddie smoothed his beard. "Ya know, there's a volunteer cherry tree out behind the house. Some time or another a bird musta dropped a cherry pit as it flew by. It took root and grew. It's a big tree now, blooms every spring. I'm sorta like that tree. I just dropped in, but Pine Crest's home now. Tom, Marty and the rest are the closest thing t' family I got."

Eddie shook the last drops out of his cup and handed it to Derek. "Thanks for the Chai 'n' conversation. I'm gonna go lay down for a while."

Eddie rested fitfully. When he woke, he immediately noticed the absence of the steady thump, thump, thump of the ship's engine. He leaped out of bed, put on his shoes and headed down the hall. He noticed two white Coast Guard cutters rocking in the water beside them as he crossed the deck on his way to Derek's lab,

So many people in the small room made the atmosphere stifling. The whine of machinery on the other side of the wall made conversation difficult. Singh and Patel raced to enter the proper codes within the allotted time. Derek joined them, glancing from screen to screen, inputting data here and checking it there.

"Is it gonna work?" Eddie asked.

Derek's eyes remained on the screens. "This machinery has never been tested."

"But it's gonna work."

"It will in theory."

Eddie slammed his hand down. "You ain't answerin' my question."

"Some questions, Mr. Beltzer, do not come with readymade answers. As a man of agriculture, you must understand what it is to plow new ground." He continued typing as he spoke. "There are only two possibilities. It either works and they come home, or it does not and they are forever lost."

Eddie mulled over what Derek said. He glanced around the room at the electronic equipment crammed into every available nook and cranny and the three men frantically coordinating the process. "So if this grand scheme of ours fails, we're the ones ultimately responsible for their deaths."

Derek rose from the console. "Incorrect. We are the ones who did everything humanly possible to save them."

Eyes on the oscilloscope above him, Singh extended his right hand and rotated a dial. He gave a tired smile and said, "There," to no one in particular.

Derek glanced at Eddie. "The timer is set and the power is coming up nicely. The moment of truth is at hand," he shouted over the sudden roar.

The two men squeezed together around a porthole. A wavering circle of blue light materialized in front of them. It expanded outward for a few milliseconds before bursting into a brilliant white arc, forcing them both to cover their eyes.

SIXTY-FOUR

Sacred Heart Medical Center, Eugene, Oregon

Someone tapped on the door of Tom's hospital room.

Claudia's head popped around the corner. "Are you decent?"

He glanced up in surprise. "What are *you* doing here?"

"It's nice to see you, too. Aren't you getting released today?"

"That's what they told me."

"Well, somebody had to pick you up. Get some clothes on." She smiled at his confused expression. "You weren't planning on walking home in a hospital gown, were you?"

"No, but I didn't expect you to come for me."

"Eddie and Derek are still at sea, everyone else was busy, and the Queen had a tea scheduled. Guess you're stuck with me."

Tom rose from the chair shaking his head. "I can't believe you came all this way."

"Yeah, I always get the grunt work," Claudia said with a shrug. "But it was kinda on my way. I was in Vancouver, BC yesterday when the *Voyager* docked. I'm scheduled for Coos Bay today and San Francisco tomorrow."

"Did you see Marty?" Tom's voice was tinged with hope.

"Marty, Marty who?"

"Marty...Martha Jenkins, my wife!"

She had to bite her lip to keep from grinning. "Oh, *her*. Don't recall seeing her, but there were an awful lot of people milling around. I probably just missed her."

"How could you not have looked for her?"

"Hey, I was busy. Maybe somebody around here knows where to find her. I'll check." Claudia opened the door. "Well, son of a gun, look who's here."

Marty entered the room and ran into Tom's waiting arms.

Claudia allowed them time to greet each other then crossed

the room. "You had us worried there for a while." She rested her arm on his shoulder and gave him a peck on the cheek. "You're looking pretty chipper for a dead guy. I'd give you a ride home, but the doctors say no flying for six months. There's a transport ambulance waiting for you downstairs."

She took their hands in hers and squeezed. "I'll see you guys when you get home. Have a good trip."

The flight from Eugene to North Bend was a short one and Claudia's plane landed well ahead of the ship. Representing Paradise Getaways Ltd., she and her brother, Brian, met with each family privately. She also held a general press conference where she read a prepared statement and answered questions. When the meetings concluded, she joined the families on the dock prior to the *Voyager's* arrival.

Eddie and Derek stood near the bow as tugs shepherded the *Thomas G Jenkins* in for its triumphant arrival. A fireboat welcomed them near Pigeon Point and led the way spraying giant arcs of water. The *Paradise Voyager,* with Admiral Schoonover aboard, came next followed by a Coast Guard Cutter. Two red-orange HH65A Dolphin helicopters from Coast Guard Air Station North Bend shadowed their progress.

People lined the channel, cheering as the ships passed. One at a time they navigated the north bend of the Coos Bay, passed beneath the McCullough Bridge, and steamed toward the Coos Bay docks. The families of the Mothers of Song waited along the boardwalk, anxiously monitoring the *Voyager's* progress. Various officials, both state and local, a Coast Guard Honor Guard, high school bands, newsmen and camera crews, along with a crowd of well-wishers overflowed the dock area and filled the street. Barricades on either end of the city re-routed traffic on US 101.

A transport ambulance pulled up minutes before the

Voyager docked. They parked and helped Tom into a wheelchair.

"Everything okay?" Claudia asked.

Marty smiled. "The trip from Eugene tired him out. I suggested we go straight home, but he insisted on making an appearance."

"By now you'd think he'd learn to listen to you."

A voice in the crowd called to Claudia. She scanned the rows of faces and eventually found Billy Nevins, grinning and waving. She raised her arm and motioned him to come join her. Grabbing his mother's hand, Billy elbowed his way through the crowd. His mother trailed behind, murmuring apologies in his wake.

A policeman blocked their access.

"They're friends of mine," Claudia told the officer. "Can you sneak them through?"

He lifted the tape barrier and they slipped under.

"Hi, Claudia." Billy grabbed her hand and pumped it. As usual, his voice was several notches higher than necessary. He introduced his mother then asked, "What are you doing here?"

She hesitated, finally settling on, "Mr. J is a friend of mine. When I heard about the celebration, I decided to drop by."

It satisfied Billy's curiosity. He looked up and shouted, "Here come the ships." He joined the surge toward the dock, forsaking his mother and Claudia in his excitement.

Kate Nevins took her hand. "He talks about you all the time. It meant so much to him when you helped stuff inserts."

"I'm glad he enjoyed it. It's a day I'll forever hold in my heart."

"I understand." Kate Nevins sighed. Not as a sign of frustration, disappointment or fatigue, but of acceptance. "Life with Billy has been like getting on an airplane headed for Spain and finding out you've landed in Holland instead. You'll never see any bullfights, but eventually you come to appreciate the lovely windmills. Don't ever change." She kissed Claudia's cheek.

Tom enjoyed the festivities, even though the surge of the crowd tired him. He sought out Derek, shook his hand and made him commit to a long visit before he returned home to India.

Next he tracked down Eddie. "How did you do it?"

"Do what?"

"Get me out of the woods."

"Thank your lucky stars I got my new leg. The old one woulda never stood the strain." Eddie laughed. "Our rottin' carcasses would still be layin' out there in the woods."

"I meant how did you manage to bring a dead man back to life?"

Eddie moved the toe of his boot in aimless circles. "Piece a cake, actually. Remember that Australian singin' group from the 70's, the BeeGees?"

"Yeah, why?"

He began to snap his fingers. "All ya gotta do is sing that song of theirs 'n' keep doin' those compressions in time."

"What song is that?"

He winked. "*Stayin' Alive.*"

Eddie turned to Marty. "I think this guy's pretty well tuckered out. I'll drop by for a visit after they wrap things up here."

They returned to Pine Crest in the transport ambulance. When they pulled into their driveway they saw Tommy waiting on the porch swing. Leaning on a cane, Tom started up the walk. He heard a familiar woof.

Charlie painfully rose and limped across the porch. Tommy held the leash, preventing him from descending the steps to greet Tom and Marty. The dog waited at the edge of the stairs, whining impatiently as his two favorite people approached.

Tom sat on the top step and reached out to Charlie. The dog pressed against him, tail wagging. A rubber drainage tube still poked out from the bandages wrapped around the dog's mid-section. Tom carefully put his arm around the dog's shoulder and hugged him tightly. Charlie responded by licking his face.

Before he left, Tommy gave Tom a hand up and helped him into the house. Taking it from there, Marty let him lean on her as they walked to the bedroom. She threw back the spread, loosened his shoes, and helped him into bed. Tom was asleep almost as soon as his head hit the pillow. She smoothed the covers over him and tiptoed away. On her way out, she passed Charlie coming in. She paused in the doorway to see what the dog would do.

He walked to her side of the bed and tentatively raised a paw onto the spread. Feeling a sudden pang of conscience, he turned and glanced back at her.

"I shouldn't be setting new precedents," she said, "but go ahead."

Charlie eagerly threw his other paw on the bed and strained to push himself up. He struggled mightily, but couldn't lift himself onto the bed. He sagged onto the floor beside the bed looking forlorn and defeated.

"Let me help." Marty disappeared into the closet and returned with the two-step stool she used to reach the top shelf. She unfurled a beach towel beside Tom, opened the stool, and stepped aside.

Charlie cocked his head and studied the steps for a moment. Then he walked up and onto the bed in one easy motion. He settled down next to Tom, sighed, and closed his eyes. Marty eased the door shut with a chuckle, leaving two wounded warriors alone for a well-deserved rest.

While they slept, Marty wandered through the house like a stranger. She moved slowly, stopping often to relive the memories a knick knack or picture elicited. She turned over magazines and reread a to-do list she'd never completed. She walked her fingers along the back of the couch, went to the window and silently gazed out at the mountains. Turning, she glanced around the room cataloging forgotten details. Her eyes told her nothing had changed, yet her heart insisted nothing would ever be the same.

She went into the kitchen and chuckled when she saw an old note she'd made on the calendar. The Mothers of Song were scheduled for Chadwick's Nursing Home the following Sunday. Beside the handle, she recognized the card she'd left under Tom's pillow. Multiple smudges marred the front and one corner had curled and begun to fray from frequent use.

Marty remembered the words she'd written and brushed aside a tear. She started to turn away, but stopped when she noticed two strips of paper taped to the refrigerator door. *Strange*, she thought. They were little slips from inside fortune cookies. She wondered about their unusual message.

Eddie's knock interrupted her musing.

She greeted him with a hug. "Tom's taking a nap. Can you stay a while and visit?"

"Happy to."

She put a hand on his elbow. "Come into the living room and get comfortable. I want you to tell me everything that went on while I was gone. And don't overlook a thing."

They passed through the kitchen on their way, and Marty directed his attention to the refrigerator. "Can you shed any light on these?" she asked, pointing at the two strips of paper.

Eddie nodded and smoothed his beard. "Oh, I believe I can. Let's get settled in the livin' room."

They sat across from each other; she in the recliner and he on the couch.

He bit his lip and rubbed his palms together, wondering where to begin. He rocked forward with a smile and rested his elbows on his knees. "By any chance does the name Viktor Frankl mean anything to ya?"

AUTHOR'S NOTES

I hope you enjoyed reading *LOST* as much as I did creating it. Nominally, *LOST* is my eighth book. It has a long and checkered history and completing it was especially satisfying because I was never certain I could pull it off. I wrote it a number of years ago and gave all 175,000 words of it to a group of first readers. They wasted no time informing me it wasn't quite ready for Prime Time.

However, I had one character with a well-developed back story and decided to extract and expand her story as a stand-alone novel. The character was Claudia Monet and the result was *PROMISES*. Meanwhile, the remainder of the manuscript lay under my bed gathering dust.

In 2007 I decided to make another run at it. I hacked, whittled and edited, but it never jelled. In between my Seeds of Christianity™ books, I made another failed attempt in 2009. I *knew* there was a book there, but it continued to elude me.

After *APOSTLE,* the third book in the Seeds Series, was released I decided to make a fourth try. I started with the thrice-edited chapters, adding here, deleting there. When the smoke cleared, I was surprised to see I'd found what was *LOST*.

People often ask how much, if any, of *LOST* is based on fact. I'm happy to say there's quite a lot of fact woven into the fiction. As with all of my novels, one of my goals was to create a strong sense of place, in this case, the Southern Oregon Coast. The mythical town of Pine Crest is an amalgam of several small towns. Coos Bay, North Bend, Shore Acres Park, Charleston, etc., are real, as is Bay Area Hospital, Coast Guard Air Station North Bend and the Southwest Regional Airport in North Bend. Derek's stories from the Panchatantra, by the way, are also real.

I was deliberately vague about the processes Dr. Maheshwari (Derek) used. It would have been very easy for *LOST* to drift into the Science Fiction or Thriller genre. But I wanted to weave the multiple storylines together in a character-driven plot: Tom's love for Marty that, despite having heart problems, caused him to stake his life on a chance to bring her back; the deep friendship and sense of obligation between Eddie and Tom, Claudia's necessity to juggle career and motherhood while facing adverse publicity and the support she found in unexpected places, the quiet heroism of Shiri and Derek, etc.

Like all of my books, it also contains a certain amount of humor and irony. Laughter is important. Laura Ingalls Wilder said, "A good laugh overcomes difficulties and dissipates more dark clouds than anything else." And Bill Cosby wrote "If you can find humor in anything, you can survive it." I try to never let my protagonists take themselves too seriously.

So far I've talked about my goals and what the book is not. That leaves two questions unanswered. First, do ships really disappear? The answer is unequivocally, Yes. The chapter in which Tom's son-in-law, Mark Grant, shares his research is completely factual. The ships and people truly existed and the ships really vanished as depicted. The *tithe* of one ship lost per week is a factual number. Scary, isn't it?

The final question people usually have is, "Can solid objects be made to disappear?" After all, the *cloaked ship* and *alternate dimension* are staples of shows such as Star Trek, Stargate, and other Sci-Fi series. Stargate SG1 had an invisibility device that a person wore and Harry Potter had his cloak of invisibility.

This ubiquity of cloak technology and alternate universes was the reason I inserted the scene in which Shiri asks, "So you discombobulate all the atoms, convert them into an energy beam, and transport them into an alternate universe like they do on the Sci-Fi channel?"

Derek shakes his head. "Sorry to disappoint you, but I used no transporter beams. Dr. Hawking would easily understand the physics behind what I did. It becomes more difficult to explain it to a layperson such as yourself."

Shiri nods in understanding. "So where did the ship go?"

"Nowhere." He shrugged. "We are playing an elaborate game of blind man's bluff here. Only in this case, everyone else is

AUTHOR'S NOTES

blindfolded and the central participant remains clear-eyed."

My research uncovered several instances of a group or individual suggesting that solid objects can become invisible. One article stated "A Japanese company already has developed a system that can make individual objects disappear from certain vantage points, simple versions have been used by illusionists..."

Another inventor claims tanks, Humvees, even individual soldiers can become invisible. He does this by covering their surface with lenses that receive, transmit, and reflect light from the object's surroundings. By transmitting an image of what is behind a person or object to lenses in front of them, an observer would, in effect, see through them. Similarly, lenses on their back would have to be simultaneously transmitting an image of what is in front of them, lenses on the right would transmit what's to their left, lenses on the left would transmit what's on their right and so on, ad infinitum. Makes me tired just thinking about it.

Yet another source says researchers at the University of California, Berkeley are using grants from the military to develop special polymers that can bend visible light around objects. Building on work done at Imperial College London with electromagnetic radiation, researchers at Berkeley are said to be developing materials that control light's direction of travel. Underlying this work is the idea that bending visible light around an object hides it. Our vision, after all, depends upon objects reflecting the light which hits them. No reflected light, no object.

So perhaps, just perhaps, the idea is not as preposterous as it appears at first glance.

Each time I sit down at the computer, my fervent hope is that my writing will entertain, inform, and inspire my readers. Which means the most important thing is, as I said in the beginning, that you enjoyed reading *LOST*.

It all begins in Appalachian Kentucky

PROMISES

By

E. G. Lewis

Book One
of the
Mountain Memories Series

Reviewers say: "Just keeps getting better and better"...'A very satisfying read, indeed."..."I highly recommend it"..."A great love story"

A Recipe for Trouble:

Take one jilted Supermodel on the rebound
Add an unscrupulous businessman who'll do anything to save his floundering business
Agitate until both are steaming, then keep at a low simmer.

When looking for love you sometimes find it...and sometimes you don't! A novel of Love, Betrayal and Revenge, *Promises* combines coming of age, romance and suspense in a totally satisfying way.

Smooth as a sip of Kentucky Bourbon, it eases you into the

Appalachian hill country. That wonderfully wild place of mountains and hollows, creeks and rivers, with its hardscrabble life and whiteboard churches where roots go deep, family matters, and Granny Wright is never wrong. A place where King Coal still rules, and beneath its veneer of respectability lies a hidden web of treachery.

Mary Jane Combs may have gotten her Momma's good looks, but her strong-willed determination came straight from Daddy. Growing up in Kentucky she dreamed of a simple life with a loving husband, a home of her own, and healthy kids. But fate has some tricks up its sleeve and her life turned out to be anything but simple.

Instead of a housewife, Mary Jane's become an International Supermodel. She's swapped the Appalachian coal country for New York City's Upper West Side, traveling the world in her private jet and staying in the best hotels. Things are going along fine until mystery man, Michael Cole, enters her life. He's an unscrupulous businessman with connections to the Russian Mafia who'll do anything to save his floundering business, including marrying her. When she catches on to what Cole's up to and dumps him, he sets out to destroy her along with everything she's accomplished.

Never one to give up without a fight, she circles her wagons and mounts a counter attack. The evidence she needs to bring down her ex-husband remains in their London penthouse. To get it, she decides break in and access his computer files.

And that's when things start to get dicey. Cole unexpectedly returns and she suddenly finds herself crouched beneath his desk while her ex seduces another woman atop it.

Throughout her battle two questions remain unanswered. Can she do what needs to be done and still remain true to the promises she made at her mother's deathbed? And when the dust settles, will she at last find the loving relationship she always dreamed of?

PROMISES

I stood at the window of my condominium watching snow blanket Central Park. Despite the apartment's warmth, I tugged my mother's shawl tighter and crossed my arms protectively. I wasn't working today. I never do on this, my least favorite day of the year.

It hasn't always been like this. I loved winters as a little girl. Every fall I'd check out the wooly bears' coats and spy on the squirrels to see how many nuts they'd gathered, searching for clues about the coming winter.

In Eastern Kentucky where I grew up, the weather turned frigid after Christmas. In January we had frost on the inside of the windows, extra quilts on the bed, and the *Warm Morning* heat stove in the living room set to high. January also brought snow, deep snow that filled the hollows and drifted over the back porch steps.

Those deep snows meant no school and going sledding with my younger brothers. Even today, I smile when I recall coming inside cold, wet and invigorated. We'd hang our gloves, coats and knit hats on a rack in front of the stove to dry and hurry to our rooms to change. When we returned Momma always had mugs of hot cocoa waiting on the kitchen table. She warned us to take baby sips so we wouldn't burn our tongues.

We, of course, never listened.

Sometimes, if the snow was just right, she'd send me outdoors with a big spoon and a bowl. After carefully scraping away the crusty top layer so I didn't get soot from the chimney, I'd fill the bowl and Momma would turn it into snow ice cream. I'll never forget how soothing it felt on my sore tongue.

Those were happy times for us all, me, my two brothers, and Momma and Daddy. Life seemed simple then and the future looked as perfect as perfect can be. Everything changed the year I turned fifteen and Momma took sick. She died the following January.

Folks back home say I look just like her, that we could be twins. It's true; more and more when I look in the mirror it's her I see. Those same people think I rely upon her good looks to earn my living. In a way, I suppose I do. But it takes more than good bones and a nice figure to make it to the top as a model.

On melancholy days such as today I remind myself that Momma was not so much taken from me, as she was given to me...even if only for a short while. She guided me in life and continues to guide me in death. A few days before she passed over, I sat at her bedside and made certain promises. Promises I've done my level best to keep.

The thought that I might have fallen short, that I somehow let her down, never ceases to haunt me.